The Collected Stories
Volume 1

Liam O'Flaherty

The Collected Stories

Volume 1

Edited and introduced
by A.A. Kelly

St. Martin's Press
New York

LIAM O'FLAHERTY: THE COLLECTED STORIES

Copyright © 1999 by Liam O'Flaherty

St. Martin's Press, Scholarly and Reference Division,
175 Fifth Avenue, New York, N.Y. 10010

First published in the United States of America in 1999

Printed by MPG Books Ltd., Bodmin, Cornwall

Volume 1 ISBN 0-312-22903-8
(Volume 2: ISBN 0-312-22904-6
Volume 3: ISBN 0-312-22905-4
Three-volume set: ISBN 0-312-22906-2)

Library of Congress Cataloguing-in-Publication Data
O'Flaherty, Liam, 1896–
        [Short stories]
        The collected stories / Liam O'Flaherty; edited by A.A. Kelly.
        p. cm.
        Includes bibliographical references and index.
        ISBN 0-312-22903-8 (cloth:v. 1). − ISBN 0-312-22904-6 (cloth:
        v. 2). − ISBN 0-312-22905-4 (cloth: v. 3)
        1. Ireland–Social life and customs–Fiction. I. Kelly, A.A.
        (Angeline A.) II. Title.
        PR6029.F5A6   1999   Vol 1
        823' .912–dc21
                                                        99-41722
                                                        CIP

Contents

Volume II

Contents: *Introduction, Red Barbara, Birth, Prey, Mackerel for Sale, The Fall of Joseph Timmins, The Fairy Goose, The Alien Skull, The Sinner, The Black Rabbit, The Letter, The Little White Dog, The Stream, The Strange Disease, The Stone, The Child of God, The Renegade, The Last Horse, Making a Home, Non-Stop, Pay on Cruiser, The Lost Child, Two Lovely Beasts,* An Luchóg, *The Mouse, The Bath,* Teangabháil, *The Touch,* An Chearc Uisce, *The Water Hen, The Flute-Player,* An Beo, *Life, Grey Seagull, The Lament, Light, The Tide, The Challenge, The Seal,* An Chulaith Nua, *The New Suit, The Wedding, The Parting, The Eviction, The Old Woman, The Beggars, Galway Bay, A Public Scandal, The Night Porter, An Extraordinary Case, A Dublin Eviction, One Hundred Pounds, The Library, Unclean, The Wild Swan, Brosnan, Sources.*

Volume III

Contents: *Introduction, The Test of Courage,* Oifig an Phoist, *The Post Office,* An Scáthán, *The Mirror,* An Buille, *The Blow, Moving, The Intellectual, The Cutting of Tom Bottle, The Cake, The Backwoodman's Daughter, Idle Gossip, Limpets, The Accident, The Good Samaritan, The Tinkerwoman's Child, In Each Beginning is an End, A Public House at Night, Tidy Tim's Donkey, Indian Summer, A Grave Reason, The Black Cat, An Ounce of Tobacco,* Dúil, *Desire, Match-making,* Díoltas, *The Pedlar's Revenge, All Things Come of Age,* Mearbhall, *The Fanatic, Patsa, or the Belly of Gold, Wild Stallions, The Mermaid,* Uisce Faoi Dhraíocht, *Enchanted Water, Lovers, The Flood, The Salted Goat, The White Bitch, Proclamation, Field of Young Corn, The Blacksheep's Daughter, For Love or Money,* An tAonach, *A Tin Can, Bohunk, A Crow Fight, King of Inishcam, Timoney's Ass, Fishing, The Arrest, The Caress, Sources.*

LIAM O'FLAHERTY

Born in 1896 on Inishmore, the largest of the Aran Islands, Liam O'Flaherty grew up in a world of awesome beauty, echoes from his ancestors and the ancient pagan past. From his father, a Fenian, O'Flaherty inherited a rebellious streak; from his mother, a noted *seanchai*, came the deep spirituality and love of nature that has enraptured readers through the decades.

In France in 1917, O'Flaherty was severely shell-shocked. After eight months' recuperation, he spent several restless years travelling the globe. In 1920 he supported the Republican cause against the Free State government. Influenced by the Industrial Workers of the World's programme of social revolution, O'Flaherty organised the seizure and occupation of the Rotunda Theatre at the top of Dublin's O'Connell Street in 1922. He hoisted the red flag of revolution, calling himself the 'Chairman of the Council of the Unemployed', but fled three days later to avoid bloodshed. Later that year he moved to London, where his writing skills came to the attention of critic Edward Garnett, who recommended to Jonathan Cape the publication of O'Flaherty's first novel. For the next two decades, O'Flaherty's creative output was astonishing. Writing in English and Irish, he produced novels, memoirs and short stories by the dozen. Remarkable for their literary value and entertainment, O'Flaherty's books are also crucial in their charting of the ways and beliefs of a peasant world before it was eclipsed by modernity.

Like the work of many authors of his time much of O'Flaherty's work was banned in Ireland. Liam O'Flaherty died in Dublin in 1984, aged 88 years, having enriched forever Irish literature and culture.

A.A. KELLY was born in London of Irish/Scottish parentage. She has a Doctorate in English Literature and has taught and lectured in Europe and the US. Her published work includes: (as author) *Mary Lavin: Quiet Rebel, Liam O'Flaherty: The Storyteller* and *Joseph Campbell: A Critical Biography*(with Norah Saunders); (as editor) *Wandering Women: Two Centuries of Travel out of Ireland, Pillars of the House: An Anthology of Verse by Irish Women from 1690 to the present, The Wilderness* by Liam O'Flaherty, *The Pedlar's Revenge and Other Stories* by Liam O'Flaherty (selected and introduced), *The Wave and Other Stories* by Liam O'Flaherty (selected and introduced), and *The Letters of Liam O'Flaherty* (selected and introduced).

INTRODUCTION

Here for the first time readers can enjoy the whole body of Liam O'Flaherty's short-story writing, composed 1922–1958. The stories are not presented in any particular order. Those curious about their dates of publication can refer to the source where each title is listed either under its first collection or, if uncollected, under first publication. George Jefferson's bibliography of O'Flaherty (Wolfhound, 1993) gives further details.

Most of these stories have previously been published in seven different collections (1922–1976), plus one Irish language collection of eighteen stories *Dúil* (Sáirséal agus Dill, 1953). Irish stories have here been placed next to their English language version with the exception of 'Fód' (uncollected), 'An tAonach' and 'An Charraig Dhubh (never translated). At least two of the Irish stories 'Daoine Bochta' and 'An Fiach' (both written in 1925) were originally composed in Irish. The other stories in Irish were translated or recomposed into their English language version. Until the 1950s it was difficult to get Irish language work published.

Those new to O'Flaherty will soon notice the contrast between his lyrical, somewhat mystical, and his brutally realistic work. He is best known for his depiction of nature and life on Aran. His deep love and understanding of nature, the islanders and their way of life in his youth, are unique and will endure. He also enjoys writing about off-beat characters such as Patsa or Stoney Batter, and the excitement of the chase or race-course. Tempered in that crucible of the Battle of the Somme, horrors emerge at times and are expressed in the stark realism shown by his half dozen war stories, the first of which, 'The Sniper' (1922), brought him his initial fame.

Since I wrote the introduction to *The Pedlar's Revenge* collection (1976) more stories have come to light, such as 'The Cutting of Tom Bottle', tucked away in an unknown 1933 miscellany, and the manuscripts of 'One Hundred Pounds' and 'For Love or Money'. Others were discovered in research connected with editing O'Flaherty's collected letters (Wolfhound, 1996).

At the age of seventy-eight O'Flaherty wrote 'my rose has still too many thorns of unfulfilled desire', yet he wrote no more short stories after the age of about sixty. The mysterious creative impulse, so painfully ardent a fire in his youth and middle age, cooled to leave these immortal embers. His work lives yet.

A.A. Kelly

SPRING SOWING

It was still dark when Martin Delaney and his wife Mary got up. Martin stood in his shirt by the window a long time looking out, rubbing his eyes and yawning, while Mary raked out the live coals that had lain hidden in the ashes on the hearth all night. Outside, cocks were crowing and a white streak was rising from the ground, as it were, and beginning to scatter the darkness. It was a February morning, dry, cold and starry.

The couple sat down to their breakfast of tea, bread and butter, in silence. They had only been married the previous autumn and it was hateful leaving a warm bed at such an early hour. They both felt in a bad humour and ate, wrapped in their thoughts. Martin with his brown hair and eyes, his freckled face and his little fair moustache, looked too young to be married, and his wife looked hardly more than a girl, red-cheeked and blue-eyed, her black hair piled at the rear of her head with a large comb gleaming in the middle of the pile, Spanish fashion. They were both dressed in rough homespuns, and both wore the loose white frieze shirt that Inverara peasants use for work in the fields.

They ate in silence, sleepy and bad humoured and yet on fire with excitement, for it was the first day of their first spring sowing as man and wife. And each felt the glamour of that day on which they were to open up the earth together and plant seeds in it. So they sat in silence and bad humour, for somehow the imminence of an event that had been long expected, loved, feared and prepared for, made them dejected. Mary, with her shrewd woman's mind, munched her bread and butter and thought of . . . Oh, what didn't she think of? Of as many things as there are in life does a woman think in the first joy and anxiety of her mating. But Martin's mind was fixed on one thought. Would he be able to prove himself a man worthy of being the head of a family by doing his spring sowing well?

In the barn after breakfast, when they were getting the potato seeds and the line for measuring the ground and the spade, a cross word or two passed between them, and when Martin fell over a basket in the half-darkness of the barn, he swore and said that a man would be better off dead than . . . But before he could finish whatever he was going to say, Mary had her arms around his waist and her face to his. 'Martin,' she said, 'let us not begin this day cross with one another.' And there was a tremor in her voice. And somehow, as they embraced and Martin kept mumbling in his awkward peasant's voice, 'pulse of my heart, treasure of my life,' and such traditional phrases, all their irritation and sleepiness left them. And they stood there embracing until at last Martin pushed her from him with pretended roughness and said: 'Come, come, girl, it will be sunset before we begin at this rate.'

Still, as they walked silently in their raw-hide shoes, through the little hamlet, there was not a soul about. Lights were glimmering in the windows of a few cabins. They sky had a big grey crack in it in the east, as if it were going to burst in order to give birth to the sun. Birds were singing somewhere at a distance. Martin and Mary rested their baskets of seeds on a fence outside the village and Martin whispered to Mary proudly: 'We are first, Mary.' And they both looked back at the little cluster of cabins, that was the centre of their world, with throbbing hearts. For the joy of spring had now taken complete hold of them.

They reached the little field where they were to sow. It was a little triangular patch of ground under an ivy-covered limestone hill. The little field had been manured with seaweed some weeks before, and the weeds had rotted and whitened on the grass. And there was a big red heap of fresh seaweed lying in a corner by the fence to be spread under the seeds as they were laid. Martin, in spite of the cold, threw off everything above his waist except his striped woollen shirt. Then he spat on his hands, seized his spade and cried: 'Now you are going to see what kind of a man you have, Mary.'

'There now,' said Mary, tying a little shawl closer under her chin. 'Aren't we boastful this early hour of the morning? Maybe I'll wait till sunset to see what kind of a man have I got.'

The work began. Martin measured the ground by the southern fence for the first ridge, a strip of ground four feet wide, and he placed the line along the edge and pegged it at each end. Then he spread fresh seaweed over the strip. Mary filled her apron with seeds and began to lay them in rows, four, three, four. When she was a little distance down the ridge Martin advanced with his spade to the head eager to commence.

'Now in the name of God,' he cried, spitting on his palms, 'let us raise the first sod!'

'Oh, Martin, wait till I'm with you!' cried Mary, dropping her seeds on the ridge and running up to him. Her fingers outside her woollen mittens were numb with the cold, and she couldn't wipe them in her apron. Her cheeks seemed to be on fire. She put an arm round Martin's waist and stood looking at the green sod his spade was going to cut, with the excitement of a little child.

'Now for God's sake, girl, keep back!' said Martin gruffly. 'Suppose anybody saw us traipsing about like this in the field of our spring sowing, what would they take us for but a pair of useless, soft, empty-headed people that would be sure to die of the hunger. Huh!' He spoke very rapidly, and his eyes were fixed on the ground before him. His eyes had a wild, eager light in them as if some primeval impulse were burning within his brain and driving out every other desire but that of asserting his manhood and of subjugating the earth.

'Oh, what do we care who is looking?' said Mary; but she drew back at the same time and gazed distantly at the ground. Then Martin cut the sod, and pressing the spade deep into the earth with his foot, he turned up the first sod with a crunching sound as the grass roots were dragged out of the earth. Mary sighed and walked back hurriedly to her seeds with furrowed brows. She picked up her seeds and began to spread them rapidly to drive out the sudden terror that had seized her at that moment when the first sod was turned up and she saw the fierce, hard look in her husband's eyes, that were unconscious of her presence. She became suddenly afraid of that pitiless, cruel earth, the peasant's slave master, that would keep her chained to hard work and poverty all her life until she would sink again into its bosom.

Her short-lived love was gone. Henceforth she was only her husband's helper to till the earth. And Martin, absolutely without thought, worked furiously, covering the ridge with black earth, his sharp spade gleaming white as he whirled it sideways to beat the sods.

Then as the sun rose the little valley beneath the ivy-covered hills became dotted with white frieze shirts, and everywhere men worked madly without speaking and women spread seeds. There was no heat in the light of the sun, and there was a sharpness in the still thin air that made the men jump on their spade hafts ferociously and beat the sods as if they were living enemies. Birds hopped silently before the spades, with their heads cocked sideways, watching for worms. Made brave by hunger they often dashed under the spades to secure their food.

Then when the sun reached a certain point all the women went back to the village to get dinner for their men, and the men worked on without stopping. Then the women returned, almost running, each carrying a tin can with a flannel tied around it and a little bundle tied with a white cloth. Martin threw down his spade when Mary arrived back in the field. Smiling at one another they sat under the hill for their meal. It was the same as their breakfast, tea and bread and butter.

'Ah,' said Martin, when he had taken a long draught of tea from his mug, 'is there anything in this world as find as eating dinner out in the open like this after doing a good morning's work? There, I have done two ridges and a half. That's more than any man in the village could do. Ha!' And he looked at his wife proudly.

'Yes, isn't it lovely,' said Mary, looking at the black ridges wistfully. She was just munching her bread and butter. The hurried trip to the village and the trouble of getting the tea ready had robbed her of her appetite. She had to keep blowing at the turf fire with the rim of her skirt, and the smoke nearly blinded her. But now sitting on that grassy knoll, with the valley all round glistening with fresh seaweed and a light smoke rising from the freshly turned earth, a strange joy swept over her. It overpowered that other feeling of dread that had been with her during the morning.

Martin ate heartily, revelling in his great thirst and his great hunger, with every pore of his body open to the pure air. And he looked around at his neighbours' fields boastfully, comparing them with his own. Then he looked at his wife's little round black head and felt very proud of having her as his own. He leaned back on his elbow and took her hand in his. Shyly and in silence, not knowing what to say and ashamed of their gentle feelings, for peasants are always ashamed of feeling refined, they finished eating and still sat hand in hand looking away into the distance. Everywhere the sowers were resting on little knolls, men, women and children sitting in silence. And the great calm of nature in spring filled the atmosphere around them. Everything seemed to sit still and wait until midday had passed. Only the gleaming sun chased westwards at a mighty pace, in and out through white clouds.

Then in a distant field an old man got up, took his spade and began to clean the earth from it with a piece of stone. The rasping noise carried a long way in the silence. That was the signal for a general rising all along the little valley. Young men stretched themselves and yawned. They walked slowly back to the ridges.

Martin's back and his wrists were getting a little sore, and Mary felt that if she stooped again over her seeds that her neck would break, but neither said anything and soon they had forgotten their tiredness in the mechanical movement of their bodies. The strong smell of the upturned earth acted like a drug on their nerves.

In the afternoon, when the sun was strongest, the old men of the village came out to look at their people sowing. Martin's grandfather, almost bent double over his thick stick, stopped in the lane outside the field and, groaning loudly, he leaned over the fence.

'God bless the work,' he called wheezily.

'And you, grandfather,' replied the couple together, but they did not stop working.

'Ha!' muttered the old man to himself. 'Ha! He sows well and that woman is good, too. They are beginning well.'

It was fifty years since he had begun with his Mary, full of hope and pride, and the merciless soil had hugged them to its bosom ever since each spring without rest. But he did not think of that. The soil gives forgetfulness. Only the present is remembered in the spring, even by the aged who have spent their lives tilling the earth; so the old man, with his huge red nose and the spotted handkerchief tied around his skull under his black soft felt hat, watched his grandson work and give him advice.

'Don't cut your sods so long,' he would wheeze, 'you are putting too much soil on your ridge.'

'Ah, woman! Don't plant a seed so near the edge. The stalk will come out sideways.'

And they paid no heed to him.

'Ah,' grumbled the old man, 'in my young days, when men worked from morning till night without tasting food, better work was done. But of course it can't be expected to be the same as it was. The breed is getting weaker. So it is.'

Then he began to cough in his chest and hobbled away to another field where his son Michael was working.

By sundown Martin had five ridges finished. He threw down his spade and stretched himself. All his bones ached and he wanted to lie down and rest. 'It's time to be going home, Mary,' he said.

Mary straightened herself, but she was too tired to reply. She looked at Martin wearily and it seemed to her that it was a great many years since they had set out that morning. Then she thought of the journey home and the trouble of feeding the pigs, putting the fowls into their coops and getting the supper ready and a momentary flash of rebellion against the slavery of being a peasant's wife crossed her mind. It passed in a moment. Martin was saying, as he dressed himself:

'Ha! My soul from the devil, it has been a good day's work. Five ridges done, and each one of them as straight as a steel rod. Begob, Mary it's no boasting to say that ye might well be proud of being the wife of Martin Delaney. And that's not saying the whole of it, my girl. You did your share better than any woman in Inverara could do it this blessed day.'

They stood for a few moments in silence looking at the work they had done. All her dissatisfaction and weariness vanished from Mary's mind with the delicious feeling of comfort that overcame her at having done this work with her husband. They had done it together. They had planted seeds in the earth. The next day and the next and all their lives, when spring came they would have to bend their backs and do it until their hands and bones got twisted with rheumatism. But night would always bring sleep and forgetfulness.

As they walked home slowly Martin walked in front with another peasant talking about the sowing, and Mary walked behind, with her eyes on the ground, thinking.

Cows were lowing at a distance.

BÁS NA BÓ

Rugadh marbh an lao. Tháinig sé in aghaidh a chos agus luigh sé ar an bhféar glas ina mheall dearg sleamhain, a cheann casta siar ar a dhroim.

Sheas siad timpeall air, ag craitheadh a gceann, gan focal astu. 'Sé toil Dé é,' adúirt bean an fhir ar leis an bhó.

Thosnaigh an bhó ag éagaoine; ar mire le tinneas beirthe. Ansin chas sí go tromchosach, a crúba ag brú síos na talún faoi mheáchan a coirp.

Chrom sí ar an lao, ag éagaoine agus í á bholú. Ansin thosnaigh sí á liachaint lena teanga gharbh go grámhar.

Do chimil an bhean clár éadain na bó agus bhris deor faoina súil: ba mháthair í féin.

Chinn an phian ar an mbó ansin. D'imigh sí ón lao. Sheas sí agus a ceann fúithi, a hanál ag teacht go tiubh as a polláirí. Do tháinig a hanál i gcolúna fada caola, mar bheadh dhá ghath gréine ag sileadh isteach imeasc breacsholais teampaill, trí fhuinneog ghloinedhaite.

Dhíbrigh siad siar í go ceann na páirce. Sheas sí, a ceann thar an gclaí, go tuirseach, ag lascadh a taobhanna lena heireaball.

Rug siad ar an lao agus thug leo é trasna na páirce go dtí an claí; á tharraingt ar an talamh, amach tríd an gclaí go páirc eile, amach trí chlaí eile fós, suas ardán féarach go bruach na haille.

Chaitheadar síos sa bhfarraige é.

Thit sé ina mheall gan cruth ar charraig. Thógadar na clathacha arís go cúramach agus tháinig siad ar ais go dtí an bhó.

Thairg an bhean deoch mhin choirce dhi ach dhiúltaigh sí an deoch. Rugadar uirthi ansin, agus dhoirteadar an deoch síos a scornach trí adharc thairbh. Shlog an bhó leath na dí. Chuir sí uaithi an chuid eile den deoch, ag casadh a béil go fiánta.

D'imigh siad abhaile ansin, an bhean ag caoineadh an lao agus ag déanamh a gearáin le Dia. D'fhan a fear leis an mbó ag faire an tsalachair. Chuir sé an salachar faoi charnán cloch. Ansin thóg sé beagán créafóige ina láimh agus rinne comhartha na croise leis ar thaobh dheis na bó.

D'imigh seisean abhaile.

D'fhan an bhó i bhfad ag dearcadh thar an gclaí gur laghdaigh a tinneas.

Chas sí go tobann, gur lig géim is gur chraith a ceann. Thug sí rith te reatha, a cosa ag snapadh. Sheas sí arís. Ní fhaca sí rud ar bith léi sa bpáirc. Ansin rith sí thart fán chlaí, ag cur a cinn thairis anseo is ansiúd agus ag géimneach go fiánta agus go cráite. Níor freagradh í. An macalla féin níor tháinig ar ais chuici. Chuaigh sí chun fiántais, do réir mar tháinig tuiscint di go raibh a lao ar iarraidh. Bhí a súile ag éirí ruaimneach agus iad ar nós súl tairbh. Thosnaigh sí ag smúracht na talún agus fuirse siúil fúithi, á treascairt sna tomacha féir.

Seo é an áit ar luigh sí roimh an bhreith, ar thaobh ardáin, an féar brúite faoi mheáchan a coirp. Siúd é an áit ar rugadh an lao; an talamh tochailte ag cosa na bhfear agus an chréafóg dhonn le feiscint aníos tríd an bhféar feoite.

Fuair sí boladh an lao san áit ar thit sé. Bhreathnaigh sí ina timpeall go fíochmhar. Chuir sí srón le talamh. Lean sí lorg coirp an lao tríd an bhféar go dtí an claí. Stad sí ag an gclaí, ag smúracht ar feadh i bhfad agus iontas uirthi cá ndeachaigh an lorg thairis sin. Ar deireadh bhrúigh sí roimpi an claí. Leag meáchan mór a coirp é. Ghearr na clocha a hucht, ach bhrúigh sí níos déine le neart uafáis, go ndeachaigh sí tríd an mbearna. Gearradh a hioscad chlé in aice an útha. Níor thug sí aird ar an bpian ach chuaigh ar aghaidh a smut le talamh.

Neartaigh a siúl. Anois agus arís chroch sí a ceann, gur lig búir — búir fhada, thruamhéileach; mar bheadh meall gaoithe ag timpeallú coirnéil.

Ag an dara claí stad sí arís. Ansin bhrúigh sí ar aghaidh. Thit sé roimpi. Ar dhul tríd an mbearna gearradh gach taobh léi sa mbléin. Do shil an fhuil anuas go casta, ag deargadh stríoca geal a bhí ar a taobh clé.

Seo suas an t-ardán í go dtí barr na haille. Thosnaigh sí ag craitheadh. Chas sí go tobann i leataobh, nuair chonaic sí an fharraige agus nuair chuala sí an torann trom thíos amach: na tonntracha móra ag briseadh ar an gcarraig agus na héanacha ag scréachaíl go géar garg. Do bholaigh sí an t-aer, agus iontas uirthi. Chuaigh sí ar aghaidh go mall iar sin. Ar bhruach na haille, áit a raibh críoch leis an bhféar agus sraith gairbhéil ag fánadh thar bruach, rith sí i ndiaidh a cúil, ag géimneach ar mire. Tháinig sí ar ais arís. Chuir sí an dá chrúib thosaigh go haireach ar an ngairbhéal agus bhreathnaigh sí amach. Bhí deireadh le lorg a lao anseo. Níorbh fhéidir léi a leanúint níos faide. Bhí sé caillte sa doimhneas amuigh thar an mbruach. Shíl sí an t-aer a smúracht, ach níor tháinig faic go dtí na polláirí ach boladh goirt na farraige.

Thosnaigh sí ag éagaoine, a taobh ag at agus ag creathnú le rith na hanála. Ansin bhreathnaigh sí síos agus chonaic sí a lao caite ar an gcarraig fúithi.

Ghéimnigh sí go lúcháireach. Rith sí soir siar ar bharr na haille, ag cuartú bealach le dhul síos chuig an lao, ag smúracht thall agus abhus, ag dul ar a glúine, ag deasú síos.

Ach ní raibh strapa le fáil. Tháinig sí ar ais arís, a cosa deiridh ag lascadh sa rith, go dtí an áit ar caitheadh síos an lao.

Is fada a d'fhan sí ag féachaint síos air gan cor aisti. Ansin do ghéimnigh sí in ard a cinn, ach freagra ní bhfuair sí. Chonaic sí an taoille ag teacht isteach, ag timpeallú na carraige ar a raibh an lao. Do ghéimnigh sí arís. Tháinig na tonntracha ar shála a chéile, timpeall ar an gcorp. Thosnaigh sí ag búirthíl agus ag casadh a cinn go fiánta, mar bheadh sí ag iarraidh an fharraige a chur ar gcúl lena hadharca.

Ansin tháinig maidhm mór millteach isteach. Scuab sé an lao den charraig.

Chuir an bhó búir aisti agus síos léi.

THE COW'S DEATH

The calf was still-born. It came from the womb tail first. When its red, unwieldy body dropped on the green-sward it was dead. It lay with its head doubled about its neck in a clammy mass. The men stood about it and shook their heads in silence. The wife of the peasant who owned the cow sighed and said, 'It is God's will.' The cow moaned, mad with the pain of birth. Then she wheeled around cumbersomely, her hoofs driving into the soft earth beneath the weight of her body. She stooped over the calf and moaned, again smelling it. Then she licked the still body with her coarse tongue lovingly. The woman rubbed the cow's matted forehead, and there was a tear in her eye; for she too was a mother.

Then the cow, overcome once more with the pain, moved away from the calf and stood with her head bent low, breathing heavily through her nostrils. The breath came in long pale columns, like sunbeams coming through the window of a darkened church. They drove her away to a corner of the field, and she stood wearily with her head over the fence, lashing her flanks with her tail restlessly.

They seized the calf and dragged it by the feet along the field to the fence, out through the fence into another field, then through another fence, then up the grassy slope that led to the edge of the cliff. They dropped it downwards into the sea. It lay in a pulped mass on the rocks. They rebuilt the gaps in the stone fences carefully and returned to the cow. The woman offered her a hot drink of oatmeal, but she refused it. They seized her and poured the drink down her throat, using a bull's horn as a funnel. The cow half swallowed the drink, half tossed it away with her champing mouth.

Then they went home, the woman still moaning the dead calf and apologising to God for her sorrow. The peasant remained with the cow, watching until she should drop the bag. He buried it under a mound of stones. He dug his heel in the ground, and taking a handful of the brown earth, he made the sign of the cross on the cow's side. Then he too went home.

For a long time the cow stood leaning over the fence, until the pain lessened. She turned around suddenly and lowered and tossed her head. She took a short run forward, the muscles of her legs creaking like new boots.

She stopped again, seeing nothing about her in the field. Then she began to run around by the fence, putting her head over it here and there, lowing. She found nothing. Nothing answered her call. She became wilder as the sense of her loss became clearer to her consciousness. Her eyes became red around the rims and fierce like a bull's. She began to smell around on the ground, half running, half walking, stumbling clumsily among the tummocks of grass.

There was where she had lain in travail, on the side of a little slope, the grass compressed and faded by the weight of her body. There was where she had given birth, the ground trampled by many feet and torn here and there, with the brown earth showing through. Then she smelt where the calf had lain. There were wet stains on the grass. She looked around her fiercely, and then she put her nose to the ground and started to follow the trail where they had dragged the calf to the fence. At the fence she stopped and smelt a long time, wondering with her stupid brain whither the trail led. And then stupidly she pressed with her great bulk against the fence. The stones cut her breast, but she pressed harder in terror and the fence fell before her. She stumbled through the gap and cut her left thigh near the udder. She did not heed the pain, but pressed forward, smelling the trail and snorting.

Faster she went, and now and again she raised her head and lowed — a long, mournful low that ended in a fierce *crescendo*, like a squall of wind coming around a corner. At the second fence she paused again. Again she pressed against it, and again it fell before her. Going through the gap she got caught, and in the struggle to get through she cut both her sides along the flanks. The blood trickled through jaggedly, discolouring the white streak on the left flank.

She came at a run up the grassy slope to the cliff. She shuddered and jerked aside when she suddenly saw the sea and heard it rumbling distantly below — the waves seething on the rocks and the sea birds calling dismally with their noisome cackle. She smelt the air in wonder. Then she slowly advanced, inch by inch, trembling. When she reached the summit, where the grass ended in a gravel belt that dropped down to the sheer slope of rock, she rushed backwards and circled around wildly, lowing. Again she came up, and planting her feet carefully on the gravel, she looked down. The trail of her calf ended there. She could follow it no further. It was lost in the emptiness beyond that gravel ledge. She tried to smell the air, but nothing reached her nostrils but the salt smell of the sea. She moaned and her sides heaved with the outrush of her breath. Then she looked down, straining out her neck. She saw the body of her calf on the rocks below.

She uttered a joyful cry and ran backwards, seeking a path to descend. Up and down the summit of the cliff she went, smelling here and there, looking out over the edge, going on her knees and looking down and finding nowhere a path that led to the object on the rocks below. She came back again, her hind legs clashing as she ran, to the point where the body had been dropped over the precipice.

She strained out and tapped with her fore hoof, scratching the gravel and trying to descend, but there was nothing upon which she could place her feet — just a sheer drop of one hundred feet of cliff and her calf lay on the rocks below.

She stood stupidly looking at it a long time, without moving a muscle. Then she lowed, calling to her calf, but no answer came. She saw the water coming in with the tide, circling around the calf on the rocks. She lowed again, warning it. Wave after wave came in, eddying around the body. She lowed again and tossed her head wildly as if she wanted to buffet the waves with her horns.

And then a great wave came towering in, and catching up the calf on its crest swept it from the rocks.

And the cow, uttering a loud bellow, jumped headlong down.

BENEDICAMUS DOMINO

The college clock struck once. It was five minutes to one. The lay brothers began to march into their refectory from the long hall where they had assembled, the long hall with a stone floor on the left side of the college quadrangle. They moved very slowly, because Brother Silas, the shoemaker, went first and his deformed left leg forced him to go down the four stone steps sideways into the refectory, which Brother Euphronius, the laundryman, said was 'more like a cellar than a refectory.' And in fact it was very bare and sunk into the ground, so that the two windows on the far side from the door only let in a stray ray of sunshine. Sitting at table the brothers' eyes were on a level with the gravel drive that led to the college reception room and very often some of them were scandalised by seeing the legs of lady visitors pass, 'with those shocking silk stockings they wear nowadays,' as Brother Cornelius used to say with a twinkle in his eyes.

They all dipped their fingers in the Holy Water font within the door as they entered and then they filed to their places at the long table in the middle of the room. They all sniffed as they entered and some sneezed, for the gas jet was lit and there was always a leakage at dinner hour, when the light was turned low. But if it were turned on full strength Brother Matthias, the housekeeper, promptly turned it down again, and as it was winter, it was impossible to see without it. So they sniffed and stood behind their covers, with their hands folded within their habit sleeves and their heads bent, shivering with the cold. Brother Silas mounted the rostrum at the rear and turned up the shaded light over it. Then he placed his 'Life of Saint Theresa' on the stand and took up the Martyrology to find the passage. He was the reader for the day.

His life would be perfectly tranquil and happy if he didn't have to read aloud to the brothers at three meals once every eleven days. There were eleven other brothers and they all took turns, except Cornelius, the book-brother, who was the brother-in-charge and was exempt from reading. Old Silas had spent all the forenoon preparing his reading, for there were numerous foreign words and Latin quotations and there was always a titter when he made a mistake. And when Brother Cornelius rang his bell and called out

'Silentium' to reprimand those who tittered, there was still more tittering, for 'Silentium' was Silas's nickname, because of his religious name Silas and his morose and taciturn character. He opened the huge Martyrology and found out those who had been martyred on that date November 25th. 'Gracious me,' he muttered. There were more than half a dozen important people, given to the lions, crucified, and torn by wild horses at various dates and they all had indescribable names in Latin. He lifted his little black round skull cap and scratched his bald head with the little finger of his left hand. He put his wrinkled old face so near the open page that his spectacles touched the book and he could see nothing. So he took them off and began to wipe them with his handkerchief.

Brother Julian, standing at the end of the table beneath the rostrum, looked up at Silas and felt pity for 'the old fool.' For Brother Julian was already tired of wearing a lay brother's habit and looked upon the whole business with disgust. He pitied old Silas because the other brothers poked fun at him. He himself had been but six months in the Order and he had long since recovered from the religious fit that suddenly took possession of him one night in Paris, when he rushed from his studio and went to confession and joined the Order on the advice of the priest to whom he confessed. He was the youngest man in the room, no more than thirty. In fact there was something indecent about his youth, in that assembly of old and withered men; just as if a racehorse in the pride of its youth were sent to stables with a number of worn-out cab-horses. Of course he would not be sent to that college, by the authorities at headquarters in Paris, nor indeed admitted into the Order, for only men past their youth were admitted, but Brother Julian was a good painter and the college required a great deal of painting to be done. And Brother Julian, looking at the round of beef at the far end of the table, waiting to be carved and distributed to the brethren by Brother Cornelius, thought that he had made an unfortunate mistake that night in Paris. All on account of a chit of a girl that didn't care a straw about him. He reflected now that he had chosen a very ridiculous and melodramatic form of revenge for her flirtation with the American sculptor Foster. And he was then almost on the verge of success. Of course they said his painting lacked imagination. But the technique was excellent. See how they exploited him here. Not only had he painted the main chapel, but the Grotto of the blessed Virgin down by the lake in the grounds, and the priests' refectory. Hundreds of pounds worth. Work that might bring him fame in civilian life. And he could not even claim it. The rules ordered that his work should be unknown. Known only to God. The priests would show it to visitors as work 'done by one of our brothers.' And they treated him as a servant. His ashy pale face went yellow as he thought of it, and Brother John who stood three covers down from him on the right-hand side looked at him and thought that he was struggling with a temptation and murmured a prayer to Saint Joseph to assist him.

But the thought that Brother Julian was being tempted thrust Brother John's thoughts back upon his own past life. His black round cap perched at the back of his skull accentuated the death-likeness of his head. There were only bones and skin, yellow, thin-lipped, hollow-eyed and ghastly. And there was a horrifying expression in his withered old body that was almost bent double, and in his lips that perpetually moved in prayer. But his mind was not listening to his prayers, in spite of all the devices that he used to drown its murmurings. It kept saying, 'Brother Julian is being tempted, tempted, tempted, just as I, forty years ago, when I killed Jack Ryan, my cousin, when I caught him with my wife, and fled to France, to fight the Prussians, to forget, and never to forget; those potatoes will be cold, before Brother Cornelius comes to say grace, my God, my God, night and day, night and day, his face is always there, Jesus, Mary and Joseph, and now he's tempted.' And he suddenly began to strike his breast fiercely.

Everybody looked at Brother John and there was a smile on the faces of some, for some thought that he was mad to carry his devotion to such an extent. For they knew he wore a hair shirt and scourged himself and spent nights in the chapel on his knees in front of the tabernacle and ran around the lake three times every day at Angelus time. And others bowed their heads, for they considered him a saint and praised God that had brought them so near to such a saint. But Brother Joseph, who sat next to him, chuckled to himself and said, 'Saint John the Baptist has got the tantrums today, so he'll leave his wine to me.' For brother Joseph, the stout little old orchard brother was a staid, placid German brother, who was more interested in wine and good living than in devotion to religion. His sallow face frowned as he looked around the table and saw that there was no cake for desert that day, and he realised that it was Thursday and not Wednesday as he thought when coming up from his orchard. He reflected that it was awfully mean of the Father Superior to allow the brothers cake only on Wednesdays and Sundays. He was very fond of cake. He always soaked it in his wine and let it melt in his mouth. But then he cheered up again, for as it was Thursday he could go into the town for seeds. He always went on Thursday. Yes, he would bring a present of choice pears to . . .

Just then a woman's voice was heard outside the door and the door opened. The Dean of Discipline, Fr McPhillip, was showing a visitor around the college. He was an aristocratic priest, slightly given to dissipation they said. He looked around the room, cracked the thumb and forefinger of his right hand and said, 'This is the brothers' refectory.' A brown fur muff appeared around the door, then the rim of a black hat, then a rosy-cheeked face with pouting lips, and a sweet voice said, 'How delightfully interesting.' Fr McPhillip smiled, coughed behind his hand and went out pulling the door after him. As the door closed the brethren heard the sweet voice say, 'Why do they eat in a cellar? It makes me feel so . . .'

Brother Aloysius who served in the students' refectory raised his eyebrows and nodded his head at Brother Euphronius, the laundryman. Brother Euphronius pursed up his lips and nodded his head in reply. The nodding was done in a melancholy fashion as became such old and responsible brothers as Euphronius and Aloysius, for the cause of the nodding was the fact that Brother Euphronius found a lady's handkerchief with the initials 'C.S.' embroidered in gold letters in the corner among Fr McPhilip's linen the week before last, and he communicated the fact to Brother Aloysius. And Brother Aloysius gazed meditatively at his plate and reflected that women are the cause of all evil, women and young students. For the young students threw pellets of bread at him, behind his back, in the refectory, and were always complaining of the tea being too weak, and the porridge being cold of a morning. And they made fun of his red wig and his long nose. And he was sorry just then, as he waited in the cold refectory for the clock to strike one and Brother Cornelius to come and say grace before the meat was cold, that he had not stayed as butler to Mrs Norris of Closheen instead of becoming a brother. But he shrugged himself and murmured an Ave Maria against the temptation.

'How ridiculous that red wig looks on Brother Aloysius,' thought Brother Euphronius, the laundryman. 'I wonder is he related to Fr Brown the Bursar? He was a wig just like him. But what a lazy man is Fr Brown!' For Fr Brown had a string attached to the bolt of his door, and he pulled the string to open the door when anybody knocked, so as to save him rising. And Brother Euphronius reflected that the priests had a far easier time than the brothers, and began to worry his head about two bed sheets belonging to Fr McNamara that had got lost in the laundry the week before. He might get into trouble about them.

Brother Matthew, the cellar-man, standing at the left-hand side of Brother Cornelius's place at the head of the table, felt his hip pocket under his habit. He had a pint bottle of cognac in his pocket. That was for Brother Cornelius. Brother Cornelius sold chocolates to the students at his book shop every Wednesday and Sunday. And Brother Matthew was very fond of chocolates. And Brother Cornelius was very fond of cognac.

Brother Simon, the carpenter brother, who had just arrived from France, and was trying to learn English, began to stroke his brown beard and looked around the table, saying to himself, 'Meat, that is meat, plate, knife and fork, glass, *du vin*, *qu'est ce que ça*, *ah oui*, wine, *pommes de terre*, pot-pot-potta-toes, puteatoes, *non*, *non*, putatoes, salt, *moutarde*.'

Everybody looked up as the door opened and Brother Cornelius entered. His girdle was too small for his girth and his head was too small for his body. He had soft white hands like a woman. He marched to the head of the table throwing his toes sideways like a policeman. He smelt the gas, then he smelt the meat, then he sighed and folded his hands in his habit sleeves. Everybody coughed and Brother Julian drew in a deep breath through his nose. At that moment he decided to run away from the college and go back into the world.

The college clock struck four times. Then it struck once. It was one o'clock. The brothers took off their skull caps and held them in front of their breasts. They crossed themselves and bent their heads. Brother Cornelius began to say grace.

THE WAVE

The cliff was two hundred feet high. It sloped outwards from its grassy summit, along ten feet of brown gravel, down one hundred and seventy feet of grey limestone, giant slabs piled horizontally with large slits between the slabs where sea-birds nested. The outward slope came to a round point twenty feet from the base and there the cliff sank inwards, making a dark cavern along the cliff's face into the bowels of the earth. At the mouth the cavern was twenty feet high and at the rear its roof touched its floor, a flat rock that stretched from the base of the cliff to the sea. The cavern had a black-slate roof and at the rear there was a large streak of yellow gravel.

The cliff was semicircular. And at each corner a black jagged reef jutted from its base out into the sea. Between the reefs there was a little cove. But the sea did not reach to the semicircle of the cliff. Only its waves swept up from the deep over the flat rock to the cliff. The sea had eaten up the part of the cliff that rested on that semicircle of flat rock, during thousands of years of battle.

It was nearly high tide. But the sea moved so violently that the two reefs bared with each receding wave until they seemed to be long shafts of black steel sunk into the bowels of the ocean. Their thick manes of red seaweed were sucked stiff by each fleeing wave. The waves came towering into the cove across both reefs, confusedly, meeting midway in the cove, chasing one another, climbing over one another's backs, spitting savage columns of green and white water vertically, when their arched manes clashed. In one monstrous stride they crossed the flat rock. Then with a yawning sound they swelled up midway in the cliff. There was a mighty roar as they struck the cliff and rebounded. Then they sank again, dishevelled masses of green and white, hurrying backward. They rose and fell from the bosom of the ocean, like the heavy breathing of a gluttonous giant.

Then the tide reached its highest point and there was a pause. The waves hardly made any noise as they struck the cliff, and they drivelled backwards slowly. The trough of the sea between the reefs was convulsing like water in a shaken glass. The cliff's face was black, drenched with brine, that streamed from its base, each tiny rivulet noisy in the sudden silence.

Then the silence broke. The sea rushed back. With the speed and motion of a bladder bursting it sprang backwards. Then it rose upwards in a concave wall, from reef to reef, across the cove, along whose bottom the slimy weeds of the ocean depths were visible through the thin sheet of water left to cover the sea's nakedness by the fury of the rising wave.

For a moment the wave stood motionless, beautifully wild and immense. Its base in front was ragged uneven and scratched with white foam, like the debris strewn around a just-constructed pyramid. Then a belt of dark blue ran from end to end across its face, sinking inwards in a perfect curve. Then came a wider belt, a green belt peppered with white spots. Then the wave's head curved outwards, arched like the neck of an angry swan. That curved head was a fathom deep, of a transparent green, with a rim of milky white. And to the rear, great lumps of water buttressed it, thousands of tons of water in each lump.

The wave advanced, slowly at first, with a rumbling sound. That awful mass of water advanced simultaneously from end to end of its length without breaking a ripple on its ice-smooth breast. But from its summit a shower of driven foam arose, from east to west, and fell backwards on to the shoulders of the sea, that came behind the wave in mountains pushing it to the cliff. The giant cliff looked small in front of that moving wall of blue and green and white water.

Then there was a roar. The wave sprang upwards to its full height. Its crest broke and points of water stuck out, curving downwards like fangs. It seemed to bend its head as it hurled forward to ram the cliff. In a moment the wave and the cliff had disappeared in a tumbling mass of white water that yawned and hissed and roared. The whole semicircle of the cliff vanished in the white water and the foam mist that rose above it blotting out the sky. Just for one moment it was thus. In another moment the broken wave had fallen, flying to the sea in a thousand rushing fragments. The cliff appeared again.

But a great black mouth had opened in its face, at the centre, above the cavern. The cliff's face stood ajar, as if it yawned, tired of battle. The mouth was vertical in the cliff, like a ten-foot wedge stuck upwards from the edge of the cavern. Then the cliff tried to close the mouth. It pressed in on it from either side. But it did not close. The sides fell inwards and the mouth grew wider. The whole centre of the cliff broke loose at the top and swayed forward like a tree being felled. There was a noise like rising thunder. Black dust rose from the tottering cliff through the falling foam of the wave. Then with a soft splash the whole centre of the cliff collapsed into the cavern. The sides caved in with another splash. A wall of grey dust arose shutting out everything. The rumbling of moving rocks came through the cloud of dust. Then the cloud rose and went inland.

The cliff had disappeared. The land sloped down to the edge of the cove. Huge rocks stood awkwardly on the very brink of the flat rock, with the rim of the sea playing between them. Smoke was rising from the fallen cliff. And the wave had disappeared. Already another one was gathering in the cove.

THE TRAMP

There were eight paupers in the convalescent yard of the workhouse hospital. The yard was an oblong patch of cement with the dining-room on one side and a high red-brick wall on the other. At one end was the urinal and at the other a little tarred wooden shed where there was a bathroom and a wash-house. It was very cold, for the sun had not yet risen over the buildings that crowded out the yard almost from the sky. It was a raw bleak February morning, about eight o'clock.

The paupers had just come out from breakfast and stood about uncertain what to do. What they had eaten only made them hungry and they stood shivering, making muffs of their coat sleeves, their little back woollen caps perched on their heads, some still chewing a last mouthful of bread, others scowling savagely at the ground as they conjured up memories of hearty meals eaten some time in the past.

As usual Michael Deignan and John Finnerty slouched off into the wash-house and leaned against the sink, while they banged their boots on the floor to keep warm. Deignan was very tall and lean. He had a pale melancholy face and there was something the matter with the iris of his right eye. It was not like the other eye, but of an uncertain yellowish colour that made one think, somehow, that he was a sly, cunning, deceitful fellow, a totally wrong impression. His hair was very grey around the temples and fair elsewhere. The fingers of his hands were ever so long and thin and he was always chewing at the nails and looking at the ground, wrapped in thought.

'It's very cold,' he said in a thin, weak, listless voice. It was almost inaudible.

'Yes,' replied Finnerty gruffly, as he started up and heaved a loud sign. 'Ah —' he began and then he stopped, snorted twice to clear his nose, and let his head fall on his chest. He was a middle-sized, thick-set fellow, still in good condition and fat in the face, which was round and rosy, with grey eyes and very white teeth. His black hair was grown long and curled about his ears. His hands were round, soft and white, like a schoolmaster's.

The two of them stood leaning their backs against the washstand and stamped their feet in a moody silence for several minutes and then the tramp, who had been admitted to the hospital the previous night, wandered into the wash-house. He appeared silently at the entrance of the shed and paused there for a moment while his tiny blue eyes darted around piercingly yet softly, just like a graceful wild animal might look though a clump of trees in a forest. His squat low body, standing between the tarred doorposts of the shed with the concrete wall behind the grey sky overhead, was after a fashion menacing with the power and vitality it seemed to exude. So it seemed at least to the two dejected, listless paupers within the shed. They looked at the tramp with a mournful vexed expression and an envious gleam in their eyes and a furrowing of their foreheads and a shrinking of their flesh from this fresh dominant coarse lump of aggressive wandering life, so different to their own jaded, terror-stricken lives. Each thought, 'Look at the red fat face of that vile tramp. Look at his fierce insulting eyes, that stare you in the face as boldly as a lion, or a child, and are impudent enough to have a gentle expression at the back of them, unconscious of malice. Look at that huge black beard that covers all his face and neck except the eyes and the nose and a narrow red slit for the mouth. My God, what throat muscles and what hair on his chest, on a day like this too, when I would die of cold to expose my chest that way!'

So each thought and neither spoke. As the tramp grinned foolishly — he just opened his beard, exposed red lips and red gums and stray blackened teeth scattered about them and then closed the beard again — the two paupers made no response. The two of them were educated men, and without meaning it they shrank from associating with the unseemly dirty tramp on terms of equality, just as they spent the day in the wash-house in the cold, so as to keep away from the other paupers.

The tramp took no further notice of them. He went to the back of the shed and stood there looking out of the door and chewing tobacco. The other two men, conscious of his presence and irritated by it, fidgeted about and scowled. At last the tramp looked at Deignan, grinned, fumbled in his coat pocket, took out a crumpled cigarette and handed it to Deignan with another grin and a nodding of his head. But he did not speak.

Deignan had not smoked a cigarette for a week. As he looked at it for a moment in wonder, his bowels ached with desire for the little thin, crumpled, dirt-stained roll of tobacco held between the thumb and forefinger of the tramp's gnarled and mud-caked hand. Then with a contortion of his face as he tried to swallow his breath he uttered, 'You're a brick,' and stretched out a trembling hand. In three seconds the cigarette was lit and he was inhaling the first delicious puff of drug-laden smoke. His face lit up with a kind of delicious happiness. His eyes sparkled. He took three puffs and was handing the cigarette to his friend with the tramp spoke. 'No, keep it yerself, towny,' he said in his even, effortless, soft voice. 'I've got another for him.'

And then when the two paupers were smoking, their listlessness vanished and they became cheerful and talkative. The two cigarettes broke down the barriers of distrust and contempt between themselves and the tramp. His unexpected act of generosity had counteracted his beard and the degraded conditions of his clothes. He was not wearing a pauper's uniform, but a patched corduroy trousers and numbers of waistcoats and tattered coats of all colours, piled indiscriminately on his body and held together not by buttons but by a cord tired around his waist. They accepted him as a friend. They began to talk to him.

'You just came in for the night?' asked Deignan. There was still a condescending tone in the cultured accents.

The tramp nodded. Then after several seconds he rolled his tobacco to the other cheek, spat on the floor and hitched up his trousers.

'Yes,' he said, 'I walked from Drogheda yesterday and I landed in Dublin as tired as a dog. I said to myself that the only place to go was in here. I needed a wash, a good bed and a rest, and I had only ninepence, a piece of steak, a few spuds and an onion. If I bought a bed they'd be all gone and now I've had a good sleep, a warm bath, and I still have my ninepence and my grub. I'll start off as soon as I get out at eleven o'clock and maybe walk fifteen miles before I put up for the night somewhere.'

'But how did you get into the hospital ward?' asked Finnerty, eyeing the tramp with a jealous look. The cigarette had accentuated Finnerty's feeling of hunger, and he was irritated at the confident way the tramp talked of walking fifteen miles that day and putting up somewhere afterwards.

'How did I get in?' said the tramp. 'That's easy. I got a rash on my right leg this three years. It always gets me into the hospital when I strike a workhouse. It's easy.

Again there was a silence. The tramp shuffled to the door and looked out into the yard. The sky overhead was still grey and bleak. The water that had been poured over the concrete yard to wash it two hours before, still glistened in drops and lay in little pools here and there. There was no heat in the air to dry it.

The other six paupers, three old men with sticks, two young men and a youth whose pale face was covered with pimples, were all going about uncertainly, talking in a tired way and peering greedily in through the windows of the dining-room, where old Neddy, the pauper in charge of the dining-room, was preparing the bread and milk for the dinner ration. The tramp glanced around at all this and then shrugged his shoulders and shuffled back to the end of the wash-house.

'How long have you been in here?' he asked Deignan.

Deignan stubbed the remainder of his cigarette against his boot, put the quenched piece in the lining of his cap and then said, 'I've been here six months.'

'Educated man?' said the tramp. Deignan nodded. The tramp looked at him, went to the door and spat and then came back to his former position:

'I'll say you're a fool,' he said quite coolly. 'There doesn't look to be anything the matter with you. In spite of your hair, I bet you're no more than thirty-five. Eh?'

'That's just right about my age, but —'

'Hold on,' said the tramp. 'You are as fit as a fiddle, this is a spring morning, and yer loafing in here and eating yer heart out with hunger and misery instead of taking to the roads. What man! You're mad. That's all there's to it.' He made a noise with his tongue as if driving a horse and began to clap his hands on his bare chest. Every time he hit his chest there was a dull heavy sound like distant thunder. The noise was so loud that Deignan could not speak until the tramp stopped beating his chest. He stood wriggling his lips and winking his right eye in irritation against what the tramp had said and jealousy of the man's strength and endurance, beating his bare hairy chest that way on such a perishing day. The blows would crush Deignan's ribs and the exposure would give him pneumonia. 'It's all very well for you to talk,' he began querulously. Then he stopped and looked a the tramp. It occurred to him that it would be ridiculous to talk to a tramp about personal matters. But there was something aggressive and dominant and yet absolutely unemotional in the tramp's fierce state that drove out that feeling of contempt. Instead Deignan felt spurred to defend himself. 'How could you understand me?' he continued. 'As far as you can see I am all right. I have no disease but a slight rash on my back and that comes from underfeeding, from hunger and . . . and depression. My mind is sick. But of course you don't understand that.'

'Quite right,' said Finnerty, blowing cigarette smoke through his nostrils moodily. 'I often envy those who don't think. I wish I were a farm labourer.'

'Huh.' The tramp uttered the exclamation in a heavy roar. Then he laughed loudly and deeply, stamped his feet and banged his chest. His black beard shook with laughter. 'Mother of Mercy,' he cried, 'I'll be damned but you make me laugh, the two of you.'

The two shuffled with their feet and coughed and said nothing. They became instantly ashamed of their contemptuous thoughts for the tramp, he who a few minutes before had given them cigarettes. They suddenly realised that they were paupers, degraded people, and contemptible people for feeling superior to a fellow man because he was a tramp. They said nothing. The tramp stopped laughing and became serious.

'Now look here,' he said to Deignan, 'what were you in civilian life, as they say to soldiers, what did you do before you came in here?'

'Oh the last job I had was a solicitor's clerk,' murmured Deignan, biting his nails. 'But that was only a stopgap, I can't say that I ever had anything permanent. Somehow I always seemed to drift. When I left college I tried for the Consular Service and failed. Then I stayed at home for a year at my mother's place in Tyrone. She has a little estate there. Then I came to Dublin here. I got disgusted hanging around at home. I fancied everybody was pitying me. I saw everybody getting married or doing something while I only loafed about, living on my mother. So I left. Landed here with two portmanteaux and eighty-one pounds. It's six years ago next fifteenth of May. A beautiful sunny day it was too.'

Deignan's plaintive voice drifted away into silence and he gnawed his nails and stared at the ground. Finnerty was trying to get a last puff from the end of his cigarette. He was trying to hold the end between his thumbs and puckered up his lips as if he was trying to drink boiling milk. The tramp silently handed him another cigarette and then he turned to Deignan.

'What did ye do with the eighty-one quid?' he said.

'Did ye drink it or give it to the women?'

Finnerty, cheered by the second cigarette which he had just lit, uttered a deep guffaw and said, 'Ha, the women blast them, they're the curse of many a man's life,' but Deignan started up and his face paled and his lips twitched.

'I can assure you,' he said, 'that I never touched a woman in my life.' He paused as if to clear his mind of the horror that the tramp's suggestion had aroused in him. 'No, I can't say I drank it. I can't say I did anything at all. I just drifted from one job to another. Somehow, it seemed to me that nothing big could come my way and that it didn't matter very much how I spent my life, because I would be a failure anyway. Maybe I did drink too much once in a while, or dropped a few pounds at a race meeting, but nothing of any account. No, I came down just because I seemed naturally to drift downwards and I couldn't muster up courage to stop myself. I . . . I've been here six months . . . I suppose I'll die here.'

'Well I'll be damned,' said the tramp. He folded his arms on his chest, and his chest heaved in and out with his excited breathing. He kept looking at Deignan and nodding his head. Finnerty who had heard Deignan's story hundreds of times with numberless details shrugged his shoulders, sniffed and said: 'Begob, it's a funny world. Though I'm damn sure that I wouldn't be here only for women and drink.'

'No?' said the tramp. 'How do you make that out?'

'No, by Jiminy,' said Finnerty, blowing out a cloud of blue smoke through his mouth as he talked. 'I'd be a rich man to-day only for drink and women.' He crossed his feet and leaned jauntily back against the washstand, with his hands held in front of him, the fingers of the right hand tapping the back of the left. His fat round face, with the heavy jaw, turned sideways towards the doorway, looked selfish, stupid and cruel. He laughed and said in an undertone, 'Oh boys, oh boys, when I come to think of it.' Then he coughed and shrugged his shoulders. 'Would you believe it,' he said turning to the tramp, 'I've spent five thousand pounds within the last twelve months? It's a fact. Upon my soul I have. I curse the day I got hold of that money. Until two years ago I was a happy man, I had one of the best schools in the south of Ireland. Then an aunt of mine came home from America and stayed in the house with my mother and myself. She died within six months and left mother five thousand pounds. I got it out of the old woman's hands, God forgive me, and then . . . Oh well,' Finnerty shook his head solemnly, raised his eyebrows and signed. 'I'm not sorry,' he continued, leering at a black spot on the concrete floor of the wash-house. 'I could count the numbers of days I was sober on my fingers and thumbs. And now I'd give a month of my life for a cup of tea and a hunk of bread.' He stamped about clapping his hands and laughing raucously. His bull neck shook when he laughed. Then he scowled again and said, 'Wish I had a penny. That's nine o'clock striking. I'm starving with the hunger.'

'Eh? Hungry?' The tramp had fallen into a kind of doze while Finnerty had been talking. He started up, scratched his bare neck and then rummaged within his upper garments mumbling to himself. At last he drew forth a little bag from which he took three pennies. He handed the pennies to Finnerty. 'Get chuck for the three of us,' he said.

Finnerty's eyes gleamed, he licked his lower lip with his tongue and then he darted out without saying a word.

In the workhouse hospital a custom had grown up, since goodness knows when, that the pauper in charge of the dining-room was allowed to filch a little from the hospital rations, of tea, bread and soup, and then sell them to the paupers again as extras at nine o'clock in the morning for a penny a portion. This fraudulent practice was overlooked by the ward-master; for he himself filched all his rations from the paupers' hospital supply and he did it with the connivance of the workhouse master, who was himself culpable in other ways and was therefore prevented by fear from checking his subordinates. But Finnerty did not concern himself with these things. He dived into the dining-room, held up the three pennies before old Neddy's face and whispered 'Three.' Neddy, a lean wrinkled old pauper with a very thick red under-lip like a Negro, was standing in front of the fire with his hands folded under his dirty check apron. He counted the three pennies, mumbling, and then put them in his pocket. During twenty years he had collected ninety-three pounds in that manner. He had no relatives to whom he could bequeath the money, he never spent any and he never would leave the workhouse until his death, but he kept on collecting the money. It was his only pleasure in life. When he had collected a shilling in pennies he changed it into silver and the silver in due course into banknotes.

'They say he has a hundred pounds,' thought Finnerty, his mouth dry with greed, as he watched Neddy put away the pennies. 'Wish I knew where it was. I'd strangle him here and now and make a run for it. A hundred pounds. I'd eat and eat and eat and then I'd drink and drink.'

The tramp and Deignan never spoke a word until Finnerty came back, carrying three bowls of tea and three hunks of bread on a white deal board. Deignan and Finnerty immediately began to gulp their tea and tear at the bread, but the tramp merely took a little sip at the tea and then took up his piece of bread, broke it in two, and gave a piece to each of the paupers.

'I'm not hungry,' he said. 'I've got my dinner with me, and as soon as I get out along the road in the open country I'm going to sit down and cook it. And it's going to be a real spring day, too. Look at that sun.'

The sun had at last mounted the wall. It was streaming into the yard lighting up everything. It was not yet warm, but it was cheering and invigorating. And the sky had become a clear pure blue colour.

'Doesn't it make ye want to jump and shout,' cried the tramp, joyously stamping about. He had become very excited, seeing the sun.

'I'm afraid I'd rather see a good dinner in front of me,' muttered Finnerty with his mouth full of bread.

'What about you, towny?' said the tramp, standing in front of Deignan. 'Wouldn't ye like to be walking along a mountain road now with a river flowing under yer feet in a valley and the sun tearing at yer spine?'

Deignan looked out wistfully, smiled for a moment dreamily and then sighed and shook his head. He sipped his tea and said nothing. The tramp went to the back of the shed. Nobody spoke until they had finished the bread and tea. Finnerty collected the bowls.

'I'll take these back,' he said, 'and maybe I might get sent over to the cookhouse for something.'

He went away and didn't come back. The tramp and Deignan fell into a contemplative doze. Neither spoke until the clock struck ten. The tramp shrugged himself and coming over to Deignan, tapped him on the arm.

'I was thinking of what you said about . . . about how you spent your life, and I thought to myself, 'Well, that poor man is telling the truth and he's a decent fellow, and it's a pity to see him wasting his life in here.' That's just what I said to myself. As for that other fellow. He's no good. He's a liar. He'll go back again to his school or maybe somewhere else. But neither you nor I are fit to be respectable citizens. The two of us were born for the road, towny. Only you never had the courage of your convictions.'

The tramp went to the door and spat. Deignan had been looking at him in wonder while he was talking and now he shifted his position restlessly and furrowed his forehead.

'I can't follow you,' he said nervously and he opened his mouth to continue, when again he suddenly remembered that the man was a tramp and that it would not be good form to argue with him on matters of moral conduct.

'Of course ye can't,' said the tramp, shuffling back to his position. Then he struck his hands within his sleeves and shifted his tobacco to his other cheek. 'I know why you can't follow me. You're a Catholic, you believe in Jesus Christ and the Blessed Virgin and the priests and a heaven hereafter. You like to be called respectable and to pay your debts. You were born a free man like myself, but you didn't have the courage . . .'

'Look here, man,' cried Deignan in a shocked and angry voice, 'stop talking that rubbish. You have been very kind about — er — cigarettes and food, but I can't allow you to blaspheme our holy religion in my presence. Horrid. Ugh.'

The tramp laughed noiselessly. There was silence for several moments. Then the tramp went up to Deignan, shook him fiercely by the right arm and shouted in his ear, 'You're the biggest fool I ever met.' Then he laughed aloud and went back to his place. Deignan began to think that the tramp was mad and grew calm and said nothing.

'Listen here,' said the tramp. 'I was born disreputable. My mother was a fisherman's daughter and my lawful father was a farm labourer, but my real father was a nobleman and I knew it when I was ten years old. That's what gave me a disreputable outlook on life. My father gave mother money to educate me, and of course she wanted to make me a priest. I said to myself, I might as well be one thing as another. But at the age of twenty-three when I was within two years of ordination a servant girl had a child and I got expelled. She followed me, but I deserted her after six months. She lost her looks after the birth of the child. I never clapped eyes on her or the child since.' He paused and giggled. Deignan bit his lip and his face contorted with disgust.

'I took to the road then,' said the tramp. 'I said to myself that it was a foolish game trying to do anything in this world but sleep and eat and enjoy the sun and the earth and the sea and the rain. That was twenty-two years ago. And I'm proud to say that I never did a day's work since and never did a fellow-man an injury. That's my religion and it's a good one. Live like the birds, free. That's the only way for a free man to live. Look at yourself in a looking-glass. I'm ten years older than you and yet you look old enough to be my father. Come, man, take to the road with me today. I know you're a decent fellow, so I'll show you the ropes. In six months from now you'll forget you were ever a pauper or a clerk. What d'ye say?'

Deignan mused, looking at the ground.

'Anything would be better than this,' he muttered. 'But . . . Good Lord, becoming a tramp! I may have some chance of getting back to respectable life from here, but once I became a tramp I should be lost.'

'Lost? What would you lose?'

Deignan shrugged his shoulders.

'I might get a job. Somebody might discover me here. Somebody might die. Anything might happen. But if I went on the road . . .' He shrugged his shoulders again.

'So you prefer to remain a pauper?' said the tramp with an impudent, half-contemptuous grin. Deignan winced and he felt a sudden mad longing grow within his head to do something mad and reckless.

'You're a fine fellow,' continued the tramp, 'you prefer to rot in idleness here with old men and useless wrecks to coming out into the free air. What man! Pull yerself together and come over now with me and apply for yer discharge. We'll foot it out together down south. What d'ye say?'

'By Jove, I think I will!' cried Deignan with a gleam in his eyes. He began to trot excitedly around the shed, going to the door and looking up at the sky, and coming back again and looking at the ground, fidgeting with his hands and feet. 'D'ye think, would it be all right?' he kept saying to the tramp.

'Sure it will be all right,' the tramp kept answering. 'Come on with me to the ward master and ask for your discharge.'

But Deignan would not leave the shed. He had never in all his life been able to come to a decision on an important matter.

'Do you think, would it be all right?' he kept saying.

'Oh damn it and curse it for a story,' said the tramp at last, 'stay where you are and good day to you. I'm off.'

He shuffled out of the shed and across the yard. Deignan put out his hand and took a few steps forward.

'I say —' he began and then stopped again. His brain was in a whirl thinking of green fields, mountain rivers, hills clad in blue mists, larks singing over clover fields, but something made him unable to loosen his legs, so that they could run after the tramp.

'I say —' he began again, and then he stopped and his face shivered and beads of sweat came out on his forehead.

He could not make up his mind.

THE ROCKFISH

F lop. The cone-shaped bar of lead tied to the end of the fishing-line
dropped into the sea without causing a ripple. It sank rapidly through
the long seaweed that grew on the face of the rock. It sank twenty-five feet
and then struck the bottom. It tumbled around and then lay on its side in a
niche at the top of a round pool. The man on top of the rock hauled in his
line until it was taut. The bar of lead, bobbed up and down twice. Then it
rested straight on its end in the niche. Three short plaits of stiff horsehair
extended crookedly like tentacles from the line above the leaden weight at
regular intervals. At the end of each plait was a hook baited all over with
shelled periwinkle. A small crab, transfixed through the belly, wriggled on
the lowest hook. The two upper hooks had a covering of crushed crab tied
by thin strings around the periwinkles. The three baited hooks swung round
and round, glistening white through the red strands of broad seaweed that
hung lazily from their stems in the rock face. Dark caverns at the base of the
rock cast long shadows out over the bottom of the sea about the hooks. Little
bulbous things growing in groups on the bottom spluttered methodically as
they stirred. The man sitting above on the top of the rock spat into the sea.
Resting his fishing-rod in the crutch of his right arm, he began to fill his
pipe, yawning.

A little rockfish came rushing out from a cavern under the rock. He
whisked his tail and stopped dead behind a huge blade of seaweed when he
saw the glistening baits. His red scaly body was the colour of the weed. It
tapered from the middle to the narrow tail and to the triangular-shaped head.
He stared at the baits for a long time without moving his body. His gills rose
and fell steadily. Then he flapped his tail and glided to the upper hook. He
touched it with his snout. He nibbled at it timorously three times. Then he
snatched at the top of it and darted away back into the cavern with a piece
of periwinkle in his mouth. The man on the rock sat up excitedly, threw his
pipe on the rock, and seized the rod with both hands, breathing through his
nose.

Several rockfish gathered around the little fellow in the cavern. They
tried to snatch the piece of periwinkle from his mouth. But he dived under a

ledge of rock and bolted it hurriedly. Then, all the rockfish darted out to the hooks. The little ones scurried around hither and thither. Three middle-sized ones stood by the two upper hooks, sniffing at them. Then they began to nibble carefully. One little rockfish stood on his head over the bottom hook and sniffed at it. But the crab wriggled one leg and the rockfish darted away at a terrific speed. All the rockfish darted away after it into the cavern. Then one of the middle-sized ones came back again alone. He went up to the highest hook and grabbed at it immediately. He took the whole bait from it. The hook grazed his lower lip as it slipped from his mouth. The rockfish dropped the bait, turned a somersault, and dived into the cavern.

The man on the rock swung his rod back over his head, and dropped it forward again with an oath when he found the line coming slack. 'Missed,' he said. Then the leaden weight slipped back again into the niche. A crowd of rockfish quarrelled over the pieces of periwinkle fallen from the middle-sized fellow's mouth. The pieces, too light to sink, kept floating about. Then they disappeared one by one into the fishes' mouths.

A huge rockfish prowled in from the deep. He stood by the corner of a rock watching the little ones quarrel over the pieces of fallen bait. He was as big as all the others together. He must have been three feet long and his middle was as thick as a bull-dog's chest. The scales on his back were all the colours of the rainbow. His belly was a dun colour. He stood still for a time, watching like an old bull, his gills showing large red cavities in his throat as they opened. Then he swooped in among the little ones. They dived away from him into the cavern. He gobbled the remaining pieces of bait. Then he turned around slowly twice and swam close to the bottom towards the hooks. He saw the crab wriggling on the lowest hook. With a rush he swallowed the crab and the hook, turned about and rushed away with it, out towards his lair in the deep. The leaden weight rushed along the bottom with him. The line went taut with a snap over his back. The fishing-rod was almost wrenched from the hands of the man on the rock. Its tip touched the water. Then the man heaved the rod over his head and grasped the line. The hook was wrenched back out of the rockfish's gullet and its point tore through the side of his mouth.

The rockfish was whirled about by the wrench and dragged backwards headlong. With a swishing sound he heaved straight through the water towards the cavern. Then the line went taut again as the man hauled in. The rockfish was tugged up along the face of the rock. He jumped twice and heaved. He tore a strip of the soft thick skin in which the hook was embedded from his jaw at one end. Hanging to the hook by his strip, he came up gasping through the hanging weeds. The man groaned as he heaved.

Then the bared top hook got caught in a broad blade of seaweed. It combed its way through to the hard stem and then got stuck. The man heaved and could draw it no farther. The rockfish hung exhausted from the bottom hook. The man stuck his right foot against a ledge and leaning back with the line held in his two hands across his stomach he pulled with all his might. The top hook broke. The line jerked up. The rockfish reached the surface. He tried to breathe with wide open mouth. Then he hurled himself into the air and dived headlong downwards. The hanging strip of skin parted from his jaw. He was free.

THE LANDING

Two old women were sitting on the rocks that lay in a great uneven wall along the seashore beyond the village of Rundangan. They were knitting. Their red petticoats formed the only patch of colour among the grey crags about them and behind them. In front of them stretched the sea, blue and calm. It sparkled far out where the sun was shining on it. The sky was blue and empty and the winds were silent. The only noise came from the sea, near the shore, where it was just low tide. The water babbled and flopped along the seaweed on the low rocks that lay afar out, black strips of rocks with red seaweed growing on them. It was a spring evening and the air was warm and fresh, as if it had just been sprinkled with eau de cologne or something. The old women were talking in low voices sleepily as they knitted woollen stockings. 'Ah yes,' said one of them called Big Bridget Conlon, an old woman of seventy, a woman of great size and strength, with big square jaws like a man, high cheekbones, red complexion and wistful blue eyes that always seemed to be in mourning about something. She made a wedge of a corner of the little black shawl that was tied around her neck and cleaned out her right ear with it. 'I don't know,' she said, 'why it is, but I always get a pain in that ear when there's bad weather coming. There it is now, just as if there was a little stream running along inside in it. My grandmother, God have mercy on her, suffered the same way.'

'Yes,' said the other woman, with a lazy and insincere sigh, 'there is no going against tokens that are sent that way.' The other woman, Mary Mullen, was only sixty-five and her reddish hair had not yet turned very grey. She had shifty grey eyes and she was very thin about the body. She was greatly feared in the fishing village of Rundangan for her slandering tongue and her habit of listening by night at other people's doors to eavesdrop on their conversation.

'Heh, heh,' said Big Bridget, looking out mournfully at the sea, 'sure, we only live by the Grace of God, sure enough, with the sea always watching to devour us. And yet only for it we would starve. Sure, many a thing is a queer thing, sure enough.' She stuck the end of a knitting needle against her teeth and leaned her head against it. With brooding eyes she looked out at the sea that way, as if she were trying to explain something to herself.

The two old women lapsed into silence again and knitted away. The tide turned and it began to flow. From where the woman sat the land stretched out on either side into the sea. To the east of them, it stretched out in high cliffs, and to the west it ran along almost level with the sea for about a mile, a bare stretch of naked grey rock strewn with boulders. Farther west it rose gradually into high cliffs. Now a light breeze crept along the crags in fitful gusts, here and there, irregularly. The women did not notice it.

Then suddenly a sharp gust of wind came up from the sea and blew the old women's petticoats in the air like balloons. It fluttered about viciously for a few moments and then disappeared again. The old women sniffed anxiously and rolled up their knitting by a common impulse before they spoke a word. They looked at one another with furrowed brows.

'What did I say to you, Mary?' said Big Bridget in an awed whisper, in which however there was a weird melancholy note of intense pleasure. She covered her mouth with the palm of her right hand and then made a motion as if she was throwing her teeth at the other woman. It was a customary gesture with her. 'That pain in my ear is always right,' she continued; 'it's a storm sure enough.' 'God between us and all harm,' said Mary Mullen, 'and that man of mine is out fishing with my son Patrick and Stephen Halloran. Good mother of mercy,' she whimpered uneasily as she got to her feet, 'they are the only people out fishing from the whole village and a storm is coming. Amn't I the unfortunate woman. Drowned, drowned they will be.' Suddenly she worked herself into a wild frenzy of fear and lamentation and she spread her hands out towards the sea. Standing on the summit of the line of boulders with her hands stretched out and wisps of her grey hair flying about her face, while the rising and whistling wind blew her red petticoat backwards so that her lean thighs were sharply outlined, she began to curse the sea and bemoan her fate.

'Oh, God forgive you, woman of no sense,' cried Big Bridget, struggling to her feet with difficulty on account of the rheumatic pains she had in her right hip; 'what is this you are saying? Abandoned woman, don't tempt the sea with your words. Don't talk of drowning.' There was a sudden ferocity in her words that was strangely akin to the rapid charges of the wind coming up from the sea about them, cold, contemptuous and biting, like bullets flying across a battlefield fired by unknown men against others whom they have never met, the fierce and destructive movement of maddened nature, blind, and rejoicing in madness. And Mary Mullen, with her hands outstretched, paid no heed to Big Bridget, but shrieked at the top of her voice 'Drowned,

drowned they will be.' She also seemed to be possessed with a frenzy in which sorrow and joy had lost their values and had intermingled in some emotion that transcended themselves. The sea began to swell and break its back with rivulets of foam.

People came running down to the beach from the village as the storm grew in intensity. They gathered together on the wall of boulders with the two old women. Soon there was a cluster of red petticoats and heads hooded in little black shawls, while the men stood about talking anxiously and looking out to sea towards the west. The sea was getting rougher with every wave that broke along the rocky beach. It began to growl and toss about and make noises as if monstrous teeth were being ground. It became alive and spoke with a multitude of different yells that inspired the listeners with horror and hypnotised them into feeling mad with the sea. Their faces set in a deep frown and their eyes had a distant fiery look in them. They shouted when they spoke to one another. Each contradicted the other. They swore angrily. They strutted about on the boulders with their hands behind their backs, looking at the sea suspiciously as if they thought it was going to rush up each minute and devour them.

Stephen Halloran's wife squatted down on a boulder beside Mary Mullen and the two women, whose men were out fishing, became the centre of interest. They arrogated to themselves a vast importance from the fact that their men were in danger of death from a common enemy, the sea. Their faces were lengthened with an expression of sorrow, but there was a fierce pride in their sharp eyes that looked out at the sea with hatred, like the wives of ancient warriors who watched on the ramparts of stone forts while their men fought in front with stone battle-axes against the enemy. Stephen Halloran's wife, a weak featured, pale faced woman with weak eyes that were devoid of eyelashes and were red around the rims, kept rolling her little head from side to side as she searched the sea to the west, looking out from under her eyebrows and from under the little black shawl that covered her head. 'Ah yes,' she was saying, as she rocked her head, 'I told him this morning when he was setting his hooks in order, not to attempt going out, on account of the day that was in it, because it was this day twenty year ago, if anybody remembers it, that my grandfather died of pneumonia.'

'Drowned, drowned they will be,' shrieked Mary Mullen. She had gone on her two knees on a boulder and she had put on a man's frieze waistcoat. She looked like a diver in it, the way it was buttoned up around her neck and three sizes too big for her.

The crashing of the waves against the cliff to the east was drowning the wind. The wind came steadily, like the rushing of a great cataract heard at a great distance, but the noises of the sea were continually changing, rising and falling, with the stupendous modulations of an orchestra played by giants. Each sound boomed or hissed or crashed with a horrid distinctness. It stood apart from the other sounds that followed and preceded it as menacing and overwhelming as the visions that crowd on a disordered mind, each standing apart from the others in crazy independence.

Then the curragh with the three men rowing in it hove into sight from the west. A cliff jutted out into the sea, forming a breakwater where its sharp wedge-shaped face ended. Around that cliff the curragh appeared, a tiny black dot on the blue and white sea. For a moment the people saw it and they murmured in an awed loud whisper: 'There they are.' Then the curragh disappeared. It seemed to those on the beach that a monstrous wave surmounted it callously and that it had been engulfed and lost for ever, swallowed into the belly of the ocean. The women shrieked and threw their hands across their breasts and some said, 'Oh Blessed Virgin, succour us.' But the men simply said to one another, 'That was the 'Wave of the Reaping Hook' that came down on them.' Still the men had their mouths open and they held their breaths and their bodies leaned forward from the hips watching for the curragh to appear again. It did appear and there was an excited murmur. 'Hah, God with them.'

From the promontory where the curragh had just passed there was a lull in the water for a long way and the people could see the curragh coming along it all the time without losing sight of it. They could see the men rowing in it. They said, 'That's Stephen Halloran in the stern. It's a mistake to have him in the stern. He's too weak on his oars for a rough day.' They began to move cautiously down to the brink of the sea, where the curragh would have to effect a landing. As the moment when the curragh would have to risk the landing and the black rocks, on which the three men might be dashed to pieces by the ferocious sea, came near, the men on the beach grew more exited and some shivered. The women began to wail. A great babble of voices rose from the beach, harsh and confused, like the voices of demented people. All gave advice and none took heed of the advice given.

The place where the curragh would have to effect a landing was in the middle of the little cove. It was a jagged rock with a smooth space at the brink of the left-hand corner, where a slab had been cut out of it by a thunderclap a few years before. In calm weather the sea just reached level with the rock at half tide and it was easy to land a curragh there. But now the waves were coming over it like hills that had been overturned and were being rolled along a level plain speedily. The men on the beach stood at the edge of the rock and the line of boulders, fifty yards away from the edge of the sea. Yet the waves were coming to their feet when the sea swelled up. They shook their heads and looked at one another.

Peter Mullen's brother, a lanky man with a lame leg, made a megaphone of his hands and shouted to the men in the curragh, 'Keep away as long as ye can, ye can't come through this sea,' but he couldn't be heard ten yards away on account of the noise of the sea and of the wind. The curragh approached until it was within two hundred yards of the landing-place. The people on the beach could see the faces of the rowers distinctly. Their faces were distorted and wild. Their bodies were taut with fear and they moved jerkily with their oars, their legs stiff against the sides of the boat, their teeth bared. Two hundred yards away they turned their boat suddenly sideways and began to row away from the landing-place. Silence fell on those on the beach. The men looked eagerly out at the boat. The women rose to their feet an clasped one another. For half a minute there was silence that way while the men in the boat manoeuvred for position.

Then simultaneously a cry arose from the men on the beach and from the men in the boat. With a singing sound of oars grating against the polished wet wood of the gunwale the curragh swung around to the landing. The singing sound of the oars and the ferocious snapping of the men's breath as they pulled could be heard over the roar of the sea, it came so suddenly. The boat swung in towards the rocks. In a few moments the rowers would be smashed to pieces or in safety.

Then the women standing on the boulders became mad with excitement. They did not shrink in fear from looking at the snaky black canvas coated boat, with three men in her, that was cutting the blue and white water, dashing in on the rocks. They screamed and there was a wild, mad joy in their screams. Big Bridget's eyes were no longer mournful. They were fiery like a man's. All the women except Mary Mullen and Stephen Halloran's wife looked greedily at the curragh, but at the same time they tore their hair and screamed with pretended fear. Mary Mullen fell on her face on the boulder and resting her chin on her hands, she kept biting her little finger and saying in a whisper to herself, 'Oh noble son of my womb.' Stephen Halloran's wife rolled herself in her shawl low down between two boulders and went into hysterics.

And the men in the rapidly advancing boat yelled too, a mad joyous yell, as if the rapidity of their movement, the roaring of the sea, the hypnotic power of the green and white water about them and the wind overhead screaming, had driven out fear. In the moment of delirium when their boat bore down on death they no longer feared death.

The boat, the crew, the men on the beach, the women on the boulder were all mingled together for a wild moment in a common contempt of danger. For a moment their cries surmounted the sound of the wind and sea. It was the defiance of humanity hurled in the face of merciless nature. And then again there was a strained pause. The noise of voices vanished suddenly and silence came.

On the back of a wave the boat came riding in, the oars stretched out, their points tipping the water. Then the oars dipped. There was a creak, a splash, a rushing sound, a panting of frightened breath, a hurried mumble of excited voices rose from the men on the beach. The men on the beach waited in two lines with clasped hands. The foremost men were up to their waist in water. The boat rushed in between the two lines. They seized the boat. The wave passed over their heads. There was a wild shriek and then confusion. The boat and the foremost men were covered by the wave. Then the wave receded. The boat and the crew and the men holding the boat were left on the rock, clinging to the rock and to one another, like a dragged dog clings to the earth.

They rushed up the rock with the boat. They had landed safely.

BEAUTY

They paused to take breath. They had almost run up the steep slope of the field from the rear of the house. On fire with passion they had been unconscious of the stiff climb. In the stillness of the warm summer night their breathing sounded liked the thudding of two propellers heard distantly from the bowels of a ship. His arm was about her waist. His moist fingers crushed the silk of her dress. Her head leaned against his shoulder. They were both flushed with wine. Their eyes gleamed lasciviously. Between breaths they both laughed lowly and thickly.

He glanced back, down the slope towards the house. He could see the lights through the trees of the orchard. They flickered as if they were grinning, through the waving leaves. Sounds of music came. He shut one eye as his face contorted with lust. His fiancée was in there. 'Bah,' he thought, 'I'm tired of her.' Until that evening he had thought there was no other woman in the world. She had brought back the feeling of youth, of clean living, of the fresh air, of purity that he had thought dead in him. And at dinner he had met the woman beside him. He had avoided his fiancée's eyes during dinner. The other woman's eyes were always on his. She looked at him with clenched teeth when she raised her glass to her lips. The contour of her full figure, clothed in clinging black silk, brought a thick hot mist before his eyes. That mist shut out youth, purity, love, freshness, everything but passion. A glance, a nod, a whispered word and he was slinking with her through the orchard, without thought.

He looked down at her. Her face resting against his shoulder was turned to the sky. Her eyes were closed. He could hardly see her lips through the darkness. 'Come on,' he said, 'farther.' They moved through a gap in a hedge into a level field. They advanced towards a line of tall trees in front. 'Over there,' she panted, 'under those trees.' 'All right,' he mumbled. They walked in silence hurriedly. Their shoulders brushed as they side-stepped to avoid the tall thistles. She moved like a cat, her body twisting at the hips. He moved crouching. His dark face was scowling. His open lips stood red against his black clipped moustache.

Then the trees loomed up in front of them. Her right heel slipped on a hoof mark. She halted with a gasp and gripped her ankle. He swore silently at the delay and bent over her stooping body. His left hand moved over her bare neck, above the cape of her wrap. He trembled at the touch of her soft flesh. 'Are you hurt?' he said.

'It's nothing,' she replied standing upright. Her right arm went about his waist. She pressed him to her. His left arm encircled her neck. They both trembled. She looked around eagerly from tree to tree. 'There,' she said pointing at the two farthest. They were about to move towards them in silence, when she gripped his coat lapel with her left hand. 'Look,' she said, 'aren't they wonderful?' He looked fiercely at the two trees. 'Curse the woman,' he thought. He was not in a mood to pay attention to wonderful trees. And yet . . .

Suddenly the form of the two trees gripped his soul. Something rushed from every corner of his body, from his legs, stomach, head, hands and heart, to the centre of his chest and then straightforward to the trees. For a moment he was spellbound. Then his brain cleared. It seemed to make a noise like a screen being swept hurriedly from a window. He saw the two trees stand out against the background of blue sky, with darkness between him and the trees, and between the trees and the sky. He forgot they were trees. They appeared to be alive. The right tree was tall and slim. Its branches hung evenly on the trunk. They were wrapped around it, leafily, like a soft sinuous cloak. It was hiding behind the cloak. The left tree was reaching out to it. The top of the trunk leaned forward eagerly. A forked branch, like a giant's hands, tried to grip it. The huge knots on its stem stood out like vast muscles, as if it were straining forward trying to embrace the other tree. And the other tree hid between its cloak. The left tree was unable to reach it. They appeared to him to have been struck dead in that position. By what? 'By sin' flashed across his mind, and he shivered. The woman shivered too. But she shivered sensuously, making a hissing noise between her teeth. 'Wonderful,' she said in a voice whose sound suddenly repelled him like the hiss of an unclean reptile. 'Like, like jasmine against, against . . .' She swallowed her breath and her hand crept up about his neck, softly like a cat's paw. Then she turned her face up to his. He looked down into it, his nostrils twitching. His eyes swept over her face. He saw the dark circles under her half-closed eyes. He saw her puffed neck moving flabbily. Then his eyes darted back to the trees. Their cold rigid bodies seemed to crack with strength, as the light breeze licked their trunks. Their pure beauty made him feel a lump in his throat. The woman shook him irritably. 'Come,' she said.

He gripped her shoulders suddenly and stared into her eyes savagely. He shook with fury. His fingers dug into her flesh until she screamed. Then he flung her away from him and, holding his hands to his eyes, he staggered around groaning. Then he threw back his head and began to laugh wildly. He held his sides and laughed. The woman hissed out 'you cur' and began to run towards the house. He started at the words and looked with wide open mouth after her. Her form was already indistinct. He could only hear the swish of her silk dress. Then his eyes smiled tenderly and sadly. He tiptoed up to the right tree. He put his arms around the dark dewy trunk. He kissed it. Then he rushed headlong back to his fiancée.

THE BLACKBIRD

He was standing on the top of a stone fence singing as loud as he could. He was trying to drown the harsh babble of the sparrows that were perched in the ivy that grew on the face of the tiny cliff behind him. On three sides the tiny cliff encircled him, making a green sloping grassy valley about him and in front of him. Beyond the valley stretched a wide plain.

With his beak in the air and his throat swelling with sound he poured out his voice over the valley. The shrill chirping of the sparrows grated on his ears as it came from behind him in a confused babble. But he rejoiced, for his own delicious warble re-echoed again and again, high above every other sound in the valley. When the echo of his voice came back to him, with its loudness silvered into an enchanting softness by the creviced cliffs, he became so drunk with pride that he swayed on his slender legs and made his wing feathers flutter. He shut his eyes and bent forward his beak again and again to sing with greater strength. It seemed to him that his throat would melt.

The sun had set. The blue twilight was darkening in the valley. It was time for him to be asleep. But he sang on, drunk with pride. So intent was he on his song that he never noticed the sudden silence that fell on all the birds that had been singing, chirping and twittering behind him. Silence came suddenly except for the nervous, questioning, protracted whisper of a robin that hopped from stone to stone in the little rocky field beneath the cliff, thrusting out his breast defiantly with each hop. The ivy on the cliff face had been a moment ago alive with sound, and the ivy leaves had been shaking and fluttering as birds rushed hither and thither through them. Now the ivy was still. Not a bird moved. But the blackbird standing on the fence sang on.

A cat had entered the valley. He came over the brow of the little cliff, scrambled noiselessly down a crevice that was covered with moss and trotted swiftly along under the cliff until the birds stopped singing and chirping. As soon as their voices stopped the cat halted. He stopped dead with his right fore paw raised, his long black body half hidden in a hummock of grass he was passing through, his big eyes already gleaming in the half darkness.

Then he began slowly to tip the grass around him with his snout as if he were going to eat it. He curled his tail up under him. He lay down slowly on his stomach, just for one moment, and then with a fierce flashing of his eyes, he took a short rush forward close to the earth. He saw the blackbird singing on the fence that stretched across his path in front. The rush brought him as far as the fence where it ended in the cliff. Carefully planting paw after paw on the stones, and shaking each paw as he raised it to climb farther, he mounted the fence until he reached the top with his head. His large round whiskered head appeared over the top of the fence and began to roll around with an awful slowness. Again his eyes reached the blackbird singing on his right, ten yards in front of him. His eyes blinked and he made a little bored movement with his head from side to side as if he were heaving a sigh. He licked his paw. Then with a sudden and amazing spring he drew his body noiselessly to the top of the fence and rushed along it for five yards with his tail outstretched, his eyes blazing with an intense ferocity. The robin set up a piercing cry. The cat stopped dead.

The blackbird, conscious of the silence behind him, was full of vanity. He thought that he had overcome the sparrows and that they were listening in rapturous silence to his delicious warbling. He heard the robin shriek and he thought that the warning shriek was a cry of jealous rage. He shook himself and let all the feathers on his dun body sway with the light breeze that came up from the valley across his round breast. Then pushing his head backwards until his neck was almost joined with his back he broke out into another peal. The cat began to smell the little patch of blackened moss that grew on a stone in front of him on the fence.

Then there was silence for several moments. The robin had suddenly taken fright and flew southwards into the darkness that seemed to hang in the distance. The blackbird was listening to the answering call of his own voice coming back to him. The cat crouched down very low with his head moving from side to side in an apologetic manner, the light breeze making little whitish ridges through the dark fur on his back. Then he moved forward again.

He moved forward just as the blackbird broke once more into song. His long black body, moving sinuously along the pointed grey stones, looked ghoulish. The rippling notes coming from the blackbird's full throat rose in a wild peal of joy as the cat stole nearer inch by inch until at last he was within striking distance. He measured the round dun body of the blackbird with his eyes, and he raised his right fore paw carefully to thrust it forward to a little round stone whence he intended to spring. His body shivered and then it stretched out. The right fore paw landed on the round stone and . . .

Just then a gust of wind struck the blackbird sideways and made him shiver. It was the first gust of the night wind. It filled him with cold and with the sudden realisation that he was making a fool of himself singing out there in complete darkness when all the other birds were gone to bed. Suddenly he thought the silence was on account of the darkness having fallen and not on account of his wonderful music. He was filled with disgust and, uttering three loud peals of bravado, he rose from the fence just as the cat plunged forward to grasp him. A claw landed in his tail and three little feathers fluttered behind as he flew away, his heart panting with fright, afraid to look behind him.

Behind him the cat lay at the foot of the fence, where he had fallen after his fruitless plunge. His head was turned sideways, he was half fallen on his haunches and he was growling savagely. The sparrows began to twitter in the ivy.

SELLING PIGS

M rs Derrane was banging a sod of turf vigorously on the hearthstone. The sod was very hard, and when at last it broke one piece flew up in the air, hit the pot-hooks that hung on the chimney hanger and then descended on the half-baked cake that lay in the griddle.

'My soul from the devil,' said Mrs Derrane angrily, picking it out of the griddle, 'everything is upside down in this house. Poverty, poverty, poverty. Get out of that, you child of misfortune,' she cried, hitting the black cat that lay curled in the ashes with the piece of turf.

The cat me-owed, darted to the dresser, and looked at her viciously while he licked his paw. Then he shook his paw and fled out of the door.

'Phew!' said Mrs Derrane's husband, 'we are in a temper this morning. Phew! You have a bad heart, my girl. By all the oaths in the Holy Book you have.' 'Oh, you lazy lout of a man!' cried the woman, jumping to her feet and arranging her hair furiously. 'It's a pity ye didn't find that out the day you married me. Troth it is. I wish to God it was on some other finger you put your threepenny-halfpenny ring!'

'Now, Mary — '

'Oh, hold yer tongue, Michael Derrane.'

Mary bustled around the kitchen doing nothing, dusting the dresser, rattling the milk can, throwing clothes about, banging the shovel that stood at the back door. Then she went to the door and stood with her arms akimbo, looking out. She was a handsome young woman, black-haired, red-cheeked and with high cheek-bones. Her dark eyes were flashing like a young colt's. She wore a check apron over her red petticoat.

Her husband sat by the fire watching her and stroking his brown beard. Now and again he giggled, and his brown eyes sparkled with merriment. He, too, was handsome, and as he giggled his splendid muscles moved rhythmically beneath his blue sweater. Then he jumped to his feet and laughed. His wife took no notice of him, but kept looking out of the door, twitching her shoulders. 'Mary, I say.' Mary did not reply. He moved up to her, smiling, and put his arm about her waist. 'Go away from me,' she said, bending her head and at the same time turning around to him.

'Yerra, where can I go, Mary?' said Michael, crushing her to his bosom. 'Amn't I tied to you for life; oh, pulse of my heart?'

Mary raised her lips to his and they kissed passionately. The smile faded from his face and he looked into hers tenderly.

'What's the trouble, my white love?' he said.

'Oh, come in from the door,' said Mary coyly, 'the whole village will see us, and we six months married. Oh, Michael!'

He lifted her in his arms and sat on the hearth stool with her in his lap.

'Was it about the pigs, Mary?'

'Yes,' she gasped, fiddling with the breast of his jersey. 'You know well I have nothing in the house, and I want to go to the mainland to buy a chair for the room and a warm blanket for the winter, and a stone of wool to make the frieze, and lots of things. And it's time to sell them, Michael. They say prices are going to fall next week.'

'Well, well, now, and why didn't you tell me that? Sure I thought it was how you were getting tired of me.'

They both laughed childishly. They were really a foolish couple and a disgrace to Inverara, where people never carry on like that after being married six months.

'Will ye sell them today, Michael?' murmured Mary, and her voice came up from somewhere in his chest.

'Yerra, I'd sell my soul to please you. Although they'd be in better condition in another month. But what the devil is the difference? Get up, you lazy girl, and boil the kettle. We better wash them right away. The jobber, I heard, is on his way over from Kilmurrage. Come on; move, lazy bones!'

Michael, holding on to her apron-strings, began to caper around the kitchen.

'Let me go, you fool,' laughed Mary, 'how can I do anything while you are hanging on to me? Go on and fix the fire, while I strain the milk. Kiss me first.'

They prepared a tub of hot water and went to the sty at the back of the cabin to wash the pigs. The sty was a little square hut covered with a sloping roof of zinc with a little square yard in front, floored with concrete and surrounded by a high double stone fence. As soon as they entered the yard, three pigs rushed out grunting, with their snouts in the air smelling. Mary emptied a pail of mashed potatoes and sour milk in the trough in the middle of the yard, and the pigs dived into it biting one another. Then she and her husband began to wash them with soapy water.

'They are three fine pigs, God bless them,' said Michael.

'How much are you going to ask for them?' said Mary. The tender tone had left her voice now. It had a businesslike ring.

Michael scratched his beard.

'It would be a mortal sin to take a penny less than sixteen pounds.'

'Say fifteen pounds ten, Michael. He'd never give more than that.'

'I won't cross yer word, Mary. Fifteen pound ten it is.'

They finished washing the pigs and came back to the cabin. Mary hurried about, sweeping the earthen floor and the hearth, polishing the dresser and tidying the pots that lay against the back door.

Suddenly Michael, who was standing at the door, looking out, said: 'Hist, here he is up the road.' 'Lord save us,' said Mary. 'You better go and have a look at the sheep. It's always best to pretend not to expect him. Stay away an hour.' She bundled him out of the cabin hurriedly and then sat on a stool by the dresser, knitting.

Presently the pig-jobber came up the yard, shouting loudly to somebody, who was a long way off, about the weather. He walked very fast and with an air of being rushing around all the time, oppressed with business. He was a small man, with grey chin whiskers, a crooked red nose, with a great red knob stuck between his two eyes, on account of a fall from a cliff. His left leg had been broken in the same fall, and it bent outwards in a semicircle as he walked. 'God save all here,' he said, coming into the cabin. 'And you, too,' said Mary. 'Ye're welcome, Peter Mullen. Take a seat by the fire here. Well, now, and how's your family?'

'Splendid, Mrs Derrane, and how's Michael?'

Oh, sure there's no use complaining, but I'm glad to see ye.'

The jobber sat by the hearth and began lighting his pipe while Mary bustled, filling the kettle with water. When the jobber saw her approaching the fire with it he expostulated.

'Now, Mary, don't offer me anything, I —'

'Oh, will ye hold yer whist; sure ye wouldn't think of leaving my house without tasting something, if it were only a mouthful of tea.'

'Well, well, now,' said the jobber with a laugh, 'it is kind mother for you to be hospitable.'

There was silence for a minute, while Mary began to lay the table.

'Where is Michael?' said the jobber, at length. 'Oh, he is out somewhere,' said Mary casually. 'Ye didn't want him, did ye?'

'No-o,' said the jobber, heaving a sigh. 'I was just passing, so I thought I might look at his slips of pigs. I might need a few shortly. Though your pigs are very young, I hear.'

'Well, we aren't thinking of selling them for another month or so, but sure you can have a look at them. Or maybe ye'd rather wait for himself. He'll be in any minute.'

The jobber tapped nervously with his stick, obviously anxious to get away, but Mary kept chattering unconcernedly about everything. The kettle boiled. The tea was made. The jobber supped his tea hurriedly and swallowed an egg and ate some griddle cake. Still there was no sign of Michael.

'I'm afraid I must be going,' he said.

'Oh, sit down, man,' said Mary, 'he be in any minute. Sure it's not afraid you are that he'd think you were courting me.'

They both laughed and the jobber sat down again, and Mary kept chattering, until at last Michael, who had been sitting in a neighbouring cottage, came in.

'Ha, my soul from the devil!' he cried, 'I'm glad to see you, Peter Mullen.'

'I thought I'd see how your slips of pigs are getting on,' said the jobber.

'Slips d'ye call them, Peter?' cried Michael. 'I'll lay my oath there aren't three better pigs in the island. But I'm not selling them yet, for all that. But sure ye can have a look at them.'

The three of them went out to the pigsty and entered the yard. The pigs were lying on their sides in the sun. They grunted, but did not rise. The jobber beat them with his stick and they struggled to their feet.

'They're not bad slips, God bless them,' said the jobber. He walked around them several times. Then he measured the girth of each with his arms. Then he felt their hips, their flanks, their ears, pulled their tails, and laid his stick along their backs measuring them. Then he stood with his arms folded, looking at the ground.

'Well,' said Michael, 'what do you think of them?'

The jobber shook his head, took his pipe from his pocket and stuck his finger down the bowl. Then he tapped the ground three times with his stick and then leaned on it.

It was a habit he had.

'There is no fall to their flank,' he said.

'No fall to their flank!' cried Michael, curling his nether lip outwards and wrinkling his forehead. 'Why, where did you ever see a flank like that? And look at their thighs. Why, man, you could take shelter on a rainy day under their thighs. Look at that clear skin. Did you ever see an ear like that, as transparent as running water. There's a snout for you, as well moulded as a blood mare's nostrils. Why, man, they are —'

'Now don't be talking,' interrupted the jobber. 'A pig is a pig and weight is weight. Where is their weight, will ye tell me?'

'Is it their weight that's troubling ye? Well, now, I am surprised that a knowledgeable man like yerself would talk that way. Sure ye're not thinking that a sloppy, grease-swilling pig would weigh as heavy as a tight, well-balanced pig that's fed with the hand on the cleanest sour milk and the best of potatoes and the best bran that could be bought for money. Listen to what I'm going to tell ye. There isn't a loose inch in one of them three pigs. Their flesh is so packed that you couldn't drive a spear through it. What man? Is it out of your senses you are?'

'Oh, hold yer whist, will ye, Michael Derrane,' said the jobber, moving out towards the door of the yard. 'Don't try to tell me anything about a pig.' He rushed back and hit one of the pigs on the hind hoof with his stick. 'D'ye see that hoof?' he cried. 'But ye're young yet. Ye're young, and ye have a lot to learn.'

'What's the matter with that hoof?' cried Michael and Mary together.

'That's the surest sign of a pig's weight,' said the jobber, leaning learn-edly on his stick with his crooked leg thrust out. 'If a hoof is not spread, there is no weight in the pig.'

'Arrah, go away with ye,' said Michael.

'If he doesn't like them, why doesn't he leave them?' cried Mary. 'I hope ye're not thinking of selling them, Michael. Take care, would you. The bran will last another month.'

'Listen here,' said Michael, striking his right fist into his left palm, 'listen here.'

'Now, wait a minute,' said the jobber, seizing his beard in his hand and looking at Michael, 'I am a man of one word. Is fifteen pounds the price of the pigs as they stand or is it not?'

'It isn't,' said Michael shortly. 'I wouldn't sell them for a penny less than sixteen pounds, if I were so long without bread that I'd mistake a dogfish for a wheaten loaf.'

'Well, now, that settles it,' said the jobber, spitting on the crutch of his stick and setting off out of the yard in an awful hurry.

Mary and Michael followed him out of the yard, and as they were shutting the door Mary whispered to Michael: 'Don't let him go.' Michael looked at her and smiled. The jobber paused half-way down the yard and turned about.

I'm telling ye, Michael Derrane,' he said, 'you'll be sorry to turn down my offer. There isn't another jobber in the county will give ye within one pound of the money a week from today. And yer pigs show no signs that they are going to improve.'

'There is nothing in that but fool's talk,' Michael called out. 'Why not be a man and give the sixteen pounds?'

The jobber walked back hurriedly. He spat on his right hand and held it out to Michael.

'Are ye going to break a gentleman's word?' he said loudly. 'Say fifteen pounds —'

Michael turned away from the outstretched hand and shook his head. The jobber waved his stick and turned to Mary.

'My good woman,' he said, 'I have done my best, what more can I do? Although I would hate to think I would leave your mother's daughter's house without buying them.'

'Oh, wait now,' said Mary, smiling coquettishly, 'sure, as the men can't arrange the bargain, maybe a woman could step in and settle the difference. Don't go back on a woman's word and split the difference.'

'Spoken like a woman,' cried the jobber, stamping on the ground with his foot. 'I was never a man to go against a word from the lips of a beautiful woman. Split it is as far as I am concerned. Are you satisfied, Michael?'

'Put it there,' cried Michael, holding out his hand. 'The bargain is made. Fifteen pound ten it is.'

The three of them went into the pigsty again and the jobber put his mark on the pigs' backs with his scissors. Then he hurried away waving his stick, glad he had got the pigs for ten shillings less then he had intended to give. Michael and Mary entered the cabin.

'Oh, Michael,' said Mary, 'now we can go to town on Thursday and I'll get everything we want and we'll have a great time, won't we? Now what's the matter, Michael? What is it you're thinking about?'

Michael was looking at the ground with his hands behind his back. He was scowling at the floor.

'It's nothing,' he said, shrugging his shoulders. 'I was wondering whether Peter Mullen would have given another ten shillings if I had held out a little longer. I'd hate to have it said that he bested me. But, sure, the ten shillings won't matter, Mary. Give me ten kisses instead.'

BLOOD LUST

The idea came in a flash. One moment he was looking into the green sea thoughtlessly, as it swung past the anchored boat, and the next moment he wanted to kill his brother. The idea entered at the top of his head, where the hot sun played on his skull and it came straight down into the centre of his brain.

There it stayed and a red spot came before his eyes. The birthmark that ran across his upper lip twitched and his nostrils expanded. He looked at his brother, who sat with his back to him in the stern of the boat.

Staring stupidly at his brother's back he tried to think, but he failed to think. Thinking was difficult. His consciousness was dead except for the red spot in front of his eyes and the idea transfixed in the centre of his brain, standing immovable, saying: 'Kill you brother.' He put his hand to the top of his skull where the idea had entered and rubbed it and then caught the two fishing lines, that hung one on each side of the boat, and letting his lower lip hang, tried not to be conscious of the red spot and the idea.

But his hands soon left the lines, refusing to obey the weak command of his will. They came back to his chest and crossed on it and then pressed tightly into his armpits, and he dimly became aware that they were cleansing themselves of the brine and the fish slime that had gathered on them. He found himself looking at them — two great rough hands, each finger hanging stiffly from the joints and a great black, half-healed scar across the back of the right hand. Then he found himself looking from the hands to his brother's back, then up along the back to his brother's neck. When the red spot became fixed on his brother's neck, he found his lips curling up sideways towards his left ear and his eyebrows strained up towards his forehead. He felt himself drawing in his breath through his nostrils and snarling slowly. A nerve in the left side of his neck twitched. His hands clenched and a trembling shiver went upwards from his hands along the wrists to the shoulders and then all through the body, until it was rigid. He hung there on the seat waiting without breathing.

Then the idea standing in the centre of his brain began to ferment. It began to talk. It said: 'Your brother has a beautiful body. You have a birthmark on your upper lip and your left leg is shorter than the right. You are ugly. No woman will look at you. Your brother gets everything good in life. Kill him.' And the idea laughed within him.

Placing his hands on either side of him on the seat, he attempted to rise to go to his brother, but he paused. A cunning look came into his eyes. He looked around. Behind him lay the open sea, rising and falling smoothly. In front of him rose the towering cliffs. There was nobody in sight. Even the sea birds were asleep on their perches in the cliffs. There was perfect silence. He listened to the silence excitedly. Then the idea surged again forward, striking against the wall of his forehead.

He placed his right foot in front of him to move and it hit the basket that lay in the centre of the boat. The basket irritated him. It prevented him from going forward directly and clasping his brother's neck with his great hands. He looked at it snarling and frowning. His eyes were two points. The basket confused him. He could not explain its presence. Its removal was a physical act that might shatter that idea. He looked at it stupidly for a moment or two. Then he saw the long knife stuck in the corner of it. He smiled and reached out for it, at the same time looking cunningly at his brother. His right hand went about the handle of the knife. He gripped it and putted it out. Then he started. His brother had moved. He yawned, stretched his arms and then lay idly on his lines again.

Again the idea fermented. It began to circle around his brain, hurting the centre of his skull. At last it stopped again, pushing against the rear wall of his forehead. He drew in his breath deeply and paused that way, with his chest expanded. His lower lip began to tremble. His right knee began to tremble. Then the trembling spread all over his body. He felt a desire to yell, but he repressed the desire. The hand holding the knife began to move. He tried to hold it back, but it strained forward. The muscles gripped the handle like a vice. His arm stiffened to the shoulder and his whole body leaned forward following the hand holding the knife. His right foot circled the basket cautiously. He lay, his left hand on the gunwale of the boat and, balancing his body he prepared to cross the basket. He stood there astride the basket with the sharp teeth of the dried willows hurting the juncture of his loins. He made an effort to go forward and failed. Just when he tried to plunge forward his muscles refuse to act. Another idea struck him at that moment, disconcerting him. Fear came and hit him in the chest, making his breathing hard. Then it went from his chest up into his brain, assaulting the other idea. The two ideas struggled for a moment, and then fear gained the mastery. He withdrew his leg and fell in a heap on the seat.

Then fear fled and the other idea became again predominant. His hand shot forward once more and stiffened. He decided to go forward from the seat to his brother's back in one rush. He drew back and fixed his gaze on the hollow beneath his brother's shoulder blade, just beneath the bulge where the bone stuck out against the shirt. The red point had now fixed on that spot. He contorted his face into a savage snarl. He shut the left eye until his cheekbone hurt him. He drew his right hand holding the knife backwards, to the full reach of his shoulder joint.

Then suddenly the fishing line to the left twanged and went taut. He dropped the knife, and seizing the line hauled it in. Presently a glittering, gasping fish landed in the bottom of the boat. He placed it between his knees and crushed, crushed, until it was a pulped shapeless mass. He dug his thumbs in through the eye sockets. Then he sighed. His blood lust was satisfied.

HIS FIRST FLIGHT

The young seagull was alone on his ledge. His two brothers and his sister had already flown away the day before. He had been afraid to fly with them. Somehow when he had taken a little run forward to the brink of the ledge and attempted to flap his wings he became afraid. The great expanse of sea stretched down beneath, and it was such a long way down — miles down. He felt certain that his wings would never support him, so he bent his head and ran away back to the little hole under the ledge where he slept at night. Even when each of his brothers and his little sister, whose wings were far shorter than his own, ran to the brink, flapped their wings, and flew away he failed to muster up courage to take that plunge which appeared to him so desperate. His father and mother had come around calling to him shrilly, upbraiding him, threatening to let him starve on his ledge unless he flew away. But for the life of him he could not move.

That was twenty-four hours ago. Since then nobody had come near him. The day before, all day long, he had watched his parents flying about with his brothers and sister, perfecting them in the art of flight, teaching them how to skim the waves and how to dive for fish. He had, in fact, seen his older brother catch his first herring and devour it, standing on a rock, while his parents circled around raising a proud cackle. And all the morning the whole family had walked about on the big plateau midway down the opposite cliff, taunting him with his cowardice.

The sun was now ascending the sky, blazing warmly on his ledge that faced the south. He felt the heat because he had not eaten since the previous nightfall. Then he had found a dried piece of mackerel's tail at the far end of his ledge. Now there was not a single scrap of food left. He had searched every inch, rooting among the rough, dirt-caked straw nest where he and his brothers and sister had been hatched. He even gnawed at the dried pieces of spotted eggshell. It was like eating part of himself. He had then trotted back and forth from one end of the ledge to the other, his grey body the colour of the cliff, his long grey legs stepping daintily, trying to find some means of reaching his parents without having to fly. But on each side of him the ledge ended in a sheer fall of precipice, with the sea beneath. And between him and his parents there was a deep, wide chasm. Surely he could reach them without flying if he could only move northwards along the cliff face? But then on what could he walk? There was no ledge, and he was not a fly. And above him he could see nothing. The precipice was sheer, and the top of it was perhaps farther away than the sea beneath him.

He stepped slowly out to the brink of the ledge, and, standing on one leg with the other leg hidden under his wing, he closed on eye, then the other, and pretended to be falling asleep. Still they took no notice of him. He saw his two brothers and his sister lying on the plateau dozing, with their heads sunk into their necks. His father was preening the feathers on his white back. Only his mother was looking at him. She was standing on a little high hump on the plateau, her white breast thrust forward. Now and again she tore at a piece of fish that lay at her feet, and then scraped each side of her beak on the rock. The sight of the food maddened him. How he loved to tear food that way, scraping his beak now and again to whet it! He uttered a low cackle. His mother cackled too, and looked over at him.

'Ga, ga, ga,' he cried, begging her to bring him over some food. 'Gaw-ool-ah,' she screamed back derisively. But he kept calling plaintively, and after a minute or so he uttered a joyful scream. His mother had picked up a piece of the fish and was flying across to him with it. He leaned out eagerly, tapping the rock with his feet, trying to get nearer to her as she flew across. But when she was just opposite to him, abreast of the ledge, she halted, her legs hanging limp, her wings motionless, the piece of fish in her beak almost within reach of his beak. He waited a moment in surprise, wondering why she did not come nearer, and then, maddened by hunger, he dived at the fish. With a loud scream he fell outwards and downwards into space. His mother had swooped upwards. As he passed beneath her he heard the swish of her wings. Then a monstrous terror seized him and his heart stood still. He could hear nothing. But it only lasted a moment. The next moment he felt his wings spread outwards. The wind rushed against his breast feathers, then under his stomach and against his wings. He could feel the tips of his wings cutting through the air. He was not falling headlong now. He was soaring gradually downwards and outwards. He was no longer afraid. He just felt a bit dizzy. Then he flapped his wings once and he soared upwards. He uttered a joyous scream and flapped them again. He soared higher. He raised his breast and banked against the wind. 'Ga, ga, ga. Ga, ga, ga. Gaw-ool-ah.' His mother swooped past him, her wings making a loud noise. He answered her with another scream. Then his father flew over him screaming. Then he saw his two brothers and his sister flying around him, curveting and banking and soaring and diving.

Then he completely forgot that he had not always been able to fly, and commenced himself to dive and soar and curvet, shrieking shrilly.

He was near the sea now, flying straight over it, facing straight out over the ocean. He saw a vast green sea beneath him, with little ridges moving over it, and he turned his beak sideways and crowed amusedly. His parents and his brothers and sister had landed on this green floor in front of him. They were beckoning to him, calling shrilly. He dropped his legs to stand on the green sea. His legs sank into it. He screamed with fright and attempted to rise again, flapping his wings. But he was tired and weak with hunger and he could not rise, exhausted by the strange exercise. His feet sank into the green sea, and then his belly touched it and he sank no farther. He was floating on it. And around him his family was screaming, praising him, and their beaks were offering him scraps of dog-fish.

He had made his first flight.

An Charraig Dhubh

Bhí an taoille chomh íseal sin go raibh iomlán na carraige móire duibhe nochtaithe, síos go dtí an fheamainn dhearg lonrach a bhí crochta, mar bheadh cuirtín, amach ar aghaidh an íochtair tollta. Síos uaidh sin fós, i ndoimhneacht dorcha na mara, tháinig bodhar-thorann cráite ón uisce a bhí ag unfairt go leisciúil mall, sa bprochlais stóránach a bhí gearrtha amach as an seanchloch ag neart feargach na dtonn; ag bualadh agus ag bualadh gan sos, leis na mílte agus na mílte bliain.

Suas ó bhruach an uisce go dtí mullach maol na carraige bhí mórghleo ag an iomad ainmhí; iad ag ithe go santach agus ag déanamh aeir faoi sholas glégeal na gréine. Bhí éadan na feamainne go léir luchtaithe le créatúir bheaga. Bhí míola mara ag lámhacán anonn agus anall ar na dois agus ag smalcadh an sú ramhar a bhí ag sileadh leis an bhfeoil bhog. Bhí bairnigh bheaga greamaithe de na slata agus iad ag luascadh, mar bheadh rinceoirí, gach uair a chrochadar a gcuid sliogán droma, le fliuchán an bhídh shúite a shacadh uatha. Níos faide suas, imeasc na bhfréamh, bhí mealltracha móra dúilicíní ag oscailt agus ag dúnadh dhá leath a gcorp, mar bheadh boscaí ceoil á n-oibriú.

Bhí bun scailpe, de leithead agus doimhneacht mhór, go díreach os cionn fréamh na feamainne. D'at an charraig amach ar gach aon taobh den bhun seo, mar bheadh dhá leath tóna. Bhí na másaí móra clúdaithe le caonach buí slíocaithe, a bhí chomh mín le síoda. Shílfeá gur daite a bhí an chloch. Bhí na mílte frídí ag déanamh siamsa go haerach ar na másaí; iad ag léimneach go mear ó áit go háit agus á dtarraingt féin le fonn tochais tríd an gcaonach teolaí.

Chuaigh an scailp chun caoladais ag gabháil trasna thar an lag a bhí idir na másaí agus mullach na carraige. Bhí a híochtar brataithe le polláin chomh tanaí sin go raibh formhór an uisce tirimithe le teas na gréine agus salann geal ag lonradh timpeall ar a mbruacha. Ní baileach go raibh a ndóthain le snámh a dhéanamh ag na dois feamainne a bhí ag fás iontu. Bhí faochain bheaga ghleoite ag soláthar bídh imeasc na ndos, dath bándearg ar a gcuid sliogán agus a gcuid adharca ag treabhadh an aeir amach rompu go luaithneach mar bheadh méaracha ceoltóra. Bhí cuid eile de na polláin an oiread seo troigh ar doimhneacht agus a dtaobha cruinne lán ó bhun go barr le huarsain, a bhí sacaithe isteach go dlúth ina gcuid cupáin chloiche sciútha, faoi chosaint a gcuid sleá. Thíos imeasc na gcarnán cloch ag tóin na bpoll bhí éiscíní beaga faiteacha ag rith anonn agus anall go deifreach; cruacháin agus eascoin agus mongaigh a bhí rólag fós le farraige a thabhairt dóibh féin. As doimhneacht na scailpe, áit a raibh smugairlí róin á luascadh le súiteán an bhéil toinne, shiúil portáin mhóra mhillteacha suas go dtí an leac réidh a bhí faoi mhullach na carraige. Bhuail teaspach iad ar an gcloch thirim ghrianmhar. Thosnaigh cuid acu ag suirí agus cuid eile ag troid; lucht na troda ag déanamh ar a chéile go leataobhach agus a gcuid súl ataithe le buile. Nuair a chuaigh na trodairí i dteannta, baineadh torann as an tromchulaith chatha a bhí ar a ndroim. Thosnaíodar ag iomrascáil le chéile ansin; na crúba beaga ag iarraidh an namhad a threascairt agus na crúba móra crochta suas, mar bheadh siosúir oscailte, ag faire le buille marfach a tharraingt ar áit neamhchosanta.

D'éirigh an mullach suas deich dtroithe os cionn na leice seo. Bhí cumraíocht phéiste móire, a fuair bás sa gcianaimsir, gearrtha amach ar thaobh cruinn na cloiche, chomh fíor agus dá mba lámh scuiltéara a rinne an múnlú. Bhí rian dearg an iarainn le feiscint freisin san ábhar. Thuas ar cheartlár an mhullaigh bhí faoileán bán ina sheasamh ar leathchois, a cheann faoi sciathán agus é ina chodladh. Bhí conablach ronnaigh, gan scioltar ar na cnámha, i ngar dhó ar an gcloch. Ní raibh cor as an éan, seasta go ríoga ansin thuas, mar bheadh seod geal álainn ar choróin mhullaigh na carraige.

D'iompaigh an taoille. D'éirigh an fharraige go tobann. Isteach léi sa bprochlais agus lasc sí a taobha. Rinne torann a buailte macalla glotharnach. Caitheadh múr geal de uisce cáite suas go hard san aer, agus é ag sioscadh ar nós bagairt ghéabha. Crochadh amach an fheamainn ar bharr toinne. Bhí na dois fhada ag lúbadh agus ag síneadh go dian le luasadh an tsrutha. Nuair a dhruid an tuile síos arís, tar éis an chéad iarraidh sin, tháinig torann beag toirnigh as bun thiar na spéire. Is ar éigin ab fhéidir é a chloisint agus bhí aiteall ina dhiaidh. Ansin arís, do phléasc an toirneach agus í go leor níos láidre. Bhí an torann seo trom agus bodhar, mar bheadh urlár na mara á reabadh thíos ar an doimhneacht.

Is gearr gur dhubhaigh an spéir. Chuaigh an t-aer chun fuaradais. Thosnaigh cuaifeacha gaoithe ag rith go mear os cionn droma na farraige; iad ag casadh anonn agus anall mar bheadh an tslí amú orthu. Bhris cúr ar chír gach lonna. Anois bhí an toirneach ag pléascadh gan sos, thuas in airde mhór na spéire. D'at an fharraige go huafásach mear, nó go raibh brachlannaí ag gabháil ar an tír agus torann a mbriste ag coimhlint leis an toirneach. Neartaigh an ghaoth agus thosnaigh sí ag screadaíl.

Dhúisigh an faoileán agus bhreathnaigh sé ina thimpeall go faiteach. Ghlaoigh sé os íseal. Ansin do scar sé a chuid sciathán go tapaidh agus d'éirigh sé ón gcarraig. Chuir sé timpeall trí bhabhta agus é ag bordáil suas tríd an spéir faoi lán eitill. Nuair a bhí sé sách ard, thug sé aghaidh ar thír agus scaoil sé a sciatháin leis an ngaoth, a bhí ag teacht go tréan ina dhiaidh aniar. Rugadh isteach ón bhfarraige é mar bheadh cleite; gan cor as na sciatháin sínte agus a chuid cos as sliobarnadh.

Scanraigh na portáin. Thréigeadar an tsuirí agus an troid. Síos leo go deifreach sa scailp; na boic ag iompar a gcarad suirí agus an dream eile ag cliobadh le teann faitís gach ar tháinig sa mbealach orthu. D'éirigh na frídí freisin as a siamsa. Bhuaileadar amach as an gcaonach ina bplod mór mill-teach agus rinneadar ar an tír chomh tréan agus a bhí iontu. Bhí cuma coirbe fada ar a léimneach reatha. Dhún na dúilicíní dorais a gcorp agus rug na bairnigh greim daingean ar an gcloch le bruacha na sliogán. Chuaigh gach uile rud beo i bhfolach roimh an mbuile dhamanta. Ansin ní raibh cor dá laghad as na hainmhithe a bhí fanta ar an gcarraig, agus bhíodar ar fad ina dtost. Bhí deireadh curtha ag an ngairfean leis an rírá sámhach a bhain teas na gréine as an slua iomadach.

Scairt lasair tintrí go tobann os cionn na carraige agus chuaigh a brí i dtalamh ar an mullach maol. Thosnaigh iomlán na cloiche ag craitheadh. Ansin tháinig scréach fada uaithi, mar bheadh na mílte agus na mílte de bhraitlíní á stróiceadh in éineacht. Phléasc sí ó thóin go ceann na scailpe. Caitheadh anuas an mullach agus thit sé isteach sa bhfarraige. D'oscail na másaí móra, mar bheadh cairín conablaigh ar uair a scoilte. Tharraing an taoille siar i bhfad agus d'eirigh sí suas ina brachlainn chumasach. Bhí a bolg uaithne folamh agus bhí a cír gheal sáite amach roimpi; í an-ard ar fad agus meall tréan uisce teannta léi aniar. Isteach léi agus an toirneach ag pléascadh go díreach os a cionn. Bhris sí go tréan idir an dá mhása leathnaithe.

Tar éis an bhuille mharfach sin, d'iompaigh na másaí droim ar ais agus slogadh síos iad go tóin an phoill. Réabadh an charraig ar fad agud d'éirigh múr mór millteach uisce cháite suas go hard, sular thit sé anuas arís ar éadan fiuchta na brachlainne briste.

D'fhan dois feamainne agus caonach agus coirp bheaga bhídeacha na marbh ag imeacht ar bharr uisce san áit a sheas an charraig, nó gur chaith brachlann eile suas faoi thír iad.

A SHILLING

Three old men were sitting on the slash wall of Kilmillick pier with their backs to the sea and their faces to the village and the sun. A light breeze came from the sea behind them, bringing a sweet salt smell of seaweed being kissed by the sun. The village in front was very quiet. Not a movement but the lazy blue smoke curling slantwise from the cabin chimneys. It was early afternoon, Sunday and all the young men and women were in Kilmurrage at a football match. The three old men were telling stories of big fish they had caught in their youth.

Suddenly there was a swish of canvas and a little white yacht swung around the corner of the pier and came alongside. The three old men immediately got to their feet and advanced through the turf dust to the brink of the pier looking down at the yacht. Patsy Conroy the most active of the old men seized the mooring rope and made the yacht fast. Then he came back and joined the other two watching the yachtsmen getting ready to go ashore. 'She's a lovely boat,' said old Brian Manion, the old fellow with the bandy right leg and the bunion behind his right ear. 'Heh,' he said scratching the small of his back, 'it must cost a lot of money to keep that boat. Look at those shiny brasses and ye can see a carpet laid on the cabin floor through that hatchway. Oh boys!'

'I'd like to have her for a week's fishing,' said Mick Feeney, breathing loudly through his long red nose. His big red-rimmed blue eyes seemed to jump in and out. He gripped the top of his stick with his two hands and looked down at the yacht with his short legs wide apart.

Patsy Conroy said nothing. He stood a little apart with his hands stuck in his waist-belt. Although he was seventy-two, he was straight, lithe and active, but his face was yellow and wrinkled like old parchment and his toothless red gums were bared in an old man's grin. His little eyes beneath his bushy white eyebrows roamed around the yacht cunningly as if they were trying to steal something. He wore a yellow muffler wound round and round his neck up to his chin, in spite of the heat of the day.

'Where is the nearest public-house?' drawled a red-faced man in a white linen shirt and trousers from the yacht deck.

The old men told him, all together.

'Let's go and have a drink, Totty,' said the red-faced man.

'Right-o,' said the other man.

When the red-faced man was climbing the iron ladder on to the pier a shilling fell out of his hip pocket. It fell noiselessly on a little coil of rope that lay on the deck at the foot of the ladder. The red-faced man did not notice it and he walked up the pier with his friend. The three old men noticed it, but they did not tell the red-faced man. Neither did they tell one another. As soon as the shilling landed on the little coil of rope and lay there glistening, the three of them became so painfully conscious of it that they were bereft of the power of speech or of coherent thought. Each cast a glance at the shilling, a hurried furtive glance, and then each looked elsewhere, just after the manner of a dog that sees a rabbit in a bush and stops dead with one paw raised, seeing the rabbit although his eyes are fixed elsewhere.

Each old man knew that the other two had seen the shilling, yet each was silent about it in the hope of keeping the discovery his own secret. Each knew that it was impossible for him to go down the iron ladder to the deck, pick up the shilling and ascend with it to the pier without being detected. For there was a man who wore a round white cap doing something in the cabin. Every third moment or so his cap appeared through the hatchway and there was a noise of crockery being washed or something. And the shilling was within two feet of the hatchway. And the old men, except perhaps Patsy Conroy, were too old to descend the ladder and ascend again. And anyway each knew that even if there were nobody in the cabin, and even if they could descend the ladder, that the others would prevent either one from getting the shilling, since each preferred that no one should have the shilling if he couldn't have it himself. And yet such was the lure of that glistening shilling that the three of them stared with palpitating hearts and feverishly working brains at objects within two feet of the shilling. They stared in a painful silence that was loud with sound as of a violent and quarrelsome conversation. The noise Mick Feeney made breathing through his nose exposed his whole scheme of thought to the other two men just as plainly as if he explained it slowly and in detail. Brain Manion kept fidgeting with his hands, rubbing the palms together, and the other two heard him and cursed his avarice. Patsy Conroy alone made no sound, but his very silence was loud and stinking to the other two men, for it left them in ignorance of what plans were passing through his crafty head.

And the sun shone warmly. And the salt, healthy smell of the sea inspired thirst. And there was excellent cool frothy porter in Kelly's. So much so that no one of the three old men ever thought of the fact that the shilling belonged to somebody else. So much so indeed that each of them felt indignant with the shameless avarice of the other two. There was almost a homicidal tendency in the mind of each against the others. Thus three minutes passed. The two owners of the yacht had passed out of sight. Brian Manion and Mick Feeney were trembling and drivelling slightly at the mouth.

Then Patsy Conroy stooped and picked up a pebble from the pier. He dropped it on to the deck of the yacht. The other two men made a slight movement to intercept the pebble with their sticks, a foolish unconscious movement. Then they started and let their jaws drop. Patsy Conroy was speaking. 'Hey there,' he shouted between his cupped hands.

A pale-faced gloomy man with a napkin on his hip stepped up to the second step of the hatchway. 'What d'ye want?' he said.

'Beg yer pardon, sir,' said Patsy Conroy, 'but would ye hand me up that shilling that just dropped out a' me hand?'

The man nodded, picked up the shilling, muttered 'catch' and threw the shilling on to the pier. Patsy touched his cap and dived for it. The other two old men were so dumbfounded that they didn't even scramble for it. They watched Patsy spit on it and put it in his pocket. They watched him walk up the pier, sniffing out loud, his long, lean, greybacked figure with the yellow muffler around his neck, moving as straight and solemn as a policeman.

Then they looked at each other, their faces contorted with anger. And each, with upraised stick, snarled at the other:

'Why didn't ye stop him, you fool?'

THREE LAMBS

Little Michael rose before dawn. He tried to make as little noise as possible. He ate two slices of bread and butter and drank a cup of milk, although he hated cold milk with bread and butter in the morning. But on an occasion like this, what did it matter what a boy ate? He was going out to watch the black sheep having a lamb. His father had mentioned the night before that the black sheep was sure to lamb that morning, and of course there was a prize, three pancakes, for the first one who saw the lamb.

He lifted the latch gently and stole out. It was best not to let his brother John know he was going. He would be sure to want to come too. As he ran down the lane, his sleeves, brushing against the evergreen bushes, were wetted by the dew, and the tip of his cap was just visible above the hedge, bobbing up and down as he ran. He was in too great a hurry to open the gate and tore a little hole in the breast of his blue jersey climbing over it. But he didn't mind that. He would get another one on his thirteenth birthday.

He turned to the left from the main road, up a lane that led to the field where his father, the magistrate, kept his prize sheep. It was only a quarter of a mile, that lane, but he thought that it would never end and he kept tripping among the stones that strewed the road. It was so awkward to run on the stones wearing shoes, and it was too early in the year yet to be allowed to go barefooted. He envied Little Jimmy, the son of the farm labourer, who was allowed to go barefooted all the year round, even in the depths of winter, and who always had such wonderful cuts on his big toes, the envy of all the little boys in the village school.

He climbed over the fence leading into the fields and, clapping his hands together, said, 'Oh, you devil,' a swear word he had learned from Little Jimmy and of which he was very proud. He took off his shoes and stockings and hid them in a hole in the fence. Then he ran jumping, his bare heels looking like round brown spots as he tossed them up behind him. The grass was wet and the ground was hard, but he persuaded himself that it was great fun.

Going through a gap into the next field, he saw a rabbit nibbling grass. He halted suddenly, his heart beating loudly. Pity he hadn't a dog. The rabbit stopped eating. He cocked up his ears. He stood on his tail, with his neck craned up and his fore feet hanging limp. Then he came down again. He thrust his ears forward. Then he lay flat with his ears buried in his back and lay still. With a great yell Little Michael darted forward imitating a dog barking and the rabbit scurried away in short sharp leaps. Only his white tail was visible in the grey light.

Little Michael went into the next field, but the sheep were nowhere to be seen. He stood on a hillock and called out 'Chowin, chowin,' three times. Then he heard 'Mah-m-m-m' in the next field and ran on. The sheep were in the last two fields, two oblong little fields, running in a hollow between two crags, surrounded by high thick fences, the walls of an old fort. In the nearest of the two fields he found ten of the sheep, standing side by side, looking at him, with their fifteen lambs in front of them also looking at him curiously. He counted them out loud and then he saw that the black sheep was not there. He panted with excitement. Perhaps she already had a lamb in the next field. He hurried to the gap leading into the next field, walking stealthily, avoiding the spots where the grass was high, so as to make less noise. It was bad to disturb a sheep that was lambing. He peered through a hole in the fence and could see nothing. Then he crawled to the gap and peered around the corner. The black sheep was just inside standing with her fore feet on a little mound.

Her belly was swollen out until it ended on each side in a sharp point and her legs appeared to be incapable of supporting her body. She turned her head sharply and listened. Little Michael held his breath, afraid to make a noise. It was of vital importance not to disturb the sheep. Straining back to lie down he burst a button on his trousers and he knew his braces were undone. He said, 'Oh, you devil,' again and decided to ask his mother to let him wear a belt instead of braces, same as Little Jimmy wore. Then he crawled farther back from the gap and taking off his braces altogether made it into a belt. It hurt his hips, but he felt far better and manly.

Then he came back again to the gap and looked. The black sheep was still in the same place. She was scratching the earth with her fore feet and going around in a circle, as if she wanted to lie down but was afraid to lie down. Sometimes she ground her teeth and made an awful noise, baring her jaws and turning her head around sideways. Little Michael felt a pain in his heart in pity for her, and he wondered why the other sheep didn't come to keep her company. Then he wondered whether his mother had felt the same pain when she had Ethna the autumn before. She must have, because the doctor was there.

Suddenly the black sheep went on her knees. She stayed a few seconds on her knees and then she moaned and sank to the ground and stretched herself out with her neck on the little hillock and her hind quarters falling down the little slope. Little Michael forgot about the pain now. His heart thumped with excitement. He forgot to breathe, looking intently. 'Ah,' he said. The sheep stretched again and struggled to her feet and circled around once stamping and grinding her teeth. Little Michael moved up to her slowly. She looked at him anxiously, but she was too sick to move away. He broke the bladder and he saw two little feet sticking out. He seized them carefully and pulled. The sheep moaned again and pressed with all her might. The lamb dropped on the grass.

Little Michael sighed with delight and began to rub its body with his finger nails furiously. The sheep turned around and smelt it, making a funny happy noise in its throat. The lamb, its white body covered with yellow slime, began to move, and presently it tried to stand up, but it fell again and Little Michael kept rubbing it, sticking his fingers into its ears and nostrils to clear them. He was so intent on this work that he did not notice the sheep had moved away again, and it was only when the lamb was able to stand up and he wanted to give it suck, that he noticed the sheep was lying again giving birth to another lamb. 'Oh, you devil,' gasped Little Michael, 'six pancakes.'

The second lamb was while like the first but with a black spot on it right ear. Little Michael rubbed it vigorously, pausing now and again to help the first lamb to its feet as it tried to stagger about. The sheep circled around making low noises in her throat, putting her nostrils to each lamb in turn, stopping nowhere, as giddy as a young schoolgirl, while the hard pellets of earth that stuck to her belly jingled like beads when she moved. Little Michael then took the first lamb and tried to put it to suck, but it refused to take the teat, stupidly sticking its mouth into the wool. Then he put his finger in its mouth and gradually got the teat in with his other hand. Then he pressed the teat and the hot milk squirted into the lamb's mouth. The lamb shook its tail, shrugged his body, made a little drive with its head and began to suck.

Little Michael was just going to give the second lamb suck, when the sheep moaned and moved away again. He said 'chowin, chowin, poor chowin,' and put the lamb to her head, but she turned away moaning and grinding her teeth and stamping. 'Oh, you devil,' said Little Michael, 'she is going to have another lamb.'

The sheep lay down again, with her fore leg stretched out in front of her and, straining her neck backwards, gave birth to a third lamb, a black lamb.

Then she rose smartly to her feet, her two sides hollow now. She shrugged herself violently and, without noticing the lambs, started to eat grass fiercely, just pausing now and again to say 'mah-m-m-m.'

Little Michael, in an ecstasy of delight, rubbed the black lamb until it was able to stand. Then he put all the lambs to suck, the sheep eating around her in a circle, without changing her feet, smelling a lamb now and again. 'Oh, you devil,' Little Michael kept saying thinking he would be quite famous now, and talked about for a whole week. It was not every day that a sheep had three lambs.

He brought them to a sheltered spot under the fence. He wiped the birth slime from his hands with some grass. He opened his penknife and cut the dirty wool from the sheep's udder, lest the lambs might swallow some and die. Then he gave a final look at them, said, 'Chowin, chowin,' tenderly and turned to go.

He was already at the gap when he stopped with a start. He raced back to the lambs and examined each of them. 'Three she lambs,' he gasped. 'Oh, you devil, that never happened before. Maybe father will give me half-a-crown.'

And as he raced homeward, he barked like a dog in his delight.

A PIG IN A BEDROOM

The sanitary officer was coming down the main street of Kilmurrage at a
sharp trot. He was coming from the post office with the mail, and letters and newspapers were sticking from the pockets of his threadbare grey
tweed suit. His boots scratched along the road as he ran, and he kept cursing
to himself and pulling at his stiff linen collar with his hand, so that there was
a black smudge under his right ear. Now and again he stopped to take out
his large silver watch and look at it. Then he put it back, scratched the back
of his head and looked at the letter that he held in his right hand. 'Damn
and blast this letter,' he would say, and trot on again. He was a thin, pale-
faced man of middle age, and a very common-looking man except for his
shifty blue eyes and the funny way he had of sniffing and twisting the end of
his long sharp nose from side to side when he sniffed.

As he was going to turn to the right by the courthouse towards his own
house, a peasant jumped off a gate and hailed him. 'Mr Milligan,' said the
peasant, wiping his mouth on his sleeve, 'it's how my wife is sick and I want
a red ticket for the doctor.' The sanitary officer waved his hands in the air
and began to swear and stammer. 'Uh-uh-uh!' he cried, 'I'm relieving officer,
sanitary officer, the devil's officer, and God knows what. You and your wife
can go to the devil, d'you hear? What do you take me for?' And he ran on.
After a few yards he turned around and said, 'Go down to the house, you
fool, and I'll give you a ticket.'

The front of his house was crowded with people, standing about and
talking; they were tourists come to Inverara for the day and were waiting for
their lunch, for Milligan's wife kept an hotel. Milligan scowled at the tourists
and at the table set for lunch which he saw through the dining-room window
as he passed. 'I'll have to wait for MY chuck until all these ragamuffins are
gone,' he growled. He went through a little green wooden gate and a flagged
alley-way into the garden. His wife forbade him to enter by the front door
'when there are strangers about, you with your scowl and your dirt that's
enough to drive the devil away.' It was humiliating not to be allowed to enter
by his own front door, so he vented his anger on a hen that was rooting
among the cabbage patch and chased her around until he was breathless. His

terrier dog chained to the tool-shed began to bark and scratch the ground, so Milligan made a kick at him, missed and fell on his back. He got up and was rushing at the dog again when he thought of the letter in his hand and he went towards the kitchen door at a run.

'Letter for you, Mary,' he said putting his head and right foot into the kitchen and searching in his pockets for the letter, but nobody took any notice of him. The kitchen was in an uproar. Mrs Milligan and her two servants were rushing about preparing lunch for twelve visitors. The kitchen was very large and yet there seemed to be no room, for the three women were continually getting into one another's way, going from the range to the large deal table in the centre of the room and to the dressers and the side table where meat, vegetables and pastries were lying about ready to be cooked. The kitchen was very hot. The air smelt strongly of roast mutton and boiling cabbage. Everybody was dripping with perspiration. It was one of the warmest days that summer.

'Here's your letter,' said Milligan. 'Dublin postmark. I suppose it's from that bloomin' lawyer that's coming down for a week. See what he says, Mary.' Milligan put the letter on a sewing machine by the door and stood by it, looking at it curiously and scratching his hip.

'The devil take you and the letter,' cried Milligan's wife, rushing at him from the side table, her hands covered with dough, and her perspiring face as red as a beetroot. She was all in white and she was spotlessly clean and there was not a single portion of her body that was not pointed and angular, nothing out of place, nothing soft, nothing round, neither a loose tress of hair, nor a bit of pink ribbon showing at the neck of her blouse. Even all her teeth were white and perfect and she had the jaw of a prize-fighter. Milligan stopped scratching his hip and opened his mouth.

'You lazy lout of a man,' cried Mrs Milligan in a voice so loud and harsh that a skinny-faced lady tourist sitting on the garden seat outside the front door jumped up and said, 'Oh, my dear, what a voice!' The two servant girls standing by the range looked at one another and tittered. 'Get out of my sight,' continued Mrs Milligan, 'here I am wearing my bones out working and you are running around with your letters. Jack of all trades indeed, and the few mangy pounds you earn in the year are not enough to keep you in food. And here you come worrying me with your letters.'

'But that letter is yours, Mary.'

'Go away. Get out. Clear out,' and she stamped and her lips quivered. Milligan sighed and trotted towards a black door to the right of the range into his office. As he passed the servant girls, he shook his fist at them and said, 'What the hell are ye laughing at, you fools?' Then he banged the door behind him. Mrs Milligan shouted at the door for a few moments and then turned on the servants and knocked their heads together vigorously. 'You idle wretches,' she cried. 'You Mary Cassidy, you slattern, have you no shame left? You were thrown out of your last job for stealing a blanket, and I took ye in here because I am too soft-hearted and ye go fiddling about. Kitty Hernon, I tell ye if ye don't straighten that ugly face of yours and put those potatoes on the fire, I'll . . . I'll flay ye alive so that yer old beershark of a mother won't recognise ye.' 'Oh boys, oh boys,' murmured Milligan, listening at the keyhole. 'Now they're getting it, bad luck to them.' He giggled as if he were enjoying a great joke and walked over to his little table, with the dirty linoleum cloth on it and papers and letters strewn about on it.

'Now how the blazes am I to write out this report and send it in today?' he cried, banging the letter he held in his hand on the table. 'All on account of a bloomin' man that kept a pig in his bedroom. Well I'll be jiggered. But it must be done.' He sat down, got a sheet of paper, took up a pen and began to bite the end: 'That bloomin' Board o' Guardians is the limit. Eh? Charley Finnigan has his knife in me. That's well known. I wish *I* were a clerk and I'd settle a lot o' them. Anyhow, let's write this bloomin' report. I'll get the sack unless I send it in today. It's the third warning.' He began to write when a fresh uproar started in the kitchen, and the peasant who had asked for a red ticket rushed into the office with his hat in his hand.

'Murdher alive!' he cried, shutting the door and panting.

'Now what the —' began Milligan, jumping up. 'It's yer wife,' said the peasant, grinning and showing two rows of black teeth, 'be God, she flew at me fer nothin' at all.'

'Now what d'ye want? cried Milligan, becoming arrogant and sticking out his chin. The peasant began to shuffle and said:

'It's how my wife is sick, and the doctor, ye see, well, ye see, I told him about her, and the parish priest, I met him up the road, ye see, an' he said —'

'Man alive, are ye out of your mind? Say what ye want, man. What is it?'

'Well, ye see —'

'Hello, Mrs Milligan, dinner ready yet?' came a loud, hearty voice from the kitchen. 'Where's Joe?'

'Hellow, Mr Corbett! Isn't it hot?' came Mrs Milligan's voice affably. 'It'll be ready in a quarter of an hour. It's *so* hot. Joe is in the office. Joe, Mr Corbett wants to see ye. Mind that saucepan, Kitty.'

'All right, I just want to show him this paper,' said Corbett with a hoarse gurgle, opening the black door. 'Hellow, Joe.'

'Hellow, Mr Corbett,' said Milligan rubbing his hands, 'take a seat. What news?'

Corbett's face was so fat that he had almost to turn his lips inside out in order to break into a laugh, and when he laughed his whole body and everything on it shook, his gold watch chain, his loose brown tweed coat, his loose navy blue trousers with the grease stain on the left knee. Even his Panama hat shook. Everything shook but his tennis shirt, and the shirt strained at his throat. He laughed and crushed the newspaper against his side. The peasant opened his mouth wide and laughed too for some reason or other. Milligan began to laugh loudest of all, but he only laughed with his mouth. In his mind he was thinking, 'It's all very well for Corbett to laugh. He is a retired pig-jobber with a comfortable income, and he has nothing else to do. And he gets more respect in my own house than I get myself, and he only pays thirty bob a week for his board and lodging. I wonder has my wife anything to do with him.'

'Look at this,' roared Corbett, flattening out the newspaper on the table and leaning over it, panting.

The newspaper was the local weekly and there was an amusing paragraph about a cow that was stolen three tines and sold three times at the same fair. Milligan did not think it amusing, but he laughed loudly and said, 'Well, I'll be damned,' several times. He found great difficulty in laughing and it made him very miserable and enraged with the peasant, who was bursting his sides laughing.

'There is that lout,' thought Milligan, 'his wife is sick and he is laughing. Whatever this blasted fool Corbett means by coming in here disturbing me for no reason at all, I don't know. . . . I'll never get that report done.' And he kept on laughing.

Then Corbett suddenly stopped laughing and said in a whisper, 'What d'ye think I heard —?' He paused and glanced at the peasant. 'Come out in the garden, Joe,' he added. Milligan cursed to himself, cast a glance at the report which he had begun and followed Corbett, looking at his watch. 'Mail'll be going in three-quarters of an hour,' he muttered. 'But my wife —' began the peasant. 'Damn your wife,' hissed Milligan over his shoulder as he closed the door. The peasant shook his head and sat on a chair. Then he began to laugh again and said, 'Well, that story about the cow was funny. Anyway, it doesn't matter about the ticket. She has only the neuralgy, but she'll kill me if I don't get the doctor. They say Milligan's wife doesn't sleep with him. Well now, what a woman she is.'

Milligan had to listen to Corbett in the garden for fully ten minutes, about a rumour that the parish priest was trying to buy the widow Mullen's motor-boat. Corbett kept saying, 'Don't say a word about it.' And Milligan kept nodding his head and saying, 'Boys, oh boys, what a clever rascal,' though for the life of him he could not see anything unusual or clever or interesting in the parish priest buying a motor-boat. Then Mrs Milligan rapped on the kitchen-window and told Corbett his dinner was ready and Corbett rushed away to wash his hands, forgetting all about Milligan and the motor-boat. 'Christ,' said Milligan, 'I'll never get that report written,' and he was running through the kitchen to his office when his wife ran out of the dining-room with an empty vegetable dish in her hand and caught him by the arm.

'Run quick,' she panted, 'half a dozen bottles o' Guinness. Be quick, man. The steamer'll be going in half an hour. They want to take them with them.'

'But I have to write a report —' began Milligan as he backed to the door.

'Be off,' cried Mrs Milligan, stamping her foot.

It was only one hundred yards to Moroney's public-house, but Milligan was buttonholed twice on the way and he wasted five minutes. Moroney's was crowded by peasants who had just sold some pigs and were drinking one another's health. It was another ten minutes before he could get out with the half-dozen bottles. He was exhausted when he got back to his office. He had only a quarter of an hour left. He began to write. 'Beg your pardon,' said the peasant, 'but —'

'Oh my God!' cried Milligan, 'what *do* you want? Here, here, and be gone. Oh Mother of God,' and he rummaged among his papers until he got the ticket. He signed it and threw it at the peasant. The peasant began to laugh when he got into the garden. Milligan again began to write, but the impossibility of getting the report finished in time for the post struck him. He threw down the pen, tore up the paper and stuck his thumb in his mouth. Then he struck the table and said, 'I have it, begob.' On a fresh sheet of paper he wrote, 'Making fresh investigations *re* pig in bedroom. Next post. In haste. Milligan.'

And hatless and breathless he just reached the steamer as she was casting off. He gave the letter to the steward.

'Just saved my bacon this time,' he murmured.

THE WREN'S NEST

It was a summer's evening just before sunset. Little Michael and Little
Jimmy, both twelve year old boys, set out to look for birds' nests. They
were both dressed alike, except that Little Michael's blue sweater and grey
flannel trousers were of better quality than Little Jimmy's, since the latter
was the son of a farm labourer and Little Michael's father was the magistrate
and a retired army officer. They were both barefooted, with cuts on their
toes, and each had a bandage on the big toe of the right foot. They skir-
mished along south of the village, crossing the crags, picking berries and
talking about the nests they had. No use looking for a nest until one came to
the hollow there beyond Red Dick's potato garden. There was a cliff there
overlooking a grassy glen. The cliff was awfully hard to climb and so was
unexplored, and there was where they were going to search. It would be a
great feat to climb the cliff anyway, since the only person who had climbed it
was Black Peter, the bird catcher, and of course he was sold to the devil and
could do anything. No boy had ever been able to climb it beyond the little
ledge about a quarter of the way up, a ledge that was always covered with
bird dirt and discoloured with cliff water that dripped on to it from a spring
in the cliff face.

The two boys came to the cliff face and looked up. Then they looked at
one another, their mouths open. 'You go first,' said Little Michael. 'No, you
go,' said Little Jimmy. 'No, you go.' They argued a long time about it, but
neither moved. 'Aw,' said Little Michael, 'I think it's too late to climb it
anyway today. Let us wait until tomorrow, and put on stockings. Black Peter
always wears stockings. Stockings stick to the cliff face.' 'You're afraid,' said
Little Jimmy, wiping his nose with the sleeve of his coat. 'Who is afraid? My
father fought in ten battles.' 'Climb it, then.' 'All right, let's climb it together.' 'Then who'll watch. We might be caught. Your father would sum-
mon me. That's certain.' They kept silent for a minute and then lay on their
stomachs on the grass looking up at the cliff. Sparrows were chirping hidden
in the ivy. Right at the top, about sixty feet above the level of the glen, there
was a deep slit in the cliff and several broods of starling were croaking there.

'There must be twenty nests there,' said Little Michael. 'There are forty.'

I counted them the other day,' said Little Jimmy. 'Let's throw stones at them.' They threw a few stones up into the ivy and a number of birds flew out screaming. Then they lay down again on the grass and watched. Suddenly Little Jimmy said 'Hist!' His dirty face was lit up with sudden excitement. 'What's that?' whispered Little Michael. 'Hist!' said Little Jimmy, 'I see a wren. Look.' He pointed to a point far down in the cliff about five feet from the ground, where just a shred of ivy was growing, an offshoot from the main growth farther up. Little Michael nearly shut his eyes looking closely and saw a little brown ball moving slightly. The two boys held their breaths for a long time, lying quite still. Presently a tiny head peered out of the ivy. Then it disappeared again. Then it appeared again, looked around, and presently a wren flew out, circled around a little and landed on the fence to the left. Then it chirped lowly and sped away. Another little wren came out of the cliff in answer to the chirp and followed it.

'It's a nest,' gasped both the boys together. They jumped to their feet and raced to the cliff, each trying to get there first.

They arrived at the cliff together and each thrust a hand into the little clump of ivy to get at the nest. There was a rustle of green leaves, a panting of breaths, and then their hands met in the ivy and they paused. They looked at one another and there was poisoned hatred in their eyes. 'I got it first,' said Little Michael. 'I touched it first.' 'Ye're a liar,' said Little Jimmy, 'I saw the wren first.' 'You call me a liar and your father was in jail twice.' 'I can beat you. I beat Johnny Derrane, and he beat you.'

'Oh, you just try.' They stood back from the cliff and looked one another up and down, each afraid of the other. The situation was intensely embarrassing, but just then one of the wrens flew back over the fence carrying a little wisp of moss in its mouth and saved the situation. They both looked at the wren, and said 'Hist!' glad of some excuse to prevent them from fighting. The wren alighted on a fence to the left and became very busy pretending to have a nest in the fence. 'Come away,' said Little Michael, 'if he sees us looking at the nest he will forsake it, and a forsaken nest doesn't count. That's well known.'

'Oh, let's see how many eggs in it,' said Little Jimmy. 'Nobody will believe us if we can't say how many eggs in it.' 'You leave it alone,' said Little Michael; 'that's my nest. If you look at it, I'll tell my father.' 'Ha, spy,' said Little Jimmy. Little Michael became very conscious of having made a fool of himself and didn't know what to say or do. He had an impulse to hit Little Jimmy, but he was afraid to hit him. No use fighting anyway when nobody was looking. Nobody ever heard of anybody fighting when there was nobody looking unless two brothers maybe, or a boy and his sister. 'Maybe you think I'm afraid,' he said at last. 'Take care now, Little Jimmy, that you'd think I'm afraid.' 'Aw, I don't care,' said Little Jimmy, dabbing his toe into the grass with a swagger. 'I'm going to look at this nest anyway.' He moved forward and Little Michael caught him by the two hands and they struggled. 'Let me go,' cried Little Michael. 'You let me go' cried Little Jimmy. The two wrens were now hovering about screaming in an agonised state, but the boys took no heed of them. Each was trying to grab at the nest and the other trying to prevent him. The ivy was soon torn from the cliff and a little round hole became visible, a beautiful little round hole, suggestive of beauty within, and around the little round hole was a house built of moss. Then Little Jimmy grabbed at the nest caught it in the tips of his fingers, and as Little Michael pulled him suddenly, the nest came out of the niche and tumbled to the ground. It fell on the ground on its side and a little egg, a tiny egg, tumbled out. It was so light that it landed between two blades of grass and stayed there poised. The wrens on the fence set up a terrible chatter and then flew away high above the ground. They would never come back.

The two boys looked at the nest in silence. 'Now see what you've done,' said Little Michael; 'the nest is no use to us.' 'It's all your fault,' said Little Jimmy; 'you were afraid to look at it.' 'Who was afraid?' said Little Michael heatedly; 'what do I care about a wren's nest,' and he kicked the nest with his foot. The structure of dried moss burst in two pieces and several eggs scattered around. Both boys laughed, and began to kick the pieces of the nest and then tore them to shreds. The inside was coated wonderfully with feathers and down, interlaced with an art that could not be rivalled by human beings. The boys tore it into shreds and scattered the shreds. Then they pelted one another with the eggs, laughing excitedly. Then they paused, uncertain what to do, and they both sighed, from satisfaction. They were friendly again, the cause of their quarrel had vanished, destroyed by their hands.

'I got a rabbit's nest with three young ones in it,' said Little Jimmy.

'Show it to me,' said Little Michael and I'll show you a blackbird's nest with three eggs in it.' 'All right,' said Little Jimmy and they scampered off, over the fence where the wrens flew away. Two fields farther on they passed the wrens, already looking for another niche, but they did not recognise them. If they had they would probably have thrown a few stones at them.

THE BLACK MARE

I bought the mare at G — , from a red-whiskered tinker and, if the truth were only known, I believe he stole her somewhere in the south, for he parted with her for thirty shillings. Or else it was because she was so wild that there was not another man at the whole fair had the courage to cross her back with his legs and trot her down the fair green but myself, for it was not for nothing that they called me Dan of the Fury in those days. However, when I landed from the hooker at the pier at Kilmurrage and, mounting her, trotted up to the village, they all laughed at me. For she was a poor-looking animal that day, with long shaggy hair under her belly, and the flesh on her ribs was as scarce as hospitality in a priest's house. She didn't stand an inch over fourteen hands, and my legs almost touched the ground astride of her. So they laughed at me, but I paid no heed to them. I saw the fire in her eyes, and that was all I needed. You see this drop of whiskey in this glass, stranger? It is a pale, weak colour, and it would not cover an inch with wetness, but it has more fire in it than a whole teeming lake of soft water. So the mare.

I set her to pasture in a little field I had between two hills in the valley below the fort. I cared for her as a mother might care for an only child, and all that winter I never put a halter in her mouth or threw my legs across her back, but I used to watch her for hours galloping around the fields snorting, with her great black eyes spitting fire and her nostrils opened so wide that you could hide an egg in each of them. And, Virgin of the Valiant Deeds, when she shed her winter coat in spring and I combed her glossy sides, what a horse she was! As black as the sloes they pick on the slope of Coillnamhan Fort, with never a hair of red or white or yellow. Her tail swept to the ground, and when the sun shone on her sides you could see them shimmering like the jewels on a priest's vestments; may the good God forgive me, a sinner, for the comparison. But what is nearer to God than a beautiful horse? Tell me that, stranger, who have been in many lands across the sea.

And then the day came when all the unbroken mares of Inverara were to be shod. For it was the custom then, stranger, to shoe all the young mares on the same day, and to break them before they were shod on the wide sandy beach beneath the village of Coillnamhan.

There were seven mares that day gathered together from the four villages of Inverara, and there were good horses among them, but none as good as mine. She was now a little over fifteen hands high, and you could bury a child's hand between her haunches. She was perfect in every limb, like a horse from the stable of the God Crom. I can see her yet, stranger, standing on the strand stamping with her hind leg and cocking her ears at every sound. But it's an old saying, talk of beauty today, talk of death tomorrow.

I kept her to the last, and gave her to a lad to hold while I mounted a bay mare that my cousin had brought from Kilmillick, and I broke her in three rounds of the strand, although she had thrown three strong and hardy men before I seized her halter. And then my mare was brought down, and then and there I offered three quarts of the best whiskey that could be bought for money to the man that could stay on her back for one length of the strand. One after the other they mounted her, but no sooner did they touch her back than she sent them headlong to the ground. She would gather her four legs together and jump her own height from the ground, and with each jump they flew from her back, and she would run shivering around again until they caught her. I smiled, sitting there on a rock.

Then Shemus, the son of Crooked Michael, spat on his hands, tightened his crios around his waist, and said that if the devil were hiding in her bowels and Lucifer's own step-brother riding on her mane, he would break her. He was a man I never liked, that same son of Crooked Michael, a braggart without any good in him, a man who must have come crooked from his mother's womb, and his father before him was the same dishonest son of a horse-stealing tinker. 'Be careful,' I said to him; 'that mare is used to have men about her that didn't drink their mother's milk from a teapot.' And when I saw the ugly look he gave me I knew that there was trouble coming, and so there was.

He got up on her all right, for, to give the devil his due, he was agile on his limbs and, although no horseman, there were few men in the island of Inverara that he couldn't throw with a twist of the wrist he had. But as soon as his legs rubbed her flanks she neighed and gathered herself together to spring, and just as she was that way doubled up he kicked her in the mouth was his foot. She rose to her hind legs and before she could plant her fore feet on the ground again to jump, I had rushed from the rock and with one swing of my right arm I had pulled him to the ground. I was so mad that before he could rush at me I seized him by the thigh and the back of the neck, and I would have broken every limb in his putrid body if they didn't rush in and separate us. Then the craven son of a reptile that he was, as soon as he saw himself held, he began to bellow like a young bull wanting to get at me. But I took no heed of him. My father's son was never a man to crow over a fallen enemy.

They brought the mare over to me and I looked at her. She looked at me and a shiver passed down her flank and she whinnied, pawing the sand with her hind hoof.

'Take off that halter,' said I to the men.

They did. I still kept looking at the mare and she at me. She never moved. Then coming over to her as she stood there without saddle or bridle, stepping lightly on my toes, I laid my right hand on her shoulder. 'Pruach, pruach, my beautiful girl,' I called to her, rubbing her shoulders with my left hand. Then I rose from the strand, leaning on the strength of my right hand and landed on her back as lightly as a bird landing on a rose bush. She darted forward like a flash of lightning from a darkened sky. You see that strand, stretching east from the rock to where it ends in a line of boulders at the eastern end. It is four hundred paces and it rises to the south of the boulders into a high sand bank underneath the road. Well, I turned her at the sand bank with a sudden flash of my hand across her eyes, leaning out over her mane. And then back again we came, with a column of sand rising after us and the ground rising up in front of us with the speed of our progress. 'Now,' said I to myself, 'I will show this son of Crooked Michael what Dan of the Fury can do on horseback.'

Raising myself gently with my hands on her shoulders, I put my two feet square on her haunches and stood straight, leaning against the wind, balancing myself with every motion of her body, and as she ran, stretched flat with her belly to earth, I took my blue woollen shirt off my back and was down again on her shoulders as light as a feather before we reached the western end, where the men stood gaping as if they had sent a priest performing a miracle. 'God be with a man,' they cried. And the women sitting on the hillock that overlooks the beach screamed with fear and enjoyment, and of all the beautiful women that were gathered there that day there was not one that would not have been glad to mate with me with or without marriage.

Back over the strand again we went, the black mare and I, like lightning flying from the thunder, and the wave that rose when we passed the rock in the west had not broken on the strand when we turned again at the sand bank. Then coming back again like the driven wind in winter I rose once more, standing on her haunches, and may the devil swallow me alive if I hadn't put my shirt on my back again and landed back on her shoulders before we reached the rock. There I turned her head to the sea and drove her out into it until the waves lapped her heaving belly. I brought her back to the rock as gentle as a lamb and dismounted.

Ha! My soul from the devil, but that was a day that will never be forgotten as long as there is a man left to breathe the name of Dan of the Fury. But all things have their end, and sure it's a queer day that doesn't bring the night, and the laugh is the herald of the sigh. It was two years after that I got this fractured thigh. Well I remember that four days before the races where I got this broken limb, I met red haired Mary of Kilmillick. As I was looking after her, for she had shapely hips and an enticing swing in them, my horse stumbled, and although I crossed myself three times and promised to make a journey to the Holy Well at Kilmillick, I'll swear by Crom that the spell of the Evil One was put on the mare. But that is old woman's talk. Mary promised me the morning of the races that if the black mare won I could put a ring on her finger, and as I cantered up to the starting point I swore I would win both the race and the girl if the devil himself were holding on to the black mare's tail.

Seventeen horses lined up at the starting point. I took up my position beside a bay stallion that the parish priest, Fr John Costigan, had entered. He was a blood stallion and had won many races on the mainland, but the parish priest was allowed to enter him, for who could go against a priest. Then, as now, there was nobody in Inverara who was willing to risk being turned into a goat by making a priest obey the rules of a race. Six times they started us and six times we were forced to come back to the starting point, for that same braggart, the son of Crooked Michael, persisted in trying to get away before the appointed time. At last the parish priest knocked him off his horse with a welt of his black-thorn stick and the race started.

We were off like sixteen claps of thunder. We had to circle the field three times, that big field above the beach at Coillnamhan, and before we had circled it the second time, the bay stallion and the mare were in front with the rest nowhere. Neck to neck we ran, and no matter how I urged the mare she would not leave the stallion. Then in the third round of the field I caught a sight of Mary looking at me with a sneer on her face, as if she thought I was afraid to beat the priest's horse. That look drove me mad. I forgot myself. We were stretching towards the winning post. The stallion was reaching in front of me. Mad with rage I struck the mare a heavy blow between the ears. I had never struck her in my life and as soon as I had done it I started with fright and shame. I had struck my horse. I spoke to her gently but she just shivered from the tip of her ears to her tail and darted forward with one mighty rush that left the stallion behind.

I heard a shout from the people. I forgot the blow. I forgot the mare. I leaned forward on her mane and yelled myself. We passed the winning post, with the stallion one hundred yards or more behind us. I tried to draw rein. Her head was like a firm rock. I cursed her and drew rein again. I might have been a flea biting her back. At one bound she leapt the fence and swept down the beach. She was headed straight for the boulders. I saw them in front of me and grew terrified. Between us and the boulders was the sand bank, fifteen feet high. She snorted, raised her head and tried to stop when she saw the fall. I heard a shout from the people. Then I became limp. We rose in the air. We fell. The mare struck the rocks and I remembered no more.

They told me afterward that she was shattered to a pulp when they found us, and sure it's the good God that only gave me a broken leg.

AN FIACH

Bhí creag mhór sínte le farraige agus gleannta caola féaracha ag lúbadh anseo agus ansiúd idir na leacracha, ó bharr na haille. Tháinig gadhar buí isteach sa gcreag. Sheas sé ar thrí cosa agus shín a eireaball. Fuair sé boladh coinín. Thug sé rith te reatha suas an gleann; a shrón le talamh. Sheas sé arís — ar craitheadh — a chluasa bioraithe.

Ansin chas sé isteach imeasc na scailp, ag léimneach anonn is anall, ag casadh go dlúth arís agus arís eile, ag smúracht an bholaidh the a bhí fágtha ar na leacacha glasa sleamhna ag cosa an choinín. Fá dheireadh sheas sé de thaghd ar aghaidh dhá chloch a bhí seasta guala le gualainn agus poll caol eatarthu. Chonaic sé coinín suite sa bpoll. Bhí droim donn an choinín i bhfogas dhá shlat dá shróin. Dhírigh a chorp agus thit a dhá chluais a bhí bioraithe roimhe sin.

Tháinig torann tobann tapaidh, ar nós línéadaigh róthirim a réabfaí go mear, nuair d'éirigh an coinín amach as dídean na gloch. Léim sé thar an leic a bhí idir é féin agus an gleann. Chas sé agus a thaobh le talamh, ar nós báid fholaimh a leagfaí faoi ghaoth láidir.

Lig an gadhar sceamh agus osna. D'éirigh sé den leic. Le neart a choirp agus le cuthach a léime stróic sé slisíní den leic lena chosa deiridh. Ag gabháil scarachosach tríd an aer, lig sé sceamh eile. Bhuail sé talamh sa ngleann. Baineadh treascairt as le saint a shiúil agus thit sé i ndiaidh a uchta. Ach bhí sé ina sheasamh arís ar bhualadh boise. Seo suas an gleann é i ndiaidh an choinín, a eireaball sínte uaidh, a bholg le féar agus sruth gealchúrach na feirge ag sileadh lena dhrad.

Bhí ardán féarach ag trasnú na creige ó chlaí go claí, tuairim is fiche slat ar leithead. Bhí iallach ar an gcoinín an t-ardán a thrasnú chun a choinicéar a shroichint, in aice claí thoir na creige, amuigh ar bhruach na farraige. Nuair a chas an coinín as an ngleann, soir in aghaidh an ardáin, bhí an gadhar i bhfogas dhá shlat dá eireaball.

Ghéaraigh siúl an ghadhair. Thus sé amhóg. Shíl sé droim an choinín d'aimsiú. Chas an coinín siar. Bhí an gadhar ina dhiaidh aniar. Chas an coinín de phlimp isteach faoi bholg an ghadhair. Chuaigh said timpeall ar a chéile trí huaire, ag iompó chomh mear sin nárbh fhéidir craiceann buí an ghadhair d'aithint ó chraiceann donn an choinín. Suas leis an gcoinín arís. Suas leis an ngadhar ina dhiaidh. Bhuail sé srón ar an gcoinín san aer. Buaileadh an coinín ar spéice i mbéal an choinicéir. Thit an gadhar ina mhullach.

Tháinig sian bheag thruamhéileach ón gcoinín agus tafann lúcháireach ón ngadhar.

Bhí an marú déanta.

SPORT: THE KILL

With a wild rush of scraping feet, the rabbit darted in under the flat rock. His right hind leg spat up a sliver of stone from the crag and disappeared, just as the dog's snout landed with a thud at the hole. The dog yelped as he tumbled head over heels with the force of his mad rush. The rabbit crawled along the straight groove in the crag under the rock. His claws made a rasping sound as, one after the other, his legs thrust his body forward. He left a trail of brown fur behind him. Midway he halted, panting. He saw the dog's black nose twitching and snorting at the far end of the groove in front. He painfully drew up his legs under his belly, twisted around his head so that he could see both entrances to the groove and waited. His sides pressed against the rock as they heaved.

A boy came bounding along from the left, skipping over the boulders that lined the cliff top. In his right hand he carried a dried long willow rod. He halted on a boulder and looked about him. The dog raised his head, looked at the boy, wagged his tail and barked. The boy whooped and rushed along the crag to the rock. The dog growled joyously and, throwing back his head, he scraped madly at the hole, clawing the limestone crag impotently. The boy threw himself flat at the other end where the rabbit had entered, shut one eye and looked in. When his eye pierced the gloom and he saw the rabbit, he too growled.

The rabbit, seeing enemies on both sides, tried to stick his head through a tiny crevice to his left, where the rock rested on two cone shaped spurs of the crag. His head entered as far as the ears and could go no farther. He lay still, one ear bent double, the other ear flat on his back, the tip quivering, fanned by the dog's breath, that came through the damp groove in a pale blue column. Then a scratching sound reached him, coming towards his hind-quarters. The boy lying on his side was pushing the dried willow rod along the groove.

The end of the rod touched the rabbit's left haunch gently. It slipped up over the haunch and tipped the rock. Then it twisted with a grating sound and got stuck in the soft fur to the left of the tail. It twisted again. The skin on the rabbit's haunches went taut as it gathered around the tip of the rod.

The rabbit started, held his breath and pulled his head suddenly from the crevice. He was stretching back his right hind leg to crawl away from the rod when he saw the dog's red tongue lolling between white fangs at the far end in front of him. With his right hind leg crooked at the thigh, he paused, his eyes blinking, his whiskers twitching, his ears pressed down into his contracted neck. Again the rod grated and twisted. The skin of his stomach was drawn up to the ball of skin and fur that was gathering around the tip of the rod. Again the rod twisted. The skin around his crutch went taut.

The boy cursed. A spur of the crag had bruised his hip. He grunted and said 'Hs-s-s-s' fiercely. The dog thrust his muzzle abruptly at the hole and barked. The bark re-echoed through the groove and the fur on the rabbit's neck quivered. The rabbit closed his eyes and bent down his head. The strong smell of the dog's breath was stifling him. Then the boy drew in a deep breath and tried to twist the rod again. His sweating hands slipped on the dried willow. The rod was too taut to turn. All the skin on the rabbit's body was as taut as the skin of a drum. The claws of his right hind leg gripped the crag with such force that their points were blunted. The dog raised his head and walked back a few paces to smell a snail that was crawling along the crag. Then he came back to the hole again, raised his left fore paw and cocked his head sideways.

Slowly, carefully, the boy began to pull the rod. For a few moments the pressure was so gradual that the rabbit did not feel himself being pulled. Then suddenly his right hind leg that was bearing the weight of his body slipped backwards with a scraping sound that ended in a thud. His whole body began to slip, bumping against the crag, the fore feet pawing the ground. He allowed himself to slip back gradually, too dazed to resist. The dog sniffed cautiously at his hole. Then fiercely. He thought the rabbit was escaping. Darting across the rock to the boy, he yelped and thrust his snout down between the boy's face and the hole. Then he whined and darted back again to his own hole.

The rabbit was within a foot of the boy's hand, at the mouth of the hole when the rod caught in a cleft, where the rock rested on a spur of the crag just within the mouth of the groove. The boy cursed and gave the rod a jerk. It failed to move. Then he pushed it back. The rabbit drew up his hind legs under him feeling the tension relaxed. Then the boy tried to give the rod another twist to free it. He had twisted it around slightly when the skin on the rabbit's left haunch burst with a snap. The rabbit jerked his head up and down suddenly and, striking the crag with his four feet, thrust himself forward with a wild squeal. The dog thrust his body at his hole furiously, cutting his muzzle against the crag. Then he lay on his belly, his eyes watery, his jaws slightly open. The boy jumped to his knees and, seizing the rod with both hands, he wrenched it clean out of the groove with a large patch of the rabbit's skin at its tip. The rabbit blinded by the pain crawled straight ahead heedless of the dog. The dog drew back his snout. His tail stretched out. His eyes half closed. His chest shivered. the rabbit's head appeared. There was a smothered squeal and then a low crack as the dog's fangs met through the rabbit's neck.

The dog tossed the rabbit in triumph over his head as the boy leaped across the rock. The boy grabbed the rabbit's hind legs and kicked the dog fiercely on the ribs. The dog dropped the rabbit and ran back whining. The boy held up the body heaving as if is were leaping fences in its death agony. 'High' he hissed through his teeth.

Then he bashed the rabbit's head on the rock.

THE SNIPER

The long June twilight faded into night. Dublin lay enveloped in darkness, but for the dim light of the moon, that shone through fleecy clouds, casting a pale light as of approaching dawn over the streets and the dark waters of the Liffey. Around the beleaguered Four Courts the heavy guns roared. Here and there through the city machine guns and rifles broke the silence of the night, spasmodically, like dogs barking on lone farms. Republicans and Free Staters were waging civil war.

On a roof-top near O'Connell Bridge, a Republican sniper lay watching. Beside him lay his rifle and over his shoulders were slung a pair of field-glasses. His face was the face of a student — thin and ascetic, but his eyes had the cold gleam of the fanatic. They were deep and thoughtful, the eyes of a man, who is used to looking at death.

He was eating a sandwich hungrily. He had eaten nothing since morning. He had been too excited to eat. He finished the sandwich, and taking a flask of whiskey from his pocket, he took a short draught. Then he returned the flask to his pocket. He paused for a moment, considering whether he should risk a smoke. It was dangerous. The flash might be seen in the darkness and there were enemies watching. He decided to take the risk. Placing a cigarette between his lips, he struck a match, inhaled the smoke hurriedly and put out the light. Almost immediately, a bullet flattened itself against the parapet of the roof. The sniper took another whiff and put out the cigarette. Then he swore softly and crawled away to the left.

Cautiously he raised himself and peered over the parapet. There was a flash and a bullet whizzed over his head. He dropped immediately. He had seen the flash. It came from the opposite side of the street.

He rolled over the roof to a chimney stack in the rear, and slowly drew himself up behind it, until his eyes were level with the top of the parapet. There was nothing to be seen — just the dim outline of the opposite house-top against the blue sky. His enemy was under cover.

Just then an armoured car came across the bridge and advanced slowly up the street. It stopped on the opposite side of the street fifty yards ahead. The sniper could hear the dull panting of the motor. His heart beat faster. It was an enemy car. He wanted to fire, but he knew it was useless. His bullets would never pierce the steel that covered the grey monster.

Then round the corner of a side street came an old woman, her head covered by a tattered shawl. She began to talk to the man in the turret of the car. She was pointing to the roof where the sniper lay. An informer.

The turret opened. A man's head and shoulders appeared, looking towards the sniper. The sniper raised his rifle and fired. The head fell heavily on the turret wall. The woman darted toward the side street. The sniper fired again. The woman whirled round and fell with a shriek into the gutter.

Suddenly from the opposite roof a shot rang out and the sniper dropped his rifle with a curse. The rifle clattered to the roof. The sniper thought the noise would wake the dead. He stopped to pick the rifle up. He couldn't lift it. His fore-arm was dead. 'Christ,' he muttered, 'I'm hit.'

Dropping flat on to the roof, he crawled back to the parapet. With his left hand he felt the injured right fore-arm. The blood was oozing through the sleeve of his coat. There was no pain — just a deadened sensation, as if the arm had been cut off.

Quickly he drew his knife from his pocket, opened it on the breastwork of the parapet and ripped open the sleeve. There was a small hole where the bullet had entered. On the other side there was no hole. The bullet had lodged in the bone. It must have fractured it. He bent the arm below the wound.

The arm bent back easily. He ground his teeth to overcome the pain.

Then, taking out his field dressing, he ripped open the packet with his knife. He broke the neck of the iodine bottle and let the bitter fluid drip into the wound. A paroxysm of pain swept through him. He placed the cotton wadding over the wound and wrapped the dressing over it. He tied the end with his teeth.

Then he lay still against the parapet, and closing his eyes, he made an effort of will to overcome the pain.

In the street beneath all was still. The armoured car had retired speedily over the bridge, with the machine gunner's head hanging lifeless over the turret. The woman's corpse lay still in the gutter.

The sniper lay for a long time nursing his wounded arm and planning escape. Morning must not find him wounded on the roof. The enemy on the opposite roof covered his escape. He must kill that enemy and he could not use his rifle. He had only a revolver to do it. Then he thought of a plan.

Taking off his cap, he placed it over the muzzle of his rifle. Then he pushed the rifle slowly upwards over the parapet, until the cap was visible from the opposite side of the street. Almost immediately there was a report, and a bullet pierced the centre of the cap. The sniper slanted the rifle forward. The cap slipped down into the street. Then, catching the rifle in the middle, the sniper dropped his left hand over the roof and let it hang, lifelessly. After a few moments he let the rifle drop to the street. Then he sank to the roof, dragging his hand with him.

Crawling quickly to the left, he peered up at the corner of the roof. His ruse had succeeded. The other sniper, seeing the cap and rifle fall, thought that he had killed his man. He was now standing before a row of chimney pots, looking across, with his head clearly silhouetted against the western sky.

The Republican sniper smiled and lifted his revolver above the edge of the parapet. The distance was about fifty yards — a hard shot in the dim light, and his right arm was paining him like a thousand devils. He took a steady aim. His hand trembled with eagerness. Pressing his lips together, he took a deep breath through his nostrils and fired. He was almost deafened with the report and his arm shook with the recoil.

Then, when the smoke cleared, he peered across and uttered a cry of joy. His enemy had been hit. He was reeling over the parapet in his death agony. He struggled to keep his feet, but he was slowly falling forward, as if in a dream. The rifle fell from his grasp, hit the parapet, fell over, bounded off the pole of a barber's shop beneath and then cluttered on to the pavement.

Then the dying man on the roof crumpled up and fell forward. The body turned over and over in space and hit the ground with a dull thud. Then it lay still.

The sniper looked at his enemy falling and he shuddered. The lust of battle died in him. He became bitten by remorse. The sweat stood out in beads on his forehead. Weakened by his wound and the long summer day of fasting and watching on the roof, he revolted from the sight of the shattered mass of his dead enemy. His teeth chattered. He began to gibber to himself, cursing the war, cursing himself, cursing everybody.

He looked at the smoking revolver in his hand and with an oath he hurled it to the roof at his feet. The revolver went off with the concussion, and the bullet whizzed past the sniper's head. He was frightened back to his senses by the shock. His nerves steadied. The cloud of fear scattered from his mind and he laughed.

Taking the whiskey flask from his pocket, he emptied it at a draught. He felt reckless under the influence of the spirits. He decided to leave the roof and look for his company commander to report.

Everywhere around was quiet. There was not much danger in going through the streets. He picked up his revolver and put it in his pocket. Then he crawled down through the sky-light to the house underneath.

When the sniper reached the laneway on the street level, he felt a sudden curiosity as to the identity of the enemy sniper whom he had killed. He decided that he was a good shot whoever he was. He wondered if he knew him. Perhaps he had been in his own company before the split in the army. He decided to risk going over to have a look at him. He peered around the corner into O'Connell Street. In the upper part of the street there was heavy firing, but around here all was quiet.

The sniper darted across the street. A machine gun tore up the ground around him with a hail of bullets, but he escaped. He threw himself face downwards beside the corpse. The machine gun stopped.

Then the sniper turned over the dead body and looked into his brother's face.

TWO DOGS

Feeney, the fisherman, had two dogs. One was a mongrel, a black dog, deep-chested and ferocious. The other was a yellow greyhound, thin and beautiful. The two dogs were deadly enemies. The mongrel was five years old when Feeney bought the greyhound as a pup. Before the greyhound's arrival the mongrel shared his little cottage with Feeney, followed him each day to the cliffs to fish and hunted rabbits. Whenever he killed one, which was not very often because he was not fast, he brought it in his mouth to Feeney and wagged his tail proudly. He was very fond of Feeney, and he was quite happy. Everybody feared his ferocity, and all the dogs in his own village and along the countryside fled when they saw him coming.

Then the pup came to the cabin, and the mongrel was no longer happy. He hated to see Feeney fondle it and feed it with milk, while he himself had to be content with potatoes and rockfish heads. He would sit on his haunches watching the long-legged pup sniff around the floor or tear at Feeney's trouser leg, and whenever he got a chance he bit at him. But Feeney beat him whenever he bit the pup, and he often had to lie on his back and allow the young greyhound to tear at his throat fur and gambol over him. He would yawn savagely and loll his tongue, unable to satiate his rage.

Then the pup grew up and began to accompany Feeney to the cliffs to fish. He was still growing and ugly, and whenever a strange dog came near him he threw himself on his back and whined. So the mongrel despised him and felt sure Feeney would not prefer such an ugly cowardly creature to himself. One day Feeney beat the young greyhound for running away from a mangy terrier that was blind in one eye, and the mongrel was quite happy. He began to snap at the greyhound in the presence of his master without being interfered with. The young greyhound began to hate the mongrel and grew madly jealous of his deep chest, his strength, and his courage.

Then the greyhound grew to his full size, and he was beautiful to look at. He was almost twice the mongrel's height, and his snout was so long and pointed that he could lick milk from the bottom of a tumbler without touching the sides. His yellow coat was as glossy as silk, and he could outdistance anything. Almost without moving a muscle, he could jump from a standing position and go clean over Feeney's head without touching it. Feeney was delighted with him, and all the neighbours stopped to praise him, so that the mongrel grew vicious with jealousy and took to howling at nights, until Feeney had to get up one night and give him a stiff thrashing with a broom handle.

But when the rabbit season came in again the mongrel turned the scales against the greyhound. The greyhound was slow to pick up a scent and could not follow one when he did get one. So while the mongrel methodically nosed along the rabbit's trail, the greyhound rushed about furiously, mad with excitement, jumping stone walls with his head in the air and absolutely useless. Then when the mongrel started the rabbit, the greyhound outdistanced him in a few strides, but was unable to catch the rabbit because of his own terrific speed and the rocky ground, which cut his delicate paws and made him stumble. And it always happened that the hound turned the rabbit into the mongrel's mouth, for the mongrel was old and cunning and knew his ground perfectly and the habits of rabbits. He knew when to follow over a fence and when to wait behind. He knew which side a rabbit would turn and when he was going to turn. So that he caught all the rabbits and the hound caught none. Nearly every day he came up to the cliff-top with a rabbit in his mouth and dropped it beside Feeney. Then he would gambol about, make a savage rush at the greyhound, and come back again barking joyously as much as to say, 'There's that useless greyhound.' Feeney began to think the greyhound was worthless and took a dislike to him. When the greyhound crawled up to him and put his head under his armpit after a kill by the mongrel, Feeney gave him a sharp blow on the side with his bait hammer and sent him away.

Then one summer morning, just after dawn, when the rocks were still shimmering with evaporating dew and there was such a freshness in the silent air that it made each living thing throb with joy at the very fact of living, Feeney was going along up the slope of Coillnamhan Fort towards his usual fishing perch on the cliff-top. The two dogs were rushing about over the crags mad with the joy of early morning, sniffing at every hole and making desperate rushes at hummocks of grass, pretending that they concealed a rabbit. And at last the mongrel started one two fields below the cliffs, at the base of a steep slope that ended in the brink of a precipice that dropped two hundred and fifty feet to the sea. The greyhound was some distance behind, but the rabbit went through a hole in a high fence, and while the mongrel was running to a low part to jump, the greyhound cleared the high fence without touching it and got in the lead. The next field was very craggy, and the greyhound fell twice and cut himself in several places, so that the rabbit reached the next fence before the greyhound could get up to him. That fence was a low one, and the greyhound took it at a flying leap and landed in front of the rabbit. The rabbit turned back into the field he had just left and was going through the hole just as the mongrel was jumping the fence. The greyhound doubled back over the fence and turned the rabbit once more, and the mongrel, who had cunningly waited the cliff side of the fence, tried to grab at the rabbit when he came through the hole the second time. But his foot caught in a crevice and he missed him. The rabbit raced up the grassy slope to his burrow on the cliff-top. The mongrel ran after him. The greyhound doubled back again over the fence with his head in the air and his tongue hanging. He whined and raced up the slope with his nose to the ground. Feeney threw down his basket and began to yell.

The mongrel suddenly saw the cliff-top and slowed down and began to bark. But the greyhound flew past him like a thunderbolt, and nosed the rabbit just as he was going to dip around the little rock at the cliff-top into his burrow. There was a muffled yelp from the hound and a scream from the rabbit, as they both went whirling over the cliff to the sea two hundred and fifty feet below. The mongrel ran up to the brink of the cliff and looked down. He sniffed and let his ears droop. Then he began to bark joyfully and ran around trying to catch his tail.

THE HOOK

The seagull was very hungry. He was soaring above the fishing village with his legs hanging down, his wings perfectly still, his head turned to one side and his sharp little eyes blinking. Above him and a little to the right, a large white flock of seagulls was cackling and diving about furiously. He alone was sailing on his own, very near the ground and perfectly silent. He saw something that he didn't want the other seagulls to see until he should get an opportunity of securing it for himself.

There it was, perched enticingly on a low stone fence, the fat red liver of a fish, about three inches long and as thick as it was long. The seagull ravened for it. He would swoop down immediately and bite at it, but he wanted to bring a share to his mate that was sitting on the eggs, on the ledge in the cliff. So he was waiting for an opportunity to rest for a moment on the fence, eat his own share and take the rest between his beak northwards to the cliff.

But he could not get an opportunity. The fence on which the liver rested bordered the lane that led from the well to the wide flat crag where the village women were washing and cleaning and salting the fish that had been caught the previous night. Young girls continually passed along the lane carrying buckets of water to their mothers. And the seagull was slightly bewildered by all the noise and bustle on the crag, with the women in their red petticoats and little back shawls around their heads squatted on their heels, and their sharp knives making the white scales fly in little flaky showers from the fishes' backs. Their harsh cries, the flashing of the knives in the bright morning sun, the glittering piles of fish slipping about, all made the seagull's head swim with excitement and hunger and desire and fear.

At last he heard a hoarse 'ga-ga-ga' close by him and another seagull swooped past the fence where the liver rested and then, banking a little farther on, doubled back, cackling aggressively as he came. The first seagull knew that the liver was discovered. He must wait no longer. He swooped upwards slightly, flapped his wings twice and then came straight down with a tearing sound. He landed lightly on the fence, took fright suddenly and looked about him, uttered a queer faint shriek and was going to spread his wings to fly again when he heard a swish and the other seagull landed beside him. The first seagull lost all fear, grabbed at the liver and tried to swallow the whole piece. He got it into his mouth in two gobbles, while the other seagull picked at its end and screamed. Then with a wild yell a number of small boys who had been hiding under the fence a few yards to the right, jumped up and began to wave their arms. The second seagull screamed and darted away. The first seagull made a last violent gobble at the liver and got it completely in his mouth and then with a fierce swing of his wings he rose sideways.

But he did not rise far. With a smothered scream he came tumbling backwards. A hook had been hidden in the liver. Its barb was sticking through the seagull's mouth, in the soft part behind the lower bill, and a piece of string protruded from his mouth and was tied to a stone in the fence. The seagull was trapped.

He fell with wings outstretched inside the fence. He lay dumbfounded for two seconds, lying on his side, his little eyes motionless with fear and pain. Then a boy leaned over the fence and tried to grab at him. He fluttered away a yard or so to the full reach of the string and then when the hook jerked him back again, he uttered a fierce cry as if spurred to madness by the renewal of pain. Bending his head he rose with the graceful and powerful movement of an advancing wave. He rose in a twirling curve. There was a slight snap, a downward jerking of his beak, then he uttered a joyful scream like a loud sigh and he flew upwards with a curling piece of string hanging from his beak. He had burst the string and left the small boys staring after him and cursing the weak string that had robbed them of their prey.

Higher and higher he whirled, upwards from the village and northward towards his ledge on the cliff and his mate. As he whirled and banked and plunged forward the string kept dangling and going through funny little convolutions, as if it were a long worm being carried off and trying to wriggle its way out of the seagull's mouth. And the whole flock of seagulls followed the hooked one, making a tremendous noise, screaming at one another and blinking their little eyes in amazement at the hook sticking from the trapped one's bill and the string dangling.

At last the seagull reached his ledge midway down a precipitous cliff. The sea grumbled far away beneath, and as his mate sat on her eggs her bill protruded over the sea, the ledge was so narrow. The trapped seagull landed beside his mate. She wearily stretched out her beak for food and then uttered a wild scream as she saw the hook. And breasting the ledge the whole flock soared about cackling. The trapped one, stupefied by all the cackling, hid one leg under his wing and let his head fall until the tip of his bill touched the ground. A little drop of blood trickled along the bill and fell on the rock.

Then the female bird seized the string in her beak and, without rising from her eggs, she began to tear at it furiously, cackling shrilly the while, like a virago of a woman reviling a neighbour. The wounded bird sank down on his breast and let his head go limp, while the whole flock of birds hovered nearer and became more subdued with their cries. Some landed on neighbouring ledges and craned their necks to watch the female bird's furious pecking.

Soon the string was cut. Then she seized the hook by the barb that protruded from beneath the bill. She pulled. The male bird spluttered a cry and flapped his wings, but the female bird arched her neck and wrenched again. The hook came with her almost. But its circular end with the string tied to it remained in the male's beak. A little stream of blood ran out. Then the male bird, unable to endure the pain any longer, tried to wrench himself clear. He pulled backwards fiercely and left the hook in his mate's bill. There was wild and victorious cackling as the freed bird staggered to his feet, shook his beak, and then uttering a weak, plaintive, surprised scream, dipped it into a little pool of water on the ledge.

His mate lay back on her eggs, smoothed her feathers with a shrug and closed her eyes in a bored fashion.

THE DOCTOR'S VISIT

Maurice Dowling lay flat on his back in his little narrow bed. He gripped the bedclothes in his two hands and held his hands up under his chin. He lay so flat and he was so slim that his figure was barely outlined against the bedclothes. But his feet stuck up at the end of the bed because the blankets were too short. His feet, covered by a rather soiled white cotton sheet, pressed against the black iron support. A yellow quilt lay sideways across his body, all crumpled up in the middle. The hospital attendant had arranged it several times during the night and warned Dowling each time not to touch it again, but Dowling always kicked it away from his chest. He wouldn't touch it with his hands to throw it away and he wouldn't endure having it near his mouth. He had an idea that the quilt was full of fleas.

His head, half buried in the white pillow, was very thin. His hair was black and cropped close. But even though it was cropped close, it was not stiff and bristly as close-cropped hair usually is. It lay matted on his skull in little ringletty waves. His face was deadly pale and his high cheekbones protruded in an ugly fashion from his hollow cheeks.

His large blue eyes kept darting hither and thither restlessly, never stopping for a moment. And his large mouth also moved restlessly.

Dowling was terribly afraid of the patients who were with him in the hospital ward. He had just come in the previous midnight. This was his first morning in the ward. All the patients were awake now waiting for the doctor's visit at ten o'clock. Ever since it became light and he could see their faces he became seized with a great horror of them. During the night he had heard queer sounds, wild laughter, whisperings and bestial articulations, but he thought he was merely suffering from the usual nightmares and noises in his head. Now, however, that he could see them he knew that it could not be a freak of the imagination. There were about forty of them there. His own bed was in the centre of the ward, near a large black stove that was surrounded by wire netting on all sides. Then both sides of the ward were lined with low iron bedsteads, little narrow beds with yellow quilts on them. All the beds were occupied except two by the glass door in the middle of the left-hand side of the ward, the door leading on to the recreation lawn. And the two patients who slept in those two beds were sitting in their grey dressing gowns at a little bamboo table playing chess. At one end of the ward there was a large folding door and the other end was covered by a window through which the sun was shining brightly. Through the window, trees and the roofs of houses could be seen. Beyond that again, against the blue sky line, there were mountain tops.

Suddenly a patient began to cough and a silence fell on all the other patients. Tim Delaney had begun his usual bout of coughing preparatory to the doctor's visit. He did it every morning. The other patients enjoyed the performance. But Dowling was horrified by it. It gave him a nauseous feeling in his bowels, listening to the coughing. Tim Delaney was sitting up in bed, his spine propped against the pillow and all the bedclothes gathered up around his huddled body. He wore a white nightshirt with a square yellow patch between the shoulder-blades. His bed was only five yards away from Dowling on the right-hand side and Dowling could see his face distinctly. The face skin was yellow. The skull was perfectly bald. The eyes were blue and red around the rims on the insides. The whole head was square and bony like a bust of Julius Cæsar's head. When he coughed he contorted and made a movement as if he were tying to hurl himself forward and downward by the mouth. His cough was hard and dry. Delaney had an idea that he was a cow and that he had picked up a piece of glass while eating a bunch of clover. According to himself the piece of glass had stuck in his throat and he could not swallow any solid food on that account. 'That fellow must be mad,' thought Dowling, as he looked at the queer way Delaney opened his jaws and bared his yellow teeth when he coughed. Dowling experienced the sensation of being gradually surrounded by black waves that presently crowded up over his head and shut out everything. A buzzing sound started in his ears and he forgot Delaney. He stared at his upright feet without blinking. A fixed resolution came into his head to tell the doctor everything. He decided that it was positively no use trying any longer to keep up the pretence of being ill. He was better off outside even if he died of starvation. He could not possibly endure the horror of being in such an environment. He had schemed to get into hospital in order to get something to eat and now that he was in hospital he could not eat. But then he had not expected to get into such a hospital, among these terrible wild-eyed people, these narrow sordid-looking beds, this dreary bare ward, with a big fat man in a blue uniform and a peaked laced cap, continually walking up and down, shaking a bunch of keys behind his back and curling his black moustache. And the food was so coarse. He had been given a tin mug full of sickly half-cold tea and a hunk of coarse bread without butter for breakfast. Naturally he couldn't touch it, desperate as his circumstances had been for the past six months. Instead of that he had expected to get into a hospital where there were pretty nurses, who smiled at a man and whose touch was soothing and gentle. He had expected kindness, quiet, rest, sleep, delicate food, treatment for the heaviness behind his eyes and his insomnia and the noises he heard in his ears. It was cruel torture to suffer from hunger, to starve in his tenement room, alone and without anybody to whom he could talk when he felt ill at night. But anything was better than this. He would endure anything if he could only be alone again. So he thought, looking at his feet.

Then the attendant came up to Delaney's bed and shook his keys in Delaney's face. Delaney stopped coughing. The attendant clasped his hands behind his back and marched slowly up the ward towards the folding door through which the doctor would enter at any moment. All the patients cast suspicious and lowering glances at the attendant as he passed them. The attendant examined each bed with a melancholy and fierce expression in his blue eyes. He seemed to be totally unconscious of the existence of human beings in the beds, or of the malicious glances directed towards him. In silence he would point a finger at a tousled sheet or a blanket or a piece of paper lying on a coverlet. The patient in question would tidy the place pointed at with jerky eagerness. Not a word was spoken. A deadly silence reigned in the ward. There was an air of suspense.

Suddenly the silence was broken by the sound of loud laughter coming from the outside of the folding door through which the doctor was to enter. Then the two wings of the door swung open simultaneously. The doctor and his attendant nurse appeared, each inviting the other to enter first. The nurse, a tall, slim, pretty, red-haired young woman of twenty-six, with a devilishly merry twinkle in her blue eyes, held her case sheets in a bundle under her right arm, while she held the door open with her left hand. The doctor, Francis O'Connor, was a middle-sized, middle-aged fat man, dressed in a grey tweed suit, with a gold watch-chain across the top button of his waistcoat. He waved his stethoscope at the nurse with his left hand, while the short fat white fingers of his right hand pushed back his side of the door. His jovial fat face was creased with laughter and little tears glistened in his grey eyes.

'Miss Kelly,' he gasped, between fits of apoplectic laughter that shook his fat girth, 'upon my soul there isn't a word of a lie in it. Go ahead. Ladies first.'

Then he himself entered first, still laughing. The nurse followed him, coughed, took up the fountain pen that hung from her waistband and dabbed at her hair with the end of it. The attendant came up at a smart pace, saluted and whispered something to the doctor. The doctor's face became serious for a moment. He glanced in Dowling's direction. Then he began to smile again, rubbed his palms together and looked at the ceiling, at the floor, at the walls, at the windows, smelling, everywhere.

'Upon my soul,' he said at last, turning to the nurse, 'does my old nose — sniff, sniff — deceive me or can I smell roses?'

The nurse nodded, swallowing her breath modestly. She pointed to the glass door that led to the recreation lawn. 'It's from that bush that grows by the wall,' she murmured, 'I saw three there last night.' 'Hm' said the doctor and he walked over to the first bed, throwing out his feet sideways without moving the middle of his body.

Dowling's heart had begun to beat wildly when the doctor entered the ward. He was delighted and relieved, for the moment, of all anxiety. Now everything would be all right. He could transfer all his worries to that jolly man, with the kind fat face.

And what a pretty nurse! Though her face was rather hard. Dowling began feverishly to prepare his confessions. He would explain everything. Then they would discharge him immediately. And in all probability the doctor would take an interest in his case and find him employment suitable to an educated man of good family. He became absorbed in the contemplation of what would happen after that. With his pale cheeks flushed and the extremities of his limbs throbbing with excitement, his mind soared off into a day dream, building castles in the air.

The doctor pulled the clothes back off the first patient's chest. He put his stethoscope to his ears and bent down to listen without looking at the man's face. The patient, formerly a peasant farmer named John Coonan, lay perfectly still with his hands lying flat on his abdomen. He stared at the ceiling through little fiery grey eyes that were set close together with a little pointed yellow nose between them. He imagined himself to be hatching twelve eggs in his stomach and he insisted on lying perfectly still, least he should disturb the formation of the birds.

The doctor's face gradually lost its merry creases as he listened here and there and tapped here and there. His eyes became sharp. Then they began to blink. Then his whole face looked cross and he straightened himself and cleared his throat. 'Now my man . . .' he began absent-mindedly and then he stopped, puffing out his cheeks. He turned to the nurse and whispered to her, holding her arm as he walked to the next bed: 'Now how can ye explain that? That man was getting better yesterday and today he's a foregone conclusion. Well, well. It's very queer.' He went up to the next bed.

The patients in the ward had been silent and attentive until then, but suddenly they seemed unable to concentrate any longer on the doctor's presence. They began to practise with voice and limb the grotesque imitations of whatever their crazed imaginations conjectured themselves to be. Dowling was startled out of his reverie by the gradual renewal of insane sounds about him. Again the true fact of his environment became real to him. He began to tremble violently. The doctor was proceeding rapidly down the ward, casually examining the fairly healthy patients. Dowling could catch the doctor looking at himself now and again. Whenever he caught the doctor's eyes looking at him, the doctor turned away hurriedly. 'He'll soon be here,' thought Dowling excitedly, 'and I can see he's interested in me already. He sees I'm different from the rest. Now how am I going to commence to talk to him?'

The doctor paused to look at the two old patients who were playing chess. The players never took any notice. Their gaze was concentrated on the board intently. One old fellow had his fingers on a black queen, making tentative excursions in all direction and then coming back again to his starting point. He had his lips sucked far into his toothless mouth. The other old man, clasping his dressing-gown about his withered body, looked on murmuring endlessly: 'Five minutes' pleasure and I have to suffer a life-time for it. Five minutes' pleasure and I . . .' The doctor walked away, followed by the nurse and the attendant.

They passed Dowling without looking at him. This irritated Dowling. He felt slighted. He ceased to tremble and his face darkened. The doctor went to the end of the ward and then came back rapidly up the other side. When he was just at the far side of Dowling's bed, he stood at the distance of a yard behind Dowling's head. He began to laugh and told the nurse a funny story about a greengrocer named Flanagan who had made a large fortune through contracts for the new government, in which he had relatives. This fellow Flanagan, a lean, stingy, mean, ignorant peasant, according to the doctor, went off from Harcourt Street Station every Sunday morning with his golf sticks, to play on his, Dr O'Connor's club links. He was a great joke, this fellow Flanagan. The doctor went on telling anecdotes about Flanagan, laughing violently in a subdued tone while he talked. But all the while he kept examining Dowling's head while he talked and laughed. Dowling's body was twitching in the bed with vexation.

The doctor finished his story and again he moved on and passed Dowling's bed without looking at Dowling. Dowling saw him pass and could restrain himself no longer. He called out angrily: 'I say, doctor, I want to speak to you.' The doctor turned about sharply and looked at Dowling seriously. The attendant came up to Dowling and whispered in his low passionless voice: 'You must wait your turn.' Then the doctor moved away again from bed to bed, talking, answering questions, examining the patients and joking with the nurse. Dowling watched him, boiling with rage. He decided that he would tell the doctor nothing. He wanted to kill somebody. Why should they persecute him like this? Could nobody in the world be kind to him?

At last the doctor reached the end of the ward and turned back. He came down towards Dowling hurriedly, his face creased in a smile. When he was within five yards of Dowling he held out his right hand and called out: 'How are you, Mr Dowling? Now I can attend to you.' Dowling immediately became soft and good humoured and smiled, a wan smile. The doctor sat down on the bed, still holding Dowling's hot thin right hand in his own fat two hands. He was looking into Dowling's wild, strained, big blue eyes with his own little half serious, half merry, half sharp eyes. A mist came before Dowling's eyes. He swallowed his breath and then he began to talk rapidly, pouring a volume of words out without stopping for breath.

'This is how it happened,' he began. The doctor bent down his head, he kept fondling Dowling's hand and listened. Dowling described how his mother died young while he was in his last year of college studying for the Indian Civil Service. His mother, a government official's widow, had an annuity that expired with her death. So Dowling, who had no other means of support, had to leave college and get employment as a newspaper reporter. That was eighteen months ago.

'I tell you,' whispered Dowling, lowering his voice and almost shutting his eyes, 'that what got on my nerves was . . . er . . . a queer thing and it may appear silly but . . . you know I couldn't give expression to something that was in me . . . somehow . . . I don't know how to tell you . . . of course I'm not a genius . . . but every man you know . . . of a certain class, of course, doctor . . . I don't know your name . . . every man has some creative power . . . and reporting work is awful . . . telling lies and rubbish day after day . . . and nobody understood me . . . everybody seemed to think that I was cocky and thought myself, on account of my family and that sort of thing, you know, better than the others . . . so that I chucked it six months ago and knocked about since . . . and then, desperate, I pretended to be ill so that I could get into hospital . . .'

He had been talking at a terrific pace and stopped suddenly to draw breath. Speaking rapidly, the doctor interrupted him in the same jerky low tone. 'And then, of course, you went to kill the editor, just to make people believe you were ill,' murmured the doctor.

Dowling suddenly stiffened in bed. He dragged his hand from the doctor's two hands. He held his two hands clenched in front of his face. His face contorted into a demoniacal grin. His eyes distended and then narrowed to slits. His body began to tremble. Gibbering, he began to mutter. Then he became articulate.

'I'll kill the bastard yet,' he screamed, 'I'll kill him. Where is he? Where is he?'

Screaming he tried to jump out of bed, but the attendant's giant hands were about him. He felt himself pressed down into the bed, flat on his back. Gibbering, he lay there trembling. Then another fit overcame him and he roared. The ward became filled with sound. All the other patients began to scream and cry and babble.

'Padded cell,' murmured the doctor to the attendant. Then he sighed and walked away to the door.

THE WILD SOW

Old Neddy the fisherman, of Kilmillick, bought a sow pig one day in Kilmurrage. He put the pig in a bag, dropped it into one of his donkey's creels and brought it home to his cabin. It was just six weeks old, a little black pig, with a long back, and big ears that dropped over it eyes and a little tail curled up in a knot.

The neighbours were surprised when they heard that Neddy had bought the pig, for he was an old man and lived alone in his two-roomed cabin and he had no land except a little patch in front of his door that grew enough potatoes to last him the year round. He was, too, very fond of drink, and whenever he had any money he stayed in Kilmurrage until he had spent it. So that the neighbours wondered what possessed him to buy the pig. In fact Martin Conroy came into Neddy's cabin and said, 'Brother, it's plain that they fooled you into buying that young pig, so if ye'll throw ten rockfish into the bargain with it, I'll give you a pound for it.'

Neddy hitched up his belt, glanced at Conroy with his little grey eyes and told him to get out of his cabin. Then he shook his fist after Conroy and said, 'I'll have money while I have that pig and that's why I bought it. So may the devil choke the lot of you.'

He made a straw bed for the little pig in the corner of his kitchen and sawed off the lower part of a barrel in which he salted his fish to make a trough for it. For a while he looked after it carefully and gave it plenty of potatoes, dry fish and whatever sour milk he could get from the neighbours. So that the sow got big and fat until it was six months old and fit for sale. But when a jobber came to look at it and asked Neddy what price did he want, Neddy told him to get out of his cabin. 'I have money,' he said, 'while I have that pig, so I'll keep it.'

That was in the month of April and Neddy's stock of potatoes had been all eaten by the sow and most of his dried fish along with the potatoes, so he turned the sow loose on the roadside to eat grass, saying, 'Now feed yerself and may the devil choke you.' And he took his basket and his fishing lines and went away to fish.

The sow wandered about on the road all the forenoon, smelling at everything, snorting furiously and making little short runs that made her foot joints snap under her fat body like hard biscuits being cracked, when a horse or a peasant driving a cow went past. She rooted among the grass until her head was caked with earth up to her eyes. Then towards her feeding time at midday she trotted back to the cabin, but the door was locked. For a time she waited at the door grunting and with her ears cocked listening to every sound, sniffing the air with her twitching hairy snout and tossing her head now and again in vexation. Then, when nobody opened the door, she began to whine with the hunger. She stood there motionless and whining until Neddy came back at dusk and let her into the cabin. He only gave her fish guts and potato peelings for her supper. 'From now on,' he said, 'you'll have to fend for yourself, and may the devil choke you.'

That went on for a fortnight with Neddy away fishing every day, and then the sow got thinner and wild with hunger. She began to eat grass by the roadside and roamed over the crags picking nettles and everything she could get hold of. She no longer snorted when horses or cows passed her. Her bristles grew rough and strong and her ears lost their tender transparency. Her eyes were hardly visible through the caked dirty that gathered around them. She used to run out of the cabin in the morning and never come near it again until dusk.

At first she roamed about the village of Kilmillick, eating grass and nettles, tearing up the ground for roots, chewing everything she found in rubbish heaps, old fish bones, rags, boots and potato skins.

Then, as the summer grew, the heat and the long days tempted her farther, down to the beach and along the lanes and the road leading to Kilmurrage. Often she never came back to the cabin for two or three days at a stretch, but would spend the night among the sandhills about the beach where the wild grass was very sweet and there was always a dog-fish or a piece of mackerel cast up by the sea among the weeds. Her bristles were now as stiff and thick as needles, and her black skin beneath them was cracked by the sun and scarred in places where dogs bit her or boys struck her with stones and dried sea rods when they cornered her in narrow lanes. All her flesh had hardened into muscle. She was lean like a hound and nearly as tall as a year-old donkey.

Towards the end of summer a jobber came again to Neddy and asked him would he sell the sow. 'She's not much good now,' said the jobber, 'so I'll give ye a pound for her. I might be able to soften her a bit and get a litter from her.' 'Get out of my cabin,' said Neddy, 'and may the devil choke you. I have money while I have that pig, so I'll keep the pig.' But the fishing was bad that year and he had to sell his donkey in order to buy flour for the winter. Still he wouldn't sell the pig. 'It's like having money in a bank,' he would say, 'a pig is always money. I often heard my father say so.'

But when winter came on and the ocean winds swept the crags viciously and sea foam was falling like snow over the cabins, the sow could go out no more, but sat on her haunches on her straw litter in Neddy's kitchen grunting and whining with the hunger.

Then one stormy day Neddy went into Kilmurrage to sell his dried pollock. He turned the pig out of the cabin and locked the door. Then he went away. The sow roamed about for a while shivering with the cold and weak with hunger. Her stomach was drawn up into her back so that she looked like a cat that is stretching itself. She could discover nothing to eat around the village so she came back to the cabin.

She got on her knees at the door and began to gnaw at the bottom until she made a hole for her snout; then she seemed to go mad and tore at the door with her teeth and battered it with her head until she burst it off its hinges and she pushed right under it into the cabin. The door hung on one hinge and the sow's right ear was gashed down the middle by a nail in the jamb.

She stood in the middle of the kitchen grunting, with her snout to the ground and with blood dripping from her ear in a steady stream. Then she tossed her head and rushed at Neddy's bedroom door.

Sticking her snout at the bottom near the jamb, she pushed and burst the string with which the door was fastened and got into the bedroom. Neddy's potatoes were lying in the far corner with a little wall of stones around them. His sack of flour stood against the wall near the potatoes. His dried rockfish were stacked on pieces of paper under the wooden bedstead. The sow began to eat. Snorting and tossing her head she ran from the flour to the potatoes and then to the rockfish, swallowing huge mouthfuls without chewing, and making a noise like a horse pulling her hoof out of a bog, until her stomach swelled out to a point at each side.

Then a big potato stuck in her throat.

When Neddy came in that evening he found her lying on her side, stone dead.

A POT OF GOLD

It was a moonlight night in July. The sky was very big, blue and silent. The valley of Rossmore, lying between towering rocky mountains that rose on either side of it, was peaceful. It was covered with a light grey mist, calm, as if it slept. A very long way off frogs croaked in a marsh.

Just before midnight four men came up the lane from the hamlet of Rossmore, going towards Mount Simon. As they crossed the flat stretch of hunchbacked moor, through which the lane ran before it reached the foot of the mountain road, they halted. They had been walking, owing to the narrowness of the lane, in single file. John Gillan, who was in front, pulled up suddenly and then the other three, one by one, had to halt suddenly, thrown one on top of the other, with their hands thrust out in front of them to protect themselves from falling, panting with terror of the weird, silent night and of the sombre, empty mountainside.

John Gillan was a thickset man, wearing a raincoat that had been washed to a whitish colour and reached from his throat to the insteps of his black heavy boots. A black slouch hat fell about his face. The moonlight shone on his fat red face and on his long grey beard as he turned sideways to talk to Barney Rogers who came behind him. Leaning on a light crowbar he held in his two hands with its end resting on the grass, he bent his head and whispered. 'Have ye got the black-handled knife?' he said.

Barney Rogers was a slight, tall, young man, dressed in an old blue suit, with the coat reaching down to the middle of his thighs in Irish fashion and a grey tweed cap perched at the back of his curly black head. He was so thin that the cartilages in his neck were visible as he strained forward his head towards Gillan. His little grey eyes opened wide and his little snub nose quivered. He clapped his hand on his left trousers pocket, felt the pocket and then he whispered: 'Sure I have. Here it is under my hand.'

'Make sure,' whispered Gillan. 'It's very important, the black-handled knife. We're not safe without it.'

'Here she is,' whispered Rogers pulling out a little black-handled pocket-knife. 'Ye can see for yerself.'

Gillan crouched down and peered at the handle. The other two men crowded around, with a swishing noise of heavy boots coming through grass. The three men, breathing loudly and murmuring, bent down, feeling the knife handle and peering at it. Rogers, with his head and shoulders outlined in the moonlight above the stooping forms of the other three men, winked both eyes and wrinkled up his face at the sky, as if he were bursting with suppressed laughter.

'She is black, sure enough,' said Gillan at length.

'She is,' whispered the other two men. They were two brothers called Higgins and they worked on Gillan's farm. They were big men dressed in grey frieze trousers and blue jerseys. They stood with their mouths open and a wild look in their black eyes. The two of them carried hammers in their hands.

Rogers carried nothing in his hands. He was a stone-cutter. He lived alone in a little cabin and he was rather a notorious character.

The four of them moved off again in single file, Gillan leading. They turned to the left, along the road that went up the side of Mount Simon until it reached the Reservoir. About half-way up Rogers said 'Hist' and tapped Gillan on the right shoulder Gillan stopped with a start and looked behind him sideways.

'We leave the road here and turn on to the crags to the left,' whispered Rogers. 'The rock is within two hundred yards of here.'

Gillan took off his hat and blessed himself. The Higgins brothers did likewise, murmuring the prayer aloud as they crossed themselves. After a little pause Rogers also took off his cap and blessed himself.

'Let's sit down for a minute,' said Gillan.

'We had better open the bottle,' said Rogers.

'Very well,' said Gillan, 'but mind, it's to be only a short swig.'

He fumbled within his raincoat and took out a quart bottle of whiskey. The four of them crouched under the little low stone fence as if they were hiding from something. The moon shone brightly on the white narrow road, the grey fence and the mountain side getting blacker and blacker as it faded away in the distance. Gillan had drawn the cork in the house but he was fooling with it a long time before he could draw it again. At last it came out with a soft sound. The sweet fragrance of the whiskey rushed out into the still night air.

They all drank, Gillan first. Then Gillan put the bottle back. The Higgins brothers kept peering over the top of the fence to the left with their mouths open. Gillan buttoned up his raincoat and then gripped Rogers by the left knee. Rogers was kneeling on his right knee with his left knee doubled up and his elbow resting on it.

'Now are ye sure ye dreamt of it three nights running?' said Gillan.

'As sure as I have an immortal soul,' whispered Rogers fiercely, taking off his cap and holding it with both hands to his breast. 'Three nights running I've seen that flat rock with red moss growing on a corner of it. Then the rock is raised up in the dream and there is a dead black cat lying under it and then down below that again, down far into the ground, through the rocks, there is a black iron pot on three legs and that pot is full of gold sovereigns. Full to the brim and the top ones are rusty.'

Gillan and the two Higgins brothers listened with awe.

'Can ye say how far down the pot is?' said one Higgins, the one called Pat, a man with large red ears, and warts on his hands.

'Shut yer mouth, Pat Higgins,' hissed Gillan, angry that his farm labourer should ask questions on the matter in his presence. 'Can't ye see that I'm talkin'?' he added arrogantly after a pause. Then he turned to Rogers and said in a stern tone: 'Now look here, Barney Rogers. Ye've make me buy a quart bottle of the best whiskey and ye've brought me out here at dead of night, to the danger of my immortal soul with believing in yer dreams, so, be the Cross of Macroom, if yer fooling me about the rock and the cat and the pot of gold . . . well, ye may look out for yerself. That's all. Come on, men. You go ahead, Rogers. Lead the way to yer rock.'

To the left of the road the side of the mountain was bare and broken. Limestone rocks, deeply creviced, protruded everywhere unevenly, with here and there a little clump of withered heather or grass. The ground was jagged in places. They walked slowly. Several times Rogers halted, holding up his hand behind him to the others. Then he would bend down on his hands and knees examining the ground about him. At last he said, 'Ha!' excitedly and darted forward to a little eminence. The eminence was crowned by an oblong flat rock.

'Exactly as in my dream,' cried Rogers, getting down on his two knees on a little bunch of withered heather beside the rock. He took off his cap with one hand and pointed to the rock with the other. 'Look at the red moss,' he whispered to Gillan.

Gillan's voice died in his throat as he tried to say something. Then he nodded his head and got on one knee beside Rogers, holding the crowbar upright in his right hand. The Higgins brothers sat on their heels with their hammers in their hands and their mouths open. They kept darting their eyes around in terror. All kept silent for several seconds. Their breathing was loud in the silence. The sound of each man's breath was distinct from the others, with the four sounds mingling irregularly. Gillan's shadow fell across the rock, his long beard sticking across the short shadow of the crowbar.

'Let's have another drink before we begin,' whispered Rogers at last.

In silence Gillan took out the bottle and uncorked it. When the cork came out with a flop the Higgins brothers started violently. All drank. Gillan took off his raincoat and rolled the bottle in it.

'In the Name of God,' he said, 'let's begin. Are we to break the rock or turn it?'

'Turn it, turn it,' said Rogers. 'You three turn it. I'll stand here with the black-handled knife in my hand.'

Rogers stood up, opened his knife and, holding it out in front of his body in his right hand, he said: 'Now turn it.' The three men, brushing against one another roughly, gripped the rock and heaved with all their might. The rock skidded and turned a complete somersault off its bed. All looked at the bed.

A dead black cat lay stretched there, with his yellow eyes open.

The Higgins brothers yelled and ran over the crags to the road, their heavy boots slipping among the stampeding cattle. Gillan had not screamed, but he jumped back and he put his hand to his throat and gripped his chest, just above the pit of his stomach, with the other hand. Just there his Scapular of the Sacred Heart was hanging on a cord. He murmured a prayer. Rogers stood behind and it was impossible to see the expression on his face in the darkness. He made no sound. At last Gillan spoke.

'It's the black cat,' he whispered, 'he's there. D'ye see him?'

'I see him,' whispered Rogers. 'It's him sure enough. There he lies, just as he lay in the dream guarding the treasure.'

'How are we going to get him out of it?' asked Gillan fearfully. 'Who is going to touch him and maybe be burned alive, Lord between us and all harm.'

'I'll do it,' said Rogers, 'I'll do it. Give me the bottle. It'll be the devil to touch him.'

'There, take a good drink,' said Gillan, handing him the bottle.

Rogers took a long swig. Then he rested, smacking his lips. Then he took another swig. Gillan, excited and looking at the cat, took no notice of him. Rogers cast a glance at Gillan and then he hastily put the bottle to his head again, took a little hurried swig and rammed in the cork. The two Higgins brothers arrived back just then, walking on their toes, with their hands raised outwards like men walking a tight rope. Gillan shook his fist at them and scowled for some reason or other.

Rogers stood up, holding the black-handled knife open in his right hand. With a sudden movement he swept his cap from his head and threw it from him to the ground. Gillan and the two brothers watched every movement breathlessly. Then, holding the knife over the cat, Rogers stooped down and grasped it by the tail. He lifted the tail. The cat came up, stiff and flat like a pancake. There was a burnt spot, a spot as big as a shilling, on the cat's left side below the shoulder. Pat Higgins, staring wild-eyed at the cat, saw the yellow spot and started slightly. Then he shivered and looked at Gillan. Rogers walked away five paces on tiptoe and then placed the cat gently on the ground. Then he wiped his forehead with the back of his hand and came back to Gillan, looking exhausted.

'Yer a brave man, Barney,' whispered Gillan in an awed tone.

'Give me . . . a drink,' mumbled Rogers, dropping on one knee and wiping his forehead.

He took the bottle in his hand and pulled the cork. Then he turned to Gillan and said: 'Now it's safe for ye to go ahead and dig. But be careful. If ye see a bone or a feather don't touch it. Tell me and I'll take away the spell with my knife. I'll sit here and watch, for fear the cat 'd change into a devil and burn ye alive. As long as I keep looking at him with the whiskey in me hand, he is helpless. Now hurry up and begin to dig.'

'Right,' cried Gillan excitedly, standing up.

'Come on, men,' he hissed; 'get to work and bend yer backs at it. I'll loosen the stones with the crowbar.'

Under the flat rock the stones were small and loose for about six inches, and under that there were thin layers of stone with black earth in between. The three men, panting and perspiring, cleared away the loose stones and then Gillan began to dig the layers with his crowbar and the two Higgins brothers tore away the loosened stones with their hands, breaking one now and again with their hammers. Rogers, kneeling on one knee with the open bottle in his hand, asked now and again, 'D'ye see any sign of the pot?' and as each time Gillan replied that he didn't, Rogers said, 'Work harder,' and he took another swig at the bottle.

Gillan dug like a madman, his eyes gleaming avariciously down into the hole. Already he pictured himself digging his hands into the golden sovereigns, clutching handfuls of them.

Then suddenly Rogers held up the bottle to the moonlight. It was half empty. He glanced around him hurriedly, and bared his teeth in a grin. He got to his feet. He moved away towards the road three paces backwards. Then he paused and called out: 'Dig, dig, something tells me ye are within a foot of the pot. Dig, dig like hell.' Then he turned and ran on his toes like a deer to the road without making a sound. If he made as much noise as a tramcar the three men digging would not have heard him at that moment. Then Rogers vaulted the low fence into the road and disappeared.

The three men worked away for a long time. At last Pat Higgins paused to take breath and looked behind him at the spot where Rogers was kneeling. He started and nudged Gillan. Gillan turned about and looked where Higgins was pointing. Rogers had disappeared. Soon the three of them had dropped their tools and were standing about, looking everywhere with wonder in their face, silently. Nobody spoke for at least a full minute. At last Pat Higgins swore out loud and clenched his fists.

'What is it, you fool?' cried Gillan angrily.

'It's my Aunt Mary's cat,' yelled Higgins. 'Ye've been made a fool of, John Gillan. I know the yellow spot on his side now. Oh, by the . . .' and he began to swear a terrible string of oaths as he rushed over to the old dead black cat and lifted him up. There was the same yellow burnt spot. They all looked at it.

Gillan raised his clenched fists above his head and stuttered, unable to speak with rage.

'Three days ago the cat disappeared and nobody knew what happened to him. It's how Rogers killed him. He should be arrested for it.'

'Arrested,' yelled Gillan, suddenly becoming articulate and turning on Higgins, 'd'ye want my name all over the county? Don't speak a word of this or I'll have yer lives. Don't give it to say to the dirty illegitimate son of a tramp that he made a fool of me. Oh, holy mother of God, how am I going to live the shame and disgrace of it?'

All the way home he kept wringing his hands and crying aloud.

THE FIGHT

Black Tom, a peasant, leaned against the counter of Mulligan's public-house. In spite of his large mouth being open, his breath going in and out through his nostrils sounded like steam hissing from a kettle. His upper teeth stuck out. A lock of hair hung down over his forehead beneath his tam-o'-shanter cap. All his bones and limbs were awkward and he was so tall that he looked slim. Nobody knew how tall he was. He must have been six feet and three inches.

As he leaned against the counter, his body seemed to be melting like snow, it looked so loosely knit together, and he changed his weight from leg to leg restlessly. His dim blue eyes strained wide open, stared stupidly at the counter. He was very drunk. It was the first time he had been drunk in six months. He had sold a pig at the fair in Kilmurrage for five pounds. He gave four pounds to his wife and told her to go home. She begged for the fifth, so he had to give her a few cuffs on the ear to get rid of her. Then he had drunk six pints of Guinness's porter in Mulligan's.

'Another pint,' he said to the barmaid, and as he spoke, he hiccuped. Then he heard somebody laugh behind him, and wheeling around cumbersomely, like a horse carrying a great weight, he saw his enemy Bartly Sweeney enter the bar with two friends. He tried to think why Bartly Sweeney was his enemy, and for the life of him he could not remember why he was, but he felt certain that he was. So he said 'Hello Bartly, hello there, boys, what are ye havin'?'

Each of the three men wiped his mouth and said, 'Mine is a pint!' Bartly Sweeney a square young man in a grey frieze trousers and blue sweater with a horsewhip stuck in his belt, spat on his hand and took Black Tom's in his.

'How are you, Tom?' he said.

'Fine, how's yerself?' said Tom, trying to smile and only succeeding in looking stupid, like a child looking at a stranger.

The barmaid brought Black Tom his fresh pint and he ordered three more for Sweeney and his friends. Sweeney began to talk to the barmaid, bantering her, and then Black Tom drew in a great breath that almost burst his nostrils, they swelled so much. He knew at that moment why Sweeney was his enemy. He was jealous of Sweeney, because Sweeney was a good-looking fellow and a great favourite among the women. It was common knowledge that Kitty Cooney, Black Tom's wife, was in love with Sweeney before she married Black Tom. Perhaps she is in love with him yet, thought Black Tom, staring at his pint. He despised his wife, but it was another matter having her in love with Sweeney, perhaps having children by him, same as he had heard it said women did in the United States. And Sweeney had been in the United States.

He felt a sudden desire to hit Sweeney on the top of the head, but just then Sweeney turned to him laughing over something he had just said, and Black Tom laughed too, shifting his weight to his other leg, and spitting out with a great noise in his throat. He knew now that Sweeney had followed him in to fight him.

'Here's luck.' 'Good luck.' 'Long life.'

They all drank. While he had his pint to his lips Black Tom was seized with a sudden fury and finished his pint at a draught. He would show this fellow Sweeney that even though he was ugly and had two teeth sticking out over his lips, that he was a strong man and able to drink his liquor. He dropped his empty pint on the counter with a bang, wiped his mouth with the back of his hand and tightened his belt, but nobody took any notice of him.

Sweeney was still talking to the barmaid and the other two men were listening to him. Black Tom felt irritated because nobody took any notice of him. He looked at the barmaid. She was leaning on the counter on her elbows, with her head cocked slantwise. Her breasts nearly showed above the neck of her blouse, as they pressed against the counter and her elbows. Her fuzzy hair was neatly piled on her head and her cheeks were flushed, listening to Sweeney's jokes. Black Tom suddenly felt a desire for her. Why the devil had he not married her instead of Kitty Cooney? Why, Sweeney had all the women in the island after him and he was not married at all. The dog. He looked at Sweeney.

Sweeney's sleek face was clean shaven and ruddy. His jaws were fresh and pink after the lather. The lines of his lips under his well-trimmed moustache were clear cut and regular. There was a nonchalant deviltry in his blue eyes, half covered by his eyelids. The very pose of his well-made body leaning far to the left was insulting. Black Tom could stand it no longer. He struck the counter with his clenched fist and roared. The barmaid started, put her hands to her throat and said 'Jesus, Mary, and Joseph.' But strangely enough, neither Sweeney nor his two friends took any notice whatsoever. Black Tom roared again. Sweeney turned around, put his hands under his armpits and looked at him. There was silence for three seconds. Black Tom was debating furiously in his mind what he should say to Sweeney.

'What's that ye said to me last year?' he screamed at last. 'Are ye as good a man now as ye were last year?'

Sweeney put his back to the counter and leaned an elbow on either side of him. Then he cracked the third finger and thumb of both hands.

'I don't care what I said last year or this year,' said Sweeney.

There was silence for several seconds, while the two men stared furiously at one another. Then Black Tom stamped on the floor with his right foot and yelled again.

'There isn't a man in Inverara as good as me,' he cried. 'I could beat all the measly, rat-whiskered, pock-marked sons of drunken priests in Kilmurrage with my little finger.'

Then he roared again and began slowly to unbutton his waistcoat, finding great difficulty in keeping himself steady on his feet.

'I'll tell you what's the matter with you,' sneered Sweeney, his face set in a contemptuous grin. 'You need somebody to wipe your nose.'

Black Tom growled, stamped with both his feet, ground his teeth and moved back a pace to spring or something, and fell on his buttocks on an empty barrel. Then he commenced to howl as if he were weeping.

'I'm alone,' he wailed, 'I'm alone among three of them, and there is nobody to hold my coat while I knock both the eyes out of his head. For God's sake, why don't somebody hold me back before I kill him.'

Then Sweeney seeing that his enemy was getting panic-stricken, tightened his belt around his waist, threw away his horsewhip, a penknife, three fishing hooks and an Agnus Dei. He stood in the middle of the floor and stamped with his right foot in a bellicose manner.

'I'm standing as God made me,' he cried, addressing the barmaid with a conceited look in his eyes, 'and I haven't a weapon on me and no man is going to raise to hand to help me. And what's more I can knock the life out of any man that was ever conceived by a drunken father, and there's one present.'

The other two men sniggered and Black Tom, having by now exhausted all his rage against Sweeney, for by nature he was a good-tempered man, roared again to show everybody that he was not afraid. He jumped to his feet and with a final effort threw off his waistcoat. It fell on the counter and knocked down a pint. Everybody rushed to pick up the pint and everybody shouted 'Don't break the house.'

'I'll break everything,' cried Black Tom, and, avoiding Sweeney, he rushed around the room hitting the walls with his head, biting the chairs with his teeth, kicking wildly. Sweeney moved over to the counter, eager to avoid coming into contact with him. The barmaid began to scream. The other two men, brave because they were not expected to fight, caught hold of Black Tom and tried to expostulate with him. But as soon as they seized him, Black Tom became really angry. He became savage. He became conscious of his great strength. He seized one of them in each hand and with one swing sent them crashing against the wall, where they fell in a heap. Then he rushed at Sweeney, but Sweeney stepped aside skilfully. Black Tom crashed against the counter, where he lay in a heap while Sweeney stood warily waiting with his fists doubled by his side. Black Tom lay on the counter for a long time. His brain began to work again. He became afraid. He felt that he was making a fool of himself. He might get arrested. What was Sweeney doing over there behind him?

Why were they all silent? He pretended to be very drunk, although he was now almost sober. He spluttered and hiccuped and threw his hands about him on the counter aimlessly. Then he struggled to an erect position, and pretending not to see Sweeney, tore at his shirt and blubbered, 'There isn't a man — '

Then Sweeney, nervous with fear that Black Tom was going to seize him and crush him to death in his mighty arms, hit him suddenly in the jaw and he fell in a heap to the floor.

After a while he came to his senses and heard them talking.

'Poor man,' said the barmaid, 'there's no harm in him, only he loses his reason when he has a little drop taken.'

'Nobody was sayin' a word to him,' said Sweeney.

'If it was anybody else threw me like that —' said one of the men.

Black Tom felt ashamed of himself, but he was too weak to assert his dignity by fighting. Instead he drank two glasses of whiskey hurriedly and left the public-house. On his way home he wept loudly. He would stand in the middle of the road and grind his teeth and swear that he would kill Sweeney some day.

When he got home he broke all the delft in the house. He whittled out a stick to thrash Sweeney and finally fell asleep on the hearth. Next morning he had a sick head when he went to work.

He did that twice every year.

COLIC

It was Saturday afternoon in the village of Cregg. There had been a little pig fair that morning and everybody was drinking his neighbour's health. It was a June day and very hot. From end to end of the Main Street people were standing outside the doors of the public-houses, with pint glasses full of black cold porter clutched in their strong red hands. There was loud laughter, hearty oaths and the smacking of thirsty lips. Here and there a man was drunk and singing some ridiculous song as his wife tried to bring him home.

The only two thirsty and unhappy men in the village of Cregg were Tom Hanrahan and his friend Mick Finnigan. They had no money. Their credit was valueless because of their liquor debts. None of the farmers would treat them, since neither of them had any land and were therefore people of no account. Hanrahan was a kind of botch carpenter and Finnigan always acted as his labourer.

They leaned against the fence outside Mrs Curran's public-house. Hanrahan had his hands in the pockets of his ragged old dungaree overalls. He wore an old blue coat, very shiny at the elbows and with a big tear, unmended, over the right pocket. The uppers of his light unpolished shoes were level with the ground on the outside of each heel and the inside of each heel was almost as high as when it was bought. So that when he walked he had to lift his feet up high, like a Chinaman wearing slippers without heels on a cobbled street. His shoulders slouched and he had a slight hump, less by nature than because of his habit, when he cracked a joke, of bunching himself together with his mouth wide open and his elbows dug into his sides as if he were hugging himself. He was a short, thin man with little blue eyes, a sharp, long nose, a big mouth and a sallow complexion.

Finnigan, on the other hand, was a huge heavy man, with a rosy, fat face, sleepy blue eyes and a sandy moustache. He never smiled. He hardly ever spoke, and when he stood still anywhere he always crossed his arms on his massive chest. He once drank four pints of Guinness's porter without drawing breath.

Suddenly Hanrahan clapped his hands together, opened his mouth wide and began to laugh without making any noise. Tears began to glitter in his little eyes. Finnigan looked at him stupidly with his mouth open.

'What's up?' said Finnigan.

'I know how we can get drinks,' gasped Hanrahan at last. Tears had begun to run down his sallow cheeks with laughter. Then he was seized with another fit and doubled up against the fence, mumbling: 'Oh, my side, I'm afraid I laughed too much, oh, my side.'

'Foo,' said Finnigan, shifting his back to get a more comfortable stone in the fence for the support of his shoulder blades. Then he opened his mouth again to speak, but forgot what he was going to say before he could say it, owing to laziness and the heat of the day. He subsided against the fence in silence, like a bladder out of which the wind is escaping slowly. He crossed his legs and dropped his chin on his neck.

Then Hanrahan suddenly became serious. He came over to Finnigan. Putting one hand on Finnigan's chest and the other hand on the fence he reached up and began to whisper in Finnigan's ear. He was whispering a long time rapidly. When he had finished Finnigan shook his head several times, scowled and said 'No,' with great emphasis. 'Now look here,' said Hanrahan in an irritated tone, 'listen to me.' He began to whisper again. Gradually the look on Finnigan's face changed. The scowl vanished. The fat, red cheeks, with little white flakes on them from sunburn, broke into creases. He opened his mouth and guffawed three times, just like this: 'Haw,' then a gasp and then again 'Haw.'

'D'ye see?' said Hanrahan, digging him in the ribs with his elbow.

'Yes,' blubbered Finnigan, laughing down in his chest heavily. 'I . . . I see what ye mean now.'

'Well, are ye game to do it?' said Hanrahan.

'Would I get arrested?' asked Finnigan, with his forehead wrinkled and a suspicious look in his eyes.

'Devil a fear of ye,' said Hanrahan. 'Who's to know the difference.'

They were both silent for a long time, almost a minute. Hanrahan was watching Finnigan's face anxiously. Finnigan was looking at the ground, his forehead wrinkled, his mouth open, his eyes staring vacantly at something to the left of him. At last he looked up and said, 'All right I'll do it. Where?'

'Here. Here where ye stand,' cried Hanrahan excitedly. 'Now mind what I told ye. Just do what I told ye. Now go ahead. It's dead easy. Leave the rest to me. Just do what I told ye. Hurry. Go ahead, man.

Finnigan cast a suspicious glance about him and then he let himself fall heavily down by the side of the fence. He made a terrific, crumbling, brushing dull noise falling. He was wearing grey heavy frieze trousers, a navy blue jersey and heavy hobnailed boots that were white with caked mud and dust. He lay in a cumbersome soft mass on the ground, lying on his stomach. He gripped his stomach and began to yell. He bellowed like a bullock. Hanrahan rushed over to him, tried to turn him on his back, shook him and then jumped to his feet.

He ran out into the middle of the road, waved his hat into the air and began to shout: 'Help, help. A doctor, or he's dead. Help, help.' People rushed out of Mrs Curran's public-house crying: 'What's the matter, what's the matter?'

'He's got the colic,' shouted Hanrahan, rushing over to Finnigan and going down on his knees. 'He's got the colic. My God, if I had only a drop of brandy for him.' He began to rub Finnigan's stomach furiously. Finnigan writhed and bellowed with monotonous regularity.

'What is it?' cried Mrs Curran, a short, stout woman in a black dress, with a silver watch hanging on her right bosom from a black satin strap. Her son had become a General in the Free State Army and she gave herself 'airs,' as the people said. She pushed up through the crowd until she faced Hanrahan and Finnigan.

'Mrs Curran,' cried Hanrahan pathetically, as he took off his hat. The crown of his head was completely bald. Some half-drunken man in the crowd giggled and cried: 'Oh sweet Virgin, isn't the full moon out early this quarter.' 'Mrs Curran,' continued Hanrahan, holding his hat in his hand, 'may yer soul rest in Heaven and save his life with a drop of brandy. An' didn't he soldier under yer son General Curran an —'

'Mary,' called Mrs Curran shrilly, 'bring out a noggin o' brandy, quick.'

Hanrahan raised his hands and eyes to Heaven and murmured a blessing on Mrs Curran. At the same time he nudged Finnigan with his right knee. Finnigan bellowed and began to kick the ground with his heels. He made a noise like an earthen floor being beaten with a heavy hammer. The same half-drunken man who had remarked on Hanrahan's baldness began to laugh, but somebody else told him to shut up and asked him whether he was a Turk or what. A quarrel started and the greater part of the crowd surged away down the road after the two men who had begun to quarrel.

Then the girl came running out with a noggin of brandy in a tumbler. Hanrahan grasped the tumbler. Holding the tumbler in his hand he began to thank Mrs Curran again. But the sight of the brandy was too much for Finnigan. He stopped bellowing and gripping his stomach. He sat up suddenly.

'I must drink yer own sweet health, Mrs Curran, first —' Hanrahan was saying, when Finnigan reached out over his shoulder and grasped the tumbler.

A few drops of the brandy spilled as Finnigan wrenched the tumbler from Hanrahan's hand. Then at one gulp he swallowed it, every drop of it.

'Scoundrel,' yelled Hanrahan, gripping Finnigan about the body and biting at him with his teeth all over the chest. 'Son of a wanton,' he hissed between bites, 'robber, may yer bones be sucked dry in hell by hungry little devils, you —'

But Finnigan jerked himself up and swung Hanrahan aside against the fence. He rose to his feet slowly and ponderously with Hanrahan hanging to his jersey. He looked around him foolishly.

'I'll have ye arrested, the two of you,' cried Mrs Curran, beside herself with rage at the trick that had been played on her. The crowd was laughing.

Finnigan, as soon as he heard the word 'arrested,' opened his eyes and his mouth, looked about him wildly, struck at Hanrahan blindly and missed him.

Then he yelled and started off at a bound through the crowd, headed westwards towards the road leading to his native village four miles away. He left a large strip of his blue jersey and of his cotton shirt in Hanrahan's bony fingers. He ran up the road, the hobnailed soles of his boots almost hitting him in the broad back as he ran, his back all ripped open and naked in parts, with remnants of his clothes slithering about his body. The people yelled with laughter. Even Hanrahan forgot his anger and laughed.

But Mrs Curran did not laugh. She kept shaking her fist at Hanrahan and shouted: 'I'll have ye arrested for fraud unless ye pay me for that noggin of brandy. So I will.'

'Yerrah, is it out of yer mind ye are, woman?' cried a fat farmer, with white side-whiskers. 'Is it a mangy drop o' brandy ye'd put in front of a good laugh. Here an' be damned to ye is the price of yer whiskey. Come on,' he added to Hanrahan, 'begob, yer worth a drink for that.' And he burst out laughing again.

'Begob an' he's worth another from me,' cried another farmer. 'Have one on me too, the curse o' God on ye for a humorous cratur, Hanrahan.'

Laughing, shouting, cheering, Hanrahan was led off to another public-house by the delighted farmers. As he was going away he turned on the re-treating and discomfited Mrs Curran and cried: 'To hell with the upstart General Curran and up the Republic.'

JOSEPHINE

It was an afternoon in June. The sun stood over the town of Kilmurrage like a ball of fire and everybody was going about perspiring and cursing. Down by the sea on the eastern outskirts of the town, the house of the retired district inspector of police lay sheltered from the heat. The sun played on its back furiously, but the front of it, facing the sea, was in the shade. The retired district inspector was a man of taste and regularity, and the front of his house was arranged skilfully to give comfort in warm weather. A verandah supported by four concrete pillars was covered with ivy, rosebushes and evergreens. The garden, surrounded by a low wall of concrete, was neatly arranged in flower beds and all the beds were in bloom. In the centre of the garden was a little avenue covered with brown, yellow, and black sea pebbles, while beneath, separated from the house only by the limestone road and a sloping beach of coloured sand and pebbles, the sea murmured, gently fanned by the breeze.

But the couple sitting on folding chairs, beneath the verandah in front of the dining-room window, were utterly unconscious of their good fortune in being so favourably situated on such a sultry day. The intoxicating mixture of smells, of flowers and the sea that was wafted up to them in the shade by the gentle breeze seemed only to make them gloomy. In fact the girl who sat on the right, Josephine Johnston, the daughter of the retired district inspector of police, was crying. She was sitting deep down in the chair, with her knees high up and pressed together, while her head was cast down on her lap and her two hands held a handkerchief to her eyes. And her body heaved spasmodically as she sobbed. Sitting on the left was George O'Neill, son of the principal shopkeeper in Kilmurrage, and a medical student in his final year in Dublin. He was not crying, but he was blowing his nose violently. And his face, which was naturally a brick-red colour, seemed to be about to burst with the exertion. His long, flabby, well-fed body was stuffed into the chair and it seemed to protrude from it at certain points like a badly made up parcel. He was evidently going somewhere, for in spite of the heat of the day, he was wearing a heavy blue suit, a light grey overcoat and a starched collar. Then he stuffed his handkerchief into his sleeve, crossed his leg and said, 'Oh, damn that sea,' looking viciously in front of him.

The girl took no notice of him, but she stopped crying. Then after a moment she raised her head and looked out at the sea. The breeze blowing against her white linen skirt showed her long, bony legs, bared to the knees, and even her body that was sunk in the chair seemed to be bony. In fact when she bent her head a moment later to cough into her handkerchief, the bone at the back of her neck stuck out like a pointed cone. But her face redeemed the bony appearance of the rest of her. She had an intellectual face, deep blue eyes, broad forehead and freckled cheeks and . . .

But George O'Neill was in no mood to take an interest in her intellectuality. 'Josephine,' he mumbled and blushed to the roots of his neck at hearing himself breathe her Christian name. 'Josephine, don't make a scene. Now look here. Damn it, what is it all about? I don't know. I come here to say good-bye and . . . Now Josephine you know quite well . . . Oh, why in the name of goodness do you sit there saying nothing?'

He raised his voice trying to appear injured and impressive, but he was obviously very embarrassed. The apple in his neck was hitting against his collar every time he drew breath and he tore at his collar nervously.

'I suppose I am foolish,' said Josephine, and the sight of her intellectual, cultured face looking so dejected and meek before the vulgar son of the shopkeeper would move a cinema audience of women to tears, more specially since she was twenty-eight, a Master of Arts and a brilliant woman, and he was only twenty-four, rather stupid and more acquainted with the racecourses and the bar-rooms off O'Connell Street haunted by students, than he was with the products of human culture.

'Hadn't we better talk it over,' continued Josephine, gathering courage and daring to look sideways at O'Neill.

'But what is there to talk over? I came here to bid good-bye. You immediately get into a fuss and start crying. Goodness gracious, what is there . . . Oh, here, don't start again for God's sake.'

Josephine had again taken her handkerchief to her eyes and her shoulder blades showing through the clinging muslin of her dress jerked upwards as she stifled a sob. Then suddenly she dropped her handkerchief to the ground, wheeled around in her chair towards O'Neill, scattering the pebbles with her right heel as she dug it into the earth. The meek expression left her face. It became imperious and aristocratic, and her voice too when she spoke was hard.

'Do you forget yesterday, Mr O'Neill?' she said.

O'Neill looked at her stupidly and his mouth fell open and he opened his eyes wide.

'Yesterday? How yesterday? Oh-h-h, I see.'

'Oh, do you? Did you think that you could play with a woman . . . that you could . . . kiss me and then forget it the next moment?'

'But good gracious, Josephine,' spluttered O'Neill, wrinkling up his forehead and waving his hands, 'what is in a kiss. Everybody kisses. You know very well all that bunkum is all . . . all very well for storybooks. You said so yourself.'

'How dare you take advantage of what I said? You cad.'

'You call me a cad, do you?' cried O'Neill angrily, jumping to his feet. 'You the daughter of a damn police inspector call on O'Neill a cad.'

He stood over her with his fists clenched and then suddenly looked towards the gate and then darted his eyes around looking for his hat. Then Josephine, terrified that he was going to leave her, jumped to her feet and caught him by the coat lapels with both hands and put her face up to his. She trembled all over and her lips twitched.

'Oh, don't go, George,' she cried; 'don't leave me. Sit down. I'm sorry. Do you hear? I'm sorry. I didn't mean what I said. Sit down and listen. I want to tell you something.'

O'Neill puckered up his forehead and sat down again with his hands in his overcoat pockets and Josephine sat staring in front of her at the sea, with her hands in her lap. For a few seconds there was silence but for the sibilant murmur of the sea on the beach and two peasants going along the road to the left laughing loudly.

'You see,' began Josephine, 'you don't understand how lonely it has been for me here. Three winters now all alone with my father. If you could only hear the sound the sea makes on that beach at night in winter. It's dreadful, and then the biting wind and the silence in spite of the wind, each dull bleak day followed by a dark night. Oh God, it has cut into my heart.'

'But you as an educated woman could find amusement in reading and thinking,' said O'Neill, afraid that some plot lay behind this picture of loneliness, and eager to minimise it.

'And then you came back this spring,' continued Josephine, paying no heed to his remark, 'and I thought that . . . Oh, George, can't you see that I love you?'

She had leaned far out of the chair towards him as she spoke, and her eyes looked at him passionately and her red lips were open and the lower lip twitched. For a moment she looked at him that way passionately and longingly and then suddenly she flushed, became embarrassed and dropped her eyes. He had merely stared at her coldly in return.

'Don't you think this is a bit theatrical, Josephine; sentimental, in fact,' he said. She shrugged her shoulders. 'Damn it,' he cried querulously and struck his knee with his fist. Her silence gave him courage and his weak mouth almost set firmly. 'Look here, Josephine, you have taken an advantage of me, that's what it is, and then you turn around and call me a cad. You're no child, you know. They tell stories about you in Dublin. You didn't give a damn then what you did to a fellow. Lots of them broke their hearts about you and there isn't a man that knew you that doesn't say . . . There you are now. As soon as I say a damn word you start crying. Say Joe, I'm sorry, but you can't have it all your own way.'

'But George, you are the first man —'

'Oh yes, and suppose the other fellows took the point of view that you were the first woman.'

'But George, you kissed me.'

'Just once.'

'No, three times.'

'Well, what's the difference? We are both bored here. We go for a walk. You with your talk of free life, free love, free woman and all that kind of thing. It would be different if there had been anything serious, but you know yourself, quite well, that there was nothing!'

He waited for her to speak, but she was silent, looking at the pebbles. He noticed that her breasts made no impression against her dress and he shuddered slightly.

'Well,' he said, 'is that all you have to tell me?' As he waited he wondered how he could have been such a fool as to flirt with her. What a change three years had wrought in the woman that had been the rage of all the young men in Dublin. Her high cheek bones, the rings around her eyes, her long legs.

'Yes, I have something to tell you,' she said weakly; 'but as it makes no difference to you that I love you —'

'Of course it makes a difference,' he said, thinking that it put him in an embarrassing position. But Josephine was twenty-eight, *passé* and foolish, and she thought that he had spoken meaning that he . . .

'Oh George' she said, 'I am glad. How happy you make me when you —'

'But good gracious —'

'What I wanted to tell you was that Chris Nolan wants to marry me.'

'Christ Nolan of Ballymullan?'

'Yes.'

'Ha. Well?'

'What am I to say to him, George?' She waited, tapping the pebbles with her toes, and her finger toyed nervously with the cross that hung on her breast, while she kept looking to the left away from O'Neill. O'Neill tore at his collar. The apple in his throat ran up and down and in and out. His brick-red face became purple. He kept moving the muscles in the calf of his right leg and through his brain were running a mixture of thoughts, of relief and embarrassment. Chris Nolan was the proper man for her. Forty and fairly wealthy. It would relieve himself of all feeling of guilt. But would she make a scene if he told her to marry Nolan. Damn it, that would be awful. In a moment he was tempted to make her his mistress and then leave her, but he thought of her long bony legs and the breasts that made no impression against her dress and . . . 'Well,' he said at length, looking at the top button of his overcoat 'Really, I don't think that's a fair question to ask me. After all, that's your own business and . . . I'm only twenty-four and haven't qualified yet, and it's very possible that I'll fail my final in September and . . . I say, Josephine, you could do worse things than marry Nolan. He has money.'

'Oh, damn money,' said Josephine, stamping with both her toes. 'I don't care if you never qualify, George. I can work. We can just live together.' 'Good God, Josephine.' O'Neill put his handkerchief to his forehead. 'Surely you're not thinking that I . . . I merely mean that I was not fitted to advise you as to marrying Nolan. I hope you didn't think that I had any intention of . . . After all, my career . . . Oh, damn it.' He bit his lip, conscious that he was making a fool of himself. He began toying with his collar. Then he looked at Josephine and started. Her face was set in a cold stony stare. Her hand hung limply by her side and she was nodding her head, as if in answer to some question that her brain was asking.

'Josephine, I say, Josephine. I didn't mean to hurt you.'

Josephine laughed, not mirthlessly but mirthfully. There was a sparkle in her eyes as she laughed. 'Go away, George,' she said lowly and calmly.

O'Neill stood up awkwardly and took his hat. He reached out his hand. 'Good-bye Josephine,' he said.

'Good-bye, George,' said Josephine without moving.

O'Neill waved his arms and turned to go, but as he was stooping to go out under the verandah on to the drive, he felt his coat tail being pulled. He turned around. Josephine was still sitting in the chair, looking up at him, her face set in a passionate stare. 'Kiss me,' she said shortly, reaching out her hands. 'There is plenty of time,' she added as O'Neill bent down to her.

Again the thought of making her his mistress came into his head and he paused with his mouth near her lips. He made a gurgling sound in his throat. She was looking at him with desire, her body passive, a gleam in her eyes. He shuddered slightly. He brushed her lips with his. Then he turned away hurriedly. As he went down the path, he rubbed his mouth with the back of his hand. Her lips had felt so dry and sticky.

Josephine sat still, looking in front of her while he was going down the drive, dimly listening to the crunch, crunch of his shoes on the pebbles. Then when the gate banged to and she heard the bolt shoot into the niche in the concrete post, she raised her head hurriedly and looked at him. He saw her through a corner of his eyes, but pretended not to see and walked away furiously to the right in the direction of the pier. As he walked, he felt a ticklish feeling in his thighs and down the backs of his calves as if he were walking in a field with his back to a bull. Then he dipped into a hollow of the road.

Josephine spring to her feet when she lost sight of him. She ground her teeth and a look of hatred came into her eyes. She felt she could drive a dagger into his heart. She did in fact make a motion with her right hand as if she was driving a dagger. Then she saw his head coming around the turning of the road. She noticed the bald spot behind his right ear. She had never noticed it before. His shoulders came into view. She noticed for the first time that he had a slight hump. Then his whole body came into view passing a gate. She noticed that he had flat feet. Then he was lost from view again. She went back to the chair, shrugged her shoulders and laughed. Then she lit a cigarette, crossed her legs and leaning her head on her hands looked out at the sea. 'Good God, I made a fool of myself. Ugh.' She shuddered at the thought of it. Then she heard the *Duncairn* blow her whistle shrilly and she jumped to her feet. 'Gracious me, the post is gone and I promised a reply today. Hey Ellen. Ellen, you get your shawl at once,' she cried, rushing through the hall into the sitting-room. As she wrote the solitary word 'Yes' on a postcard she called out to the servant, 'Take this to the steward of the *Duncairn* and tell him to post it at once as soon as the ship reaches the mainland.' Then she placed the postcard in an envelope and addressed it to 'Chris Nolan, Esq., Solicitor, Ballymullan.'

Then, sitting down again in the chair puffing her cigarette, she watched the servant trot down towards the pier with the letter in her hand. She smiled at her thoughts. After all, Ballymullan was on the mainland within easy reach of Dublin. There would be social calls, weekend trips and a liberal allowance. And Chris Nolan? She shuddered when she thought of his bald head and the noise he made in his throat when he was eating. But anything was better than Inverara in winter.

And perhaps the curate in Ballymullan . . .

And Josephine smiled again.

THE STRUGGLE

The sea was dead calm. There was no wind. The sun stood high in the heavens. Seamus O'Toole and Michael Halloran were coming from Kilmurrage to Rooruch in a new boat they had just bought. The fresh tar on the boat's canvas sides glistened in the sun, and the polished wooden lathes of the frame emitted a strong smell of pine. The two men were singing snatches of coarse songs as they rowed. They had drunk a lot of whiskey in Kilmurrage. They were both strong young men. Seamus O'Toole rowed in the prow. His cap resting crookedly on the back of his head, showed his white forehead above a ruddy face. His blue eyes were glassy with drink and there was a slight froth around the corners of his thick lip. Michael Halloran rowed in the stern. His bare head was shaped like a cone, shorn to the bone all round with a short glib hanging over the narrow forehead. Sweat discoloured the knees of his white frieze trousers. His shoulder blades twitched convulsively under his grey shirt as he lay forward over the oars and he kept hanging his head sideways, as if he were trying to hit his left knee.

They were passing Coillnamhan harbour about a mile from the shore, when O'Toole stopped rowing suddenly and said, 'Let us have a drink.' 'I'm satisfied,' said Halloran, letting go his oars. The boat flopped ahead with a lapping sound on the eddies of her wake. O'Toole picked up a pint bottle of whiskey that rested on his waistcoat in the prow. He uncorked it and took a swig. The whiskey gurgled going down his throat. Then his lips left the neck of the bottle with a gasp and he passed it in silence to Halloran. Halloran took a long draught and passed it back. 'That's enough for us,' he said thickly. 'Go to the devil,' said O'Toole with a rough laugh and put the bottle to his lips again. Halloran turned round in his seat and snatched the bottle. O'Toole's teeth rasped against the rim as the bottle was wrenched from his mouth. Halloran swallowed his breath hurriedly and tried to put the bottle to his lips with his right hand. He was leaning backwards, his face to the sun, his left hand on the starboard gunwale.

O'Toole cursed, drew in a deep breath, and struck at Halloran's upturned face with his right fist. His upper lip contorted as he struck. He struck Halloran between the eyes. The bottle fell to the bottom of the boat, hit a round granite stone that lay there and broke into pieces. Halloran's head hit the bottom of the boat with a hollow thud and rebounded as he clawed with his hands and legs. His bloodshot eyes glared and he shrieked as he struggled to his feet. O'Toole with his jaws wide open jumped to his feet too and snatched at his waistcoat. He pulled a knife from the pocket. He was opening it when he dropped it suddenly and whirled about. Halloran had yelled again. He was standing athwart his seat, the round stone in his left hand. He drew back his arm to take aim when the boat rolled to port, and he slipped. His right shin struck against the seat. In seizing the gunwales with both hands to steady himself the stone dropped into the sea. Its splash sounded loud in the silence. Hissing, they both stood upright, swaying gracefully with the rocking boat, as agile as acrobats in their drunken madness. They stared into one another's eyes for several seconds, their bodies twitching, their thighs taut. Each felt the other's breath hot on his face. Their breathing was loud. Each stood astride his seat.

Then the boat stopped rocking. With a roar they rushed at one another's throats. They met between the two seats, their feet against the sides, each clasping the other's throat. They stood cheek to cheek, breast to breast. They had moved so lightly that the boat did not rock. The two of them close together looked like a mast. They stood still.

Then O'Toole raised his left leg and hit Halloran in the stomach. Halloran yelled and doubled up. The boat rocked as O'Toole pressed forward and the two of them tumbled across the second seat, Halloran beneath, O'Toole sprawling on top, his hands still gripping Halloran's throat. Then Halloran heaved and struggled sideways to his knees. He threw O'Toole's legs over the port gunwale. The boat canted ominously to port. The port gunwale was almost under water. They both shrieked. Halloran's body bounded off the boat's bottom as he wrenched himself to starboard and wound his legs about the seat. The boat rocked from side to side madly. Then O'Toole tired to lift his legs on board. They were almost on board when Halloran grasped at his head and seized his ears. They swung out again with a swish. The boat rolled with them, paused for a moment with the gunwale at the water's edge and then it toppled over with a swoop. There was a muffled yell as the two men disappeared beneath the black dome of tarred canvas, Halloran's legs clinging like a vice to the seat, O'Toole's hands gripping Halloran's throat.

For half a minute the boat hopped restlessly. There was a rustling noise of something splashing in water. Then all was still. The sun glistened on the tarred bottom of the boat. A cap floated near.

Then the upturned boat began to drift slowly westwards.

WOLF LANIGAN'S DEATH

It was a frosty January night about ten o'clock. A large barge drawn by two horses was coming slowly down the Canal nearing its destination at Porto-bello Bridge, Dublin. There was no moon, but now and again glaring lights from the tramcars that rattled over the Bridge lit up the dark waters of the Canal, the grey bulk of the barge, the taut rope, the narrow gravel path and the two lean horses walking slowly in single file with their head drooping.

Then as the barge drew closer to the bank, Wolf Lanigan raised his head and shoulders behind the windlass in the bows and looked about him cautiously. 'Jump, towny,' cried the helmsman in a whisper. Wolf stood up suddenly, jumped on to the tarpaulin that covered the cargo, stooped and took a flying leap to the bank. He landed on his hands and knees, jumped to his feet, waved his hand to the barge and vaulted over the low concrete wall into the street beyond. He landed ankle deep in the mud beside the wall with a loud thud. The noise made him stiffen with his hands and back gripping the concrete wall. He listened for several seconds with out breathing. Not a sound in the dark street but the squelching of the displaced mud. He ran crouching across the street and into a dark alleyway between two houses. At the far end there was a heap of rubbish and an upturned cart in a little wooden shed. He went on his hands and knees in the shed behind the cart, took an electric torch from the pocket of his loose raincoat and flashed it about. There was nothing but a heap of straw, a torn black hat lying in a corner, and an empty sack.

He switched off the torch and placed it in the cart. The he took off his raincoat, a blue serge coat and a leather jacket. Lying between his shoulder blades on his white shirt was a Colt automatic pistol, bound by leather thongs around his neck and waist.

He loosed the thongs, placed the pistol in the cart, and dressed hurriedly. Then he switched on the torch again and placed it in the cart with the light towards him. He took the pistol, released the cartridge case, emptied the cartridges, wiped each one with a handkerchief, notched their heads with a clasp knife, returned them to the case and returned the cast to the pistol. Then he switched off the light, put it in his pocket and jumped to his feet.

He put the pistol in his left breast pocket, and with right hand on the butt he walked back into the street with stooping shoulders.

He crossed Dublin without stopping, following dark side streets, going under arches and through by-lanes. He passed over the Liffey at Butt Bridge and then hurried through a maze of slum streets until he reached Dublin's brothel quarter, north of Amiens Street. There he slackened his pace and went cautiously, stopping at every corner and convulsively pressing the butt of his pistol when anybody passed. At last he crossed a waste patch of ground that was strewn with bricks, heaps of debris and old pots and he came to the corner of Divis Street.

Peering around the corner of a deserted house at the end of the street a blaze of light struck him, running low to the ground in parallel lines until it ended in a dark lane at the far end. The light streamed from the open doorways of the two-storied brothels, shebeens, and dens of criminals on either side, while the second stories were in darkness, or with only a dim light showing through heavy blinds. The street was crowded with men and women, walking up and down and standing at the doorways, some drunk, staggering and quarrelling, others singing with clasped hands, others walking silently in couples with the measured tread of policemen. Strains of music and the sound of wild singing and still wilder laughter rose from the street in a strange inhuman melancholy roar to the still sky overhead. And yet in spite of the noise there seemed to be a deadly silence. The music, the singing, the banging of doors, the obscene curses, the drunken lascivious laughter came like a casual murmur heard from the bottom of a dark abyss.

The Wolf waited over five minutes, motionless, with his body pressed against the brick wall, watching the street. He could not move while those silent couples were pacing up and down steadily, seemingly intent on nothing but their thoughts. He knew their eyes would catch him slinking past, that guns would flash out, and deep voices bellow out 'hands up!' . . .

Then from the far end a young woman came staggering down the street, hanging on the arm of a young man. Her long, black hair flowed down about her shoulders. A loose dressing-gown was open to below her breasts. She laughed hysterically as she tried to brandish a bottle over her head. Then suddenly another woman rushed out at her from an open doorway. 'Let him go, you b —, he's mine.'

A shriek, a sudden rush and the two women were at one another's throats. The whole street gathered around, shouting. 'Now's my chance,' muttered the Wolf.

He darted along the side of the street, passed the crowd and dived into a dark doorway at the far end. On tiptoe he passed a door on the right of the hall. Sounds of drunken revelry came through the door, sounds packed close together as of a pot boiling furiously. In the hall there was the silence and darkness of death. The Wolf drew his pistol and groped for the wall with his left hand. He couldn't see his hand. At last he found the wall. He slid along it, holding the pistol behind him, facing the street. His foot came in contact with a stairway. Noiselessly he mounted step after step, sideways, with the pistol behind. He reached a landing. The roof was so low that he had to stoop. Opposite him there was a gleam of light coming through the keyhole of a door. Catlike, lifting each foot carefully and planting it flat, he reached the door. He put his ear to the keyhole and listened. Then he knocked quietly, two double knocks. There was a noise of a bed creaking and then of slippers shuffling along a boarded floor. The door opened slightly and a woman's head appeared. 'Rosie,' hissed the Wolf.

'God!' ejaculated the woman, stepping back.

The Wolf darted in after her and close the door gently and put his back to it. Turning the key with one hand, with his gun levelled, his eyes darted around the room. It was bare, low roofed, garret-like, with a table in the centre of the bare boarded floor. On the table was a white cloth with dirty crockery in a pile at one end. In the corner was a wide bed with the yellow quilt crushed, evidently where the woman had been lying on top of it. A coal fire burned brightly in the open grate. A lamp with a broken chimney hung on a nail on the wall. Not a sound was heard in the room but the lazy crackling of the fire and the distant heavy murmur from the street coming through the heavy blinds on the window. The air was heavy and thick.

The Wolf stood with his legs wide apart, crouching forward from the hips. His sallow face was contorted with excitement. A thick growth of black beard covered his square jaws and his lips. There was a patch of clotted blood over his right eye. His boots were caked with mud and there was a large rent in his right trouser leg below the raincoat, that covered his body from there to the throat. A grey tweed cap was pulled far down over his head. A bony hand covered with dirt gripped the pistol close to his hip. He stood squat, broad-shouldered, leaning forward, as if he were ready to jump through the window at the slightest sound.

The woman stood by the table staring at him with an expression of horror on her pale beautiful face. It was deadly pale. Even the open lips were pale and her large eyes were glassy and lifeless. A long plait of black hair was hanging over her right shoulder, trailing down the breast of her loose grey dressing-gown. Her hands clutched at the end of the plait. Her bare feet were stuck into a pair of heelless slippers. She stood, tall and motionless, staring wildly and intently at the Wolf's face, with compressed lips, as if hypnotised.

For several seconds they stood that way, the two of them, in the silent room. Then suddenly the Wolf spoke.

'Anybody been here?' His voice came in a hoarse, cracked whisper, the voice of a man who has spent sleepless nights in the winter air

The woman tried to speak, swallowed something and shook her head.

'What the h-ll is the matter with ye?' hissed the Wolf through his yellow teeth. 'Aren't ye glad to see me? Eh! Has anybody been here? Ye know who I mean?'

He advanced towards her noiselessly and stood with the muzzle of his pistol pointed within an inch of her breast. But the woman, without a movement of her body and without taking her eyes from his face, just shook her head once more. Then she gasped, shivered, put her right hand to her forehead, and sank to a chair by the table, still looking at the Wolf, as if drawn by a magnet.

'Afraid of me? Eh?' said the Wolf opening his mouth wide and bursting into a noiseless laugh. His head and shoulders shook, but he made no sound. 'Do I look funny? Eh? Come on, move, an' get me somethin' t' eat. I'm starved. D'ye hear? Didn't eat this two days. Move, blast ye.'

He watched the woman get to her feet and walk to the cupboard near the fireplace. Then he moved on the flat of his feet to a chair by the table facing the door. He laid the pistol in front of him. The woman was putting a kettle on the fire.

'Don't mind that kettle, I tell ye,' he said. 'Give me somethin' t' eat. I don't want any tea. Haven't ye got any grub?'

Without a word she dropped the kettle and went back again to the cupboard. The Wolf took off his cap. His forehead was bald and sloped straight back from the eyes. There was another large patch of congealed blood where the bald spot met the hair near the top of his skull. He put his fingers to it and ground his teeth with pain. The woman put a pork pie, bread, butter and milk on the table. She moved mechanically, using only one hand, as if drive by an alien will to do something hateful. And all the time her lifeless eyes strayed to the Wolf's face. Without looking at her the Wolf began to eat ravenously. Every time a shout came from the street, he started, looked around wildly and grabbed his pistol. The woman stood by the fireplace, with her hands folded on her breast, motionless, her eyes fixed on his face.

Then he finished eating, licked his fingers and looked at the woman. His small grey eyes roamed over her face and his under lip protruded.

'Why the h-ll don't ye say somethin'?' he snarled. 'Ye heard about the racket in Mullingar, didn't ye?'

The woman's lips quivered, but she didn't speak. He jumped up, and gripped her by the right shoulder and pointed the gun at her breast.

'Listen to what I'm goin' to tell ye. I'm goin' to tell ye somethin' that'll wake ye up, dosey. D'ye know where I went four days ago? Eh? Well, me an' Chris Moloney an' the Bull Kelly went to raid a bank in Mullingar. The cops followed us from here, see? Somebody gev the game away. Chris an' the Bull got pinched, an' I'd have got pinched too, only I plugged a cop. I plugged a man, Rosie, d'ye hear? Shot him dead. Been two days comin' down in a canal boat. I'm wanted for murder, d'ye hear?'

The woman nodded her head several times and pointed to a newspaper that lay in the coal-scuttle. The Wolf darted over and picked it up. On the front page in large headlines it ran:

MULLINGAR BANK HELD UP
DETECTIVE SERGEANT CARNEY SHOT DEAD.

And underneath was the Wolf's photograph.

The Wolf swore softly, crushed the paper into a ball and stamped on it. Then he turned once more to the woman. His nostrils were expanding and contracting.

'Listen. They aren't goin' to get me by —' He pulled out the cartridge case from the pistol. 'They are all dum-dum. An' one is for mesel' and another for you. See? The rest is for the gang that comes to take me. Un'erstan'?'

There were beads of sweat on his swarthy forehead. The woman never moved or spoke. But her eyes became larger and the skin around her lips tightened. Swearing frightfully the Wolf took a bottle of whiskey from the cupboard and held it up to the light. It was nearly full. He wrenched out the cork with his teeth and drank deeply. Then he sat down again at the table facing the door, his left hand clutching the bottle, his right on his pistol butt. The woman drew a chair to the fire and sat down, still watching him.

The Wolf began to drink starting at every noise; and between drinks he stared at the table, his eyes narrowed, his forehead wrinkled into deep furrows, as if his brain were struggling with some intricate problem. The silence in the room was intense. Then gradually the Wolf's face relaxed. He began to move his limbs and nod his head. Then he struck the table with his fist, put the bottle to his head and emptied it and got to his feet. His body swayed slightly and there was a slight mist before his eyes. With his foot he drew his chair beside the woman's. He was careless now about making a noise. He sat down with a flop. He still had the gun in his hand. He put his arm around her waist. She looked into the fire and shivered.

'Say, Rosie.' His voice was loud and hoarse and there was an attempt at merriment in it. 'Be nice to me. Won't ye? Ain't I been a good pal to ye? Eh? Be the lumpin' Moses didn't I pick ye up in O'Connell Street, half starved, after that sojer friend o' years deserted ye? Amn't I after keepin' ye here two months, an' ye never had to go out once an' bring in any money same as any other girl. Eh? Ain't ye goin' to kiss me, Rosie?'

The woman never moved. He staggered against her and pressed his lips to her white cheek. She shuddered.

'Divil take ye. Yer like a dead thing. Is it how ye think I haven't got any money?' He fumbled at his shirt and pulled out a wad of bank-notes tied with a string. 'There's three hundred there. See? It takes the Wolf to get away with 'em. See? We're going' to have a good time on them, Rosie. Me an' you, Rosie. See? Soon as these cops are off the hunt, we'll ship across t' England. See? They ain't goin' to get me. See?' He jumped to his feet, suddenly furious. 'Who's goin' to get me?' His voice came like a hiss between his teeth. Then he growled like a wild animal and stalked about the room with his gun levelled. 'See? I'm the Wolf Lanigan. The Wolf. D'ye hear?'

Suddenly he staggered and put his hand to his head.

'Blast it, my head is goin' round. Must have a sleep.' He moved over to the woman and whispered, 'Rosie, I'm goin' to lie down. See? You keep watch.'

He tumbled on to the bed and lay on his back with the pistol in his right hand across his chest. The woman's eyes were fixed on the fire. She sat immovable. The Wolf's eyes began to shut, but a soon as a noise came from outside, he started up and grabbed his pistol. Then gradually a weariness seized his limbs. They became listless. The weariness crept up into his head. His eyes shut. His mouth fell open. The hand slipped off the butt of the pistol. He began to snore. He was asleep.

Then slowly the woman turned her head around towards the bed and looked at him. Her eyes opened wild like the eyes of a child brought face to face with something strange and tremendous. Gradually a look of wonder spread over her face. Her lips were parted, showing her white teeth. She stood up with her hands down by her sides. The dressing-gown slipped from her shoulders. Mechanically she slipped her hands from the sleeves and let it fall to the ground. She stood in her nightdress, her hair plaited, white like an apparition. She walked over to the bed, moving straight and stiff. She stood over the bed looking down at the Wolf's face.

Then a strange, ghastly smile crept over her lips and cheeks without touching the eyes. The eyes became cold and glassy; two large discs lit with an immeasurable hatred, while her lips smiled. Her right hand moved forward slowly until it reached the pistol. Slowly the fingers crept around the butt. Then the smile faded from her lips. Her eyeballs started from the sockets. Her teeth bared. She drew in a deep breath, pressed the pistol to the Wolf's chest and pressed the trigger.

There was a deafening roar as bullet after bullet crashed through the sleeper's breast. Then in the silence that followed, the rattling of the window, the fragments of the lamp falling to the floor sounded like the dying echo of a thunder-clap. The woman turned, dropped the smoking pistol to the floor and burst into a wild shriek of insane laughter. Then there was silence again. Little clouds of smoke roamed about the ceiling. The figure on the bed was still.

THE BLACK BULLOCK

He was two years old when he came to Inverara. But he had been hungry all his life and he was no bigger than a donkey. His owner was a boatman on the mainland opposite Inverara and he had bought the black bullock for ten shillings when the bullock was a week old. Its mother had died of the colic or something (the poor widow who owned her said it was the Evil Eye). But the boatman had no land and the bullock grew up about the cabin, more accustomed to potato skins and nettles than to hay or clover or plain grass. By day he wandered around the little fishing hamlet, rambling on the roadside, chased by dogs and pelted by children and by night he was tethered in his owner's kitchen to an iron hook in the wall by the back door. There was a deep groove around his neck where the rope rested, and the groove was deepest under his chin. For the lads of the village who visited his owner's cabin often amused themselves at night when the boatman was not looking by holding a potato in front of the bullock's mouth and retreating with it as the bullock strained after it moaning with hunger. Little boys amused themselves by riding him and sticking thistle heads in the end of his tail that only reached half-way down his legs. Yet he was by nature so healthy that his temper never soured under this ill-treatment and, in spite of hunger, his black hide was glossy and curly. He had no horns, and the tip of his skull where bullocks have horns was always cake with dried mud, for he was in the habit of playfully butting his head into the bog and wallowing like a wild one.

Then on the festival of the pagan god Crom Dubh in autumn his owner brought him to the island of Inverara to graze for the winter, in the hope that he would get fat, and be fit for sale in the following May. He gave him to a peasant named Jimmy Hernon of Coillnamhan. 'Feed him well, Jimmy,' he said, 'and I'll bring you the best boatload of turf that was ever cut in a bog when I am taking him away next May Day.' Hernon took off his hat, spat on both hands and swore by all the saints that he would keep the bullock's belly full if his own had to go empty. In the presence of the boatman he put the little black bullock to graze in a clover field with his own cow. 'There you are,' he said. 'There isn't a man in Inverara would treat your bullock so well.' And the boatman went away to the mainland highly pleased with the bargain he had made.

As soon as the little black bullock found himself loose in the luscious clover he began to eat ravenously, wagging his tail, shaking his head and snorting. When he began to eat his belly was so thin that one could transfix it with a knitting needle, but it rapidly filled out so that he looked like a little cask. He soon made friends with the cow, although at first she horned him away when he sniffed at her flanks, and they wandered up and down the field all night side by side, their coarse tongues making a noise like tearing silk as they chopped the clover. Then in the morning when the cow leaned over the gap chewing her cud and lowered now and again wanting to be milked, the little black bullock stood by, chewing his cud with his eyes half shut, perfectly content.

But Hernon came with his wife to milk the cow and began to swear ferociously when he saw the black bullock's rotund stomach. 'I'll declare,' he said with an oath, 'that he'll eat three times as much as my cow, the miserable little wretch. Out he goes to the crag this very minute.' And he drove the bullock from the clover field up a rocky lane to the cliff top, hammering him with a big stick, so that the bullock ran and stumbled and bellowed, wondering what was happening to him. Then Hernon put him to graze in a broad barren crag overlooking the sea and went away.

The bullock roamed about the crag for a long time, scarcely able to make his way over the jagged rocks and pointed loose stones. Several times he tried to nibble at the stunted grass that grew in the tiny valleys, but the grass tasted too salt and sour. And the sea roared near him. And the crag was so high and exposed that it caught every breeze and gust of wind, so that he felt very miserable and was struck with terror. For he had always been used to living among people and within sight of houses and shelter. All day he never ate anything, even of the stunted grass that grew there, but spent most of the time circling the crag trying to find a way out. The fence was not very high and he might easily jump it or knock it down by thrusting his breast against it, but his terror was so acute that he was unable to muster up courage to do so. When he passed along the brink of the cliff overlooking the sea, where there was no fence, he was continually snorting and jumping sideways with fright.

Then night came and he had nowhere to take shelter from the bitter autumn wind that rose from the sea. Next morning his hide was wet with dew and sea froth and his belly was as empty as it had been when he landed in Inverara. As day advanced the sun shone brightly, warming him, so he capered about nibbling and felt fairly comfortable, though his hoofs were sore from treading the sharp rocks.

The best grass grew in the deep crevices in the rocks and he had to scramble over the most difficult ground to reach it, sometimes even going on his knees and straining his neck down into the holes. When he had eaten sufficient he wanted to drink, and that too was difficult, for the little pools were almost dry and it was only after visiting six of them, scattered at long intervals, that he was satisfied.

He spent a week that way without seeing a soul, and every day he became hungrier, more thirsty and miserable. Then three wandering goats came on to his crag and stayed the day prancing about the cliff top. He tried to make friends with them, but when he came near them and stretched out his head and sniffed, they stamped and snorted and ran away. And in the evening they departed eastwards, jumping a low part of the fence quite easily. He stood looking over the fence where they had leaped a long time, lowing after them until they disappeared. Then, seized with fury, he pushed against the fence, knocked off a few stones and scrambled through the gap in a heap to the other side.

With his tail in the air he ran along in the direction the goats had gone until he came to a lane. There he met a donkey with a young foal. He nestled up to the donkey, but the donkey kicked him in the belly and then bared his teeth and tried to bite him. So he wandered on, until he saw a village ahead of him.

When he saw the houses and the people he thought he was home again. He began to low with joy and, tossing his head, he trotted along snorting playfully. But straying round the village smelling at gates and dunghills he was chased by dogs, and peasant women ran out and threw stones at him, so that he retired miserably to a waste plot at the back of a barn and lay down, very weary of life. For these people regarded him as a wild beast and would not let him come near them.

Then two stray dogs discovered him and chased him down to the village cross-roads where a number of young men were loafing. The young men, bored for want of amusement, herded him into a corner and tied a tin kettle to his short tail. Then they beat him and shouted 'Fe-och, fe-och' and turned him out into the road again. The tin kettle just tipped the ground, and at every step the bullock took it clattered against his heels.

He began to trot in order to get away from it. But the more he trotted the greater was the noise it made and it hit his heels all the harder. Then he got mad, lashed out with his hind legs and broke into a gallop. The dogs barked and ran alongside him, biting at his mouth and his flanks. The men yelled and urged on the dogs. The bullock ran on and on frothing at the mouth until he reached a gap in the road fence that led into a crag. He rushed through the gap and on to the crag. But the kettle made a greater noise on the limestone crag and the dogs were better able to bite him, since he had to go slower. So he began to bellow and jumped headlong down into a little glen. It was but ten feet of a fall, but his hind hoof caught in a crevice as he jumped, and he fell on his back.

When Hernon found him his spine was broken, so he had to slaughter him.

THE BLADDER

The schoolmaster was a disagreeable man. He was always interfering in other people's business and giving advice about things of which he knew nothing. So that, although he was an excellent teacher, he was disliked in the island of Inverara. Somehow or other everything he said or did was aggressive and insulting. He walked with his head thrown back on his fat, red neck, that bulged in little waves over the collar of his coat, and with his brown beard thrusting out in front of his face. He always wore grey tweeds and a little grey cap that was pulled so far down over his forehead that a little patch of his baldness could be seen at the rear of his skull. Then when he spoke to any one he kept one hand in his pocket, jingling his money, and stroked his beard with the other. He had a great deep voice, slow and pompous. 'Haw,' he would say, somewhere down in his throat, 'what did I tell you? Why didn't you take my advice?'

At lunch time he walked up and down the road in front of his school with his lunch on his right palm on a piece of newspaper, and a clasp-knife in the other hand, eating bread and cheese. The cheese was always very high, and he had a horrid way of putting a piece between his thick red lips and then making a sucking sound. And he did that, he told the police sergeant, to persuade the islanders that bread and cheese was the healthiest and cheapest diet for a midday meal.

He was always telling the peasants that they didn't till the land properly or look after their cattle properly, and the fisherman that their nets were not the correct depth or length. In the same manner he inveighed against the unhealthy food the people used — tea, poor American flour, potatoes, and salt fish. When John Feeney's son Brian had the influenza the schoolmaster met John one night and said, 'What are you feeding your son with?' Feeney scratched his head and said, 'Faith, I'm giving him the best o' nourishment. Pancakes.' 'You're a fool, Feeney,' said the schoolmaster in his bass voice; 'give him oatmeal porridge, man.' Then young Feeney's influenza turned into consumption, and the boy died. At the funeral the schoolmaster caught Feeney by the shoulder and bawled into his ear, 'What did I tell you? Why didn't you take my advice?'

After his wife died of the delirium tremens he began a campaign against intoxicating liquor. He would talk for hours in front of the church on Sunday after Mass, reading statistics to show how drink beggared the country and filled the lunatic asylums. 'And tobacco is nearly as bad,' he would say. 'Fancy a sane man making a chimney of his mouth and setting fire to his purse.'

Then one December he brought a heifer from Jim Delaney, and, since he had no land, he sent the heifer to graze on Michael Derrane's land at so much a month. The heifer was in calf when he brought her, and she was a good-looking, healthy beast of a dark red colour with a white patch underneath her stomach. 'Now we'll see how he gets on,' said the peasants, winking at one another.

The cow spent the winter in those fields Derrane had beneath the road half a mile west of the church, and all through the winter she was the main topic of conversation among the peasants in the west of the island. People were always leaning over the fence on the roadside, looking at her. Every evening after closing the school the schoolmaster went to visit her. He drove her around the field, examined her droppings and the water-tub. Then he would stoop down and look at her udder to see if she was beginning to gather milk, fully three months before she was due to calve. He became unbearable in his conversation, boasting about the cow. 'Look at her,' he would say. 'I am a schoolmaster. I grow my own potatoes, cabbages, onions, and parsnips in my garden. Now I'm going to have my own milk. That's what comes of being educated and being able to use the brains that the Lord gave me.' And he spent an amount of money on agricultural periodicals dealing with the breeding and treatment of cattle.

When the cow was due to calve he had relays of the school-children watching her by day, and he hired Tom Finnigan, the labourer, to watch her at night. Every evening he gave the cow a hot drink. 'Phew,' said the peasants, 'be Saint Michael that cow will beggar him. It's true story. Put a beggar on horseback.'

The cow went twelve days over her time, and then on Friday night just before dawn she had a speckled calf. Tom Finnigan and the schoolmaster were there, and the schoolmaster was as proud as if the calf were his first-born child instead of a little speckled beast that sprawled about on the grass, trying to stand up. 'You wait, Tom,' said the schoolmaster, 'that will be the best bullock in the island in two year's time.' Then he went home to mix another drink for the cow and left Tom to watch her.

But in their excitement they had forgotten to empty the water-tub. Tom

Finnigan had been up three nights, and overcome with weariness he fell asleep sitting under the fence, and in that condition the schoolmaster found him on his return. When Tom opened his eyes there was the schoolmaster showering blows on him and yelling like a madman. 'Scoundrel, scoundrel, I'll have the law of you.' 'Yer honour,' began Tom, jumping to his feet. Then he stopped and opened his mouth. The cow was standing in the middle of the field with her neck stretched low to the ground and her open mouth in the air. One side of her was flat and the other side swollen like a bladder. She had emptied the water-tub.

In a short while a crowd gathered and men offered advice, but the schoolmaster paid no heed to anyone. He kept roaring, 'Scoundrel, scoundrel!' and in his shirt sleeves, with froth on his beard, he rubbed and rubbed at the cow's expanded side until the red hair was coming off in handfuls. For all that, he might as well be rubbing a mountain in the hope of flattening it out. The cow began to bellow and stagger about.

At last the peasants got mad with him and said that if he didn't let them treat the cow in the proper manner they would flay him within an inch of his life. 'What good can you do to her, you scoundrels?' yelled the schoolmaster. 'Give her whiskey,' roared the peasants. The schoolmaster was terrified out of his wits and told them to go and get whiskey. A lad brought a pint. They seized the cow and poured it down her throat. Soon she began to toss her head and run about breaking wind. That evening she was as well as ever.

But the schoolmaster sold her and the calf a month later to Mick Grealish the blacksmith. Since then he never talks of cattle or farming. Neither does he give anybody advice. But the peasants have nicknamed him 'The Bladder'.

GOING INTO EXILE

Patrick Feeney's cabin was crowded with people. In the large kitchen men, women, and children lined the walls, three deep in places, sitting on forms, chairs, stools, and on one another's knees. On the cement floor three couples were dancing a jig and raising a quantity of dust, which was, however, soon sucked up the chimney by the huge turf fire that blazed on the hearth. The only clear space into the kitchen was the corner to the left of the fireplace, where Pat Mullaney sat on a yellow chair, with his right ankle resting on his left knee, a spotted red handkerchief on his head that reeked with perspiration, and his red face contorting as he played a tattered old accordion. One door was shut and the tins hanging on it gleamed in the firelight. The opposite door was open and over the heads of the small boys that crowded in it and outside it, peering in at the dancing couples in the kitchen, a starry June sky was visible and, beneath the sky, shadowy grey crags and misty, whitish fields lay motionless, still and sombre. There was a deep, calm silence outside the cabin and within the cabin, in spite of the music and dancing in the kitchen and the singing in the little room to the left, where Patrick Feeney's eldest son Michael sat on the bed with three other young men, there was a haunting melancholy in the air.

The people were dancing, laughing and singing with a certain forced and boisterous gaiety that failed to hide from them the real cause of their being there, dancing, singing and laughing. For the dance was on account of Patrick Feeney's two children, Mary and Michael, who were going to the United States on the following morning.

Feeney himself, a black-bearded, red-faced, middle-aged peasant, with white ivory buttons on his blue frieze shirt and his hands stuck in his leather waist belt, wandered restlessly about the kitchen, urging the people to sing and dance, while his mind was in agony all the time, thinking that on the following day he would lose his two eldest children, never to see them again perhaps. He kept talking to everybody about amusing things, shouted at the dancers and behaved in a boisterous and abandoned manner. But every now and then he had to leave the kitchen, under the pretence of going to the pigsty to look at a young pig that was supposed to be ill. He would stand, however, upright against his gable and look gloomily at some star or other, while his mind struggled with vague and peculiar ideas that wandered about in it. He could make nothing at all of his thoughts, but a lump always came up his throat, and he shivered, although the night was warm.

Then he would sigh and say with a contraction of his neck: 'Oh, it's a queer world this and no doubt about it. So it is.' Then he would go back to the cabin again and begin to urge on the dance, laughing, shouting and stamping on the floor.

Towards dawn, when the floor was crowded with couples, arranged in fours, stamping on the floor and going to and fro, dancing the 'Walls of Limerick,' Feeney was going out to the gable when his son Michael followed him out. The two of them walked side by side about the yard over the grey sea pebbles that had been strewn there the previous day. They walked in silence and yawned without need, pretending to be taking the air. But each of them was very excited. Michael was taller than his father and not so thickly built, but the shabby blue serge suit that he had bought for going to America was too narrow for his broad shoulders and the coat was too wide around the waist. He moved clumsily in it and his hands appeared altogether too bony and big and red, and he didn't know what to do with them. During his twenty-one years of life he had never worn anything other than the homespun clothes of Inverara, and the shop-made clothes appeared as strange to him and as uncomfortable as a dress suit worn by a man working in a sewer. His face was flushed a bright red and his blue eyes shone with excitement. Now and again he wiped the perspiration from his forehead with the lining of his grey tweed cap.

At last Patrick Feeney reached his usual position at the gable end. He halted, balanced himself on his heels with his hands in his waist belt, coughed and said, 'It's going to be a warm day.' The son came up beside him, folded his arms and leaned his right shoulder against the gable.

'It was kind of Uncle Ned to lend the money for the dance, father,' he said. 'I'd hate to think that we'd have to go without something or other, just the same as everybody else has. I'll send you that money the very first money I earn, father . . . even before I pay Aunt Mary for my passage money. I should have all that money paid off in four months, and then I'll have some more money to send you by Christmas.'

And Michael felt very strong and manly recounting what he was going to do when he got to Boston, Massachusetts. He told himself that with his great strength he would earn a great deal of money. Conscious of his youth and his strength and lusting for adventurous life, for the moment he forgot the ache in his heart that the thought of leaving his father inspired in him.

The father was silent for some time. He was looking at the sky with his lower lip hanging, thinking of nothing. At last he sighed as a memory struck him. 'What is it?' said the son. 'Don't weaken, for God's sake. You will only make it hard for me.' 'Fooh!' said the father suddenly with pretended gruffness. 'Who is weakening? I'm afraid that your new clothes make you impudent.' Then he was silent for a moment and continued in a low voice: 'I was thinking of that potato field you sowed alone last spring the time I had the influenza. I never set eyes on the man that could do it better. It's a cruel world that takes you away from the land that God made you for.'

'Oh, what are you talking about, father?' said Michael irritably. 'Sure what did anybody ever got out of the land put poverty and hard work and potatoes and salt?'

'Ah yes,' said the father with a sigh, 'but it's your own, the land, and over there' — he waved his hand at the western sky — 'you'll be giving your sweat to some other man's land, or what's equal to it.'

'Indeed,' muttered Michael, looking at the ground with a melancholy expression in his eyes, 'it's poor encouragement you are giving me.'

They stood in silence fully five minutes. Each hungered to embrace the other, to cry, to beat the air, to scream with excess of sorrow. But they stood silent and sombre, like nature about them, hugging their woe. Then they went back to the cabin. Michael went into the little room to the left of the kitchen, to the three young men who fished in the same curragh with him and were his bosom friends. The father walked into the large bedroom to the right of the kitchen.

The large bedroom was also crowded with people. A large table was laid for tea in the centre of the room and about a dozen young men were sitting at it, drinking tea and eating buttered raisin cake. Mrs Feeney was bustling about the table, serving the food and urging them to eat. She was assisted by her two younger daughters and by another woman, a relative of her own. Her eldest daughter Mary, who was going to the United States that day, was sitting on the edge of the bed with several other young woman. The bed was a large four poster bed with a deal canopy over it, painted red, and the young women were huddled together on it. So that there must have been about a dozen of them there. They were Mary Feeney's particular friends, and they stayed with her in that uncomfortable position just to show how much they liked her. It was a custom.

Mary herself sat on the edge of the bed with her legs dangling. She was a pretty, dark-haired girl of nineteen, with dimpled, plump, red cheeks and ruminative brown eyes that seemed to cause little wrinkles to come and go in her little low forehead. Her nose was soft and small and rounded. Her mouth was small and the lips were red and open. Beneath her white blouse that was frilled at the neck and her navy blue skirt that outlined her limbs as she sat on the edge of the bed, her body was plump, soft, well-moulded and in some manner exuded a feeling of freshness and innocence. So that she seemed to have been born to be fondled and admired in luxurious surroundings instead of having been born a peasant's daughter, who had to go to the United States that day to work as a servant or maybe in a factory.

And as she sat on the edge of the bed crushing her little handkerchief between her palms, she kept thinking feverishly of the United States, at one moment with fear and loathing, at the next with desire and longing. Unlike her brother she did not think of the work she was going to do or the money that she was going to earn. Other things troubled her, things of which she was half ashamed, half afraid, thoughts of love and of foreign men and of clothes and of houses where there were more than three rooms and where people ate meat every day.

She was fond of life, and several young men among the local gentry had admired her in Inverara. But . . .

She happened to look up and she caught her father's eyes as he stood silently by the window with his hands stuck in his waist belt. His eyes rested on hers for a moment and then he dropped them without smiling, and with his lips compressed he walked down into the kitchen. She shuddered slightly. She was a little afraid of her father, although she knew that he loved her very much and he was very kind to her. But the winter before he had whipped her with a dried willow rod, when he caught her one evening behind Tim Hernon's cabin after nightfall, with Tim Hernon's son Bartly's arms around her waist and he kissing her. Ever since, she always shivered slightly when her father touched her or spoke to her. 'Oho!' said an old peasant who sat at the table with a saucer full of tea in his hand and his grey flannel shirt open at his thin, hairy, wrinkled neck. 'Oho! indeed, but it's a disgrace to the island of Inverara to let such a beautiful woman as your daughter go away, Mrs Feeney. If I were a young man, I'll be flayed alive if I'd let her go.'

There was a laugh and some of the women on the bed, said: 'Bad cess to you, Patsy Coyne, if you haven't too much impudence, it's a caution.' But the laugh soon died. The young men sitting at the table felt embarrassed and kept looking at one another sheepishly, as if each tried to find out if the others were in love with Mary Feeney.

'Oh, well, God is good,' said Mrs Feeney, as she wiped her lips with the tip of her bright, clean, check apron. 'What will be must be, and sure there is hope from the sea, but there is no hope from the grave. It is sad and the poor have to suffer, but . . .' Mrs Feeney stopped suddenly, aware that all these platitudes meant nothing whatsoever. Like her husband she was unable to think intelligibly about her two children going away. Whenever the reality of their going away, maybe for ever, three thousand miles into a vast unknown world, came before her mind, it seemed that a thin bar of some hard metal thrust itself forward from her brain and rested behind the wall of her forehead. So that almost immediately she became stupidly conscious of the pain caused by the imaginary bar of metal and she forgot the dread prospect of her children going away. But her mind grappled with the things about her busily and efficiently, with the preparation of food, with the entertaining of her guests, with the numerous little things that have to be done in a house where there is a party and which only a woman can do property. These little things, in a manner, saved her, for the moment at least, from bursting into tears whenever she looked at her daughter and whenever she thought of her son, whom she loved most of all her children, because perhaps she nearly died giving birth to him and he had been very delicate until he was twelve years old. So she laughed down in her breast a funny laugh she had that made her heave, where her check apron rose out from the waist band in a deep curve. 'A person begins to talk,' she said with a shrug of her shoulders sideways, 'and then a person says foolish things.'

'That's true,' said the old peasant, noisily pouring more tea from his cup to his saucer.

But Mary knew by her mother laughing that way that she was very near being hysterical. She always laughed that way before she had one of her fits of hysterics. And Mary's heart stopped beating suddenly and then began again at an awful rate as her eyes became acutely conscious of her mother's body, the rotund, short body with the wonderful mass of fair hair, growing grey at the temples and the fair face with the soft liquid brown eyes, that grew hard and piercing for a moment as they looked at a thing and then grew soft and liquid again, and the thin-lipped small mouth with the beautiful white teeth and the deep perpendicular grooves in the upper lip and the tremor that always came in the corner of the mouth, with love, when she looked at her children. Mary became acutely conscious of all these little points, as well as of the little black spot that was on her left breast below the nipple and the swelling that came now and again in her legs and caused her to have hysterics and would one day cause her death. And she was stricken with horror at the thought of leaving her mother and at the selfishness of her thoughts. She had never been prone to thinking of anything important but now, somehow for a moment, she had a glimpse of her mother's life that made her shiver and hate herself as a cruel, heartless, lazy, selfish wretch. Her mother's life loomed up before her eyes, a life of continual misery and suffering, hard work, birth pangs, sickness and again hard work and hunger and anxiety. It loomed up and then it fled again, a little mist came before her eyes and she jumped down from the bed, with the jaunty twirl of her head that was her habit when she set her body in motion.

'Sit down for a while, mother,' she whispered toying with one of the black ivory buttons on her mother's brown bodice. 'I'll look after the table.' 'No, no,' murmured the mother with a shake of her whole body, 'I'm not a bit tired. Sit down, my treasure. You have a long way to travel today.'

And Mary sighed and went back to the bed again. At last somebody said: 'It's broad daylight.' And immediately everybody looked out and said: 'So it is, and may God be praised.' The change from the starry night to the grey, sharp dawn was hard to notice until it had arrived. People looked out and saw the morning light sneaking over the crags silently, along the ground, pushing the mist banks upwards. The stars were growing dim. A long way off invisible sparrows were chirping in their ivied perch in some distant hill or other. Another day had arrived and even as the people looked at it, yawned and began to search for their hats, caps and shawls preparing to go home, they day grew and spread its light and made things move and give voice. Cocks crew, blackbirds carolled, a dog let loose from a cabin by an early riser chased madly after an imaginary robber, barking as if his tail were on fire. The people said good-bye and began to stream forth from Feeney's cabin. They were going to their homes to see to the morning's work before going to Kilmurrage to see the emigrants off on the steamer to the mainland. Soon the cabin was empty except for the family.

All the family gathered into the kitchen and stood about for some minutes talking sleepily of the dance and of the people who had been present. Mrs Feeney tried to persuade everybody to go to bed, but everybody refused. It was four o'clock and Michael and Mary would have to set out for Kilmurrage at nine. So tea was made and they all sat about for an hour drinking it and eating raisin cake and talking. They talked of the dance and of the people who had been present.

There were eight of them there, the father and mother and six children. The youngest child was Thomas, a thin boy of twelve, whose lungs made a singing sound every time he breathed. The next was Bridget, a girl of four-teen, with dancing eyes and a habit of shaking her short golden curls every now and then for no apparent reason. Then there were the twins, Julia and Margaret, quiet, rather stupid, flat-faced girls of sixteen. Both their upper front teeth protruded slightly and they were both great workers and very obedient to their mother. They were all sitting at the table, having just finished a third large pot of tea, when suddenly the mother hastily gulped down the remainder of the tea in her cup, dropped the cup with a clatter to her saucer and sobbed once through her nose.

'Now mother,' said Michael sternly, 'what's the good of this work?'

'No, you are right, my pulse,' she replied quietly. 'Only I was just thinking how nice it is to sit here surrounded by all my children, all my little birds in my nest, and then two of them going to fly away made me sad.' And she laughed, pretending to treat it as a foolish joke.

'Oh, that be damned for a story,' said the father, wiping his mouth on his sleeve; 'there's work to be done. You Julia, go and get the horse. Margaret, you milk the cow and see that you give enough milk to the calf this morning.' And he ordered everybody about as if it were an ordinary day of work.

But Michael and Mary had nothing to do and they sat about miserably conscious that they had cut adrift from the routine of their home life. They no longer had any place in it. In a few hours they would be homeless wanders. Now that they were cut adrift from it, the poverty and sordidness of their home life appeared to them under the aspect of comfort and plenty.

So the morning passed until breakfast time at seven o'clock. The morning's work was finished and the family was gathered together again. The meal passed in a dead silence. Drowsy after the sleepless night and conscious that the parting would come in a few hours, nobody wanted to talk. Everybody had an egg for breakfast in honour of the occasion. Mrs Feeney, after her usual habit, tried to give her egg first to Michael, then to Mary, and as each refused it, she ate a little herself and gave the remainder to little Thomas who had the singing in his chest. Then the breakfast was cleared away. The father went to put the creels on the mare so as to take the luggage into Kilmurrage. Michael and Mary got the luggage ready and began to get dressed. The mother and the other children tidied up the house. People from the village began to come into the kitchen, as was customary, in order to accompany the emigrants from their home to Kilmurrage.

At last everything was ready. Mrs Feeney had exhausted all excuses for moving about, engaged on trivial tasks. She had to go into the big bedroom where Mary was putting on her new hat. The mother sat on a chair by the window, her face contorting on account of the flood of tears she was keeping back. Michael moved about the room uneasily, his two hands knotting a big red handkerchief behind his back. Mary twisted about in front of the mirror that hung over the black wooden mantelpiece. She was spending a long time with the hat. It was the first one she had ever worn, but it fitted her beautifully, and it was in excellent taste. It was given to her by the schoolmistress, who was very fond of her, and she herself had taken it in a little. She had an instinct for beauty in dress and deportment.

But the mother, looking at how well her daughter wore the cheap navy blue costume and the white frilled blouse, and the little round black hat with a fat, fluffy, glossy curl covering each ear, and the black silk stockings with blue clocks in them, and the little black shoes that had laces of three colours in them, got suddenly enraged with . . . She didn't know with what she got enraged. But for the moment she hatred her daughter's beauty, and she remembered all the anguish of giving birth to her and nursing her and toiling for her, for no other purpose than to lose her now and let her go away, maybe to be ravished wantonly because of her beauty and her love of gaiety. A cloud of mad jealousy and hatred against this impersonal beauty that she saw in her daughter almost suffocated the mother, and stretched out her hands in front of her unconsciously and then just as suddenly her anger vanished like a puff of smoke, and she burst into wild tears, waiting: 'My children, oh, my children, far over the sea you will be carried from me, your mother.' And she began to rock herself and she threw her apron over her head.

Immediately the cabin was full of the sound of bitter wailing. A dismal cry rose from the women gathered in the kitchen. 'Far over the sea they will be carried,' began woman after woman, and they all rocked themselves and hid their heads in their aprons. Michael's mongrel dog began to howl on the hearth. Little Thomas sat down on the hearth beside the dog and, putting his arms around him, he began to cry, although he didn't know exactly why he was crying, but he felt melancholy on account of the dog howling and so many people being about.

In the bedroom the son and daughter, on their knees, clung to their mother, who held their heads between her hands and rained kissed on both heads ravenously. After the first wave of tears she had stopped weeping. The tears still ran down her cheeks, but her eyes gleamed and they were dry. There was a fierce look in them as she searched all over the heads of her two children with them, with her brows contracted, searching with a fierce terror-stricken expression, as if by the intensity of her stare she hoped to keep a living photograph of them before her mind. With her quivering lips she made a queer sound like 'im-m-m-m' and she kept kissing. Her right hand clutched at Mary's left shoulder and with her left she fondled the back of

Michael's neck. The two children were sobbing freely. They must have stayed that way a quarter of an hour.

Then the father came into the room, dressed in his best clothes. He wore a new frieze waistcoat, with a grey and black front and a white back. He held his soft black felt hat in one hand and in the other hand he had a bottle of holy water. He coughed and said in a weak gentle voice that was strange to him, as he touched his son: 'Come now, it is time.'

Mary and Michael got to their feet. The father sprinkled them with holy water and they crossed themselves. Then, without looking at their mother, who lay in the chair with her hands clasped on her lap, looking at the ground in a silent tearless stupor, they left the room. Each hurriedly kissed little Thomas, who was not going to Kilmurrage, and then, hand in hand, they left the house. As Michael was going out the door he picked a piece of loose white-wash from the wall and put it in his pocket. The people filed out after them, down the yard and on to the road, like a funeral procession. The mother was left in the house with little Thomas and two old peasant women from the village. Nobody spoke in the cabin for a long time.

Then the mother rose and came into the kitchen. She looked at the two women, at her little son at the hearth, as if she was looking for something she had lost. Then she threw her hands into air and ran out into the yard.

'Come back,' she screamed; 'come back to me.'

She looked wildly down the road with dilated nostrils, her bosom heaving. But there was nobody in sight. Nobody replied. There was a crooked stretch of limestone road, surrounded by grey crags that were scorched by the sun. The road ended in a hill and then dropped out of sight. The hot June day was silent. Listening foolishly for an answering cry, the mother imagined she could hear the crags simmering under the hot rays of the sun. It was something in her head that was singing.

The two old women led her back into the kitchen. 'There is nothing that time will not cure,' said one. 'Yes. Time and patience,' said the other.

FÓD

Bhí an bóithrín an-chúng. Bhí láir srathruithe in a seasamh ann agus níor bhféidir le duine siúl thart gan cromadh faoi na cléibh do bhí ar crocadh léi ar gach aon taobh. Faoi chosaibh an chapaill bhí an bóithrín clúdaithe le gainnimh mín agus le mion chlocha. Bhí claí árd ar gach taobh de'n bhóithrín agus bhí baranna glasa fataí ag borradh amach in aice bonn an chlaí annso agus annsúd. Lá breá Earraidh do bhí ann, tuairim am dinnéir.

Bhí Pats Mhichil Pháidin ag bainnt fóide ó bhonn an chlaí ar thaobh na láimhe deise agus dá líonadh ar an gcapall. Fear cothrom aosta do bhí ann, gléusta i sean drár glas, bróga úr leathair, sean hata dubh agus léine ghorm. Bhí srón cam air agus bhí cluasa an-bheaga aige. Bhí an t-ualach in-gar do bheath líonta aige nuair do chuala sé béic. Chuir sé cois ar a spáid agus dhírigh sé é féin.

Thuas ar an árd, timcheall céad slata an taobh eile de'n chapall bhí a chol ceathrar, Micheál Bhriain Bhig, in a sheasamh ar chlaí agus é ar craitheamh a chaipín go fiáin. Fear caol árd é, agus féasóg giobach dearg air. Bhí a éadan caite agus báiníneach, agus chaith sé an chuid is mó dá aimsir ag spaisteóireacht nó ar an leaba. Deir daoine go raibh an eitinn air, deir daoine eile go raibh sé as a mheabhair. Deir a bhean go raibh leisge air.

'A chneamhaire gan choinnsias' do bhéic sé ar bhárr an chlaí. 'A goid mo chuid fóide atáir, a mhic an diabhail. Bailidh leat nó réabfaidh mé do chnámha.'

D'fháisg Pats Mhicil Pháidin a chrios faoi'n a lár agus rug sé ar an spáid. Bhuail sé failm ar an gclaí. 'Tar, a leadaí na luatha agus déanfad sa rud leat ba chóir déanamh leat an lá do rugadh thú. Is leat-sa taobh na láimhe deise, is liomsa taobh na láimhe clé den bhóithrín. Cé'n pleidhceacht atá ort?'

'Gadaí na fóide' do bhúir Micheál Bhriain Bhig agus chuaidh sé de léim anuas de'n chlaí. Rith sé anuas an bóithrín agus fuadar faoi gur shroich sé an capall. Rug sé greim adhastair uirthi agus thosnuigh sé dá maoidheamh agus dá bhualadh san ucht le na cosa. Thosnuigh an capall ag iarraidh tarraingt siar uaidh agus ag éirí ar a cosa deiridh.

'Leig don chapall, a dhiabhail' do bhéic Pats, an spáid ina lámha agus é cromtha faoi bholg an chapaill ag iarriadh teacht in aice le Micheál. Bhí an capall ina bhealach. Níor fhéad sé dul anonn. Bhí sé ina dheatach mar sin ar feadh cúig nóiméad go dtí ar deireadh, bhí na cléibh agus an t-srathar tuite den chapall, bhí giota mór den chlaí leagtha ag gach aon taobh isteach i mullach na bhfataí. Bhí an bheirt fear ag béiciú, ag feannadh ar a chéile agus ag lasgadh an chapaill do bhí eathorra ag iarraidh dul ar a chéile. Annsin do splannc an láir agus chuaidh sí de léim isteach sa ngarra fataí ar thaobh na láimhe deise. Do sheas sí ar iomaire agus í ar creathamh. Do bhreathnuigh an bheirt fhear ar a chéile agus na fiacla ag creathamh in a mbéul le fearg.

'Anois céard tá tú dul a dhéanamh,' arsa Pats.

'Céard tá tusa dul a dhéanamh,' arsa Micheál.

'Cá bhfuil tú bainnt na fóide,' arsa Micheál arís nuair nár labhair Pats.

'Annsin,' adeir Pats, 'ar mo chuid talúna féin ar thaobh na láimhe clé. Is liomsa an taobh sin den bhóithrín nach liom?'

'T'anam ó'n diabhal é, tuige nár dhúirt tú sin liom,' arsa Micheál. 'Cheapas, go rabhais dá bainnt ar thaobh na láimhe deise. Anois céard tá déanta agat le do chuid pleidhceacht. Dá labharfad in am agus rá liom. . . bheil, bheil, is bréan an rud atá déanta agat.'

THE TENT

A sudden squall struck the tent. White glittering hailstones struck the shabby canvas with a wild noise. The tent shook and swayed slightly forward, dangling its tattered flaps. The pole creaked as it strained. A rent appeared near the top of the pole like a silver seam in the canvas. Water immediately trickled through the seam, making a dark blob.

A tinker and his two wives were sitting on a heap of straw in the tent, looking out through the entrance at the wild moor that stretched in front of it, with a snowcapped mountain peak rising like the tip of a cone over the ridge of the moor about two miles away. The three of them were smoking cigarettes in silence. It was evening, and they had pitched their tent for the night in a gravel pit on the side of the mountain road, crossing from one glen to another. Their donkey was tethered to the cart beside the tent.

When the squall came the tinker sat up with a start and looked at the pole. He stared at the seam in the canvas for several moments and then he nudged the two women and pointed upwards with a jerk of his nose. The women looked but nobody spoke. After a minute or so the tinker sighed and struggled to his feet.

'I'll throw a few sacks over the top,' he said.

He picked up two brown sacks from the heap of blankets and clothes that were drying beside the brazier in the entrance and went out. The women never spoke, but kept on smoking.

The tinker kicked the donkey out of his way. The beast had stuck his hind quarters into the entrance of the tent as far as possible, in order to get the heat from the wood burning in the brazier. The donkey shrank away sideways still chewing a wisp of the hay which the tinker had stolen from a haggard the other side of the mountain. The tinker scrambled up the bank against which the tent was pitched. The bank was covered with rank grass into which yesterday's snow had melted in muddy cakes.

The top of the tent was only about eighteen inches above the bank. Beyond the bank there was a narrow rough road, with a thick copse of pine trees on the far side, within the wired fence of a demesne, but the force of the squall was so great that it swept through the trees and struck the top of the tent as violently as if it were standing exposed on the open moor. The tinker had to lean against the wind to prevent himself being carried away. He looked into the wind with wide-open nostrils.

'It can't last,' he said, throwing the two sacks over the tent, where there was a rent in the canvas. He then took a big needle from his jacket and put a few stitches in them.

He was about to jump down from the bank when somebody hailed him from the road. He looked up and saw a man approaching, with his head thrust forward against the wind. The tinker scowled and shrugged his shoulders. He waited until the man came up to him.

The stranger was a tall, sturdily built man, with a long face and firm jaws and great sombre dark eyes, a fighter's face. When he reached the tinker he stood erect with his feet together and his hands by his sides like a soldier. He was fairly well dressed, his face was clean and well shaved, and his hands were clean. There was a blue figure of something or other tattooed on the back of his right hand. He looked at the tinker frankly with his sombre dark eyes. Neither spoke for several moments.

'Good evening,' the stranger said.

The tinker nodded without speaking. He was looking the stranger up and down, as if he were slightly afraid of this big, sturdy man, who was almost like a policeman or a soldier or somebody in authority. He looked at the man's boots especially. In spite of the muck of the roads, the melted snow and the hailstones, they were still fairly clean, and looked as if they were constantly polished.

'Travellin'?' he said at length.

'Eh,' said the stranger, almost aggressively. 'Oh! Yes, I'm lookin' for somewhere to shelter for the night.'

The stranger glanced at the tent slowly and then looked back to the tinker again.

'Goin' far?' said the tinker.

'Don't know,' said the stranger angrily. Then he almost shouted: 'I have no bloody place to go to . . . only the bloody roads.'

'All right, brother,' said the tinker, 'come on.'

He nodded towards the tent and jumped down into the pit. The stranger followed him, stepping carefully down to avoid soiling his clothes.

When he entered the tent after the tinker and saw the women he immediately took off his cap and said: 'Good evening.' The two women took their cigarettes from their mouths, smiled and nodded their heads.

The stranger looked about him cautiously and then sat down on a box to the side of the door near the brazier. He put his hands to the blaze and rubbed them. Almost immediately a slight steam rose from his clothes. The tinker handed him a cigarette, murmuring: 'Smoke?'

The stranger accepted the cigarette, lit it, and then looked at them. None of them were looking at him, so he 'sized them up' carefully, looking at each suspiciously with his sombre dark eyes. The tinker was sitting on a box opposite him, leaning languidly backwards from his hips, a slim, tall, graceful man, with a beautiful head poised gracefully on a brown neck, and great black lashes falling down over his half-closed eyes, just like a woman. A womanish-looking fellow, with that sensuous grace in the languid pose of his body which is found only among aristocrats and people who belong to a very small workless class, cut off from the mass of society, yet living at their expense. A young fellow with proud, contemptuous, closed lips and an arrogant expression in his slightly expanded nostrils. A silent fellow, blowing out cigarette smoke through his nostrils and gazing dreamily into the blaze of the wood fire. The two women were just like him in texture, both of them slatterns, dirty and unkempt, but with the same proud, arrogant, contemptuous look in their beautiful brown faces. One was dark-haired and black-eyed. She had rather a hard expression in her face and seemed very alert. The other woman was golden-haired, with a very small head and finely-developed jaw, that stuck out level with her forehead. She was surpassing beautiful, in spite of her ragged clothes and the foul condition of her hair, which was piled on her tiny skull in knotted heaps, uncombed. The perfect symmetry and delicacy of her limbs, her bust and her long throat that had tiny freckles in the white skin, made the stranger feel afraid of her, of her beauty and her presence in the tent.

'Tinkers,' he said to himself. 'Awful bloody people.'

Then he turned to the tinker.

'Got any grub in the place . . . eh . . . mate?' he said brusquely, his thick lips rapping out every word firmly, like one accustomed to command inferiors. He hesitated before he added the word 'mate,' obviously disinclined to put himself on a level of human intercourse with the tinker.

The tinker nodded and turned to the dark-haired woman.

'Might as well have supper now, Kitty,' he said softly.

The dark-haired woman rose immediately, and taking a blackened can that was full of water, she put it on the brazier. The stranger watched her. Then he addressed the tinker again.

'This is a hell of a way to be, eh?' he said. 'Stuck out on a mountain. Thought I'd make Roundwood tonight. How many miles is it from here?'

'Ten,' said the tinker.

'Good God!' said the stranger.

Then he laughed, and putting his hand in his breast pocket, he pulled out a half-pint bottle of whiskey.

'This is all I got left,' he said, looking at the bottle.

The tinker immediately opened his eyes wide when he saw the bottle. The golden-haired woman sat up and looked at the stranger eagerly, opening her brown eyes wide and rolling her tongue in her cheek. The dark-haired woman, rummaging in a box, also turned around to look. The stranger winked an eye and smiled.

'Always welcome,' he said. 'Eh? My curse on it, anyway. Anybody got a corkscrew?'

The tinker took a knife from his pocket, pulled out a corkscrew from its side and handed it to the man. The man opened the bottle.

'Here,' he said, handing the bottle to the tinker. 'Pass it round. I suppose the women'll have a drop.'

The tinker took the bottle and whispered to the dark-haired woman. She began to pass him mugs from the box.

'Funny thing,' said the stranger, 'when a man is broke and hungry, he can get whiskey but he can't get grub. Met a man this morning in Dublin and he knew bloody well I was broke, but instead of asking me to have a meal, or giving me some money, he gave me that. I had it with me all along the road and I never opened it.'

He threw the end of his cigarette out the entrance.

'Been drinkin' for three weeks, curse it,' he said.

'Are ye belongin' to these parts?' murmured the tinker, pouring out the whiskey into the tin mugs.

'What's that?' said the man, again speaking angrily, as if he resented the question. Then he added: 'No. Never been here in me life before. Question of goin' into the workhouse or takin' to the roads. Got a job in Dublin yesterday. The men downed tools when they found I wasn't a member of the union. Thanks. Here's luck.'

'Good health, sir,' the women said.

The tinker nodded his head only, as he put his own mug to his lips and tasted it. The stranger drained his at a gulp.

'Ha,' he said. 'Drink up, girls. It's good stuff.'

He winked at them. They smiled and sipped their whiskey.

'My name is Carney,' said the stranger to the tinker. 'What do they call you?'

'Byrne,' said the tinker. 'Joe Byrne.'

'Hm! Byrne,' said Carney. 'Wicklow's full o' Byrnes. Tinker, I suppose?'

'Yes,' murmured the tinker, blowing a cloud of cigarette smoke through his puckered lips. Carney shrugged his shoulders.

'Might as well,' he said. 'One thing is as good as another. Look at me. Sergeant-major in the army two months ago. Now I'm tramping the roads. That's boiling.'

The dark-haired woman took the can off the fire. The other woman tossed off the remains of her whiskey and got to her feet to help with the meal. Carney shifted his box back farther out of the way and watched the golden-haired woman eagerly. When she moved about her figure was so tall that she had to stoop low in order to avoid the roof of the tent. She must have been six feet in height, and she wore high-heeled shoes which made her look taller.

'There is a woman for ye,' thought Carney. 'Must be a gentleman's daughter. Lots o' these shots out of a gun in the county Wicklow. Half the population is illegitimate. Awful bloody people, these tinkers. I suppose the two of them belong to this Joe. More like a woman than a man. Suppose he never did a stroke o' work in his life.'

There was cold rabbit for supper, with tea and bread and butter. It was excellent tea, and it tasted all the sweeter on account of the storm outside which was still raging. Sitting around the brazier they could see the hail-stones driving through a grey mist, sweeping the bleak black moor, and the cone-shaped peak of the mountain in the distance, with a whirling cloud of snow around it. The sky was rent here and there with a blue patch, showing through the blackness.

They ate the meal in silence. Then the women cleared it away. They didn't wash the mugs or plates, but put everything away, probably until morning. They sat down again after drawing out the straw, bed-shape, and putting the clothes on it that had been drying near the brazier. They all seemed to be in a good humour now with the whiskey and the food. Even the tinker's face had grown soft, and he kept puckering up his lips in a smile. He passed around cigarettes.

'Might as well finish that bottle,' said Carney. 'Bother the mugs. We can drink outa the neck.'

'Tastes sweeter that way,' said the golden-haired woman, laughing thickly, as if she were slightly drunk. At the same time she looked at Carney with her lips open.

Carney winked at her. The tinker noticed the wink and the girl's smile. His face clouded and he closed his lips very tightly. Carney took a deep draught and passed him the bottle. The tinker nodded his head, took the bottle and put it to his lips.

'I'll have a stretch,' said Carney. 'I'm done in. Twenty miles since mornin'. Eh?'

He threw himself down on the clothes beside the yellow-haired woman. She smiled and looked at the tinker. The tinker paused with the bottle to his lips and looked at her through almost closed eyes savagely. He took the bottle from his lips and bared his white teeth. The golden-headed woman shrugged her shoulders and pouted. The dark-haired woman laughed aloud, stretched back with one arm under her head and the other stretched out towards the tinker.

'Sht,' she whistled through her teeth. 'Pass it along, Joe.'

He handed her the bottle slowly, and as he gave it to her she clutched his hand and tried to pull him to her. But he tore his hand away, got up and walked out of the tent rapidly.

Carney had noticed nothing of this. He was lying close to the woman by his side. He could feel the softness of her beautiful body and the slight undulation of her soft side as she breathed. He became overpowered with desire for her and closed his eyes, as if to shut out the consciousness of the world and of the other people in the tent. Reaching down he seized her hand and pressed it. She answered the pressure. At the same time she turned to her companion and whispered:

'Where's he gone?'

'I dunno. Rag out.'

'What about?'

'Phst.'

'Give us a drop.'

'Here ye are.'

Carney heard the whispering, but he took no notice of it. He heard the golden-headed one drinking and then drawing a deep breath.

'Finished,' she said, throwing the bottle to the floor. Then she laughed softly.

'I'm going out to see where he's gone,' whispered the dark-haired one. She rose and passed out of the tent. Carney immediately turned around and tried to embrace the woman by his side. But she bared her teeth in a savage grin and pinioned his arms with a single movement.

'Didn't think I was strong,' she said, putting her face close to his and grinning at him.

He looked at her seriously, surprised and still more excited.

'What ye goin' to do in Roundwood?' she said.

'Lookin' for a job,' he muttered thickly.

She smiled and rolled her tongue in her cheek.

'Stay here,' she said.

He licked his lip and winked his right eye. 'With you?'

She nodded.

'What about him?' he said, nodding towards the door.

She laughed silently. 'Are ye afraid of Joe?'

He did not reply, but, making a sudden movement, he seized her around the body and pressed her to him. She did not resist, but began to laugh, and bared her teeth as she laughed. He tried to kiss her mouth, but she threw back her head and he kissed her cheek several times.

Then suddenly there was a hissing noise at the door. Carney sat up with a start. The tinker was standing in the entrance, stooping low, with his mouth open and his jaw twisted to the right, his two hands hanging loosely by his sides, with the fingers twitching. The dark-haired woman was standing behind him, peering over his shoulder. She was smiling.

Carney got to his feet, took a pace forward, and squared himself. He did not speak. The golden headed woman uttered a loud peal of laughter, and, stretching out her arms, she lay flat on the bed, giggling.

'Come out here,' hissed the tinker.

He stepped back. Carney shouted and rushed at him, jumping the brazier. The tinker stepped aside and struck Carney a terrible blow on the jaw as he passed him. Carney staggered against the bank and fell in a heap. The tinker jumped on him like a cat, striking him with his hands and feet all together. Carney roared: 'Let me up, let me up. Fair play.' But the tinker kept on beating him until at last he lay motionless at the bottom of the pit.

'Ha,' said the tinker.

Then he picked up the prone body, as lightly as if it were an empty sack, and threw it to the top of the bank.

'Be off, you — ,' he hissed.

Carney struggled to his feet on the top of the bank and looked at the three of them. They were all standing now in front of the tent, the two women grinning, the tinker scowling. Then he staggered on to the road, with his hands to his head.

'Good-bye, dearie,' cried the golden-headed one.

Then she screamed. Carney looked behind and saw the tinker carrying her into the tent in his arms.

'God Almighty!' cried Carney, crossing himself.

Then he trudged away fearfully through the storm towards Roundwood.

'God Almighty!' he cried at every two yards. 'God Almighty!'

MILKING TIME

Softly, softly, the milk flowed from the taut tapering teats into its own white upward-heaving froth. It flowed from the two front teats, two white columns shooting, crossing and descending with a soft swirling movement through the billowing froth. There is no soft cadence as soothing as its sound, no scent as pure as its warm smell, cow smell, milk smell, blood smell, mingling with the thousand soft smells of a summer evening.

The cow stood on the summit of a grassy knoll. Behind her was a rock-strewn ridge, making a grey horizon against the sky. In front there was a vast expanse of falling land, fallen in flat terraces to the distant sea. Close by, the land was green-bright under the rays of the setting sun, but in the distance it was covered with a white mist, as if it rolled, dust-raising, to the sea.

The cow chewed her cud, looking through half-closed luminous eyes downwards at the mist-covered land, her red flanks shivering with content, the wanton pleasure of being milked by a sweet-smelling, crooning woman, the gentle pressure of the woman's fingers against her teats, softer than a calf's gums.

And the woman milking was in an ecstasy of happiness; for it was her first time milking her husband's cow; her cow now. They had been married on Thursday. It was now Sunday evening and they had come together to milk, as was the custom among the people.

He lay on the grass watching her milk, listening to her crooning voice and the voices of the birds; thinking.

'Isn't it wonderful how your little fingers can milk so quickly?' he said.

She turned her head and shook her towering mass of black hair proudly; smooth-combed, winding tresses of black hair gleaming in the twilight, red lips smiling as they crooned; full white throat swelling with soft words; crooning, meaningless words of joy, as she looked at him.

He looked at her joyously and smiled, swallowing her breath.

'Wasn't it lovely today, Kitty,' he murmured, 'coming from Mass?'

She bowed her head, crooning dreamily.

'Everybody was looking at us, as we came out of the chapel together. We are the tallest couple in the whole parish, and I heard several people talking about us in whispers as we passed along the road between the men sitting on the stone walls. Were you shy?'

'I was. I put my shawl out over my face, so they couldn't see me. I thought I'd never get out of sight of the people.'

'After all, it's a great thing,' he said.

'What's a great thing, Michael?'

His freckled face became serious. He looked away into the distance over the mist-covered falling land to where the dim horizon of the sea dwindled into a pale emptiness.

'How tall he is,' she thought, 'and though his arms are hard like iron, he touches me gently.'

'What's a great thing, Michael?' she said again.

'Well! It's hard to say what it is, but we are here now together and there's nothing else, is there?'

'How?'

'Before, on a Sunday evening I always wanted to wander off somewhere a long way and maybe get drunk, but now I don't want anything at all only just to lie here and watch you milking the cow.'

She did not reply. She flushed slightly and bent her head against the cow's warm side, thinking of other Sundays when she sat among the village women on the green hill above the beach, singing songs as they knitted. Then she too longed for something shyly, awakening, nameless longings for a gentle strong voice and the gentle pressure of strong arms.

'But,' she said, 'men are queer,' and changing her hands she drew at the two hind teats, wetting them first with froth and pulling slowly until two fresh white streams flowed downward.

The cow raised a hoof languidly and stamped, swinging her tail. Michael laughed.

'Maybe they are,' he said.

'Michael!'

'What?'

'Sure you won't be going off again on Sunday evening to get drunk after you get tired of me?'

'I'll never get tired of you, Kitty.'

'Ah, yes, it's easy saying that now when we are only a few days married, but maybe . . .'

'No, Kitty, there's going to be no maybe with us. We'll have too much work to do to get tired of one another. It's only people who have nothing to do that get tired of one another.'

'It will be lovely working together, Michael. I love pulling potato stalks in autumn and then picking the potatoes off the ridge, and at dinner-time we'll roast a few in the ground with a fire of stalks.'

'The two of us.'

'Yes.'

'But we have all summer before that. There isn't much work in summer, only fishing. I'm going fishing tomorrow.

'Then you'll be away all day and I'll be so lonely with nobody in the house.'

'You won't feel it until I'll come back in the evening with a whole lot of fish. It would be grand to take you with me in the boat, but people would be laughing at us.'

'Won't it be grand if you get fish? I love to spill them out of a basket on a flag and see them slipping about. And they'll be my fish now. You'll catch them for me. Oh! It is grand, Michael.'

They became silent as she finished milking, passing from teat to teat, drawing the dregs, the richest of the milk. It was like a ceremony this first milking together, initiating them into the mysterious glamour of mating; and both their minds were awed at the new strange knowledge that had come to their simple natures, something that belonged to them both, making their souls conscious of their present happiness with a dim realisation of the great struggle that would follow it, struggling with the earth and with the sea for food. And this dim realisation tinged their happiness with a gentle sadness, without which happiness is ever coarse and vulgar.

She finished milking. Michael rose and spilt half the milk into a bucket for the calf.

'You take it to him,' he said, 'so that he'll get used to you.'

The cow lowed lazily, looking at them with great eyes; she walked with heavy hoofs to the fence beyond which her calf was waiting in a little field for his milk. Putting her head over the fence, she licked his upraised snout.

They pushed aside the cow's head and lowered the bucket to the calf. He dashed at it, sank his nozzle into the froth and began to drink greedily, his red curly back trembling with eagerness.

Kitty rubbed his forehead as he drank.

Then they walked home silently hand in hand, in the twilight.

BLACKMAIL

Brunton was waiting in the select bar. There was nobody else there. It was early afternoon and the sun was streaming yellowishly through the muffed windows. Only the lower parts of the windows were muffed. But the upper parts were covered with half-lowered yellow blinds to keep out the glare of the sun. Still, it was very hot in the bar and there was a heavy odour of heat and of alcohol fumes.

In spite of the heat Brunton was wearing a heavy Burberry coat that was buttoned closely about him. It was very soiled and it gave the impression that he wore it in order to hide the shabbiness of his other clothes. Only his cap, his collar and tie, the ends of his trousers and his boots could be seen. They were all shabby, though the boots were meticulously clean and polished. He was a thickset fellow and the coat seemed to be full of wind, on account of the manner in which his full rounded flesh bulged beneath it, even down along the spine, where a coat is usually hollow.

He sat brooding, with his hands in his overcoat pockets, staring at the glass of whiskey which an attendant had placed in front of him five minutes before but which he had not yet touched. His round face was very blotched. There were red flakes on the cheeks, and between the flakes tiny red veins ran through the pallid, puffed flesh. He had thick white eyebrows. His eyes were round and soft, with an expression of mute suffering in them. There was no harm in his eyes. But it seemed that another will, any evil will other than his own weak, mute will, could make those eyes cruel and callous sentinels that would cunningly watch the performance of an evil deed. And they were aware that evil deeds had been performed under their gaze. They were so mournful and reproachful; staring, faded, blue, round, liquid eyes behind the upward-heaving flesh of his flabby cheeks. His nose was thick and ill-developed, like a bulbous root grown in rocky soil. And his hopeless mouth, with drooping, thick, purple lips, looked sad; an ill-used mouth.

Three months before Brunton had been dismissed from the army. He had been a lieutenant. But he had been merely an officer out of consideration for his past services to the revolutionary movement that had put the present government in power. He was in no way fitted for the job of commanding men and doing the other silly chores that form the duties of an officer in peace-time. During the war against the British and during the Civil War he had been invaluable; a dour, silent, unthinking gunman. But now these people had no further use for him. Afterwards . . . governments and politicians become respectable, no matter what their origin and the methods by which they rose to power. They dropped him silently. They wanted smart young men. This Brunton knew too much. He was too fond of drink. He had become insolent and contemptuous of authority, under the influence of his old lawless pursuits. He would not parade. He would not salute his superiors. He got drunk often, and drunk he talked abusively of the 'b——s that were robbing the country which he and the likes of him had won for them.'

For three months he went around Dublin drinking the money they had given him and swearing to his boon companions that they would not get rid of him as easily as they thought. He knew too much about some of them. He wasn't going to keep his mouth shut very long unless they came across with the money. They had ruined his life, but now he was up for auction and the highest bidder could have him. As there were many more like him going about the public-houses with the same story, nobody took any notice of his talk. But Brunton had become desperate and there was one politician who was really in his power. He was now waiting for that man. He had sent a message into his office that morning.

At twenty minutes past three, Mr Matthew Kenneally, the politician for whom Brunton was waiting, walked into the select bar. He hardly made any noise entering, pushing the swing door inwards gently, and then pausing, with his gloved hand on the door and half his figure within it. He looked around the room casually and saw Brunton. When he saw Brunton, he raised his eyelids and creased his forehead but showed no emotion, either of surprise or of fear, in his face. Then he nodded slightly, and entering fully, closed the door behind him.

Brunton coughed and shuffled his body on his chair but did not speak. Mr Kenneally advanced up the room slowly without speaking.

Mr Kenneally was a tall, slim man with a very long, sallow face and a narrow skull that tapered at the rear to a point. There was nothing extraordinary or remarkable about his face, except the fact that it aroused no interest whatsoever when one looked at it. It was impossible to fix on any one feature, because all the features struck one at the same time, and the only impression that one received was an impression of sallowness and length. The face was more grey than sallow because the grey eyes diffused their own limpid light over all the features. His figure, however, and his clothes made a very acute impression, but an unpleasant one. His figure was so long and slim that he looked like an eel, but not like an eel after all, because an eel moves rapidly, whereas Mr Kenneally was never in a hurry and all his movements were slow and measured, noiseless, as if his joints were greased. His hands were remarkably long and he was always biting his finger-nails, as if to draw attention to the length of his fingers, or perhaps because he was ashamed of their length and couldn't help playing with them. His clothes, too, were always in tone with the colour of his face. Not grey, as one might expect, but a shade of brown, with greyish spots in it. And lastly, he had no shoulders to speak of, so that he always had his hands in his pockets in order to support their length, and he twisted himself along in a curious way, without any apparent assistance from his hands or shoulders, but simply propelling himself by a twisting movement of the hips.

Mr Kenneally was now forty-five years of age. Recently he had become a 'made man'; but everybody still remembers the time when he was 'a Sunday man,' a curious type of person that is unknown outside Dublin, a man who never pays his debts and goes abroad only on Sundays, when writs cannot be served. In those days he had an office on the quays, a lawyer's office, with a name written on a nameplate in a dark hallway and a small room up three flights of stairs, where there was a roll-top desk and a chair and where no business was done, as far as anybody could see. How he had wriggled himself into respectability and affluence nobody knows, but in times of social upheaval these characters seem to be best fitted by nature to come to the surface and lead better types. They blossom forth for a time and then wither away, leaving no trace whatever. They are neither representative of their race nor of their time; but rather an indication of the obscene instruments which humanity uses now and again to propel itself forward.

Mr Kenneally advanced along the room to the little square hole in the wall, through which the attendant served drinks. As he advanced he kept his eyes on Brunton's face and Brunton returned the look. The two of them looked casually at one another, both hiding their thoughts, making their faces masks, lest either might give an advantage to the other for the coming struggle, by the slightest indication of emotion. Mr Kenneally rung the bell, still looking at Brunton. Presently the wooden slide went up, somebody put his hand on the sill and Mr Kenneally said: 'Scotch.' And the attendant said: 'Scotch, Mr Kenneally.' Then there was a pause until the attendant returned with the drink. And during this time the two men still stared at one another. Then Mr Kenneally took his drink, paid for it, the slide slipped down and Mr Kenneally slipped along the floor to the table where Brunton was sitting.

He still stared, coldly, with lowered eyelids.

'Ye needn't keep yer eye on me, Matt,' said Brunton suddenly. 'I ain't goin' to shoot ye. It's not my game an' I sold me gun. If I wanted to plug ye it's not here I'd do it. Ye needn't bother lookin' at me.'

Brunton's voice was soft and thick. The words just rolled out from his lips without any effort and almost without any movement of the mouth. He seemed to have no interest in what he was saying, so that one expected him to stop speaking at any moment, after the second word or in the middle of a sentence. There was absolutely no emotion in his voice, just like the voice of a man whose job it is to deliver verbal messages, in which he has no interest whatever.

Mr Kenneally sat down, and then, drawing his mouth together, he rubbed the two forefingers of his right hand along his face, from the temple to the jaw, still looking at Brunton dispassionately. When he finished rubbing his face, he sniffed three times and then shrugged himself. Then he uttered a little dry laugh and put his whiskey to his lips.

'Here's luck, Mick,' he said very sarcastically.

Brunton watched him drink. He drank very little and rolled it around his palate before swallowing it, sucking his cheeks inwards as he did so. Then he slowly took a cigarette-case from his pocket, extracted a cigarette, lit it and flicked away the match, still looking at Brunton between the eyes. Then he blew out a cloud of cigarette smoke, and leaning his chin on his doubled fists, he twisted around his lips.

'Well,' he said at last. He seemed to talk through his nose, with a sniffing sound. 'I got your message. What's the important business we're going to discuss?'

'Ye know very well what it is,' Brunton said.

'I'm not God,' said Mr Kenneally. 'How should I know unless I'm told.'

'No, yer not God,' said Brunton with sudden ferocity.

Then he frowned, and seizing his glass of whiskey suddenly, he emptied it. Then he leaned forward, with an expression of fear in his face.

'Yer not God,' he said, 'but I think yer the devil.'

'Wish I were,' said Mr Kenneally, biting his finger-nails.

'Well, I'm going to tell ye what I want,' said Brunton. 'I want money.'

'Everybody does nowadays,' sighed Mr Kenneally. 'But most people have to work for it.'

'Now none o' yer coddin',' said Brunton. 'Matt, I want five hundred quid down or I'm goin' to the Minster for Justice with this.'

He pulled out a large envelope from his breast-pocket, tapped it and then put it back again hurriedly.

'What's that?' sniffed Mr Kenneally.

'There's more than enough in that to get you hung,' said Brunton fiercely. 'That's an account of a job I done for ye.'

'What job is that?' said Mr Kenneally in a whisper, glancing towards the aperture in the wall as he spoke.

Brunton did not reply for a few moments. They stared at one another. In spite of himself, Mr Kenneally's face had become an ashen colour, but his eyes did not shrink from Brunton's stare.

'Ha!' said Brunton. 'I see in yer rotten face that ye remember it. That man is dead and the curse o' God on ye for it. Look here, Matt.'

Brunton suddenly got excited and his eyes had a fearful look in them. They got big and fixed.

'I never did another dirty job but that,' he whispered. ''Twas you made me do it. See? Anything else I done was for me country. I'm not sorry and I'm not ashamed of it. But I can see that man yet. I gave him one in the head an' he lyin' on the ground, with —'

'Shut up,' snapped Mr Kenneally, suddenly seizing Brunton by the wrist.

'Let go me wrist,' said Brunton, again speaking calmly.

Mr Kenneally dropped the wrist and leaned back. Brunton also leaned back. Both their bodies relaxed and they both sighed, like two men who have been suddenly startled and are recovering from their fright. They both glanced around the room and did not look at one another again for several moments. When their eyes met again they both looked afraid, as if they had looked at a spectre. But almost as soon as their eyes had met, anger took the place of fear in both their faces.

'You're trying your hand at blackmail now,' said Mr Kenneally.

'I don't give a damn what I try my hand at,' said Brunton. 'I'm desperate. I'm fit for nothing. My life is ruined. I don't give a damn what I do. I know I'll swing for this job as well as you if I make my statement. But you'll swing with me, you b———.'

'What about your oath?' whispered Mr Kenneally.

'Damn my oath,' said Brunton. 'What about your oath? You promised to get me a job and a pension but you never lifted a hand.'

'I did my very best,' said Mr Kenneally.

'Well, ye got to do more,' said Brunton with a hoarse laugh. 'I want money or I'm marchin' off with this. Look here. I'm not goin' to waste time talkin' to ye. I want five hundred quid now. Out with the money.'

'And supposing I don't give it?' whispered Mr Kenneally.

'The evidence is here,' murmured Brunton, tapping his breast.

'Go to the devil,' hissed Mr Kenneally, with trembling lips.

Brunton started up and his hand went to his left breast-pocket in a flash. Mr Kenneally also darted his hand towards his breast-pocket, but Brunton's hand came away before it reached his pocket. 'God!' he said. His gun was not there, of course. Their bodies again relaxed. Brunton laughed dryly.

'Hech!' he said, half rising to his feet. He rested his palms on the corner of the table and leaned on them, half standing. He looked at Mr Kenneally with a curious gleam of pleasure in his eyes. 'What good is the money to me, anyway? Eh? What could I do with it — only drink it? What good is it to me to go on living like this? Where is my home — only in the streets and the pubs and the dosshouses, an' you livin' in the lap o' luxury? Sure it's no vengeance for me to take yer money, a few mangy pounds that won't make a woodpecker's hole in yer bank account. Yah! It's not money I'll take, but vengeance. Man, man, I'll make ye swing with me. The two of us'll swing together, Matt, and we'll both go to hell together, for it's not money I'll take but vengeance.'

He stood erect and his face lit up with a mad light. Mr Kenneally began to tremble. He fumbled in his breast-pocket and he muttered: 'Sit down, Mick. Sit down, Mick. Sit down. Listen to me a moment.'

'No,' said Brunton. 'I'm a man yet an' you're only a rat. Isn't it better for me to —'

'Here, here,' cried Mr Kenneally, spreading a cheque-book on the table. 'Listen. Sit down and listen.'

Brunton had stopped, seeing the cheque-book. The light faded from his face and his lips fell loose, with an expression of greed in them. His face worked, as if he were fighting this expression of greed in his lips. Then he fell on to his chair and stared at the cheque-book. Mr Kenneally watched him closely with his under-lip protruding. Then he winked his right eye slowly and took his pen from his pocket. He rapidly wrote out a cheque, tore it off, and passed it along the table to Brunton. Brunton's hand went out to it and seized it rapidly.

'That's a hundred,' said Mr Kenneally. 'I'll let you have the rest in monthly instalments. It's no good giving you the lot together. Now hand me that paper in your pocket.'

'What for?' said Brunton.

Mr Kenneally shrugged his shoulders.

'Supposing anything happened to you with that on your person?'

Brunton looked at him suspiciously.

'How do ye mean, if anything happened to me?' he said softly.

'Why,' said Mr Kenneally, raising his eyebrows, 'couldn't you drop dead in the street same as anybody else, or meet with an accident or . . .'

'How d'ye mean . . . eh? . . . meet with an accident?' said Brunton.

'Look here,' said Mr Kenneally with a show of anger, 'hand me back that cheque. I'm not going to argue with you. A bargain is a bargain, isn't it?'

Brunton drew the cheque closer to him and thought for a moment. Then he looked at Mr Kenneally closely again, and pursed up his lips.

'Now I warn ye,' he said, 'not to try any o' them accidents on me. I got friends yet. Ye can get me, maybe, but they'll get you. Don't forget that. Here. Ye can have the paper. After all . . . I'm not an informer, even though you're a rat. Here. May they burn ye. Ye'll burn anyway later on.'

He threw the envelope across the table. Mr Kenneally grabbed it. Brunton put the cheque into his pocket. He rose to his feet.

'One a month'll suit me all right,' he said. 'Where?'

'Here,' said Mr Kenneally in a low voice, as he stowed away the envelope.

'Well!' I'm going,' said Brunton.

'Good-bye,' said Mr Kenneally.

They stared at one another for a few moments and then Brunton moved off. Mr Kenneally raised his glass and had another sip. When he was near the door, Brunton suddenly stopped and came back a few steps rapidly. He thrust out his clenched fist towards Mr Kenneally and nodding his head he muttered:

'Mind what I told ye about tryin' on any o' them accidents.'

Mr Kenneally rolled his whiskey around his palate and then swallowed it. Brunton turned and rushed out of the bar. Mr Kenneally stared at the door through which he had disappeared. Then he leaned his chin on his doubled fists and stared at the table. After sitting motionless for over a minute that way, he sighed and shrugged himself.

'Have to get rid of him . . . somehow,' he muttered.

THE CONGER EEL

He was eight feet long. At the centre of his back he was two feet in circumference. Slipping sinuously along the bottom of the sea at a gigantic pace, his black, mysterious body glistened and twirled like a wisp in a foaming cataract. His little eyes, stationed wide apart in his flat-boned, broad skull, searched the ocean for food. He coursed ravenously for miles along the base of the range of cliffs. He searched fruitlessly, except for three baby pollocks which he swallowed in one mouthful without arresting his progress. He was very hungry.

Then he turned by a sharp promontory and entered a cliff-bound harbour where the sea was dark and silent, shaded by the concave cliffs. Savagely he looked ahead into the dark waters. Then instantaneously he flicked his tail, rippling his body like a twisted screw, and shot forward. His long, thin, single whisker, hanging from his lower snout like a label tag, jerked back under his belly. His glassy eyes rested ferociously on minute white spots that scurried about in the sea a long distance ahead. The conger eel had sighted his prey. There was a school of mackerel a mile away.

He came upon them headlong, in a flash. He rose out of the deep from beneath their white bellies, and gripped one mackerel in his wide-open jaws ere his snout met the surface. Then, as if in a swoon, his body went limp, and tumbling over and over, convulsing like a crushed worm, he sank lower and lower until at last he had swallowed the fish. Then immediately he straightened out and flicked his tail, ready to pursue his prey afresh.

The school of mackerel, when the dread monster had appeared among them, were swimming just beneath the surface of the sea. When the eel rushed up they had hurled themselves clean out of the water with the sound of innumerable grains of sand being shaken in an immense sieve. Ten thousand blue and white bodies flashed and shimmered in the sun for three moments, and then they disappeared, leaving a large patch of the dark blue water convulsing turbulently. Ten thousand little fins cut the surface of the sea as the mackerel set off in headlong flight. Their white bellies were no longer visible. They plunged down into the depths of the sea, where their blue-black sides and backs, the colour of the sea, hid them from their enemy. The eel surged about in immense figures of eight, but he had lost them.

Half hungry, half satisfied, he roamed about for half an hour, a demented giant of the deep, travelling restlessly at an incredible speed. Then at last his little eyes again sighted his prey. Little white spots again hung like faded drops of brine in the sea ahead of him. He rushed thither. He opened his jaws as the spots assumed shape, and they loomed up close to his eyes. But just as he attempted to gobble the nearest one, he felt a savage impact. Then something hard and yet intangible pressed against his head and then down along his back. He leaped and turned somersault. The hard, gripping material completely enveloped him. He was in a net. While on all sides of him mackerel wriggled gasping in the meshes.

The eel paused for two seconds amazed and terrified. Then all around him he saw a web of black strands hanging miraculously in the water, everywhere, while mackerel with heaving gills stood rigid in the web, some with their tails and heads both caught and their bodies curved in an arch, others encompassed many times in the uneven folds, others girdled firmly below the gills with a single black thread. Glittering, they eddied back and forth with the stream of the sea, a mass of fish being strangled in the deep.

Then the eel began to struggle fiercely to escape. He hurtled hither and thither, swinging his long, slippery body backwards and forwards, ripping with his snout, surging forward suddenly at full speed, churning the water. He ripped and tore the net, cutting great long gashes in it. But the more he cut and ripped the more deeply enmeshed did he become. He did not release himself, but he released some of the mackerel. They fell from the torn meshes, stiff and crippled, downwards, sinking like dead things. Then suddenly one after another they seemed to wake from sleep, shook their tails, and darted away, while the giant eel was gathering coil upon coil of the net about his slippery body. Then, at last, exhausted and half strangled, he lay still, heaving.

Presently he felt himself being hauled up in the net. The net crowded around him more, so that the little gleaming mackerel, imprisoned with him, rubbed his sides and lay soft and flabby against him, all hauled up in the net with him. He lay still. He reached the surface and gasped, but he made no movement. Then he was hauled heavily into a boat, and fell with a thud into the bottom.

The two fishermen in the boat began to curse violently when they saw the monstrous eel that had torn their net and ruined their catch of mackerel. The old man on the oars in the bow called out: 'Free him and kill him, the whore.' The young man who was hauling in the net looked in terror at the slippery monster that lay between his feet, with its little eyes looking up cunningly, as if it were human. He almost trembled as he picked up the net and began to undo the coils. 'Slash it with your knife,' yelled the old man, 'before he does more harm.' The young man picked up his knife from the gunwale where it was stuck, and cut the net, freeing the eel. The eel, with a sudden and amazing movement, glided up the bottom of the boat, so that he stretched full length.

Then he doubled back, rocking the boat as he beat the sides with his whirling tail, his belly flopping in the water that lay in the bottom. The two men screamed, both crying: 'Kill him, or he'll drown us.' 'Strike him on the nable.' They both reached for the short, thick stick that hung from a peg amidships. The young man grabbed it, bent down, and struck at the eel. 'Hit him in the nable!' cried the old man; 'catch him, catch him, and turn him over.'

They both bent down, pawing at the eel, cursing and panting, while the boat rocked ominously and the huge conger eel glided around and around at an amazing speed. Their hands clawed his sides, slipping over them like skates on ice. They gripped him with their knees, they stood on him, they tried to lie on him, but in their confusion they could not catch him.

Then at last the young man lifted him in his arms, holding him in the middle, gripping him as if he were trying to crush him to death. He staggered upwards. 'Now strike him on the nable!' he yelled to the old man. But suddenly he staggered backwards. The boat rocked. He dropped the eel with an oath, reaching out with his hands to steady himself. The eel's head fell over the canted gunwale. His snout dipped into the sea. With an immense shiver he glided away, straight down, down to the depths, down like an arrow, until he reached the dark, weed-covered rocks at the bottom.

Then stretching out to his full length he coursed in a wide arc to his enormous lair, far away in the silent depths.

CIVIL WAR

Day had dawned. It was the fourth day. Now everything was lost, but they would not surrender. They had crawled on to the roof and they waited for the soldiers to come as soon as it was light. They would be here shortly now. In the distance there was heavy machine-gun fire, and the sky was red in one quarter, not with the dull blaze of the rising summer sun, but with the dark red flare of flames mixed with black smoke, crackling upwards, winding and jumping in ghastly shapes, while timbers fell with monstrous jumbling sounds into the broad street, away to the right; where the Republican headquarters was surrounded and on the point of capture.

Here on the roof of a public-house, in a narrow slum street, the two men waited, waiting for death. It was terrible.

Four days. How different everything was now. There, round about, stretching away on all sides from the black dusty roof, the multitudinous roofs of the city lay like an uneven plain, silent; a great roof covering a multitude of people that slept. They slept, snoring now in peace because everything was over, the end was in sight and the Republicans were defeated. Four days and the whole surging throng of Republicans, rushing with mad eagerness in their eyes to their posts, were all scattered, jailed, killed, wounded, hiding in the hills.

The two men crouched on the roof, with their pistols in their hands, waiting for the soldiers to come. One of them was Lieutenant Jim Dolan, a slim young man of twenty-two, with his new blue suit, that he had bought especially for the rising, all torn and covered with dirt, his white young face haggard and blotched with terror of death and with want of sleep, a clerk. The other was Quartermaster Tim Murphy, an enormous low-sized work-man, with a neck like a bull and a great brown face ending in a square red jaw that stuck out like a broad upward-curving claw; little grey eyes hidden in pouched dark flesh and a snub nose; a resolute fanatical gunman; senseless, indomitable.

Murphy lay flat on his stomach with his chest resting against the low gutter of the roof, his head jammed against the chimney stack that rose erect from the corner of the roof, his pistol gripped loosely in his right hand close to his right eye, staring in front of him, waiting with desperate hatred for the first head to show. Thirty rounds left. Then death. All was lost now. There was no further need to live. Death. . . .

Dolan knelt on his right knee, with his buttock on his heel, also grasping his revolver. But the muzzle pointed at the gutter and his teeth chattered. He didn't want to die. The same hatred throbbed in his brain; hatred of the people who slept; hatred of the soldiers who were setting the distant street on fire and would come creeping through the houses towards him when the daylight spread. But he didn't want to die. The fear of death made his teeth chatter.

Thinking feverishly . . . he thought of the two corpses on the stairway, his two comrades that had been killed the day before when a passing lorry full of soldiers hurled a bomb. It burst with a deafening crash on the stairs. There were screams. The garrison went into panic. Three men bolted into the street, with their hands up, and surrendered. He, too, wanted to surrender. But Murphy was by his side at the top-floor window. Murphy fired, once, twice, three times. The three men twirled round and fell in the street. He fired again. Somebody screamed in the lorry and as it whirred away at full speed, a green-clothed body vaulted with curved spine in the middle of it and then fell among the crouching backs of the soldiers, who had fallen prone for shelter.

Now they were alone, the two of them. He was alone with Murphy and he feared him. He was in command, in charge of the post. But this bull-necked fiend was the real commander. There was no command now. They were alone. And Murphy was a devil.

Murphy had turned on him, stuck his pistol into his chest and roared, frothing, into his face: 'You bloody well stay with me. D'ye hear, you bastard? I'm in command and it's no surrender.'

That was yesterday evening. What a night! Silence, shots at a distance, rats on the stairs, thinking about his wife, Murphy prowling about muttering, two drunken men trying to enter the bar for loot, shots, curses, a scramble on to the roof just an hour ago and now . . . waiting for death. No surrender.

Dolan thought of his wife. God! How strange everything was. Was it four days or was it a thousand years? He did not love her now. Not at all. She had disappeared out of his life. There remained only memories of her thin frail hands, her delicate pink cheeks, the fair curls in bunches about her ears, her big pale blue eyes, and the absolute impossibility of making her understand anything. He hadn't told her anything. He didn't even send a message, when he rushed out of his office four days ago to take charge of his post.

She wouldn't understand . . . anything. He only thought of her, because she represented the world as compared to this wilderness, where he was cut off completely from life, on a roof with a devil.

Why, why could he not scream for help? Why could he not turn his loaded revolver on the broad back of Murphy lying prone beside him and fire, fire, fire with clenched teeth and staring eyes, ferociously, until six bullets had entered the devilish body? Then he would be free. He could rush down the stairs past the . . . No. He could not pass the corpses. God! The corpses on the stairs!

With his teeth chattering he knelt, with a terrible pain in his head and his whole body on fire, every nerve throbbing, his bowels heavy as if they were made of lead and sagging down, so that every moment he seemed to be on the point of going into a frenzied fit, during which, he thought, he would wander away for ever through an endless abyss peopled with devils who fired and screamed and cursed, endlessly.

Murphy never moved. His prone body was stiff, with the flesh lying loosely on the rigid bones, like a waiting animal at bay. Light spread, whitening, sparkling, warming the roof. Sounds approached.

At first came the rumble of rubbered wheels and the dull thumping of a motor. Then the rumbling sound stopped with a thud and there was a clatter of feet. Murphy grunted, shifted his elbows and stretched his heels out wide. Turning his head around slowly, he stared at Dolan. His eyes were bloodshot and almost closed.

'They're coming,' he said. 'Good-bye. See ye in hell.'

The puffed flesh on his cheeks trembled as he laughed silently without opening his mouth. Then he stared for a few more moments at Dolan and turned to his front, grinding his teeth and levelling his Mauser pistol slowly towards the sounds.

Dolan also went rigid. His jaws set. His eyes opened wide, staring senselessly without seeing anything. He stopped thinking. His whole body waited. What?

Trup, trap, trip. They came. They were still invisible. The narrow street curved a hundred yards to the left. They would come around that corner, past a blank wall that faced an inward-curving black-painted shop front, with J. WALSH, GROCER, painted on it in white. J. WALSH, GROCER, in white letters, brown horse-dung dried on the narrow street, and a blank wall. Dolan stared at them, first one, then the other, senselessly.

Suddenly two green-clothed men appeared, walking slowly on either side of the street, their rifles at the high port, their caps set rakishly on the sides of their heads, one man chewing a long wisp of white straw, both staring upwards at the windows of the houses. They halted, spoke to another and then one looked behind and twirled his right hand above his head. He paused with his hand raised and then shot it forward and brought it stiffly to his side. Signal. Advance. They marched on. Two more men appeared. Then three more, all marching slowly with their rifles at the high port.

Murphy growled and then his body heaved as he gurgled his laughter silently. They were walking into his trap. He was waiting until they came beneath him, at close range. Then he would fire . . .

But Dolan . . . As soon as he saw them, his heart began to beat violently and his brain again began to work. He had no fear of them. He had forgotten that they were enemies, that he had been fighting them for four days. He had ceased to be a revolutionary. He was a prisoner, he thought, at the mercy of a murderer and madman, and here was hope of delivery. He tried to cry out to them and wave his hands, but somehow, the terrible power of the man beside him clove his tongue to the roof of his mouth and rendered his hands lifeless. He could only shiver and make inarticulate movements with his pallid lips.

They came closer. He could see the buttons on their tunics glimmering and the curious casual expression on their faces, as if they were strolling along carelessly. God! Why could they not know that he was here, in danger of death? Why were they coming like that so carelessly when . . . Hell!

Murphy moved. His right arm stiffened. The squat muzzle of his gun jutted downwards sharply. He was going to fire. Dolan screamed and threw himself on the prone body. With a growl Murphy whirled around, dashing his elbow backwards into Dolan's ribs. Dolan's light frame was hurled backwards with a slithering sound on to the slates of the roof. He fell on his back and slipped sideways into the gutter, with his face upwards, the head bent forward and the eyes staring at Murphy's. Murphy pointed his gun at Dolan's face. 'Ha,' he said. Then there was a sharp crack. Dolan thought he was dead. But it was Murphy that was hit. His mouth opened wide and he fell backwards for a moment and then turned himself, twisting his body curiously all on the right side. His left side was helpless. There was a bullet in the upper part of his chest beneath the left shoulder. They had fired from the street.

Dolan threw back his head and lay flat. He still thought he was dead. His brain was whirling round and round at an amazing speed. There were revolving red circles before his closed eyes, and the extremities of his limbs seemed to be firmly bound with enormous weights that were dragging him downwards ever so slowly and yet leaving his body on the roof. He waited in terrible silence, hearing nothing.

As soon as the soldiers had fired they ran, taking shelter in a lane, a little way up the street on the left-hand side. Murphy had fired blindly, two rounds, but he had hit nobody. The bullets spattered against the edge of the black-fronted shop, making little dull white spots, side by side. Then he waited.

Suddenly there was another crack and Murphy's body shivered. His head bent backwards and he put his right hand to his throat. He was hit again, in the left shoulder near the neck. Immediately blood spurted out through his blue sweater. His mouth opened, his tongue came out and then his lips closed, gripping the end of his tongue. He closed his left eye, and with an immense effort levelled his gun at a chimney. Silence. Crack, crack, crack. He fired three times, rapidly. There was a yell and a man threw up his hands, curving inwards, with a rifle held slantwise in them. Then he fell forward and lay stretched across the chimney, writhing. Another figure jumped up and tried to drag him off, stooping low. Murphy fired again. The other figure fell back. Was he hit?

Dr-r-r-r-r. A Lewis gun spattered farther up. A whizzing stream of bullets passed in front of Murphy's face, moving from side to side in the air, as they whizzed, hot near his face. He ducked and lay still. Crack, crack, dr-r-r-r, crack. They were all at him, firing from all sides. Pieces of brick from the chimney stack and slivers of the slates from the roof pattered on his back. Still he was unhit, waiting in the gutter.

Waiting, he thought of Dolan. He would finish him off now, the traitor. He felt himself getting very weak. Only one side of him was alive. Death was coming rapidly. He would get that bastard though. Slowly he turned his head, brushing his skull against the low wall of the gutter, so as not to raise it against the background of the slates, on which the bullets were pattering. Then he had to bring his right arm around under his elbow and move his right knee up under his hip. He was a long time shuffling and groaning with the terrible pain of his wounds.

Dolan heard him move and started with terror. This movement brought him back to consciousness again, like a man waking suddenly from a nightmare on hearing a noise in his room. He thrust forward his head, opened his eyes and saw Murphy's face, all covered with blood, staring at him; and the muzzle of Murphy's pistol, veering round. He uttered a scream and, planting his elbows under his hips, he jerked backwards along the gutter. Murphy growled and made a sudden movement, raising himself a little to present his pistol and fire at the same moment. But just as he raised himself to fire, his head jerked upwards, the bullet fled from his gun harmlessly into the air above his head and he fell backwards, banging his skull against the gutter. He had been shot through the brain. He lay perfectly still.

The firing stopped. Soldiers were calling to one another from across the street. Dolan lay perfectly quiet looking at Murphy's body. Would he jump up now and raise his hands above his head? No. As soon as the thought of getting really into contact with the soldiers came into his head, his terror of them came back. He again realised that they were his enemies. A cold perspiration broke out all over his body and he crouched lower on to the roof, trying to push his body in through the slates, to hide himself. Then pressing against the roof, he lay still and shut his eyes.

Silence . . . a long silence. All was still.

Then there were footsteps on the roof behind him.

He heard them and jumped up, waving his arms above his head. Then he fell on his knees and bent forward chattering and fluttering his clawing hands.

'Take me out of this. Take me out of this. I didn't fire. I didn't fire. He was mad. My wife, my wife. I declare to God I never fired. Two men on the stairs. Murphy is his name. Take me out of this.'

There were two of them there, peering over the ridge of the roof, five feet away from his face. Only their faces, their arms and their rifles were visible. Two cruel, cold faces, staring coldly at him. Gradually he saw the faces growing colder and more cruel, the lips curling into a snarl and the eyes narrowing. Then one man said: 'Let's give it to the bastard.'

They both fired point-blank into his head.

THE FOOLISH BUTTERFLY

L ife came to the butterfly when the sun was a golden ball in the East. It crawled on moist unsteady legs from the chrysalis on to the stem of the twig. It stood there, slightly swaying, while the sun and wind dried its body. The sun's rays came to it over the sea, bearing a cool heat that was scented with the fresh morning breeze. The light caresses of the breeze polished the butterfly's long trunk and loosened the large wings that were folded like a fan. The sun's heat dried and warmed it and caused it to swell out and pulsate with the joy of newborn life.

Scarcely had it completed the act of birth when its wings unfolded and spread themselves on the air, giddily rocking at first from side to side to find their balance and then falling gracefully outwards and downwards into position. They were so large and resplendent that the trunk was hidden beneath their awning. They were all decked with colour too, so that it was hard to see what part of them was white and what part was covered with black rings that seemed to multiply before the eyes rapidly. Yet all of the two wings looked white in some strange manner. It stood there on the twig, with its wings spread, full-grown and beautiful at birth, without a sound, either of joy or of pain, to disturb the silent beauty of its mysterious creation. A godly thing.

It rose without effort from the twig, daintily stepping on to the invisible support of the air without a single sound. Not a cry, not a whisper of wings broke the amazing silence of its existence. Its wings spread on the breeze and flapped innumerable times gracefully, up and down, in leaps and bounds, as if they were playing on some instrument, jumping from key to key in an abandoned way. Gambolling like a thing tossed in a whirlwind, it rose high into the air and then fell away into the valley.

The valley was small and round and opened on a pebbly shore, with the sea stretching beyond. On the other sides there were low but sheer cliffs, their slopes covered with long grass and bushes, gorse and bracken. Everywhere there were little tiny flowers. Birds flitted about, little ones among the bushes and great seagulls soaring in the empty blue sky. Innumerable forms of life roamed in the grass and the accumulated sounds of their existence rose in a sleepy hum on the air. And round about, everywhere, fluttering and bobbing and curvetting, the butterfly beheld thousands of other butterflies like itself, all differing in colour or size, but all silent and beautiful and skipping about without rest. It joined the hurry throng of butterflies, passing from flower to flower, drinking their sap. It rested now and again under the brilliant heat of the sun. It played with other butterflies. But above all, it liked to fly and flutter in the beautiful empty air, ever moving its glittering wings in throbbing flight, up, up into the wind with a sudden leap, down to the earth in zigzag course, and away again sideways, in and out, as if it followed an interminable maze of alleyways through the firmament.

A little after noon the butterfly wandered down to the edge of the strand, where there was a cluster of scarlet pimpernels growing. It hovered about the flowers a little and then rested among them. The sun was very hot. It beat down on the hot pebbles and on the great expanse of the calm sea, that shone white under its rays. Then suddenly a fresh wind started up from the direction of the land. It was a soft fresh wind and it blew in long slow rushes. It made the heads of the scarlet flowers, on one of which the butterfly rested, lean far over, like children bowing low all together. It excited the butterfly. It rose immediately into the air. It took three long zigzag leaps upward, high into the heavens, and then it let itself be carried with the wind, revelling in the delicious pressure of the wind against its trunk and wings. Soon it soared out over the sea, leaving the land behind. It soared a long way, flapping its wings gently and gliding before the generous impulse of the ever-constant long sweeping rushes of the winds. It glided away, almost asleep with the pleasure of facile and rapid movement. Then with a sudden rapid and intricate series of wing movements, it drew itself downwards out of the course of the wind, to earth as it thought.

But there was no earth beneath it. Instead it beheld an amazing level plain, moving continually, with innumerable little waves on its surface, with their crests silvered by the light of the sun and their sides deep blue. While here and there were black patches and light green patches, and again little flecks of froth that sparkled. The butterfly thought these sparkling things were flowers and it darted down towards one of them, but when it hovered near, it did not detect the smell of flower sap, but a strong pungent smell that was unknown to it and repulsive. Then a drop of water thrown up by the concussion of two wavelets struck it in the trunk and it rose quickly, terrified. It rose far up from the sea and flew again into the wind, letting itself be carried speedily away from the strange place that was repulsive to it. Rejoicing once more in the wind and the heat and light of the sun, it forgot its terror.

All trace of land had now disappeared. The sea was encircled by the sky on all sides, the sea a level blue plain, the sky a painted cup lying mouth-downwards on the sea. And the little white butterfly, a solitary prisoner beneath that boundless cup, flew on before the wind, flitting gaily on its resplendent wings.

In a kind of languorous ecstasy it flew until the wind suddenly went down and a great calm enveloped the back of the sea and the empty air above it. The butterfly's wings grew weak and it fluttered downwards suddenly, again seeking a resting-place and the refreshing sap of some flower to invigorate it.

But again that moving plain with its pungent odour and its continual murmur repelled the butterfly. It rose, once more, terrified. But now it did not rise far. Its strength was waning. It was drawn downwards again. Again it skimmed the surface of the sea with the curved ends of its trunk. Again it rose. It performed a frenzied series of little jumps, tossing itself restlessly on the heated air, exhausting the last reserves of its strength in a mad flutter of its beautiful white wings. Then it sank slowly in spite of fierce flapping. The wings drooped, swaying as they had done at the moment of birth when they had come from the chrysalis. The trunk touched the crest of the sea. It sank into the water. The wings fluttered once and then the sea-water filtered through them, like ink through blotting-paper.

There were a few little movements of the round head. Then the butterfly lay still.

THE WILD GOAT'S KID

Her nimble hoofs made music on the crags all winter, as she roamed along the cliff-tops over the sea.

During the previous autumn, when goats were mating, she had wandered away, one of a small herd that trotted gaily after a handsome fellow, with a splendid grey-black hide and winding horns. It was her first mating. Then, with the end of autumn, peasant boys came looking for their goats. The herd was broken up. The gallant buck was captured and slain by two hungry dogs from the village of Drumranny. The white goat alone remained. She had wandered too far away from her master's village. He couldn't find her. She was given up as lost.

So that she became a wild one of the cliffs, where the sea-gulls and the cormorants were lords, and the great eagle of Moher soared high over the thundering sea. Her big, soft, yellow eyes became wild from looking down often at the sea, with her long chin whiskers swaying gracefully in the wind. She was a long, slender thing, with short, straight horns and ringlets of matted hair trailing far down on either haunch.

With her tail in the air, snorting, tossing her horns, she fled when anybody approached. Her hoofs would patter over the crags until she was far away. Then she would stand on some eminence and turn about to survey the person who had disturbed her, calmly, confident in the power of her slender legs to carry her beyond pursuit.

She roamed at will. No stone fence however high could resist her long leap, as she sprang on muscular thighs that bent like silk. She was so supple that she could trot on the top of a thin fence, carelessly, without a sound except the gentle tapping of her delicate hoofs. She hardly ever left the cliff-tops. There was plenty of food there, for the winter was mild, and the leaves and grasses that grew between the crevices of the crags were flavoured by the strong, salt taste of the brine carried up on the wind. She grew sleek and comely.

Towards the end of winter a subtle change came over her. Her hearing became more acute. She took fright at the least sound. She began to shun the sea except on very calm days, when it did not roar. She ate less. She grew very particular about what she ate. She hunted around a long time before she chose a morsel. She often went on her knees, reaching down into the bottom of a crevice to nibble at a briar that was inferior to the more accessible ones. She became corpulent. Her udder increased.

Winter passed. Green leaves began to sprout. Larks sang in the morning. There was sweetness in the air and a great urge of life. The white goat, one morning a little after dawn, gave birth to a grey-black kid.

The kid was born in a tiny, green glen under an overhanging ledge of low rock that sheltered it from the wind. It was a male kid, an exquisite, fragile thing, tinted delicately with many colours. His slender belly was milky white. The insides of his thighs were of the same colour. He had deep rings of grey, like bracelets, above his hoofs. He had black knee-caps on his forelegs, like pads, to protect him when he knelt to take his mother's teats into his silky, black mouth. His back and sides were grey-black. His ears were black, long, and drooping with the weakness of infancy.

The white goat bleated over him, with soft eyes and shivering flanks, gloating over the exquisite thing that had been created within her by the miraculous power of life. And she had this delicate creature all to herself, in the wild solitude of the beautiful little glen, within earshot of the murmuring sea, with little birds whistling their spring songs around about her, and the winds coming with their slow whispers over the crags. The first tender hours of her first motherhood were undisturbed by any restraint, not even by the restraint of a mate's presence. In absolute freedom and quiet, she watched with her young.

How she manoeuvred to make him stand! She breathed on him to warm him. She raised him gently with her forehead, uttering strange, soft sounds to encourage him. Then he stood up, trembling, staggering, swaying on his curiously long legs. She became very excited, rushing around him, bleating nervously, afraid that he should fall again. He fell. She was in agony. Bitter wails came from her distended jaws and she crunched her teeth. But she renewed her efforts, urging the kid to rise, to rise and live . . . to live, live, live.

He rose again. Now he was steadier. He shook his head. He wagged his long ears as his mother breathed into them. He took a few staggering steps, came to his padded knees, and rose again immediately. Slowly, gently, gradually, she pushed him towards her udder with her horns. At last he took the teat within his mouth, he pushed joyously, sank to his knees and began to drink.

She stayed with him all day in the tiny glen, just nibbling a few mouthfuls of the short grass that grew around. Most of the time she spent exercising her kid. With a great show of anxiety and importance, she brought him on little expeditions across the glen to the opposite rock, three yards away and back again. At first he staggered clumsily against her sides, and his tiny hoofs often lost their balance on tufts of grass, such was his weakness. But he gained strength with amazing speed, and the goat's joy and pride increased. She suckled and caressed him after each tiny journey.

When the sun had set he was able to walk steadily, to take little short runs, to toss his head. They lay all night beneath the shelter of the ledge, with the kid between his mother's legs, against her warm udder.

Next morning she hid him securely in a crevice of the neighbouring crag, in a small groove between two flags that were covered with a withered growth of wild grass and ferns. The kid crawled instinctively into the warm hole without any resistance to the gentle push of his mother's horns. He lay down with his head towards his doubled hind legs, and closed his eyes. Then the goat scraped the grass and fern-stalks over the entrance hole with her fore feet, and she hurried away to graze, as carelessly as if she had no kid hidden.

All the morning, as she grazed hurriedly and fiercely around the crag, she took great pains to pretend that she was not aware of her kid's nearness. Even when she grazed almost beside the hiding-place, she never noticed him, by look or by cry. But still, she pricked her little ears at every distant sound.

At noon she took him out and gave him suck. She played with him on a grassy knoll and watched him prance about. She taught him how to rear on his hind legs and fight the air with his forehead. Then she put him back into his hiding-place and returned to graze. She continued to graze until night-fall.

Just when she was about to fetch him from his hole and take him to the overhanging ledge to rest for the night, a startling sound reached her ears. It came from afar, from the south, from beyond a low fence that ran across the crag on the skyline. It was indistinct, barely audible, a deep, purring sound. But to the ears of the mother-goat, it was loud and ominous as a thunder-clap. It was the heavy breathing of a dog sniffing the wind.

She listened stock-still, with her head in the air and her short tail lying stiff along her back, twitching one ear. The sound came again. It was nearer. Then there was a patter of feet. Then a clumsy, black figure hurtled over the fence and dropped on to the crag, with awkward secrecy. The goat saw a black dog, a large, curly fellow, standing by the fence in the dim twilight, with his fore paw raised and his long, red tongue hanging. Then he shut his mouth suddenly, and raising his snout upwards sniffed several times, contracting his nostrils as he did so, as if in pain. Then he whined savagely, and trotted towards the goat sideways.

She snorted. It was a sharp, dull thud, like a blow from a rubber sledge. Then she rapped the crag three times with her left fore foot, loudly and sharply. The dog stood still and raised his fore paw again. He bent down his head and looked at her with narrowed eyes. Then he licked his breast and began to run swiftly to the left. He was running towards the kid's hiding-place, with his tail stretched out straight and his snout to the wind.

With another fierce snort the goat charged him at full speed, in order to cut him off from his advance on the kid's hiding-place. He stopped immediately when she charged. The goat halted too, five yards from the hiding place, between the dog and the hiding-place, facing the dog.

The dog stood still. His eyes wandered around in all directions, with the bashfulness of a sly brute, caught suddenly in an awkward position. Then slowly he raised his bloodshot eyes to the goat. He bared his fangs. His mane rose like a fan. His tail shot out. Picking his steps like a lazy cat, he approached her without a sound. The goat shivered along her left flank, and she snorted twice in rapid succession.

When he was within six yards of her he uttered a ferocious roar — a deep, rumbling sound in his throat. He raced towards her, and leaped clean into the air, as if she were a fence that he was trying to vault. She parried him subtly with her horns, like a sword-thrust, without moving her fore feet. Her sharp horns just grazed his belly as he whizzed past her head. But the slight blow deflected his course. Instead of falling on his feet, as he intended cunningly to do, between the goat and the kid, he was thrown to the left and fell on his side, with a thud. The goat whirled about and charged him.

But he had arisen immediately and jerked himself away, with his haunches low down, making a devilish scraping and yelping and growling noise. He wanted to terrify the kid out of his hiding-place. Then it would be easy to overpower the goat, hampered by the task of hiding the kid between her legs.

The kid uttered a faint, querulous cry, but the goat immediately replied with a sharp, low cry. The kid mumbled something indistinct, and then remained silent. There was a brushing sound among the ferns that covered him. He was settling himself down farther. The goat trotted rigidly to the opposite side of the hiding-place to face the dog again.

The dog had run away some distance, and lay on his belly, licking his paws. Now he meant to settle himself down properly to the prolonged attack, after the failure of his first onslaught. He yawned lazily and made peculiar, mournful noises, thrusting his head into the air and twitching his snout. The goat watched every single movement and sound, with her ears thrust forward past her horns. Her great, soft eyes were very wild and timorous in spite of the valiant posture of her body, and the terrific force of the blows she delivered occasionally on the hard crag with her little hoofs.

The dog remained lying for half an hour or so, continuing his weird pantomime. The night fell completely. Everything became unreal and ghostly under the light of the distant myriads of stars. An infant moon had arisen. The sharp rushing wind and the thunder of the sea only made the silent loneliness of the night more menacing to the white goat, as she stood bravely on the limestone crag defending her newborn young. On all sides the horizon was a tumultuous line of barren crag, dented with shallow glens and seamed with low, stone fences that hung like tattered curtains against the rim of the sky.

Then the dog attacked again. Rising suddenly, he set off at a long, swinging gallop, with his head turned sideways towards the goat, whining as he ran. He ran around the goat in a wide circle, gradually increasing his speed. A white spot on his breast flashed and vanished as he rose and fell in the undulating stretches of his flight. The goat watched him, fiercely rigid from tail to snout. She pawed the crag methodically, turning around on her own ground slowly to face him.

When he passed his starting-point, he was flying at full speed, a black ball shooting along the gloomy surface of the crag, with a sharp rattle of claws. The rattle of his claws, his whining and the sharp tapping of the goat's fore feet as she turned about, were the only sounds that rose into the night from this sinister engagement.

He sped round and round the goat, approaching her imperceptibly each round, until he was so close that she could see his glittering eyes and the white lather of rage on his half-open jaws. She became slightly dizzy and confused, turning about so methodically in a confined space, confused and amazed by the subtle strategy of the horrid beast. His whining grew louder and more savage. The rattle of his claws was like the clamour of hailstones driven by a wind. He was upon her.

He came in a whirl on her flank. He came with a savage roar that deafened her. She shivered and then stiffened in a rigid silence to receive him. The kid uttered a shrill cry. Then the black bulk hurtled through the air, close up, with hot breathing, snarling, with reddened fangs and . . . smash.

He had dived for her left flank. But as he went past her head she turned like lightning and met him again with her horns. This time she grazed his side, to the rear of the shoulder. He yelped and tumbled sideways, rolling over twice. With a savage snort she was upon him. He was on his haunches, rising, when her horns thudded into his head. He went down again with another yelp. He rolled over and then suddenly, with amazing speed, swept to his feet, whirled about on swinging tail and dived for her flank once more. The goat uttered a shriek of terror. He had passed her horns. His fangs had embedded themselves in the matted ringlet that trailed along her right flank. The dog's flying weight, swinging on to the ringlet as he fell, brought her to her haunches.

But she was ferocious now. As she wriggled to her feet beside the rolling dog that gripped her flank, she wrenched herself around and gored him savagely in the belly. He yelled and loosed his hold. She rose on her hind legs in a flash, and with a snort she gored him again. Her sharp, pointed horns penetrated his side between the ribs. He gasped and shook his four feet in the air. Then she pounded on him with her fore feet, beating his prostrate body furiously. Her little hoofs pattered with tremendous speed for almost a minute. She beat him blindly, without looking at him.

Then she suddenly stopped. She snorted. The dog was still. She shivered and looked down at him curiously. He was dead. Her terror was passed. She lifted her right fore foot and shook it with a curious movement. Then she uttered a wild, joyous cry and ran towards her kid's hiding-place.

Night passed into a glorious dawn that came over a rippling sea from the east. A wild, sweet dawn, scented with dew and the many perfumes of the germinating earth. The sleepy sun rose brooding from the sea, golden and soft, searching far horizons with its concave shafts of light. The dawn was still. Still and soft and pure.

The white goat and her kid were travelling eastwards along the cliff-top over the sea. They had travelled all night, flying from the horrid carcass of the beast that lay stretched on the crag beside the little glen. Now they were far away, on the summit of the giant white Precipice of Cahir. The white goat rested to give suck to her kid, and to look out over the cliff-top at the rising sun.

Then she continued her flight eastwards, pushing her tired kid before her gently with her horns.

THE TERRORIST

Louis Quigley crouched over the balustrade of the Upper Circle, shivering in his thin overcoat.

Overhead there was a continual pattering of feet and occasional loud thuds, as the poor people crowded into the gallery, shuffling and talking noisily, jumping along the wide tiers of wooden seats. A respectable stream of shabby genteel people filtered through the Upper Circle seeking their seats rapidly. Below in the Stalls, in the Dress Circle and in the Boxes, sombrely clad men entered slowly, with rigid hips and bored faces, inattentively glancing for their sumptuous seats. The bare powdered bosoms of their women sparkled with jewels. They dropped their luxurious wraps and sank wearily into their seats.

Quigley, leaning against his curved left arm that lay along the red velvet covering of the Upper Circle balustrade, glanced downwards at the rich who entered with intense hatred in his feverish eyes.

'Drones!' he muttered. 'Drones soured by their own luxury!'

The theatre filled, noisily above him, respectfully about him, boredly below him. It was very warm in the theatre. You could smell the artificial heat coming in waves through the brilliantly lighted hall. But Quigley shivered in his thin overcoat.

He had been waiting for two hours at the door in order to get a front seat behind the balustrade. And it had been a cold winter's night outside; a clear, frosty, starlit sky, overarching the windy streets through which the ill-clad poor went crouching.

His overcoat was buttoned about his throat, enveloping his meagre frame loosely like a bag. A shabby grey cap covered skull, down over his forehead and pressing his ears outwards. His ears were blue with the cold. His face was small, thin and pale; but there was a fever in his large, blue eyes that illuminated the paltry face and made it terrifying. The face was fixed and the vertical grooves in the skin gathered between the eyes did not twitch. His whole being was transfixed, contemplating the idea in his brain.

The idea had been with him for six days, since he first contemplated the act, in the darkness of his room at night, clutching his knees in bed, thinking.

The desire to commit the act had entered his brain suddenly without his knowing it or expecting it. When it came, he had sprung out of bed in terror. He had stood for a long time in his bare feet on the floor, stooping forward, listening. Listening he had become very tired. He had sighed. He had entered his bed again slowly, utterly exhausted. He had fallen asleep almost immediately. But in the morning he awoke to find the idea fixed in his brain; as securely fixed there as if he had been born to commit the act. All the other ideas had gone. He had no further interest in them. He read no more. He spent the six days making preparations for the act.

Watching the people enter he was quite cool. But the tips of the fingers of his left hand were embedded in the soft red velvet of the balustrade covering. And the knuckles of his left hand were white. He waited tensely until the appointed moment should come, without thinking. It seemed to him that his head was made of iron, it felt so strong. It also seemed to him that he was really sitting alone, an immeasurable distance from everybody; that he was enveloped by a cloud; and that he would hurl a thunderbolt out of that cloud, down upon the drones. An avenging God!

Before he hurled the bomb he would utter aloud his prophecy. It would go forth to all the world as a clarion call. The tocsin would be sounded that night. 'The blare of trumpets at dawn on the banks of the Po, as the squadrons of Hasdrubal's Nubian horsemen . . .' Prophets immolate themselves. His right hand was thrust into his right breast-pocket, between the second and third buttons of his overcoat.

The theatre was full. Now a dull murmur rose as thousands of words mingle in the heated air without form or meaning. People murmuring. Broken waves seething white on a rocky shore, thought Quigley.

The sound pleased him. He fancied that there below, beneath the cloud in which his body was hidden, a concourse of people babbled expectantly, waiting for his word and the sacrifice of blood. 'Somewhere and by some one that sacrifice will be made; even by one man armed with a stone.' A bomb was more fitting that a stone, because the reverberation of its explosion would resound through the earth to awake the sleepers, to urge on the tired ones; all, all marching with the prophecy on their lips. His body grew still colder and salty moisture exuded from the corners of his eyes. His eyes blurred and he could see nothing below him. People had sat on either side of him closely. That was all right. Behind him, around him and above him were his own people. Below him were the drones.

Crash! He started violently and then his body relaxed, trembling, as the soft sounds of music rose from the orchestra, the jingle-jingle of the cymbals tintinnating, tintinnating, the weird, melancholy, comic sound of the saxo-phone, the alternating boom of the drums and the choleric brasses pounding the air; all in harmony mingling. It was the mad laughter of the elements heralding the act.

He was carried away by the sound. His miserable frame collapsed with a loose palsied movement of his weak muscles; rendered incapable by the fever-ish exaltation of his mind to remain fixed and taut. The crude anger of his idea now changed. It became enveloped with a maniacal joy that transcended it. Lo! The whole theatre was transformed before his eyes. Lo! There in that box to the left of the stage two women had entered, while two men, hidden from his view, seated them. He could see the white hands of the men, with jewels shimmering on their fingers, gesticulating; while the women disposed their dresses and sat upright, laughing backwards at their men. Two tipsy courtesans. One, dark, with firm jaws and rounded, firm breasts, smiled stu-pidly, while her black eyes ogled her man. The other, with hair the light golden colour of ripe corn, the fecund colour of the fruitful earth, drooped languidly, a beautiful fawn beast exulting in her savage beauty. His blurred eyes gloated over her long stately limbs, loosened with wine and sensuality. Lo! This was not anger but an exulting joy, the slaughter of drones; society had laid before him the most gross and yet exquisite manifestation of its lordly vice so that his act might go forth. . . .

Br-r-r-r. Suddenly the drums of his ears began to hum, deafening him. His cheeks flushed a rosy colour. He half rose from his seat, trembling violently. They made a startled movement about him, shrinking away and looking in awe at his frenzied eyes. Half risen, he smiled and tried to pull forth the bomb to hurl it at the fawn beast, but . . .

In a moment the humming stopped in his ears. He became aware of the movement about him. This unbalanced him and he fell back into his seat. He wanted to look around him and say something to reassure HIS people. But he was incapable of any action but one, i.e. to hurl the bomb. Already nobody else existed in the world but himself and 'the horned spectres of the Revela-tions' down below. His stomach was becoming ill and all his members were revolting in terror from any movement. And his brain began to be afraid; afraid of the extraordinary and unexpected conduct of his stomach, which was now assuming the mastery over his brain, starting some devilry of its own, expanding and throbbing, as if at the next instant it would explode and annihilate him. Plump! He sat down, closed his eyes and held his breath.

There was a murmur about him now, about him and behind him. He heard it but he took no notice. His consciousness was impervious now to sound. Sound had become formless and meaningless to his ears. The music still continued. Down below people were swaying to its rhythm. But he no longer heard the rhythm. In the box, a man had planted his left foot on the fawn beast's lap. With a languid gesture she cast it off and made a sensual movement downwards from her loins. No, not there. His eyes were also out of control. They wandered from the box along the Dress Circle, and there they suddenly became fixed once more.

There was a row of black-clothed youths like mummies sitting erect, with stiff necks and thoughtless pallid faces, gazing inanely at the stage. His ecstasy changed once more into anger. The fever left him and he became rigid. Here, here was the most foul iniquity. Not debauch nor luxury, but young humanity drained of its intelligence, an insult to the divinity of man; 'the headless clowns sitting on the throne of wealth to sign the edicts of ghoulish fiends that trample the starving millions.'

Now he was completely in a state of unconsciousness. There was some excited movement about him and people were talking loudly and calling, but it meant nothing to him. Because the idea had repossessed him with terrific power. It had expanded in his brain until his whole entity had vanished and he had become purely an amorphous idea, crying: 'Now, now.'

He arose slowly like an automaton, with curious stilted movements. He raised his left hand. Abruptly he pulled forth the bomb. He raised his eyes to the ceiling. He cried out:

'Man has conquered the earth. He now marches triumphantly to the conquest of the Universe. The drones stand in the way. Death to . . .'

His voice ended in a choking murmur as several big men pounced on him. He felt numb immediately, and then . . . he floated away, lying, he thought, on a soft fleecy cloud, soaring over the void of the wrecked universe.

THE OLD HUNTER

Mr Stephen Mullen, the horse-dealer of Ballyhaggard, went to an auction one day. He was a tall, slim man with a red face and white eyebrows. Being a very popular man, on account of his dry wit and his good temper, he met many friends in the town where the auction was being held, and the result was that he spent the morning in the hotels drinking. Slightly intoxicated, he arrived at the auction when everything was sold except an old hunter called Morrissey.

Mr Mullen went up to the auctioneer, a friend of his, and asked him, had he anything left. The auctioneer pointed to the old hunter.

'That's the lot,' he said.

'What's that?' said Mr Mullen, shutting one eye and cocking his head sideways.

'Pooh!' said the auctioneer, 'there's enough iron in that old rascal to keep a factory going for a month. Tell you what, these bank-clerks and shop-keepers that are buying horses now with their ill-gotten gains don't know a . . .'

'Hech, hech,' said Mr Mullen, 'let's have a look at him. I might give ye the price of a drink for him.'

They walked over to the hunter. He was a finely built animal, but he looked like a man that had just left a nursing home after a serious nervous breakdown. His bones were sticking through his hide, and though he held his head proudly in the air, it was obvious that he did so out of respect for his ancestry and not because of any consciousness of his strength. He was of a bay colour and somebody had fired his left hind leg, so clumsily and in such a cruel manner that it appeared to have been done with a red-hot crowbar. The pelt was quite naked of hair and the flesh was singed in streaks.

'Look at that,' said Mr Mullen, pointing to the leg. 'Did ye get him from a tinker, or what?'

'Lord have mercy on yer soul,' said the auctioneer, 'that fellah has a pedigree as long as yer arm. Come here, I'll show ye.'

'Ye needn't bother,' said Mr Mullen. 'What good is a pedigree to a dying man? The Master o' the Hounds might give a few bob for him for the pack.'

Mr Mullen wrinkled up his face in a smile and he looked at the auctioneer with his mouth open. He really wanted the horse because he liked the old fellow's head, but he wanted to get him for next to nothing. The auctioneer also wanted to get rid of him very badly, but still, he wanted to strike a good bargain.

'Now drop the coddin', Mr Mullen,' he said, 'and buy the horse if ye want him. Sure I needn't tell you what a horse is, whether he is a horse or a mule. Man alive, sure a few square meals 'ud change that fellah so much ye wouldn't know him. Look at his . . .'

'Aye,' said Mullen coldly, 'let's have a look at them. I mean at his insides. I bet he's got a smoker's heart and a liver stitched together with the best silk thread. If I buy him, would ye get him carted home for me?'

'I can see it's out for coddin' me ye are,' said the auctioneer, turning to go away.

'Very well,' said Mr Mullen, clearing his throat, 'I'll make ye a offer for him.'

'What's that?' said the auctioneer, halting abruptly and turning around to Mr Mullen.

'I've got thirty bob on me,' said Mullen, contracting his white eyebrows. 'I'll give ye the lot, though it's good money wasted.'

The auctioneer pursed up his lips and stared at Mr Mullen for a few moments as if he were dumb founded.

'D'ye really mean it?' he said.

Mr Mullen nodded.

'Take him home, for God's sake,' said the auctioneer, waving his hands.

Mr Mullen paid for the horse and took him home. He led him along beside his own horse, and it was the devil of a job to keep him in hand. My boy, he had his head in the wind and champed along, rearing and trying to break loose.

'Good Lord,' thought Mr Mullen, 'that fellah is a corker only for his age.'

Mr Mullen went to a party that night and there was heavy drinking. In his cups he began to boast about the old hunter he had bought for thirty shillings. Everybody made fun of him about it, so Mr Mullen boasted that he would ride the old horse to the meet of the Ballyhaggard hounds next day.

'Wait till you see,' he cried. 'I'll leave you all so far behind that I'll have the fox's skin dressed before you arrive.'

Next day Mr Mullen's head was as big as a pot, and when he remembered his boast he was disgusted with himself. But he was a man of his word and he ordered the old hunter to be saddled for him. He drank a considerable amount of raw whiskey and mounted him. Off he went to the meet.

Everybody in the district turns out with the hounds, from Lord Clonmore to Mr Mulligan the butcher of Murren. All sorts of ungainly beasts appear. In fact, Mr Murchison the new Protestant curate once joined, mounted on a cart-horse, which a scoundrel called The Tiger Donnelly sold him as an Irish hunter. Since the war and the revolution all sorts of people have been thrown together in the district, so that, as Mr Mullen says, 'There's no class about anything nowadays.' But when Mr Mullen himself appeared that day on Morrissey, everybody agreed appeared that day on Morrissey, everybody agreed that such an extraordinary animal had never been seen before. It was like a mortally sick man appearing at a wedding, half drunk and insisting on being the most hilarious person present.

'Bravo, Mr Mullen,' said Lord Clonmore. 'The dead have arisen. Eh?'

Everybody laughed and Mr Mullen was mortally insulted, but when the cavalcade set off, by Jove, Morrissey behaved himself marvellously. Like a good thoroughbred of the old school, he showed every ounce that was in him. He cleared the ditches and fences as lightly as those wonderful horses for which the Galway Blazers were famous, fellows that could live for a week on a raw turnip and cross a bog without wetting their fetlocks. Mr Mullen kept refreshing himself now and again with stimulants, and as a consequence rode even more daringly than was his custom; but the old hunter carried him all day without a single stumble, until at last, just before the finish, he arrived at the drain that flows from the workhouse, about a mile outside the town. There is no more filthy or evil-smelling drain in the world. There is no necessity to describe it.

But when Morrissey arrived at this drain at full speed, he stopped dead. Undoubtedly the animal was too well bred to face it. Mr Mullen was pitched over the horse's head and he fell headlong into the stinking place. Several people pulled up, but Mr Mullen crawled out, uninjured. Seeing him, everybody went into hysterics with laughter. He was indescribable, and in fact unrecognisable. Morrissey lowered his head, sniffed at Mr Mullen and set off back at a mad canter.

'It must have turned his stomach,' laughed a red-haired farmer.

'Yer a lot of scoundrels,' shouted Mr Mullen, struggling to his feet and holding out his dripping hands that were as black and sticky as if he had dipped them in tar.

Morrissey was found again and brought back to the stables. Mr Mullen went home and had a bath, and by that time his anger had worn off and he himself was able to laugh at the joke. Next morning he went to look at Morrissey.

The poor animal was quite stiff with his efforts of the previous day. But he still had his head in the air and he whinnied joyfully when he saw Mr Mullen. That softened Mr Mullen's heart towards him.

'Damn it,' he said to the stable boy, 'he's a great old horse. I'll take him down to the shore and give him a dip in the salt water to soften his legs.'

He rode Morrissey down to the strand. It was a fine day, but there was a rather heavy ground-swell and the waves broke on the sand with a thundering noise. This thundering noise and the menacing aspect of the dark green waves, rising suddenly within a few feet of the shore and falling with a thud, terrified the horse. It was impossible to get him to walk in the tide. As last Mr Mullen managed to get him near the surf, when the tide had receded for a particularly long distance, as it does now and again, after a certain number of short waves have broken. Then as the horse was stamping about and snorting, trying to get away from the water, an enormous wave rose suddenly and almost enveloped him. Instead of trying to rush backward, he was so confused by the rush of water under his stomach that he plunged out to sea. Mr Mullen tried to head him off, but it was no use. Presently another equally large wave arose, passed right over the horse and the rider, so that they both turned a somersault. Mr Mullen was thrown from the saddle and he became entangled somehow in the horse's legs. When he came to the surface, after having saved himself, the horse was five yards away and Mr Mullen was in deep water. He swam a few strokes, struck ground and then looked behind him. There was the horse, swimming mightily out towards the open sea.

'God Almighty!' cried Mr Mullen. 'With ten pounds of a saddle on him.'

Mr Mullen dashed up on to the strand and began to call some boatmen that were there. They ran over to him.

'Hey,' he cried, 'if he drowns, will he sink or float?'

'God save us,' they cried, 'who are ye talkin' about?'

'My horse, damn it,' cried Mr Mullen; 'he's gone out to sea. Don't ye see him? Look.'

'Aw, snakes alive,' they said, when they saw the dark object, heaving along sideways, like an unwieldy porpoise.

'He'll float sure enough,' said one man, 'with the water he'll swallow.'

'All right, then,' said Mr Mullen, 'get me a boat. I want to save the saddle. The horse isn't worth his keep, but the saddle is worth money. Get a boat for me.'

They rushed down a boat and put to sea after the horse. When they had gone out almost half a mile, they met the horse swimming back towards them.

'There he is,' cried one boatman.

'He's floatin' sure enough,' said Mr Mullen. 'Get alongside him and get the saddle.'

'It's not floatin' he is but swimmin' like a warrior,' said the boatman.

'God!' said Mr Mullen.

They were all amazed and they lay on their oars, as Morrissey swept past them towards the beach, going at a terrific pace. They followed him, and when they reached the strand, Morrissey was standing there, shivering and exhausted. Mr Mullen took off his hat and struck his forehead.

'Well, that horse beats all I ever saw,' he said. 'Here. I'll buy a bottle of whiskey over this. Come on, men.'

After that Mr Mullen and the horse that went to sea became quite famous in the district. So that Mr Mullen grew fond of the horse and he kept him all that winter in his stables with plenty of food. But he made no attempt to ride him, and although the fame of the horse spread afar, still nobody made an offer for him. Because even though he was famous for having swam a mile out to sea and then swam back again, he was also famous for having thrown Mr Mullen into the workhouse drain.

Then in the following April another extraordinary thing happened to the horse. I must say that he had improved considerably during the winter. He had fattened a great deal and his hide was becoming almost glossy. The mark on his hind leg was not so outrageous, and to an ordinary person he seemed a perfectly sound horse. But to a horseman he was still an old crock. One of those game old things, whether they are old colonels who insist on wearing tight waists in their seventieth year, or old horses or old battered fighting cocks that take a step ferociously and then glare, wagging their chaps aggressively as if they were in the prime of their lives, — I say, he was one of those game old things that make a virtue of looking fit even when they might be excused drooping their heads and lying down to die. But all the buyers admired him and left him alone. Then Mr Stanley Edwards came to the town.

Mr Edwards might be called a crock as well as the old hunter. He spent a greater part of each year in a nursing home. The remainder of the year he spent in the pursuit of extravagant pleasures, not always very well considered. His money was tied up in this country, otherwise it is very probable that he would never spend a week in it. But when he had done a great bout in London, he always had to return to Ireland to get some more money. After one of those bouts and a month in hospital, he engaged a villa in Ballyhaggard to take the sea air. A few days after his arrival in the town he came to Mr Mullen. Mr Mullen looked him up and down, rather surprised that such a weakling should come to him for anything.

'Well,' he said, 'what could I do for you?'

'Look here,' said Mr Edwards, 'I have to live for a few months in this ghastly place. I'm sick and I have very little money. I have been here three days and I'm quite fed up with walking up and down the shore and talking to the lunatics around here. I want a horse. Can you get me one?'

'Let me see,' said Mr Mullen, looking at him shrewdly, 'you'd want a quiet horse, I suppose?'

'I want a horse,' said Mr Edwards pettishly. 'It doesn't matter what he is. If he breaks my neck it might be a jolly good idea.'

'I see,' said Mr Mullen. 'I think I've got the very thing that'll suit you.'

'Oh! Look here,' said Mr Edwards rather nervously. 'I don't mean I want some . . . eh . . . crazy thing. You know . . . a . . . oh, well . . .'

'You leave it to me,' said Mr Mullen. 'You can try him out before you buy him.'

Morrissey was brought out and Mr Edwards immediately mounted him and trotted off. Mr Edwards looked a very poor figure on horseback. Some wit said that he was born to be a rag-picker, because his gaunt frame went like a willow rod and his nose was so long that he could use it in the same way that an elephant uses the tip of his trunk. But such a slight weight suited the old horse and he went off very gallantly indeed, with that twirl in his right hind leg, which is a sign of old age in a horse and which warns off the cunning buyer but which is very attractive; like the smart twirl of the spurred boot which tells the swagger cavalry officer.

Mr Mullen looked after the horse, scratching his chin and thinking that he would be very glad to accept a five-pound note for him.

After an hour, Mr Edwards returned, perspiring but looking very happy. A good hour's trotting on a well-bred horse on a fine spring morning would make a corpse almost come to life again.

'Go all right?' said Mr Mullen, smiling his most engaging smile.

'Splendid,' said Mr Edwards, sitting the horse and wiping his forehead, as if he were loath to dismount. 'How much do you want for him?'

'I'll take thirty pounds at a pinch,' said Mr Mullen, after a moment's apparent thought and looking at Mr Edwards as if he were going to do him a favour, which, however, gave him a great deal of pain.

'Oh!' said Mr Edwards, a little surprised.

Then he dismounted and looked curiously at Mr Mullen.

'It's a lot,' he said.

'Oh! Well,' said Mr Mullen, making a gesture with his hands, 'a horse isn't a bicycle.'

'Quite,' said Mr Edwards. 'Now, let me see.'

He walked around the horse and passed his hand over the horse's body in various places. Mr Mullen was very glad to see that he touched the wrong places. Then Mr Edwards stood at a distance from the horse and looked at him. He seemed very loath to leave him. Mr Mullen began to feel very comfortable.

'Look here,' said Mr Edwards at length, 'I'll come back tomorrow and have another ride. May I?'

'Why, certainly,' said Mr Mullen affably. 'You can have a look at his pedigree now if you like.'

'Oh, has he got a pedigree?' said Mr Edwards.

'Lord, yes,' said Mr Mullen, 'yards of it.'

Here it must be stated, that although Mr Edwards was a wealthy country gentleman, he kept motor-cars instead of horses and knew nothing about the animals except on race-courses. So that a pedigree seemed to him as good a guarantee of perfection as the maker's name on a Rolls-Royce.

'Let's have a look at it,' he said.

Mr Mullen produced the pedigree and Mr Edwards inspected it.

'In that case,' he said, 'I'll buy the horse right away.'

'It's like taking milk from a child,' thought Mr Mullen, as Mr Edwards wrote out the cheque.

Everybody expected Mr Edwards to break his neck, and some people said the Mr Mullen played rather a scurvy trick on the poor fellow, but during the whole of that summer the horse was seen on the roads almost every day, trotting along in the pink of condition. And what was more, Mr Edwards became quite a new man. Whether it was the sea air or the riding that did it, he regained his health to an extraordinary extent. He did not become robust, but he was no longer an invalid and he led a decent healthy life. In fact, just before he went away, he came to Mr Mullen and said: 'Look here, Mr Mullen, you've saved my life.'

'Glad to hear it,' said Mr Mullen, without winking an eye.

In September Mr Edwards left the district, but instead of going to England, as was his custom, he returned to his property in County Kilkenny. Nothing more was heard of him or of the horse for two years. And then two months ago I met Mr Mullen in Dublin. We were having a drink together and talking about various things, when he suddenly gripped my arm and said:

'D'ye remember that horse, Morrissey, I had, the fellah that threw me into the drain?'

I nodded.

'Ye remember I sold him to a chap called Edwards from Kilkenny. Well, I've just been down there to a show. Met him there. He's still got the horse, going as strong as a three-year-old and . . . d'ye know what I'm going to tell ye? That horse saved his life, as he said himself. When I asked him about the horse he said: "I wouldn't part with that horse for a thousand. I haven't left this district since I saw you last, and I can drink two bottles of port now after dinner without turning a hair."'

So that, indeed, it seems that there IS something in a pedigree.

OFFERINGS

The parish priest stood within the door reading his breviary. But although he was reading and moving his lips in prayer, one of his eyes undoubtedly watched the little table that rested against the whitewashed humpy wall to the left of the door. There was a small, white, stiff, linen cloth, like a big napkin chequered with rigid creases, spread on the little table. No. It was not a table really. The home was too poor to have a table. There were only deal forms, painted red, in the house, and little three-legged green stools. So an orange-box had been placed on a stool and the priest had brought a napkin in his overcoat pocket. It was the priest's stiffly ironed napkin.

The priest was very big and his black overcoat was unbuttoned, hanging loosely about his august frame. What was he reading in his little black book?

The only other person in the kitchen was Paddy Lenehan, whose daughter they were burying. She was his only child. But she died young, just four years old. It was not really, they thought, a cause for sorrow, because they go straight to heaven at that age. And where there is not enough food, even to feed two mouths, is not the good God kind to take a third mouth out of the hungry world into the joy of Paradise? So they said at the wake, the people of the village, to the mother whose tearless eyes stared fixedly at the dead body of her treasured one. Although life had fled, the tangled red curls of the dead child still lived and shimmered in the candlelight.

It was very funny the way the people came in one by one, glanced around them sheepishly, looked at the praying priest from under their reverently lowered eyelids, curtsied to him and then placed their offerings on the table. It was very funny the way some of them gripped the coin lovingly in their thick fingers, hesitated a moment and then dropped it, grudgingly, with the rest, on the rigidly creased napkin. They curtsied to the door of the bedroom in which the dead was already coffined. Then they went out and others entered. It was very funny the way the priest's eye stole round and watched them drop the coin, a shilling, a florin, half a crown for near relations. He could afford more that man. The offerings were made in order that masses might be said for the repose of the soul of little Eileen Lenehan.

Paddy Lenehan watched each offering as eagerly as the priest. It was an insult to him if somebody offered a shilling instead of two. He was not thinking of whether a mass more or less might be said for the dead. But, you know, it is a custom, a measure of a man's social importance; if the offerings are large he is important; if the offerings are small it is an insult. What of the dead and of the house in which there was no table, nor enough food to feed three mouths? What of the tearless mother who still sat by the nailed coffin in the room? Paddy Lenehan did not think of that. Life does not end with the death of one. There are others who live on and they have customs and a common code of conduct that must be observed.

And as the people entered, dropped their coins and departed, Lenehan watched the coins and thought of other things. How kind Charley Manion, the publican, had been! You know, there is some good in every man. Lenehan was working in the village when the news was brought to him that Eileen was dead. Lenehan had been idle for many months. He just got a job from Carmody, the road contractor, to break stones for the mending of the road. And when he heard the news he crossed himself and said: 'Lord God! Isn't this a way to be? I haven't a halfpenny to buy a drop of drink for the wake, not to mind the pound to give the priest for saying Mass in the house. And where will I get pipes and tobacco?' But when he went to Charley Manion and told him about it, Charley Manion said without looking at him: 'Roll away that barrel of porter. Ye can pay me any time.' And Mr Tierney gave him pipes and tobacco on credit. And his uncle lent him a pound. Of course that would all have to be paid out of the money the pigs would fetch. But isn't anything better than to be disgraced before the eyes of all the people?

He thought of Eileen took, but in a detached way. She had gone out barefooted to turn stray sheep off the Red Crag. A shower of hailstones caught her. She came home with a chill. Next day she had pneumonia. They didn't get a doctor because he was too busy with an epidemic of typhoid in the village of Carramor. Next day she was dead. It's funny the way they die suddenly that way. Everything seemed to be very queer and very funny to Lenehan. And indeed he thought it was funny the way the priest stood that way pretending to read his little black book. He and his stiffly creased napkin. Lenehan would make a joke about it. People laughed at his jokes. He was a wit. When a man is very, very poor and life is very, very miserable, it is a nice thing to be a wit. He could get drinks in public-houses for his jokes.

Fewer people came now with their offerings. Only a stray person now and again. The priest's eye wandered more often. At last he coughed and looked out of the door. Outside people were sitting on stone walls and Paddy Lenehan's brother Michael was going around with a bucket. He had three mugs. He dipped the mugs into the bucket and offered the porter to the people. Most of them closed their throats and spat before they drank. It was very funny.

When the priest moved and looked out Lenehan's face assumed a fawning expression. He curtsied with his left knee and made a slight, subservient movement towards the priest, like a waiter. Did he want something? No; the priest did not look at Lenehan. Gloomily, his eyes sought his little black book once more. Another man approached the door, and entered. He curtsied and dropped a coin. He curtsied to the hidden dead child and departed.

That was the lot. At last the priest closed his book and put it into his pocket. Lenehan approached the table with him. Another man came in. They began to count the money. The priest counted it. As the priest counted, Lenehan thought that it would be better to give himself that money to pay for the burial. He bit his lip and hated the priest; just for a moment. Then again he thought it was very funny; he was a wit, you know.

There was a total of seven pounds fifteen shillings.

The priest had just counted the money on the napkin, using one hand only. When he had finished he took his other hand out of his pocket. He seized the corners of the napkin, folded it up loosely, so that the money was in the centre. Then he twisted the ends into a loose knot; just the way workmen carry food in a handkerchief.

He stuffed the napkin carelessly into his pocket.

THE JEALOUS HENS

Mrs Geraghty's aunt gave her a black hen as a birthday present. Mrs Geraghty put the black hen into the little yard where she kept her six other hens and one cock. She was just beginning to collect a fowl-run.

The arrival of the black hen caused a great sensation in the yard. When she was dropped on to the hard gravel-strewn floor of the yard she lay on her belly, with her head thrust out sideways and her large, fat, crimson gills touching the dust. Her legs had been tied together with string for the past three hours, while she journeyed in Mr Geraghty's trap, and she was dazed and crippled. At least, she pretended to be crippled and lay very still.

She was, however, very interested in the six hens who came running up from all quarters as soon as they saw her, with their heads reaching out and their legs kicking the air behind, as it were, just as if they were swimming. They made little clucking sounds to one another as they ran. They were all of a reddish colour, and not very large.

Behind them came a great big iron-grey cock, with long yellow legs and bright spurs. He walked, making angry noises, like an old army officer complaining about something to an inferior. Now and again he ran two or three steps. Then he broke again into a walk, winked an eye, shook his feathers, and tried to pull his head out of his neck, so to speak. At last he arrived at the spot where his six little reddish wives were gathered round about the big black hen that had just arrived.

When the black hen saw the cock out of the corner of her eye, she raised herself slightly, staggered forward, and then got to her feet. She shook one leg and then another. She made various little strained movements, as if trying to find out whether any limbs were broken. Then she shook herself fiercely pecked three times at her breast, and drew herself up to her full height. She was a beautiful black hen, with crimson gills and wonderful long yellow legs. Her breast-feathers were so black that they had a greenish shimmer in them, like a polish.

With a great hoarse cluck, like a guffaw, the cock drew himself up to his full height and shook his gills. Then he scraped the earth furiously, using one leg at a time. The hen took no notice. Then he let his wings hang down, he put his beak to the ground, and he ran around the black hen, clucking amorously. The black hen remained totally indifferent, but the other hens began to put their heads together sideways and made sinister little noises, as if they were whispering maliciously. They shut and opened their little eyes in a peculiar manner.

Then the cock suddenly stopped running. He drew himself up, and made an angry, irritated noise in this throat. The little hens stopped and looked at him. Uttering another grunt, the cock rushed among the little hens and scattered them in all directions, jumping on them with his spurs as if he were kicking them ignominiously. Screaming, they fled to different corners of the yard, running on one side, like motor-cars going at a great speed around a sharp corner. The cock scratched his breast carelessly. Then he shook himself arrogantly and turned to the black hen. With his beak to the ground he went over to her quickly, and said something in a confidential, intimate tone. The black hen seemed to assent, for she put her beak daintily within an inch of the ground, with her neck strained forward, and waited. The cock picked up a grain of corn and planted it, with a gentle cluck, in front of her beak. She took it in her beak sharply, and then meditated a second before she swallowed it. Then they both walked off together in a friendly fashion, scraping and clucking. Now and again the cock trailed his wings and ran about the black hen, clucking amorously. She graciously accepted his advances. Situated in a corner of the yard, near the roost, the other hens watched, amazed and jealous.

All through the evening the cock remained devoted to the black hen, and never once did he take any notice of the other hens, except to chase them away when they happened to come near, or when he heard their sinister little whines at a distance. The six little hens went off their food completely and spent the whole evening planning something or other, with their heads close together, standing on one leg. Then night fell, and they all went to roost. The black hen went to roost beside the cock.

But she did not get much rest all night. All night long the other hens kept pecking at her, pushing against her, scratching at her, and doing all in their power to make things uncomfortable for her. The cock did his best to terrorise them and maintain order, but in the darkness of the roost they were not afraid of him. Further, he was too sleepy, and after a while he fell asleep, leaving the black hen completely at the mercy of the little red ones.

In the morning the black hen was not so beautiful as she had been when she arrived. Her feathers were ruffled and tangled, and some of them were almost pulled out of their sockets, so that they stuck out here and there like overgrowths, in an ugly manner. And she was terrified and lonely, so that she walked timorously and without the elegant swagger of the previous day. However, the cock again resumed his intimacy with her, and paid not the slightest heed to the other hens.

The day was warm and sunny. As it progressed the black hen regained her confidence and her strength. She arranged her feathers beautifully and plucked out the ones that had been loosened. She fed assiduously and became so conceited and arrogant that towards evening she took part in some of the raids that the cock made on the other hens. But roosting-time came again, and she flew to her perch trembling with fear.

Next morning she was almost senseless. Her skin was black and punctured in scores of places. Hundreds of her feathers had been torn out. One of her eyes was closed, on account of a blow from another hen's claws. When she came down from her perch she was so weak that she could hardly stand. She kept staggering about. The cock fussed about her, but it was plain that instead of feeling pity for her he was disgusted with her for being in such a disreputable condition. And after half an hour or so, he deliberately went off clucking and scraping and shaking himself, probably in order to hide his confusion, and made advances to the other hens. They accepted him just as if nothing had happened.

When Mrs Geraghty came with the morning's food she uttered an exclamation when she saw the condition of the black hen. Then she laughed outright when she understood what had happened. She herself was a plain woman.

'I'll have to give her to Mrs O'Reilly,' she said, putting the black hen under her arm.

THE FIREMAN'S DEATH

Eight bells tolled slowly in the engine room. He marched down the iron ladder into the stokehold. The others marched rapidly in front of him, their light-shod feet pattering, their covered left hands rushing along the hot rails with a slipping sound. His feet stumbled heavily down. His hand trembled on the rail.

He was sick. He should be in bed. But he had been a fireman for twelve years without missing a watch. His pride said: 'Die before your fires rather than let a fellow-worker shed his body's sweat for you.'

When he landed in the stokehold the hot fumes struck him in the chest. He gasped, caught his eyes with his fists and staggered. His stomach muscles contracted. They crowded around him in pity, urging him to go back to his bunk. He straightened himself fiercely and thrust them away with a swinging movements of his arms. 'I'd die sooner than that,' he growled.

He marched to the fires. His thin outward-curving calves were visible passing the bright glow from the ashpits of the furnaces. His tall, slim body and his bony head were hidden in the gloom.

The retiring watch went up the ladder to the deck. Their faces were black. Their eyes were white. Their sodden trousers clung to their sweating thighs. They went up the ladder groaning curses on the sea, the fires, God, and the rich men who make slaves toil in the bowels of ships.

It was very dark. Ashes and coal-dust floated in a thick mass through the sluggish air. The electric lights glimmered like dim candles. The bulky forms of the boilers loomed out of the darkness. The engines thudded. A dull volcanic murmur came from the hidden fires.

He stripped before his fires and put his sweat-rag in his belt. Then he seized the long swaying rake to clean his low fire. He opened his furnace door. His body flashed into the firelight. He was naked to the waist. The ribs rose in ridges on his fleshless breast. The skin lay taut along his protruding jaws. His eye sockets were black. His biceps were rugged knots interlaced with sickly blue veins.

He stooped forward and thrust in the rake. A wave of heat emerged, striking him in the face. He reeled before it for a moment. Then he made a great effort and stood erect. A cold sweat poured out all over his body. That terrified him. Had the others seen? He looked cautiously. They were working furiously. They had not seen. Good.

He swore a blasphemous oath and muttered to himself: 'I'm not going to give in.' He hauled out the red-hot ashes and the jagged cakes of spent coal that clung like glue to the fire-bars. He finished one side. He changed over the live coals from the other side. He cleaned the other side. All finished. He handed the shovel to the trimmer to coal the bars. Then he walked stiffly to the ventilator.

God! Not a breath of wind came down the dusty gaping tube from the sun-baked deck. His lungs strained like inflated bladders to catch the hot air that struggled down his parched throat slowly.

And there was a great inward heaving of his sides like the panting of a tired horse.

His whole body murmured: 'Water, water, water.' But his fierce mind would not listen to the cry. He must feed the fires.

Suddenly his head seemed to whirl round and round. Madness seized him. He wrinkled up his mouth and nose. Then he laughed harshly. Rasping sounds filled the stokehold, furnace doors opening, shovels grating along the iron deck, black coal being shot in among the licking flames. It was the madness of conflict. His weakness vanished. He dashed at his shovel, seized it, spat and opened the door of his right-hand fire. 'Give it to her boys,' yelled the pot-bellied engineer, as he rushed into the stokehold. 'Steam is falling. Steam is falling. Give her a shake.'

The great fires roared and shot out whirling shafts of yellow flame to meet each shovelful of black coal that was hurled into them. He talked wildly to the fires as he hurled in the coal. He called them foul names and put out his tongue at them. He glared at them and hurled himself at them savagely. They had been his enemies for twelve years. He piled coal on them, more, more, until he smothered them under a black glistening mound. Their vast roar was submerged beneath the already reddening black mound. Then he dropped his shovel again and stepped away.

Ha! There was strength in him still.

But what was this? He could not hear. Not a sound. And everything was dim. Somebody was standing in front of him making a noise. He gripped his eyes and peered. He saw a mouth wide open and moving, spitting black coal-dust from its blood-red tongue as it spoke. That was the bloody Irishman from the starboard boiler. Telling him he looked like a corpse and should go on deck. By the slippery heels of the bald-headed Chilian deck-swabber! He ground his teeth and mustered all his strength. 'Leave me alone,' he yelled. 'I'm a Glasgow fireman and I never give in. And I NEVER will. Leave me alone.'

His voice ended in a shriek.

He groped for the slice. His hands clawed at it blindly, for he could see nothing in the gloom. The long thick iron bar swung towards him as he pulled at it. It pushed against his shoulder and he staggered back three paces. 'Steady on,' he muttered. He crouched and raised it, trembling all over. Then he groped to the fires. He opened the door and thrust the wedge-shaped point of the slice at the base of the mound. He ran it along the bars to the very end. Then he drew himself together. He must lift that mound and break it in the middle, in order to give air to the flames. He jumped with a loud gasp and landed crosswise, face downwards, on the slice, his two hands clenching the slice against his hollowed stomach. He lost conscious-ness. A terrific pain ran from his stomach to his head, making all his body numb. But his brain still thought of the fire and the mound that must be broken. It was not broken. The slice had not left the bars. It was not broken. It had merely bent slightly downwards from the middle to the end, under the impact of his body. His feet reached for the deck. He stood erect. He moved backwards two paces slowly, crouching low, all his sinews rigid, his eyeballs protruding.

Then uttering a savage yell, he jumped again on the slice. He landed once more upon it crosswise, his two hands clenching it against his hollowed stomach. The slice rose by the head. The mound broke. A huge scar appeared. Then flames shot out. With a roar they covered the mound and whirled about the door, licking the air and darting out along the slice towards the hanging body of the fireman.

He did not move. His body hung limply across the slice. His toes almost tipped the deck. His eyes were fixed. His lips were white. He was dead.

STONEY BATTER

In our part of the country the old custom of 'Confessions' still survives. Twice a year the priests visit each village in the parish. Mass is said in one house in each village and all the villagers gather into that house to hear Mass and confess their sins. The appointed house in each village undergoes a thorough cleansing and renovating prior to the visit; so that, indeed, apart from the spiritual benefits accruing from it, the custom is a very good one from a sanitary point of view. As the average number of houses in each village is twenty, each house is thoroughly cleansed once every ten years. Otherwise perhaps they might never get cleansed.

In our village there were twenty-four houses, so that twelve years passed before a house was visited a second time. During that time it was only reasonable to expect that the unvisited houses would become very disreputable. But our village was an exemplary one. The inhabitants were proud of keeping their houses in good order, and of their own free will they had a house-cleaning every Xmas. All except Stoney Batter.

Stoney Batter's house was again chosen by Divine Providence after a respite of twelve years to receive His servants. Since the last visit Stoney Batter's wife had died, leaving him a widower with three grown-up sons, whom he immediately advised to go to America as he had nothing to give them and they were now old enough to provide for themselves. They all went away, one after the other, and were never again heard of, as far as I know. Stoney was left alone in the house, and, of course, when there is no woman in the house it becomes disreputable. Had the wife lived it might have been just as bad. I don't remember what it looked like in her lifetime, but I know that she was reputed to be a thorough slattern; one of those large, healthy, easy-going women with prominent hips, who have an amazing faculty for surrounding themselves with sloppiness and who go around their yard with the tongues of their boots hanging out. But bad as she was, the house was to the dogs altogether after her death of a surfeit of colcannon.

Stoney Batter (his real name was Michael Feeney) had a small plot of land, but he never tilled it or took any notice of it whatsoever. On the land a very thin horse grazed and an equally thin cow, which Stoney's brother Peter milked, brought to the bull and otherwise utilised for his own profit, in exchange for vegetables, dried fish and other necessary foodstuffs which he supplied to Stoney. The brother also used the horse and the grazing, although Stoney very often rode the horse into the town and came back again on her, after a day or maybe two days, with his hands clasped around her neck, in a delicious state of intoxication. The only mercenary occupation he allowed himself was the purchase of a few young piglings now and again. But having bought the pigs he allowed them to forage for themselves around the village. They always grew up wild and hairy, devouring every refuse they came across; indeed, very often when a peasant woman went to the well leaving her door open in order to let the fire have a draught, she found on her return that Stoney Batter's pigs had entered her kitchen, torn up all the old clothes that were hanging on the back door and perhaps gulped down the little sack of flour which she had placed on a bench by the fire to keep it from getting damp. These pigs were always, or nearly always, seized by publicans as payments for Stoney's drinking debts.

In the face of all this, it might appear that Stoney was a thoroughly out-rageous scoundrel, but he was looked upon as a hero in our village and over the whole parish. When I was a child and he was still forty something and in the prime of his life, a huge soft man, with laughing black eyes and a brown beard that looked like a furry hames around his neck, with his red alcoholic round chin sticking out, always clean-shaven, I thought that it should be every-body's ambition in life to grow up and live like Stoney Batter.

However, when the time for 'Confessions' arrived this particular autumn and the village realised that Stoney was to be honoured by the sacred visit, everybody was scandalised. The parish priest announced the itinerary from the altar of the parish church on Sunday. A crowd of the villagers gathered outside Stoney's house after Mass discussing what should be done about cleaning the house. They were very wild about it, being, of course, a very respectable number of people, as all peasants are in our part of the country, God-fearing, upright, with a terrific *amour-propre*. They stood in the road outside, abusing Stoney Batter.

The house looked a complete wreck. It had not been thatched for years. In places the old thatch had formed a black mould and all sorts of weeds and grasses grew out of this mould, so that the roof of the house looked like a deserted garden-patch, spotted here and there with wild and useless verdure, while in other places it was barren, as if even weeds could not grow on it. The walls were still worse. The loose mortar had fallen off the stones with which it had been built. The stones were quite naked, large boulders in parts and then tiny little stones in other parts. The walls had originally been whitewashed, but the whitewash had turned green with the constant dripping from the eaves. Then the sun dried the green a yellowish colour. The previous year Stoney had a maudlin fit of drunken remorse and he decided to whitewash the house and lead a better life perhaps. But he didn't do very much, just a few heavy splashes of the brush to the left of the door. This white patch beside the door looked still dirtier and more unseemly than the rest of the wall. The yard was in the same condition of dirt and decay, and it had hardly any fence, just an irregular low mound of stones, where the fence had fallen.

While the crowd was looking at the house and wondering what should be done, Stoney's brother Peter arrived. He was a very respectable man, the most respectable man in the village, but I always hated him. He was a typical bourgeois, or the father of one, the sort of peasant root from which the bourgeois grows. He had a finger in all sorts of little undertakings, from keeping the village road in order to collecting the 'Oats money' for the curate on commission. He bought fish for the buyers and he bought pigs for the jobbers, and he always made a little on these transactions, just a very little of course, but he hoarded it carefully, and with this money he sent his two sons to Dublin to become apprenticed to the 'licensed trade.' One of them is now a publican. He wore a starched white linen shirt every day in the week, but without a collar or tie and with a bright yellow stud which bumped against his prominent Adam's apple. He had a very long, lean figure and he walked with his hands behind his back, taking long, slow strides carefully, as if he were stepping to avoid puddles. When anybody addressed him he turned his head swiftly and said 'Uh!'

When Peter arrived on the road outside the house he turned to the crowd angrily and said: 'I'm going to look after this.' Then he strode in through the yard and the crowd began to murmur among themselves and scatter.

Peter lifted the latch of the door and entered the kitchen. There was nobody there. There was hardly any furniture. In fact, there seemed to be nothing there but a smell. This was the smell of burnt peat and another smell of mustiness that one gets in a room that is never ventilated and that is shut up for a long time, so that the dust and the air and the material of the walls, floor and woodwork mingle into a combined odour that is very hard to describe and can only be felt. But even though it is hard to describe, it is a very positive and definite odour, or atmosphere, and I have even noticed it about the persons of members of the societies that root up old forts and churches about the country.

'Michael,' cried Peter angrily. He always called his brother by his given name.

There was a silence for a moment and then a rumbling noise was heard from the room to the right of the kitchen. This rumbling noise soon developed into a hoarse cough and somebody finally cleared his throat with a tremendous noise.

'Heh, heh,' came Stoney's voice at last. 'Now, what the devil . . . well now . . . oh, well now . . . who would that be, I wonder. . . . I say . . . who is shouting?'

'It's me,' cried Peter. 'Get up outa that. God Almighty is it in bed ye are at this hour of God's own Sunday?'

'Oh! Is it yerself that's in it?' came Stoney's soft, loud voice. 'Begob yer welcome, Peter.' There was a slight pause and then the sound of scratching. 'Heh! Did ye bring us a drink — eh?'

'Get up outa that,' snapped Peter. 'Come down at once. I want to talk to ye.'

'Oh! Begob,' said Stoney calmly. 'Tare an' ages, haven't I the head on me like a boiling pot. Heh!' Another pause and then the sound of a yawn. 'Eh, have ye e'er a chew o' tobacco, Peter?'

Peter did not reply. He strode to the fireplace and sat down on the edge of a three-legged stool. Stoney could be heard letting himself out of bed and groaning as he did so.

'Is it a . . . oh, me head . . . a . . . eh . . . fine mornin', Peter?'

There was no reply.

'Silence is consent,' said Stoney. 'Eh. I'll never touch a drop again. But Patcheen Tom met me last night . . . ugh . . . an' he comin' home with a new heifer he bought, an' o' course . . . oh, well . . . was I ever tellin' ye, Peter, about that cousin o' yer wife's that went to look for a woman in Dunliosa?'

'Hurry up,' growled Peter.

'Yerra what hurry are ye in?' cried Stoney heartily. 'Now, what's yer trouble anyway? Is it the old horse is dead — eh?'

While he was speaking he appeared from the room, buttoning up his trousers, with his braces trailing behind his bare feet and his shirt open on his hairy chest. He stopped in the doorway and screwed up his humorous eyes to look at his brother. Peter glared at him with his mouth open.

'Sit down,' said Peter.

'It's not the horse, then?' said Stoney, sitting on another stool.

'Who said anything about a horse?' said Peter.

'It's the 'Confessions' that'll be in yer house a fortnight from tomorrow!'

'Oh! Hell to yer soul,' cried Stoney, crossing himself. 'Is it coddin' me ye are?'

'There's no coddin' about it,' said Peter. 'Yer a disgrace to me name an' to the whole parish. Look at the house ye have to receive a priest.

'Oh! God help me, what am I goin' to do?' wailed Stoney.

'Yer to clean out yer dirty house an' get ready.'

'But sure ye know well I haven't a stiver.

'D'ye expect me to do it for ye, then?'

'Well, sure . . . ye have me grazin' an' me cow an' the use o' me horse.'

'Don't I feed ye for it? Isn't that our bargain?'

There was silence for a moment. Then Stoney broke out:

'Here. I'll give ye the place an' the land an' everything. I'll sign it down to ye before the parish priest, only . . . only put the house in a fit condition for . . .'

They began to argue for a long time. Although Peter had long been waiting for this opportunity to get hold of his brother's land, he now pretended that he didn't want it all; but at last the bargain was made and Peter departed. Stoney went back to bed again.

Next day Peter hired a woman called Louisa Derrane to do the cleaning, while he himself ordered the necessary linen and furniture in the town, that is, all that he could not lend from his own house. The following day Louisa Derrane arrived in the village.

Louisa Derrane lived in the town. She was a rather handsome woman but a generous woman, with a weakness for the male sex. She had been married to a soldier who got killed in the Boer War, and somehow or other she drifted into an immoral life. She wasn't exactly an outcast, because the best people in the parish hired her to do washing and char-work for them, but she had already two illegitimate children. The authorities did not condemn her for this because the father of both children was a highly respected land-owner in our district. But the children had been taken from her and Mr — had them brought up in some home or other at his own expense. The parish priest had made this arrangement of course. That was seven years before the time of this story, and since then Louisa had been either lucky or on her good behaviour. She had a little house in the town and she was quite com-fortable, because she was always working and earning money.

Of course, when she came to our village to renovate Stoney's house, she went to live in Peter's house, as she couldn't go back and forth to the town every day (it was eight miles away over a mountain), and it was unthinkable that she could be let live with Stoney. But even so, she was alone with Stoney all day, and the village women immediately began to talk about it. And . . .

Here it is best to skip over a period of eight months. I have no definite knowledge of what happened myself. All I know is, that the house was in perfect order for the 'Confessions' and that Stoney himself received the Blessed Sacrament and that he went to Mass every Sunday for two months afterwards. Everybody thought that he was going to lead a better life and he wore a mournful expression. But he gradually broke back again into his old ways and became the same happy old reprobate. The tongues of the village women ceased to wag and everybody had forgotten the fortnight Louisa Derrane had spent in the village.

Then after eight months Louisa came to the village again. She came over the crags at nightfall and without by your leave entered Stoney's house. Stoney happened to be at home, whether by appointment or not it is hard to say. As soon as Louisa entered they immediately got at one another's throats.

'Now,' she cried, 'what are ye goin' to do about it?'

Stoney was sitting by the fire warming his shins.

'Sit down, woman alive,' he said calmly. 'Take off yer shawl an' warm yersel'.'

'What are ye goin' to do about it?' she cried again, menacing him with her hands.

'I told ye before,' said Stoney, closing one eye and screwing up his face, 'that ye can't get wool off a goat.'

'God Almighty!' moaned Louisa. 'Look at me an' the state I am in, a respectable woman, be the likes o' ye.'

'Now sit down,' said Stoney. 'Then we'll talk it out. There's no use in jig-actin', Louisa. Sure things like these are happenin' every day, an' didn't the good God put us into the world to . . . there now. Now listen to me.'

Louisa sat down by the fire, staring at him angrily.

'Now yer blamin' me,' said Stoney shrewdly, 'but how do I know?'

'How d'ye know what?' said Louisa.

'Sure weren't ye sleeping in Peter's house?'

'Oh! Ye —'

'Now whist, whist, woman,' said Stoney. 'Now wait till I tell ye. I told ye before I have nothin'. Ye can get nothin' outa me. Begob, I can get nothin' outa mesel' for mesel', if ye prefer it that way. But Peter now . . . There's a man for ye that's got more money in the bank that ye could empty out with a spade in a day's work. Blame him for it.'

'Is it to blame Peter yer askin' me?' cried Louisa indignantly.

'O' course,' said Stoney calmly. 'What else? Weren't ye sleeping in his house?'

'Yerrah who'd believe me?'

'Foo, woman! Sure everybody'd believe ye.'

'It's in jail they'd put me.'

'Arrah sorra jail ye'd get. Haven't ye all the evidence? An' how do I know anyway but it was he did it? Will ye tell me that now?'

They argued for a long time and at last Stoney won. For of course it was clear to the woman that she could get nothing out of Stoney, except that she might compel him to marry her. But what good would that be to her? A lazy fellow who had handed over his property to his brother. She left the house and went to Peter's house.

Then there was an uproar, the like of which was never seen in the village before, since old Sheila Clogherty was arrested for opening her husband's skull with a hatchet. A great din was heard in Peter's house, and after half an hour or so Peter emerged from the house with the handle of a spade in his hand, followed by Louisa. The whole village gathered, as if they had been precisely waiting by the hearths to rush forth. Peter came into his brother's yard and stood there brandishing his spade and blaspheming, as he had never been heard to do before, while Louisa danced around him, dragging her shawl in the mud and shouting:

'Ye done it, ye hypocrite. Deny it now, ye shamefaced old rascal. It's in yer eye the truth, is ye son o' wickedness. Look at me an' the state I'm in with yer villainy.'

'Come out o' yer house, Stoney Batter,' screamed Peter. 'Ye robber! Ye reprobate! Ye scoundrel! Come out till I murder ye where ye stand.'

Stoney didn't budge until the village people came up in a body and seized Peter. It was then fairly dark. When they were dragging him away and he was well secured among them, Stoney's door opened and Stoney himself appeared, stripped to the waist and with a cudgel of some sort in his hand.

'Let me at him,' he cried, 'till I bate the rascal to the marrow of his bones. Ho! The ruffian! Is it rapin' and honest woman he's been, instead of attending to his wife. Oh! The disgrace to me name that he is.'

He rushed up, making a great show of fight, and a few more had to hold him and bring him back to his house. And there the matter ended for the night. But of course the parish priest arrived on the scene the following morning. When he arrived Peter's wife had left, bringing with her her two daughters. She went off to her father's house. The whole village was in an uproar and in spite of the efforts of the parish priest the affair was quite public and everybody knew the facts. There were conferences and discussions that lasted a whole week, but in the end it was all settled and, mark you,

Stoney had the best of it. For it was decided by the parish priest that Peter would have to pay the bastardy when the child was born. Then of course Peter's wife came back and everything went on as before.

But Peter had his revenge. He brought an action against Stoney for the possession of the house which had been deeded to him, and I remember the day well when the police arrived to evict poor Stoney. That of course turned the whole village against Peter, and then everybody believed that he was really the father of the child. They called him 'the old ram.'

But poor Stoney had a sad end. After he had been evicted from his home he wandered around from house to house, staying a week here and a month there. Very soon his dissipated life took effect on him and he went to pieces altogether. He was still the boon companion of all the young fellows who wanted to be rakes, but all they would give him was drink. Soon people began to turn him away from their houses, on account of the foul condition of his clothes, and at last he was compelled to enter the workhouse, where he died a pauper a few years ago.

THE WOUNDED CORMORANT

Beneath the great grey cliff of Clogher Mor there was a massive square black rock, dotted with white limpets, sitting in the sea. The sea rose and fell about it frothing. Rising, the sea hoisted the seaweed that grew along the rock's rims until the long red winding strands spread like streams of blood through the white foam. Falling, the tide sucked the strands down taut from their bulbous roots.

Silence. It was noon. The sea was calm. Rock-birds slept on its surface, their beaks resting on their fat white breasts. Tall sea-gulls standing on one leg dozed high up in the ledges of the cliff. On the great rock there was a flock of black cormorants resting, bobbing their long necks to draw the food from their swollen gullets.

Above on the cliff-top a yellow goat was looking down into the sea. She suddenly took fright. She snorted and turned towards the crag at a smart run. Turning, her hoof loosed a flat stone from the cliff's edge. The stone fell, whirling, on to the rock where the cormorants rested. It fell among them with a crash and arose again in fragments. The birds swooped into the air. As they rose a fragment of the stone struck one of them in the right leg. The leg was broken. The wounded bird uttered a shrill scream and dropped the leg. As the bird flew outwards from the rock the leg dangled crookedly.

The flock of cormorants did not fly far. As soon as they passed the edge of the rock they dived headlong into the sea. Their long black bodies, without stretched necks, passed rapidly beneath the surface of the waves, a long way, before they rose again, shaking the brine from their heads. Then they sat in the sea, their black backs shimmering in the sunlight, their pale brown throats thrust forward, their tiny heads poised on their curved long necks. They sat watching, like upright snakes, trying to discover whether there were any enemies near. Seeing nothing, they began to cackle and flutter their feathers.

But the wounded one rushed about in the water flapping its wings in agony. The salt brine stung the wound, and it could not stand still. After a few moments it rose from the sea and set off at a terrific rate, flying along the face of the cliff, mad with pain. It circled the face of the cliff three times, flying in enormous arcs, as if it were trying to flee from the pain in its leg. Then it swooped down again towards the flock and alighted in the water beside them.

The other birds noticed it and began to cackle. It swam close to one bird, but that bird shrieked and darted away from it. It approached another bird, and that bird prodded it viciously with its beak. Then all the birds screamed simultaneously and rose from the water, with a great swish of their long wings. The wounded one rose with them. They flew up to the rock again and alighted on it, bobbing their necks anxiously and peering in all directions, still slightly terrified by the stone that had fallen there. The wounded one alighted on the rocks with them, tried to stand up, and immediately fell on its stomach. But it struggled up again and stood on its unwounded leg.

The other birds, having assured themselves that there was no enemy near, began to look at the wounded one suspiciously. It had its eyes closed, and it was wobbling unstably on its leg. They saw the wounded leg hanging crookedly from its belly and its wings trailing slightly. They began to make curious screaming noises. One bird trotted over to the wounded one and pecked at it. The wounded bird uttered a low scream and fell forward on its chest. It spread out its wings, turned up its beak, and opened it out wide, like a young bird in a nest demanding food.

Immediately the whole flock raised a cackle again and took to their wings. They flew out to sea, high up in the air. The wounded bird struggled up and also took to flight after them. But they were far ahead of it, and it could not catch up with them on account of its waning strength. However, they soon wheeled inwards towards the cliff, and it wheeled in after them, all flying low over the water's surface. Then the flock rose slowly, fighting the air fiercely with their long thin wings in order to propel their heavy bodies upwards. They flew half-way up the face of the cliff and alighted on a wide ledge that was dotted with little black pools and white feathers strewn about.

The wounded bird tried to rise too, but it had not gone out to sea far enough in its swoop. Therefore it had not gathered sufficient speed to carry it up to their ledge. It breasted the cliff ten yards below the ledge, and being unable to rise upwards by banking, it had to wheel outwards again, cackling wildly. It flew out very far, descending to the surface of the sea until the tips of its wings touched the water. Then it wheeled inwards once more, rising gradually, making a tremendous effort to gather enough speed to take it to the ledge where its comrades rested. At all costs it must reach them or perish. Cast out from the flock, death was certain. Sea-gulls would devour it.

When the other birds saw it coming towards them and heard the sharp whirring of its wings as it rose strongly, they began to cackle fiercely, and came in a close line to the brink of the ledge, darting their beaks forward and shivering. The approaching bird cackled also and came headlong at them. It flopped on to the ledge over their backs and screamed, lying on the rock helplessly with its wings spread out, quite exhausted. But they had no mercy. They fell upon it fiercely, tearing at its body with their beaks, plucking out its black feathers and rooting it about with their feet. It struggled madly to creep in farther on the ledge, trying to get into a dark crevice in the cliff to hide, but they dragged it back again and pushed it towards the brink of the ledge. One bird prodded its right eye with its beak. Another gripped the broken leg firmly in its beak and tore at it.

At last the wounded bird lay on its side and began to tremble, offering no resistance to their attacks. Then they cackled loudly, and, dragging it to the brink of the ledge, they hurled it down. It fell, fluttering feebly through the air, slowly descending, turning round and round, closing and opening its wings, until it reached the sea.

Then it fluttered its wings twice and lay still. An advancing wave dashed it against the side of the black rock and then it disappeared, sucked down among the seaweed strands.

THE INQUISITION

There was perfect silence in the study. Twenty-seven postulants were stooping over their high desks, writing and reading, their pens moving over the exercise books with the cumbersome stupidity of boyhood, their heads held between their hands as they repeated over and over again the conjugation of some Latin or Greek noun and tried to retain it in their racked memories. In the rear desk, three auxiliary prefects wearing black soutanes worked and conversed in whispers, disobeying the law of silence which they imposed on the younger postulants. For, even in religious orders, officials disobey their own laws.

It was past six o'clock. The Angelus had been said. It was still an hour before the first auxiliary would bang his desk. Then they would all go on their knees and recite the prayer before leaving the study for the refectory and supper.

A terrible hour, thought Francis Cleary. He sat in the second desk to the left of the passage, and although he had his Euripides open on his desk, he was not reading it. He was listening to every sound with beating heart, thinking that the very next moment there would be a heavy step outside the door. Then the door would open slowly and the father director's large red melancholy face would appear. Holding his biretta in his hand, he would advance slowly down the study, picking his steps with difficulty on account of his corns. He would pause at Cleary's desk and he would tip Cleary's right shoulder gently. Then without a word he would go back again to the door and Cleary would have to follow him.

Cleary kept going over this routine of movement in his mind, and every time he came to the gentle tip on the shoulder, he started and a flow of blood went to his head that made him flush and tremble. It was terrible waiting like this. He had expected the priest every moment since five o'clock, when they entered the study from the recreation ground. Why had he not come? Why was he torturing him like this?

There were three other boys guilty and they also were waiting, but they all knew Cleary would be first. Why? Just with that instinct of boyhood and the peculiar cunning that life in a religious seminary engenders, where life is so closely scrutinised and public that each knows the others better than brothers and sisters know one another in a large family. So Cleary was known to be the most religious and devout boy in the scholasticate. The father director paid most attention to him. There were great hopes of his ultimate sanctity. Therefore he would be first. It would be through him that the guilt of the others would be made known or concealed. The others knew that. Cleary knew it and he trembled, because he felt that he would never have the courage to hold back information from Fr Harty. Already he heard the boys hissing 'spy' at him.

At last the ominous sound came. The auxiliaries stopped whispering. Cleary became absolutely numb with terror. The door opened. Cleary did not look up. He heard the slow irregular heavy footsteps approach. He felt the gentle tip on his shoulder and he heard the priest's asthmatic breathing over him. He rose immediately, and as he followed the priest's broad black back, he cast a hurried glance around him. The three faces were watching him, with terror in their eyes, but also with a peculiar warning look, as much as to say: 'You know what you're going to get if you tell.'

The father director's room was across the passage. Cleary was always terrified of that dark door that seemed to lead to a tunnel. On Saturday nights they all waited outside the door and entered into its lamp-lit gloom to kneel at the little prayer stool beside which Fr Harty sat, hidden in darkness, hearing their confessions. Now it would be another sort of confession, a more terrible one.

Fr Harty never spoke until he had lit the lamp and sunk into his easy chair by the fire. Then he put his head between his hands and rubbed his face from the temples to the chin with the peculiar melancholy movement that was customary with him. Cleary standing erect by the door felt pity and love for him. He was tender and kind to him, that priest. Why was he now afraid of him? But it seemed now that some other being was sitting in the chair instead of the good priest, who had once been a great athlete and a heavy drinker. This middle-aged man with the red face and the terrible mental suffering stamped on his red face was like an extraordinary and terrible being, merciless, insane, overpowered by a monstrous fanaticism that licked all tenderness and understanding out of his consciousness like a devilish flame licking up the tender moisture of humanity, leaving only the crusted charred bones of the dogmas that had brought that constant suffering into his face. This was not Fr Harty but a terrible fanatic.

Cleary was only sixteen. He had not yet begun to think out of his own experience. Until now he had assimilated without question all the precepts that were offered to his mind, in the lecture rooms, in the chapel and in the study, where Fr Harty gave sermons on personal conduct and the lives of the saints. Cleary's mind was hitherto just a receptacle for all these precepts and he had shrunk away in terror from any personal thought, lest it might lead him into doubt and sin. But now his consciousness had been completely roused by his terror and this first questioning of the justice of the situation in which he was placed. His superiors were not just, something suggested to him. And almost immediately his mind had begun to think independently and he doubted the wisdom of his superiors. And then a little wall had thrust itself in front of his own personality, and for the first time in his life he found himself standing behind this wall, ready to fight his superior. This was an enemy sitting in that chair. Not Fr Harty whom he loved but this embodiment of the terrible dogmas that made men do such cruel things, as this terrible torture of a youth, this fanatic. That was his enemy. With the extraordinary instinct of youthful persons whose judgements are not deflected and obscured by elaborate reasonings he could see this difference as clearly as if there were two people sitting in the chair instead of one. And from that moment, when this difference became manifest to him, Cleary had ceased to believe in God with his whole soul as he had hitherto done. He no longer loved God as an omnipotent friend and father. He now feared him.

'Well,' said the priest heavily, without looking at Cleary, 'this is terrible.'

There was a short silence. Cleary's legs trembled and his head seemed to go round and round. The sacred pictures on the walls, the gleaming gilt backs of the books on the shelves, the dark polished wainscoting, the oilcloth on the floor, all seemed occult and terrifying, to his eyes wandering about, seeking some point to which to attach themselves instead of to the recumbent heavy figure of the priest.

'How did this happen?' continued the priest sadly. 'How did this terrible craze grow within you? If you had been lukewarm and . . . and casual in your devotions I could perhaps understand your giving way to this temptation. But I had placed such faith in your purity. I had such hopes of you. Perhaps I encouraged you too much. Conceit is a terrible danger. Francis, tell me everything.'

Cleary's lips began to tremble and tears came to his eyes, but he could not speak. The gentle sadness of the priest's voice knocked down that wall of defence at one blow and Cleary felt himself an utter miscreant. The enormity of his sin appeared so frightful that he abandoned all hope and he was ready to do anything, anything, in order to lighten the grief of the priest. And yet, at the same time, his overwhelmed mind simmered with revolt against this appeal to his heart. He could not speak and he was glad that he could not speak.

'Tell me, Francis. Open your mind to me. Then this demon of temptation will be overcome. I am certain that you have been led astray by your companions. I have no doubt of it. I could not be so mistaken in your character. Others older and less pure in mind than yourself have been the cause of this. Speak, Francis.'

'I can't speak, Father,' blubbered Cleary, bursting into tears. 'I have done nothing. I have done nothing.'

'But, my child, I have just spent an hour with Fr Superior. An hour. And I tell you it was very hard on me. Very hard. You went to the dentist this morning to the town and Fr Moran saw you coming out of a tobacconist's shop. He stopped you to ask what you had bought and found a packet of cigarettes in your pocket. Do you call that nothing?'

Cleary wept, and weeping he found relief from the load of grief and terror that oppressed his heart. It seemed, too, that all his pity for the priest had been washed away with the tears. And when the father director mentioned Fr Moran the superior, Cleary knew immediately that he loathed the Fr Superior with a terrible loathing, his paunch, his fat hands, his fat red neck, his little ferret-like eyes and the syrupy tone of his voice, like the soft loathsome voice of some reptile, hissing and snakelike. And this terrible hatred, so new to his soul, made him hard and cold, so that his mind became clear and active again.

'They were not for myself,' he said. 'I don't smoke.'

'I am glad, Francis,' said the priest. 'I am very glad. But you must tell me now who they were for. It is your duty to tell me.'

The priest sat up erect suddenly and his face hardened.

'That would not be honourable,' muttered Cleary.

'Honourable!' cried the priest. 'My God! Where have you been hearing these words? In religious life there is nothing honourable but the love of God and obedience to his holy rules. Do you think it's honourable to shield the sinful acts of your fellow-postulants? My child, I command you to tell me who those cigarettes were for. As you director, I command you. You know what disobedience of my order means to your soul.'

The priest had stood up suddenly. Standing he looked enormous in the gloom. Cleary shrank away in terror. In his terror he thought that the priest was God himself, the terrible avenging God of the Old Testament, who cried: Spare neither women nor children.' His terror had become physical and he thought that he would be immediately struck dead if he did not speak. But even in that moment of terror when his lips were going to utter the words that would kill all love in his soul, his mind exulted, for it had become relieved of fear. Henceforth it would be free to exult in thought, free and hidden from observation, with a wall around it, formed by cunning and deceit, to protect it from these terrible exponents of dogmas that were now its enemies.

'They were for Michael O'Connor and John Hourigan and Paddy O'Kelly,' cried Cleary, almost in a scream.

'Michael O'Connor, John Hourigan and Paddy O'Kelly,' repeated the priest slowly, as he sat down again in his chair, groaning as he sat.

Then he placed his hands again on his temples and rubbed them slowly down over his face, as if he were erasing some picture from his memory. A phantom.

Cleary's eyes now shone wildly. His body was rigid and he was ready to jump, he thought. His face twitched. But he felt a great relief. He had come to a decision. Nothing mattered to him now. He felt a great strength in his jaws where they joined the muscles of his neck and he didn't have to blink his eyes, as he was in the habit of doing. His eyes remained wide open without effort and the lids seemed to be very cold and rigid.

The priest's attitude changed again. He began to lecture.

Cleary thoughtlessly repeated the words of the lecture to himself after the priest, while his newly functioning mind planned other things.

'In the first place, it's against the rules to go into a shop. Secondly, it's a grave sin to procure the means of sin for another soul. Thirdly, 'tis a . . .'

And his mind exulted, ravenously devouring all sorts of new ideas, let loose into the whole cosmos of things without restraint. Free now and cunning and deceitful and securely hidden behind a thick wall of deceit, through which nothing could pierce. Free and alone and hating everything. Free to found a new cosmos, to fashion a new order of thought and a new God. Through hatred to a new love. Through terrible suffering in loneliness to a new light. Through agony to a new peace. The man was growing in him.

The priest ceased. Then he said:

'Send Michael O'Connor in to me. I will speak to you later about your penance.'

Cleary bowed and left the room. He was no longer afraid entering the study. He went to the auxiliary desk and asked permission to speak to Michael O'Connor. He went to O'Connor and said: 'Fr Harty wants you.' He paid no heed to the threat that O'Connor uttered. He went to his desk and, covering his face with his hands, he smiled.

In the morning he would run away, he thought.

DAOINE BOCHTA

Bhí fuaim na mara ag filleadh go borb trí dhorchadas ciúin an mhaidneachain, fuaim fhada bhriste ag únfairt ar ghaineamh gheal na trá; fuaradas nimheanta maidin Fheabhra san aer dorcha; an guaire cois bóthair in uachtar na trá, brataithe le taisí millteacha; cothrom na talún dubhdhaite, faoi shuan.

Bhí ciumhais na mara lán le feamainn, tromualach á dhoirteadh ar an domhan dearg, scamallach, ag filleadh isteach, dos ar dhos, le gach uile mhaidhm a bhris go righin gnúsach i ndorchadas na maidne. Adhart.

Seo anuas Pádraig Ó Dioráin, píce ar a ghualainn, a bhróga úrleathair ag gíoscadh i bhfliuchán an bhóthair, báinín geal fostaithe ina chrios, a cholann chaol chaite ar craitheadh leis an bhfuacht.

Shroich sé an guaire. Tríd an mbreacdhorchadas chonaic sé an fheamainn sa taoille, á sú amach agus isteach le gluaiseacht bhríomhar, righin na farraige. Chuir sé gáir íseal lúcháireach as agus anuas leis, agus rith go rúitín sa ngaineamh bhog.

Bhí an cúigiú lá déag de Fheabhra ann agus gan sop feamainne bailithe aige, lena chuid fataí a chur. Sé seachtaine ar a dhroim ar an leaba, créachta leis an flú, a bhean lag tar éis cruatan agus anró an gheimhridh, a mhac — ina cheithre bhliain — ar leaba a bháis, an mhóin caite le mí, agus gan plúr ná bainne sa teach, ach i dtuilleamaí grá Dé na gcomharsan . . . ach . . . caithfear obair a dhéanamh. Caithfear an fheamainn a bhailiú agus na fataí a chur, mar tá geimhreadh eile ag teacht tar éis teasa an tsamhraidh, geimhreadh agus fuacht agus tinneas agus cruatan. Maide mór an bhochtanais ag lascadh a dhroma, á dhíbirt anuas an trá úd tríd an ngaineamh bhog.

Níor smaoinigh sé anois ar a bhean ná ar a mhac ná ar a ocras agus é ag cruashiúl síos, suas síos, ón adhart go dtí an guaire, ag crochadh leis an fheamainn ar a phíce agus á doirteadh ina carnán sciorrach; ag obair go santach agus a fhiacla fáiscithe in aghaidh an fhuaicht. Ní raibh ina cheann ach an cur agus an maide mór úd ag lascadh a dhroma, spiorad aireachais na mbocht, ag meabhrú dhóibh an cruatan atá le teacht; ag bodhrú an phian atá láithreach.

Tháinig fear agus fear eile den bhaile, deifir orthu ar fad, ag rith anuas tríd an ngaineamh bhog. Bheannaigh siad uilig do Phádraig agus d'fhiafraigh dhe cé an chaoi raibh a mhac.

'Á! Muise, go suarach,' ar seisean. 'Tá faitíos orm nach bhfeicfidh sé an féar ag fás arís.'

'Á, a Mhuire is trua,' ar siadsan go cráite.

Is cruaidh le bochta cruatan na mbocht.

D'éirigh an ghrian. Scairt solas an lae ar an tír, ar an trá, ar an bhfarraige. Dhúisigh éanacha an aeir agus chuireadar a gceol binn uathu ag rince trí dhoimhneas na spéire. Bhí brat feamainne ag lonradh ar an trá; dearg ar nós fola, ar a scairteann grian, in aghaidh dúghorm na farraige préachta. Bhí carnán mór bailithe ag Pádraig Ó Dioráin — deich mbord capaill. Chuaigh sé abhaile. Lag tar éis tinnis, is ar éigin a bhí sé i ndon an bóthar a shiúl agus a ioscaidí losctha leis an sáile. Agus anois ag triall abhaile, meabhraíodh dó arís an dúbhrón a bhí ansiúd ag faire air, éagaoin chráite agus uaigh á hoscailt . . .

Bhí a theach ar cheann an bhaile, teachín fada, geal, faoi bhrat aoil; an tuí go cúramach ar a cheann, gach uile rud glan piocaithe ar fuaid na sráide; craobhacha beaga glasa ag fás ag bun an tí. Bean mhaith. Fear maith.

Sa gcistin, ní raibh ach bean chomharsan ina suí ar stól os comhair tine bhriogadáin, ag iarraidh ciotal a chur ar fiuchadh. Bheannaigh sí dhó i gcogar.

'Cá bhfuil Bríd?' ar seisean.

Chuaigh sí amach ag cuartú braon bainne le haghaidh an tae. Tá an bord réitithe sa seomra mór. Gabh siar. Tá an ciotal beagnach fiuchta. Beidh sí isteach ar an nóiméad leis an mbainne.

Níor bhreathnaigh sí air. Sheas sé, a bhéal ag iarraidh labhairt, ag dearcadh ar dhoras an tseomra bhig, áit a raibh an maicín ina luí.

'A'. . . a' bhfuil aon athrú air?' adeir sé go lag.

Chraith sí a ceann.

'Gabh siar,' adeir sí arís.

'Gabhfad isteach go bhfeicfead . . .'

'Ná téirigh,' adeir sí, ag éirí go tobann, 'tá suan beag air agus ní bheidh ach briseadh croí ort ag breathnú air. Siar leat agus suigh chun boird.'

Tháinig an bhean isteach, soitheach beag faoina naprún aici. Bean bheag agus éadan cruinn uirthi, súile móra gorma leathnaithe ina ceann; a béilín oscailte, mar bheadh iontas mór ar a hintinn i dtaobh rud éigin, nárbh fhéidir léi a thuiscint. Dhearc siad ar a chéile, an fear agus an bhean, ach níor labhair siad focal. Níor ghá dhóibh labhairt. Ag dearcadh, súil ar shúil, thuigeadar araon gach ní a bhí le rá; daoine simplí, ceanúla, níor ghá dhóibh labhairt, mar níl dada le ceilt nuair atá dhá chroí pósta.

Chuaigh sé siar sa seomra agus a cheann faoi. Chaith sé dhe go craiceann, mar bhí gach uile bhall éadaigh dá raibh air fliuch ó iompar na feamainne.

Thug sí balcaisí tirime dó. Chuir sé air iad agus shuigh chun boird. Níor shuigh sí féin leis, mar nach raibh ann ach dóthain duine den arán, agus é sin féin gann go leor. Ach rinne sé dhá chuid den arán agus shín chuici cuid. 'Ní íosfad,' adeir sí. 'Ith thusa ar fad é. Níl aon ocras orm.'

Bhreathnaigh sé uirthi go cúthalach. Bhí sí ag ól cupán tae, ina seasamh le taobh an bhoird, ag dearcadh amach tríd an bhfuinneog. Ag dearcadh ar a cruth caite agus ar na féitheacha dearga sna láimhíní a bhí chomh bog sleamhain bliain nó dhó ó shoin, líon a chroí le fearg uafásach in aghaidh an tsaoil. Tháinig meall goirt aníos a scornach á thachtadh. A Dhia! Nach cruaidh? Nach dtig leis réabadh agus stróiceadh a dhéanamh, thairis a bheith fostaithe mar seo ag an mbochtanacht; fostó daingean air ag slabhra mór an ocrais.

Ach do bhris deor faoina súil. D'éirigh sé agus chuir sé a lámh timpeall uirthi.

'Ith, a Bhríd,' adeir sé go bog, 'fhad is fhágfaidh Dia ag a chéile muid, tá gach uile shórt ceart.'

D'iompaigh sí air, leag a ceann ar a ucht agus thosnaigh sí ag gol.

'Éist, éist,' adeir sé. 'Níl aon mhaith bheith ag caoineachán.'

'Maith dhom é,' adeir sí, ag cimilt a súl, 'ach tá me chomh tuirseach — agus gan againn ach mo mhaicín beag, cé an fáth nach bhfágfaí againn é?'

'Éist, a stór. Éist. Tá Dia láidir.'

D'ith sé. D'imigh sé arís i gcoinne an chapaill. Chuir sé srathar uirthi agus chuaigh sé chun na trá. Bhí an capall ag rith go fiáin, ag seitreach. Agus a cheann san aer, a cholann dearg ag creathnú le fuacht an lae, áthas an tsiúil ina chroí — mar atá áthas an tsaoil i gcroí gach ainmhí san Earrach. Ach bhí croí Phádraig chomh cruaidh le cloch, ina shuí ar chairín an chapaill, ag cuimhniú ag cuimhniú . . .

I dtráth an mheán lae bhí an fheamainn ar fad curtha amach ar an ngarraí aige. Tháinig sé abhaile arís. Bhí eagla anois air ag teacht in aice an tí. Ach nuair a d'ardaigh sé an charcair agus go bhfaca sé doras an tí agus mná an bhaile ag triall air, tháinig fuadach croí air.

Léim sé den chapall ar an sráid agus rith sé chun an dorais ag fógairt: 'Céard seo? Céard seo?'

D'fhreagair glór a mhná ar an tairseach é, measctha le iomad glór an olagóin ag éirí os íseal ar bhéala na mban a bhí ina suí timpeall an tí: caoineadh na marbh ag éirí faoi áras an tí; fuaim fhada bhriste ag únfairt le doilíos a n-anam.

Rith sé chun an tseomra bhig agus fuair sé ansin í, ar a glúine cois na leapan, ag caoineadh a mic.

Taobh le taobh do chaoineadar.

POOR PEOPLE

The sound of the sea grumbled through the calm darkness of the dawn, a long broken sound wallowing on the white sand of the beach; the poisonous cold of a February morning was in the dark air; the sandbank by the road above the beach was shrouded with mighty black ghosts; the form of the earth slept, covered in darkness.

The edge of the sea was full of seaweed, a great load spilling from the deep, red, slime-covered, dribbling in with every wave that broke slowly murmuring in the darkness of the dawn.

Patrick Derrane came running down the road with a pitchfork on his shoulder, his rawhide shoes squelching with the wetness of the road, a white frieze smock tucked into his waistbelt, his slim thin body shivering with the cold. He reached the sandbank and saw the seaweed in the tide through the darkness, being sucked in and out by the mighty slow movement of the sea. He uttered a low, joyous cry and ran down, running ankle-deep in the soft white sand.

'Praise be to God!'

It was the fifteenth day of February and he had not yet gathered any seaweed to manure his potatoes.

He had been six weeks lying on his back with influenza, his wife was weak after the hardship of winter, his four-year-old son was lying on his death-bed, the supply of peat had been all burned for the past month, there was neither flour nor milk in the house and they had to depend on the charity of their neighbours . . . but . . . work must be done . . .

The seaweed must be gathered and the potatoes must be planted because another winter was coming after the warmth of summer, another winter with cold and sickness and hardship. The great whip of poverty was lashing his back, driving him down the beach through the soft sand.

He had no thought now of his wife or of his son or of his hunger, walking rapidly back and forth from the sandbank to the tide, lifting the seaweed on his pitchfork and spilling it in a slipping heap. He worked wildly, gritting his teeth against the cold. He only remembered the crop he had to sow and that great lash of hunger, the dread spirit that ever taunts the poor, reminding them of the hardship that is to come, deadening the pain that is present.

Several other men came from the village, all in a hurry, running down the beach over the soft sand. They all saluted Derrane and asked him how his little son was.

'Ah, indeed he is very poorly,' he replied. 'I'm afraid he'll never see the grass growing again.'

'Ah, may the Virgin pity him,' they said sadly.

The poor pity the hardships of the poor.

The sun rose. Daylight sparkled on the land, on the beach and over the sea. The birds awakened and sent their sweet music dancing through the depths of the sky. The cloak of red seaweed on the beach shimmered, like freshly spilt blood on which the sun is shining, against the dark blue background of the freezing sea.

Derrane had gathered a great heap of seaweed, ten loads for a horse. He went home. Weak after his sickness, he was hardly able to walk the road. His thighs were scalded by the brine. And now that he was going home, he remembered the sadness that awaited him there, lamentation and a grave being opened . . .

His house was at the head of the village, a little long house, with whitewashed walls, the straw thatch neat, everything tidy in the yard, little green bushes growing by the walls. A good housewife. A good husband. But poverty respects nothing . . .

In the kitchen there was only a neighbouring woman sitting on a stool in front of a fire of briars, trying to get a kettle to boil. She saluted him in a whisper.

'Where is Brigid?' he said.

'She went out looking for a drop of milk for your tea. The table is set in the big room. Go in. The kettle is just boiling. She'll be in a minute with the milk.'

She did not look at him.

He stood, trying to speak, looking at the door of the little room, where his son was lying.

'Eh . . . is there any change in him?' he said weakly.

She shook her head.

'Go in,' she said again, pointing to the big room. 'I'll go and see if —' he began.

'No, don't,' she said, jumping up suddenly. 'He is sleeping now and it will only be a heartbreak for you to took at him. Go in and sit down to table.'

His wife entered with a small vessel under her apron. She was a little woman with a round face, two great blue eyes staring and her little mouth opened, as if her mind were wondering at some terrible thing which she could not comprehend. They looked at one another, the husband and the wife, but they did not speak a word. There was no need for them to speak. Looking, eye to eye, they both understood all that was to be said; simple, loving people, there was no need for them to speak. When two hearts are married there is nothing to hide. . . .

He entered the big room with downcast head. He stripped off all his clothes. They were drenched by the seaweed. She gave him dry clothes. He put them on and sat down to table. She did not sit down with him because there was only enough bread for one and even that was little enough. But he divided the bread evenly and offered her half.

'I won't eat it,' she said. 'Let you eat all of it. I'm not hungry.'

He looked at her shyly. She was drinking a cup of tea, standing by the table, looking out through the window. Looking at her haggard frame and at the red veins in her little hands that used to be so smooth and comely a year or two ago, his heart filled with anger against the world. A salt lump came up his throat, choking him. God! God! Why could he not rend and break and destroy everything, instead of being tied down like this by poverty, without power, stricken, helpless, tied, tied, by the great chain of hunger.

But instead a tear broke under his eye. He arose and put his arm about her.

'Eat it, Brigid,' he said softly. 'While God leaves us one another sure everything will be all right.'

She turned to him, dropped her head on his breast and burst into tears.

'Stop, stop, darling,' he said. 'There's no use in crying.'

'Forgive me,' she said, wiping her eyes. 'But I am so tired and I having only him, my little son, why couldn't he be left to me?'

'Stop, darling. Stop. God is powerful.'

He ate. He went away again for his horse and went to the beach. The horse ran wildly, neighing with his head in the air, his red body trembling with the cold of the day, the joy of motion in his heart, because there is the joy of life in the heart of every animal in spring. But Patrick sat on the horse's haunches, with his heart as hard as a stone, thinking, thinking, thinking . . .

About midday he had brought all the seaweed to the field. He came home. He was afraid coming near his house and as he ascended the hill in front of the village and saw several neighbour women approaching his door, his heart stopped beating.

He jumped off his horse in the yard and ran to the door crying: 'What's this? What's this?'

On the threshold he heard his wife's voice, mingled with the many voices of the death-cry rising from the lips of the village women seated round the house; a long, broken sound, wallowing with the sorrow of souls.

He ran to the little room and found her there, kneeling by the bed.

Side by side they wept.

THE TYRANT

There had been a dinner party at the house of Mr Patrick Sheridan, the barrister. The guests had all departed, but it seemed that they were yet present in the drawing-room, which was not perfectly silent, with that intense silence which follows the loud murmur of many voices, talking in small groups about a drawing-room, discussing various things. The odour of cigarette smoke still hung about the room, although the large bay window had been flung open wide and the soft, warm, autumn night air was drifting into the room silently. Silently it drifted into the silent room where a minute before there had been a babel of murmuring voices. The ash-trays on the little low tables about the room were laden with cigarette ashes and there was an American newspaper on the couch by the window where a visitor had dropped it, its leaves now being fluttered gently by the incoming humid autumn night breeze.

Mrs Sheridan, sitting alone in the drawing-room, was so exhausted that she kept thinking the guests had just gone into another room to look at a picture and that they would be back in a moment; though, of course, she knew her husband was downstairs in the hall seeing them out and she could hear motor-cars purring and people crying laughingly: 'Good night,' 'Good-bye,' '*Au revoir*.'

She shuddered, listening stupidly to the distant sounds, shuddering in her thin evening gown with the draught from the window she had opened, listening and looking at the fire that had burned low, now drowsily smouldering in its ashen embers. A dying fire in a deserted room . . .

Her green silk dress shimmered fitfully in the firelight, as flames spurted up from the smouldering fire and then died again; again and again lighting her up, as if urging her to do something. What? She was too exhausted to think, but still there was a great cloud of unformed thoughts in her brain; violent, rebellious, dour thoughts. They were yet formless thoughts. They had as yet found no expression in her beautiful, mild, white face. But her grey eyes had that staring, fixed look about them which is menacing in a woman; the eyes of a timid, gentle woman who suffers meekly and yet is beginning to revolt.

She was aware of that cloud in her brain, but all she could concentrate upon was the babel of meaningless murmuring she had heard all the evening, the clatter of plates, the terrific anxiety of preparing dinner and attending to her guests and her husband's eyes always following her; his lowered eyelids, the pouches under his eyes and his underlip licking his upper lip when he looked at her. So she sat motionless but shuddering slightly, in a chair by the fire, waiting for her husband to return, a flabby woman of forty, with a faded, white, beautiful face and a mournful look in her grey eyes; two round thick-fingered hands clasped in her lap.

She heard his footsteps on the stairs. She sat up, very stiffly. My God, what would he say? He coughed in his throat, a low, pompous sound, and then came the soft padding of his feet . . . Why should she be afraid of these sounds? She raised her head and looked around her stupidly with terror in her eyes, saw the open window and wanted to float out through it, away through the void of heaven; the passive flight of a terrified thing, an unconscious movement of limbs with a terror-striken mind urging them on, away, away. But she did not move, as if something bound her to the approaching feet and to the cougher, coughing pompously in his throat to terrify her.

He entered and closed the door behind him. Then she had to direct her eyes towards his. She saw him, a blurred figure, tall, slim, elegant, groomed, the face that had smiled affably at his guests now sallow and drawn with a malignant temper; a malignant, domineering, furious light in those suave, expressionless brown eyes and the underlip raised . . . raised to strike, a thin lip striking upwards.

As he approached her, walking slowly across the room, her face became suffused with a pale red colour and all her limbs tingled with shame. Why should she fear him? But it was no use telling herself not to be afraid. For many years now she had been quite helpless, while he approached her with his underlip raised, or spoke to her with that malignant glint in his suave eyes; or even while she knew he was thinking of her, preparing to approach her with his underlip raised.

'Helen,' he said, 'I must remonstrate with you for the last time.'

His voice was low, deep, polished. His words were measured, cultured, almost toneless, expressive of no emotion.

'Yes,' she blurted out.

Her voice was deep and soft and guttural. As soon as she had uttered the word, it seemed that her whole character had assumed a different aspect. Her voice was like a key, that opened her up and made manifest the secret of the pity which her flabby, down-trodden face excited. It was the crude, agonising voice of a beaten thing, stripped of the delicate intonation and refinement which clothes a woman's voice with many interlacing wraps, making it a mysterious intriguing harmony. The sweet, delicate voice of a woman stirs the blood with adventurous thought, but the moaning sound of Helen's voice touched the heart with pity.

'You have positively disgraced me this evening,' he continued, speaking with his hands behind his back and in a low, calm voice, as if he had no interest in what he was saying. If he only expressed anger in his voice it would be less cruel, but that cold, calm tone gave him the appearance of a martyred man who was kindly remonstrating with his torturer. 'Not once during dinner or afterwards did you make an intelligent remark. You made no effort to entertain my guests in the drawing-room. You sat there stupidly, as if I had beaten you before they came in. I can only imagine that it was deliberate. Otherwise how could you . . . Listen, Helen. We have been married ten years. In those ten years I have worked the skin off my fingers to make a career. It was all for the children that I might have had but which you didn't give me . . .'

'Oh!' blurted Helen, putting her hands to her face. But she dropped her hands immediately and stared at him again lifelessly, with her underlip trembling.

'Please don't go into hysterics,' he intoned. 'Let me finish. I am willing to pass over this. But now that these hopes are gone I am consoling myself with giving all my energy, all my talents, all achievements to the service of my country. You know very well I am a candidate for the Senate. Sir Joseph Flynn's support is vital to me. I brought him here tonight SPECIALLY that you might make a good impression on him. His support would mean that the Catholic Hierarchy would throw their whole weight in favour of my candidature. You have the reputation of being an ardent Catholic. Unfortunately my attitude towards the Church is doubtful.'

Mr Sheridan laughed dryly, a sort of callous sound, like an uttered sneer.

'But although I had definitely IMPLORED you to use all your efforts to entertain him, you were dumb. Dumb, absolutely dumb. Helen, the position is impossible. How, how do you explain it?'

He made a gesture with his arms and strode to the window. Helen tried to speak, not to explain it, or defend herself, but to give utterance to the cloud of rebellious thoughts in her brain, but she remained mute. It had been like a speech in court and there seemed to be no possibility of reply. The terrifying atmosphere of the court was in the room with him. He seemed to carry with him into his drawing-room the whole paraphernalia of terror which supported him in court. The intricate structure of society, by the cunning manipulation of which he wormed his way into prominence, even though 'his attitude towards various institutions was in doubt,' now as always weighed down her simple, stupid mind, leaving her quite dumb. He was right. She was dumb. But why could he not be kind to her and let her exercise her simple talents naturally? Was it necessary for her also to be clever? Were not peace and happiness more valuable than . . .'

These were some of the unformed thoughts in her brain which she could not utter. He went on talking, coldly and abusively. She did not understand any longer what he said, but every word struck her physically, like a hot iron, burning her flesh and causing her body to vibrate painfully with the concussion of the stroke. She became more and more confused and helpless until finally she went into a fit of silent hysteria.

At last he noticed her condition and stopped in the middle of a sentence. Instead of relenting or going to her assistance, his face grew still more sallow with anger. He struck his forehead with his palm and said:

'My God! What a burden!

Then he walked out of the room slowly without saying good night, coughing pompously in his throat, his feet padding softly over the thick carpet.

'What a burden!'

As she swam back to consciousness that phrase was repeated to her again and again. And as she began to think again clearly it was about that phrase she thought. A burden! That put the whole business in a different light. Morals! Scruples! Duty! Burden! And then another phrase which she had read or heard somewhere long ago and which she had regarded for a long time as an evil temptation: 'the inalienable right of man to life, liberty and the pursuit of happiness.'

She thought thus with her eyes shut and it was very silent in the room. It began to grow cold, as the fire faded and the night air reduced the atmosphere of the room, lately crowded with warm-breathed human beings, to its own cold, pure, odourless intensity.

The cold, pure air and the silence reminded her of something. She opened her eyes and rose stiffly, a flabby figure stiffened with sorrow. But there was now a light of determination in her cowed eyes and her brain was clear. The cloud of formless thoughts had broken and its fragments were falling like soothing, soft rain after a sultry day. Dropping softly through her body, soothing the flesh that had been lacerated by his words, falling gently in smooth, winding streams all over her, washing away everything. While through this rain of thought a new being emerged, rising upwards with cool brow and joyous heart, like a parched flower opening its petals to the rain. Her brain, released from its load of depression, was looking courageously at a means of escape from its suffering and at a new life of happiness.

She stood erect. She threw back her head and pressed her hands down by her sides.

'Do I dare?' she cried. 'Do I dare?'

And as she spoke she smiled. Here in the silence and the cold night air it was so easy to dare. The cold air was powerful, beckoning her. The night belonged to it, when it could reconquer the city and turn the turbulent maelstrom of civilisation into a cold, silent wilderness. Now it spoke to her and called her, beckoning her to fly to the solitude of the mountains, where there would be peace. It was a fitting time to go. Autumn, when the leaves were dropping and the mountain-sides had become grey again and the heather-blossoms had died. It was a fitting time for a weary one to seek a quiet place. She walked to the window and looked out. Over the roofs of the city she could see the mountains.

'I am a burthen to him,' she murmured. 'Then I am better gone. By staying I will only grow to hate him and load my soul with sin. It cannot be a sin to go. I have done my best for him.'

And she thought how loving he was when they were married first and she had to support him on her income. And thinking of that, it struck her that he had married her for her income. Her simple mind had never thought of it before. It was this new being that thought of it. In the cold purity of the night, thinking of the peace of the hills, it was possible to understand many things.

'Yes,' she said calmly, 'I will go.'

'There will be many things to do,' she added after a pause. 'Little things that I like doing. I will get some old person to live with me. Some quiet old person. I will have a cat and there will be little birds about. And we will plant things and watch them grow. And then, I'll forget all this.'

The dying fire tinkled, tinkled, cracking the last muscles of its dying embers. The couches recently bearing the impress of chattering human bodies had straightened out. Already her husband was asleep, dreaming of his ambitions.

'He rises late,' she said. 'I will pack my things now and write him a note. I will be gone before he gets up. Won't it be wonderful to have each day quiet like the last. And to come out in the morning and watch the sunbeams playing on the grey rocks and listen to the birds singing?'

THE LOST THRUSH

There was tense excitement within the open space between the tall trees below the gamekeeper's lodge. Three young thrushes that had just left their nest were hopping about there. Their parents were perched close by, on opposite rhododendrons, uttering shrill cries and bobbing their heads.

With their beaks resting languidly on their puffed breasts, the young thrushes hopped hither and thither aimlessly, resting a long while between hops. They winked their eyes. They stretched their legs backwards one by one. They tried to stand on tip-toe and flap their wings.

Then the gamekeeper's yellow dog, asleep on a brown mat at the rear of the lodge, was awakened by the chirping. He got up and nosed his way along to see what was the matter. When he saw the birds, he raised his right fore paw and watched them for a little while, sniffing. Then his belly shivered and he uttered a series of barks, looking all round him and scratching the ground furiously. Without waiting any further, he walked back to his mat, smelling the ground casually for a rabbit scent.

But he had terrified the thrushes. The parent birds dashed to the stone fence on the right. The young ones threw themselves flat on the grass. Then one by one they spread their weak wings and took flight. They flew like gorged bats, headlong, in an arc, into the undergrowth between the trees. One landed in nettles. The other two landed among young briars.

The parent birds waited in silence for some time, until they made sure the dog had gone away. Then they flew into the undergrowth and landed on an oak tree root. They began to chirp. The two young ones that had landed in the briars answered and came forth, but the other one was nowhere to be found.

Terrified by the barking of the dog, he had crawled out of the nettles and hopped along, in order to get away as far as possible. He made a short flight across an open space into some brushwood. He remained there a long time, exhausted by his unusual exercise. His little fat breast heaved in and out regularly, as he stood on a little spot of black earth beneath a laurel branch.

He fell asleep. After a while rain began to fall. Drops fell on to his back from off the slippery laurel leaves. He awoke and hopped away to escape the raindrops. But he hopped into a quite open space where he immediately got drenched. He stood still, dumbfounded and unable to escape from the monstrous attack of water. Reeling under the innumerable blows of the raindrops, he lay down and surrendered himself. His beak fell to the ground.

Then the rain stopped as suddenly as it had begun. The sun came out again. The whole surface of the earth sparkled in the sun, like a shield. Myriads of raindrops lay like jewels everywhere, on the grass, on the leaves of the trees, on the very brink of thorns. The little thrush shivered with joy when he felt the warm sun on his back. He stood up and chirped. He spread his wings to fly but the wings were quite useless. He could not even return them to their position on his back. They trailed along the ground with some of the big feathers sticking out. They had been loosened by the heavy rain from the skin that was still young and tender.

Trailing his wings, his hopped along. He wanted to keep moving. He was afraid to stand still and be alone. He hopped through a screen of leaves on to a little limestone road. The road was dotted with green leaves that had fallen during the rain. The trees joined overhead so that only shadows of the sunlight came through. It was cool there. The wet thrush began to shiver again. He felt weak. He stood by the roadside stupidly. The lower part of his beak dropped with exhaustion. He shook himself slightly and tried to close his beak again, but he only succeeded in sticking out his tongue. Then he could neither withdraw his tongue nor close his beak. He staggered.

A rabbit came out of the brushwood on the other side of the road. Dragging himself along over the moist road as if his hind part were paralysed, he began to nibble at the green leaves that had fallen. He collected several in mouth and then he sat on his thighs on a dry spot, eating the leaves. As he ate he turned his head in all directions.

There was a savage yelp and a mad rush of soft feet. The yellow dog came rushing down the road from the lodge. The rabbit bounded into the corpse. The dog lurched after him, making a noise like ice on a pond being broken by a heavy stone. The thrush sank on to the ground to hide himself.

A little boy came running down the road, yelling to urge on the dog. When he reached the spot where the dog had disappeared into the copse, he stood still, with his head cocked to one side, listening. He wiped his nose on his coat-sleeve. His coat was very ragged and much too long for him.

He was about to go back home when he saw the thrush. With a joyful cry he pounced on it. The thrush bent down his head. When the boy's hard fingers closed on his plump, soft, warm body he chirped madly.

The boy shut the beak to see would it stay shut. It did. 'He's not dyin', thought the boy. 'He's only drowned. I'll take him home and give him somethin' t'ate.'

He placed him on the low, slanting roof of the lodge and brought him breadcrumbs from the kitchen. He scattered the crumbs in front of the thrush's breast. The thrush took no notice of them. Then the boy took hold of the thrush, opened his beak and forced a crumb into his mouth. The thrush wriggled and clawed with his feet. He tried to eject the crumb with his tongue, but while doing so he tasted it and he liked the taste. He ate it, and when the boy pushed his beak to another crumb, he picked it up of his own accord and ate it also.

The boy fed the thrush until he could eat no more. Then he stood a long time watching him, prodding him in the tail with a little twig and blowing at his feathers. But the thrush was very stupid with exhaustion and he would do nothing but lie on his breast basking in the sun, drying himself and resting. The boy got bored with him. In sudden anger he hurled a large stone at the bird and walked away into the copse to hunt rabbits.

As the day wore on, the warm sun dried the thrush's body and poured strength into him. He rolled on to his side and loosened his wings, so that the heat could penetrate to every pore. Every time a fresh wave of strength and warmth reached his body he shook himself and chirped. At last he stood up and began to stretch his legs backwards under his trailed wings. He hopped along to the ridge of the roof. He began to chirp.

Presently he heard an answering chirp, a plaintive call that was very familiar to him. He cocked his head sideways and listened. He heard it again. He chirped as loudly as he could. The plaintive call answered him and almost immediately he saw his father and mother flying out of the copse and alighting on a hawthorn bush about ten yards away. He uttered a tremulous chirp and flew towards them. He had not gone half the distance before he was forced to land. But his parents swooped down to meet him.

Then there were three chirping heads close together for a long time. Wings were fluttered and choice pieces of worm were pressed into the beak of the lost one that had been found again.

THE OUTCAST

I am the Good Shepherd (Jesus Christ)

The parish priest returned to the parochial house at Dromullen, after a two months' holiday at the seaside resort of Lisdoonvarna.

He returned fatter than he went, with immense red gills and crimson flakes on his undulating cheeks, with pale blue eyes scowling behind mountainous barricades of darkening flesh and a paunch that would have done credit to a Roman emperor.

He sank into the old easy chair in the library with a sumptuous groan. He was tired after the journey. He filled the chair and overflowed it. His head sank into his neck as he leaned back and his neck-flesh eddied turbulently over the collar of his black coat, toppling down behind in three neat billowing waves. He felt the elbow-rests with his fat white palms caressingly. Great chair! It had borne his weight for ten years without a creak. Great chair! Great priest!

His housekeeper stood timorously on the other side of the table, with her hands clasped in front of her black skirt, a lean, sickly woman with a kind white face. She had followed him in. But she was afraid to disturb the great man so soon after his arrival.

He sighed, grunted, groaned, and made a rumbling internal noise from his throat to his midriff. Then he said 'Ha!' and shifted his weight slightly. He suddenly raised his eyebrows. His little eyes rested on the housekeeper's twitching hands. They shot upwards to her pale face. His mouth fell open slightly.

'Well?' he grunted in a deep, pompous voice. 'Trouble again? What is it?'

'Kitty Manion wants to see ye, Father?' whispered the housekeeper.

'Foo!' said the priest. He made a noise in his mouth as if he were chewing something soft. He grunted. 'I heard about her,' he continued in a tone of oppressed majesty. 'I heard about the slut. . . . Yes, indeed. . . . Ough! . . . Show her in.'

The housekeeper curtsied and disappeared. The door closed without a sound. The white handle rolled backwards with a faint squeak. There was silence in the library. The priest clasped his paunch with both hands. His paunch rose and fell as he breathed. He kept nodding his head at the ground. Two minutes passed.

The door opened again without a sound. The housekeeper pushed Kitty Manion gently into the library. Then the door closed again. The white handle squeaked. There was a tense pause. The parish priest raised his eyes. Kitty Manion stood in front of him, at the other side of the table, two paces within the door.

She had a month-old male child at her breast. His head emerged from the thick, heavy cashmere shawl that enveloped his mother. His blue eyes stared impassively, contentedly. The mother's eyes were distended and bloodshot. Her cheeks were feverishly red. Her shawl had fallen back on to her shoulders like a cowl, as she shifted it from one hand to another in order to rearrange her child. Her great mass of black hair was disordered, bound loosely on the nape of her neck. Her neck was long, full, and white. Her tall, slim figure shivered. These shivers passed down her spine, along her black-stockinged, tapering calves and disappeared into her high-heeled little shoes. She looked very beautiful and innocent as only a young mother can look.

The priest stared at her menacingly. She stared back at him helplessly. Then she suddenly lost control of herself and sank to her knees.

'Have pity on me, Father,' she cried. 'Have pity on me child.'

She began to sob. . . . The priest did not speak. A minute passed. Then she rose to her feet once more. The priest spoke.

'You are a housemaid at Mr Burke's, the solicitor.'

'I was, Father. But he dismissed me this morning. I have no place to go to. No shelter for me child. They're afraid to take me in in the village for fear ye might ... Oh! Father, I don't mind about mesel', but me child. It . . .'

'Silence!' cried the priest sternly. 'A loose tongue is an ill omen. How did this happen?'

She began to tremble violently. She kept silent.

'Who is the father of yer child, woman?' said the priest slowly, lowering his voice and leaning forward on his elbows.

Her lips quivered. She looked at the ground. Tears rolled down her cheeks. She did not speak.

'Ha!' he cried arrogantly. 'I thought so. Obstinate slut. I have noticed you this long while. I knew where you were drifting. Ough! The menace to my parish that a serpent like you . . . Out with it!' he roared, striking the table. 'Let me know who has aided you in your sin. Who is he? Name him. Name the father of your child.'

She blubbered, but she did not speak.

'For the sake of your immortal soul,' he thundered, 'I command you to name the father of your child.'

'I can't,' she moaned hysterically. 'I can't, Father. There was more than one man. I don't know who . . .'

'Stop, wretch,' screamed the priest, seizing his head with both hands. 'Silence! Silence' I command you. Oh my! Oh! Oh!'

The child began to whimper.

'Jesus, Mary and Joseph,' muttered the girl in a quiet whisper.

The priest's face was livid. His eyes were bloodshot. His paunch trembled. He drew in a deep breath to regain control of himself. Then he stretched his right hand to the door with the forefinger pointed.

'Go!' he thundered, in a melancholy voice. 'Begone from me, accursed one. Begone with the child of your abomination. Begone.'

She turned slowly, on swaying hips, to the door, with the foot movements of one sinking in a quagmire. She threw back her head helplessly on her neck and seized the door-handle. The handle jingled noisily. The door swung open and struck her knee. She tottered into the hall.

'Away with you,' he thundered. 'Begone from me, accursed one.'

The housekeeper opened the hall door. She was thrusting something into the girl's hand, but the girl did not see her. As soon as she saw the open air through the doorway, she darted forward with a wild cry. She sprang down the drive and out into the road.

She paused for a moment in the roadway. To the right, the road led to the village. To the left, it led to the mountains. She darted away to the left, trotting on her toes, throwing her feet out sideways and swaying from her hips.

It was an August day. The sun was falling away towards the west. A heat mist hung high up in the heavens, around the dark spurs of the mountains.

She trotted a long way. Then she broke into a walk as the road began to rise. It turned and twisted upwards steeply towards the mountains, a narrow white crust of bruised limestone curling through the soft bog-land. The mountains loomed up close on either side. . . . There were black shadows on the grey granite rocks and on the purple heather. Overhanging peaks made gloomy caverns that cast long spikes of blackness out from them. Here and there the mountains sucked their sides inwards in sumptuous curves, like seashell mouths. Long black fences raced majestically up the mountain sides and disappeared on far horizons over their peaks, with ferocious speed. The melancholy silence of a dead world filled the air.

The melancholy silence soothed the girl. It numbed her. She sat down to rest on the stunted grass by the roadside. She cast one glance at the valley behind her. She shuddered. Then she hugged her baby fiercely and traversed its tiny face with kisses. The baby began to cry. She fed him. Then he fell asleep. She arose and walked on.

She was among the peaks, walking along a level, winding stretch of road that led to the lake, the Lake of Black Cahir. A great dull weariness possessed her being. Her limbs trembled as she walked. Her heart began to throb with fear. Her forehead wrinkled and quick tremors made her shiver now and again. But she walked fiercely on, driven forward towards the lake in spite of her terror.

She reached the entrance to the valley where the lake was. She saw the lake suddenly, nestling cunningly behind an overhanging mossy-faced cliff, a flat white dot with dark edges. She stood still and stared at it for a long time. She was delirious. Her eyes glistened with a strange light.

Then she shivered and walked slowly downwards towards the lake bank, stopping many times to kiss her sleeping child. When she reached the rocky bank and saw the deep, dark waters, she uttered a cry and darted away. The child awoke and began to cry. She sat down and fondled him. He ceased crying and beat the air feebly with his hands. She kissed him and called to him strange words in a mumbling voice.

She took off her shawl, spread it on a flat, smooth rock, and placed the child in it. Then she tied the shawl into a bundle about the child. She placed the bundle carefully against another rock and knelt before it. Clasping her hands to her breast, she turned her face to the sky and prayed silently.

She prayed for two minutes, and then tears trickled down her cheeks, and she remained for a long time staring at the sky without thinking or praying. Finally she rose to her feet and walked to the lake bank quickly, without looking at her baby. When she reached the brink, she joined her hands above her head, closed her eyes, and swayed forward stiffly.

But she drew backwards again with a gasp.

Her child had crowed. She whirled about and rushed to him. She caught him up in her arms and began to kiss him joyously, laughing wildly as she did so.

Laughing madly, wildly, loudly, she rushed to the bank.

She threw back her head. She put the child's face close against her white throat, and jumped headlong into the lake.

A RED PETTICOAT

Mrs Mary Deignan and her four children were sitting around the fire in their cabin. They were very miserable. For the reason that the day was a cold one in the middle of February, and there was no food in the house. That morning they ate the last piece of oaten cake, and there was no more oats to make another cake. Their flour had given out a week before that. A dried fish that Coleman, the eldest child and the only son, had stolen off a wall where it was getting dried after being taken out of pickle, had lasted them three days for dinner. There was not a single scrap in the house. Not even a piece of potato.

'Well,' said the mother, 'what are we doing here? We must do something. God is good, no doubt, but he is good only to those who forage for themselves. Now what's to be done? Children, can none of you think of anything? Isn't it well known that the angels put wisdom into the mouths of little ones. Though, God forgive me, the four little ones I have are bigger than myself, at least as far as their stomachs are concerned. So they are.'

The four children, in spite of their hunger and their misery, began to laugh. They were really a remarkable family. The mother was remarkable and the children were remarkable. Since the father, old Mick Deignan, that had the wart on his nose, and was always sick with the influenza, and always wore a white frieze trousers that somehow or other always had a yellow burnt spot on its leg one place or another, since he died ten years before that the family had been very, very poor. They had ten acres of land, but they had no stock to put on it, so they always rented it for a few pounds a year. The mother worked at any odd job that she could find, washing, thickening frieze, and scrubbing in people's houses, and the daughters used to mend nets for the co-operative society, while the son, who was seventeen years of age, worked as a labourer. But, to tell the truth, as far as work was concerned, they were a lazy and indigent family. Maybe they would work well enough for a spell, and then for some reason or other the whole family took to idleness and sat in their cabin all day composing poems, cracking jokes, drinking tea, and having the time of their lives. So that the villagers, passing their cabin and hearing loud laughter, got mad with rage against these poor devils who were gifted by the good God who governs all things with the Divine capacity for enjoying life and their good health. For in spite of their cabin containing only one tiny bedroom where the mother and her three daughters slept, and the little kitchen where the son slept on the settle, the children were healthy. And the mother was healthy, except in cold weather when she drank too much tea and suffered so terribly from flatulence and pains all over her middle, that she was always on the point of death and moaned liked a possessed one.

But that winter things had gone badly with them until now they were at the end of their tether. Their credit was exhausted. Their solitary pig had been taken from the sty in lieu of debt by Flanagan, the grocer from Kilmurrage, 'the curse of God on his rotten Co. Mayo liver,' as Mrs Deignan said. None of them could find work anywhere. Until now they had bravely kept up courage and laughed and sang and composed poems, satires on all their enemies, but the hunger was telling on them that bitterly cold day as they sat by the fire. Barbara, the eldest daughter, aged sixteen, was trying to toast her short, fat legs at the turf fire.

She was sitting on a low stool in the corner, her short, thick black hair woven in a plait that hung over her shoulders. Her soft, open red lips and her big, black eyes were turned towards her legs that were bare to the knees, and her short, stubby little hands were moving up and down the legs, counting the 'Rockfishes' on them, that is the queer blue spots that came into them from being constantly exposed in their nakedness to the turf blaze. Mary, aged fifteen, a girl almost exactly similar in shape and face to Barbara, except that she was slightly thinner, had her left leg in her lap and with her two hands she was pulling at the big toe. She had an idea that if she pulled at her toes long enough she could make them as long and slender as her fingers and thus be a great lady. Little Margaret, the most serious of the family, aged fourteen, the one who always discovered the correct phrase when the rest of the family were in a difficulty over a poem, sat very seriously with her little hands folded in her lap, looking at the fire, with her black curls hanging about her little pale face. Coleman, a handsome boy of seventeen, with large blue eyes and long lashes like a woman, lay stretched on the form beside his mother, looking at the fire and brooding over something. He was always thinking and breathing heavily through his nose, and then all of a sudden he would slap his thigh and jump to his feet bursting with laughter, and no matter how much people asked what he was laughing at and what had come into his head, he would just shake his shoulders and say nothing.

The mother sat in the other corner opposite Barbara. She was about sixty and very thin and old-looking on account of the yellowish colour of her wrinkled face, a colour she got very presumably from her tea drinking and her bad digestion. When she had her clothes on and she was talking she looked big enough, but when she stripped going to bed she was so thin and small that it was a continual cause of wonder to Margaret that she didn't break in the middle. They called her 'Mary of the bad verses' in the village and all over the whole island of Inverara, not because her verses were bad as verses, but because they were scurrilous and abusive, and at times even indecent and in a sense immoral.

'Well,' said the mother, again, 'have you got any plans, Coleman?'

Coleman looked at his mother seriously with his big eyelashes drooping and his round, red mouth half open. Then he giggled and nestled farther down on the form like a child that is playing with its mother.

'If there are any plans to be made,' he said, still giggling, 'you better make them yourself. I'm too hungry to think about anything.'

'Yes, mother, think of something,' cried the other three children, suddenly becoming excited.

'Well,' said the mother, setting herself squat on her stool and resting her chin between her two palms, 'I might think of something. Let me see now. What is there?'

There was silence for nearly a minute. Coleman's heavy breathing could be heard distinctly. Then the mother sat up suddenly, slapped her knees with her palms and cried: 'Children, I have it. I have it. Get me my shawl quickly. Jump up, girls, and get me my shawl. Get me my shawl and my new check apron.'

She jumped up and, taking a tiny portion of her black, threadbare skirt between the thumb and forefinger of each hand daintily, she jerked her head to one side and began to dance around the room, singing as she danced: 'There was an old peddler in love with a nun, God forgive him.'

They brought her shawl and the check apron and pestered her with questions, asking her what she was going to do, but she never budged.

'Now let me alone, children,' she said, 'let my blood be on my own hands. You just stay quiet in the house and if I am not back within two hours with food and the making of a drink, ye will know where to find me, and that will be in the police barracks.'

Then she put on her apron and her black shawl, which she wore in triangular fashion, with the point of it tipping the ground behind her heels, like a steering gear. She went out, marched through the village without looking at a person, with her shawl thrown far forward over her head, and stooping slightly. She walked down the road to the next village, which was a mile away, and where Mrs Murtagh had a little general shop, that sold everything which a peasant could be expected to buy, and bought everything which a peasant could be induced to sell, except cattle, of course, and immortal souls. It was a two-storied concrete house, and even though it was only three years old it looked bedraggled and weather-stained like a ship that has been away somewhere for a long time and has come back to port covered with barnacles and scratched and wicked-looking. Mrs Deignan marched into the hall and turned to her left, into the large, long dark room that served as the shop. There was a heavy smell of sugar, soap, salty bacon, and stale biscuits all mixed up together. Behind the counter, with her arms folded on her breast, stood Mrs Murtagh. She was a handsome woman of forty-five, with a pair of hard, mercenary eyes, with a foxy look in them. Her face would have been very beautiful were it not for that foxy look in her eyes and the yellowish colour of her skin around her cheeks. Her cheeks had a rosy flush like a young girl. She looked at Mrs Deignan furtively, and nodded her head slightly, as if she were not a bit pleased to see that good woman.

'Well,' she said, in a very curt voice and with a very gross attempt at speaking in a humorous voice, 'I suppose you have come to settle up that little bill you owe me. There, now, I always said you were an honest woman, Mrs Deignan. But sure don't be in a hurry with it. Let it lie another five years.' She began to laugh in a queer manner that she had, a laugh that was almost like a hen's cackle, saving the comparison.

But the laugh died in her mouth when she saw the expression on Mrs Deignan's face. Mrs Murtagh was a hard woman, and could drive a hard bargain with a parish priest, such was her force of character, but still . . . the look on Mrs Deignan's face terrified her. Mrs Deignan had not spoken a word. She had merely let her shawl fall back from her shoulder and trail behind her. She had let her lean, wrinkled, yellow-skinned hands go limp. She had allowed her face to go lax and loose and then gradually it began to curl and form convolutions like milk just getting ready to boil in a saucepan on a slow fire. Gradually her face gathered itself together, her throat became alive, her bosom gave signs that something devilish was forcing its way upwards from her middle and finding great difficulty in reaching her throat. In fact, Mrs Deignan looked as if she was going to give birth to something awful. She did. She began to talk. The first word come out with great difficulty, emerging from her wrinkled yellow lips in curves and spirals, with the grinding sound of a knife being sharpened on a whetstone. Then her words began to gather speed until they came pouring out of her mouth, with the sweet, sharp cadence of a rushing stream.

'Hypocrite, robber, receiver of stolen goods,' she cried. 'Oh woman that has denied God, virtue, charity, and all the good deeds of the holy ones, you female devil routed from hell because Lucifer himself couldn't sleep under the same roof with such an abomination, you virago of the seven tongues, and they all cancerous with the load of foul words that come each hour across their flabby and pestilential backs; oh, daughter, shared by seven fathers and they all drunkards and vagabonds; oh, monster, oh! . . . ah!' she paused, and raised her hands and held them in front of her face like an Eastern merchant going to strike a bargain. Her eyes distended, and she frothed at the mouth, 'my tongue refuses to describe you.' Suddenly she flopped down in a chair that stood by the counter and she began to fan herself with a corner of her shawl, while her whole body shook as if she were in hysterics.

'Is it out of our mind you are?' gasped Mrs Murtagh, in a low voice. She was beside herself with rage, but she was a cautious woman and fear gained the mastery of her rage. She stood behind the counter, trembling and darting her eyes out of the window for fear a customer might come in and hear Mrs Deignan. 'Is it out of your mind you are?' she repeated. 'What have you got against me? What is it I say? Speak, woman.'

Mrs Deignan kept shaking her head and her right hand for a few moments, then she tried to open her lips, but she didn't. Encouraged by Mrs Deignan's failure to open her lips, Mrs Murtagh darted around the corner of the counter, folded her arms and glared at Mrs Deignan with ferocity.

'Speak,' she hissed, 'and say your say, or your bones will rot in jail while I have a pound to bribe a judge to keep you there.'

'Ah-h-h-h-h-h.' Mrs Deignan had opened her lips at last and given vent to a snarl like a dog. Her face became alive again and gathered in a ball. Her limp, little body became as active and mobile as a squirrel's body. Mrs Murtagh stepped back and, in spite of herself, she uttered a scream. 'You would, would you?' cried Mrs Deignan. 'You're a widow yourself, but you would stamp on another widow. We'll see-e-e-e, we'll se-e-e-e.' Then she laughed loudly, ending her laugh in a high note that she changed in some manner into a scream of triumph. Then she bent forward her head and, with her hands on her knees, she looked into Mrs Murtagh's face and said, in a low distinct voice: 'Where is the red petticoat you were wearing last Sunday night, when you went to visit the tailor?'

'Oh, Lord in heaven!' gasped Mrs Murtagh, putting her two clenched hands to her lips. Then she laughed in a hard, cold way that was quite artificial, and looked about her. Mrs Deignan kept glaring at her. Then she stopped laughing, gave a little start, and came up to Mrs Deignan and bent down to her and hissed straight at her: 'You're a liar, I wasn't wearing a red petticoat last Sunday.'

'You-are-telling-a-lie.' Mrs Deignan shot out the words separately like a schoolmaster explaining something to a stupid boy. 'I saw you with my own eyes coming out of the tailor's house wearing a red petticoat. Deny it if you can.'

'It's a lie,' cried Mrs Murtagh, suddenly straightening herself and stamping her foot. She was blood-red to the roots of her neck. 'It's a lie,' she cried again, in a short voice. 'It wasn't a red petticoat I was wearing. It was a black skirt.'

Mrs Deignan uttered an exclamation and jumped to her feet. Her face was radiant with delight.

'Ha,' she cried, in a low, strident voice, just like the sound a man might make after swallowing a rich bottle of Guinness's stout on a very hot day. 'Now, I have you. So it was you who was there, was it? I saw the black skirt as I was coming along the lane, but I wasn't sure. Ha-a-a-a-a. Didn't I find you out easily, my fine trapster? Didn't I?'

'Oh-h-h-h,' hissed Mrs Murtagh through her teeth, as she rushed at Mrs Deignan. There was a tussle and a few screams and more curses, and the two women were at one another's throats, tearing at one another like a pair of cats that have met on a moonlight night in a back garden. Things were thrown about and there was considerable noise until at last Mrs Murtagh swung her enemy and sent her reeling to the far end of the shop, where she fell against a few sacks of flour. She was going to follow up her advantage when her habitual caution again gained control of her and she paused, looking undecidedly at Mrs Deignan. Mrs Deignan, who was not at all hurt, saw her indecision out of the corner of her eye. She promptly, in the very act of getting to her feet and assuming a posture of defence, threw her hands in the air and fell in a dead faint on the floor. As she fell, she muttered distinctly and audibly 'that she was dead.'

'Good God, what have I done?' cried Mrs Murtagh. 'I've killed her.' She rushed over to Mrs Deignan and raised her up. At the same moment two women appeared at the door of the shop attracted by the noise.

'God between us and all harm,' cried one of them, 'what is it?'

'It's a fit she has,' whispered Mrs Murtagh. 'Give me a hand to take her into the parlour, poor woman; it's her stomach is bad.'

'Ah, God help the poor,' said the two neighbours with insincerity, looking at one another with a look that said plainer than words that Mrs Murtagh had refused poor Mrs Deignan credit for some food and that Mrs Deignan had very properly assaulted her for such cruelty.

However, when they revived Mrs Deignan on the parlour sofa with smelling-salts and a nip of brandy, the two neighbours were bitterly disappointed to find the poor woman very grateful to Mrs Murtagh for her kindness. Mrs Deignan sat up, rubbed her eyes with both hands, than her cheeks, then her chest, and then held out both hands to Mrs Murtagh. With tears visible in her eyes, she looked at Mrs Murtagh and said: 'Oh, may God in heaven reward you for your kindness to the poor. Neighbours,' she cried, turning to the two other women, 'it's how I came in here and told her that we didn't have a bite of food in the house for the past week, not even a bite of potato to give to the four poor orphans that the Lord gave to me as a burden. And, like the good woman that she is, she turned around and said, said she: 'Mrs Deignan, put your shawl on the counter and I'll give for the honour of God what'll stop the cry of hunger in your house for a few days, tea and sugar and flour, and whatever you like to take on six months' credit.' 'Ah-h-h-h-h, neighbours, it was too much for me. It was too much for me. Ba-a-a-a-h, it was too much for me. I took bad. Ba-a-a-a-h.' And she began to beat her middle with both hands.

The two women went out and whispered to one another outside that there was something in the wind. But what it was they couldn't make out. And they went home in a vile temper.

Ten minutes later, Mrs Deignan emerged with her black shawl turned into a wallet laid across her back, and in the round, black bottom of the shawl there were two pounds of sugar, a pound of tea, four tins of condensed milk, two stone of flour, and four loaves that had gone a bit stale. And at the door of the stop stood Mrs Murtagh looking after her customer with a look of bitter hatred. But her fear was stronger than her hatred. The one black spot on her character, her illicit affair with the bachelor tailor, was discovered by this virago of a poetess. And Mrs Murtagh kept thinking of the number of times Mrs Deignan would go away with a shawl full of groceries on her. But then, again, she thought of the tailor.

TRAPPED

Night was falling. The sun was sinking into the sea, casting a great wide red arc of light over the calm water. The cliffs that had looked grey during the daytime were now black and their faces seemed to ooze water, a sort of perspiration that pours from them during the night. Beneath them the sea was a deep, deep blue, almost black, and the little waves never broke at all but swelled in and out murmuring. It was very beautiful, silent and dreamy.

Bartly Hernon the bird-catcher had descended the cliff-path from the summit of the Clogher Mor and landed on the broad plateau that protrudes from the face of the cliff, about fifty feet above the level of the sea. To the left the cliffs curved inwards, forming a half-circle. They bellied out far over their concave bases. There were great wide clefts in them, like scars running horizontally between each massive layer of stone that formed the foundation of the earth above them. From the plateau the great height of the cliffs made the fissures look small, but a man could stand erect in some of them. And the little stones, that could be seen wedged in their mouths here and there, were really huge boulders, buttressing the upper lairs of the cliffs.

Hernon was a very big man with finely developed limbs and a square muscular head. His face was tanned brown by the elements and great strong fair hairs covered the backs of his hands. He was all fair-haired and his face had the gentle, passive expression of the man who never thinks of anything but physical things. An ever-active, fearless man, he was so used to the danger of climbing the cliffs that he was as surefooted as a goat. He carried a sack, a heavy short stick and a small basket. The sack was to carry the birds. The stick was used to club them. He stored the eggs in the basket.

In order to reach the entrance to the lower fissure, one he was to explore that night, he had to scale a very narrow and difficult path along the cliff face for a distance of about twenty yards. This path was formed by a portion of the cliff coming loose and slanting out at an angle of ten degrees or so from the cliff itself. It looked like a crazy structure of boxes, piled one on top of the other irregularly. It seemed that one had only to give it a slight push and it would topple over into the sea. Above five hundred tons of stone. Between the cliff face and this slanting pile, loose rocks had fallen.

Along these rocks Hernon had to go. He had been many times through this pass and it had never occurred to him that there was any danger in it. The broken pile had been there as long as anyone in the district could remember. It had a name and it was part of the country. So it would always be there. If it fell it would be impossible to reach those fissures where the sea-birds lived, or, having reached them, to get back to the plateau. But among our peasants it was unmanly even to think of its being dangerous to go up that way.

Hernon took off his shoes and left them on the rock. He also took off his frieze waistcoat and left it with his shoes. He would leave them there until his return in the morning. He took a piece of the bread which he carried in a red handkerchief and ate it. The remainder he placed beside the waistcoat. If he got hungry during the night, very hungry, he could suck a raw rockbird's egg. It was very strong but very good to prevent that sort of hunger-sickness which men get sometimes in the cliffs; not from hunger but begotten of the terrific solitude and darkness of the caverns. The remainder of the bread he would eat in the morning, on his return, before climbing to the cliff-top.

He tightened his belt and began to climb. All those big rocks were loose and very smooth. He had to jump from one another, gripping for footholds with his hands and toes, crouching like a dancer and then jumping, curled up in a ball, so that he landed on all fours. He got almost to the end of the pass when he missed his foothold. He swayed for a moment out over the sea. Then he gasped and swung himself in towards the cliff, grasping a pointed rock that projected. The rock held his weight until he reached another foothold in the entrance to the fissure. Then as he strained at it further to raise himself and thrust himself forward, it gave way with a rumbling noise. Terrified at finding the rock coming loose with his hands, he hurled himself forward on his face and clung to the wet floor of the fissure. He lay still.

It was the first time he had missed a foothold scaling that pass, and he was stupefied with terror. It always happens that way with a fearless man who has done daring things but has never met with an accident. He listened without looking behind him.

There was a dull rumble as the loosened rock fell with a thud against the slanting pile. Then there was silence for about half a second. Then the silence was broken by a slight snapping sound like the end of a dog's yawn. That sound changed into another and louder one, as of a soft mound bursting. Yet nothing seemed to move; until suddenly there was a tremendous crash. A cloud of dust rose in the air and the great pile of broken cliff hurtled down to the sea, casting rocks far out into the dark waters, where they fell with a pattering sound, while the bulk subsided to the base of the cliff and

became still almost immediately. When the cloud of dust cleared away the face of
the cliff was again smooth and unbroken. There was not a foothold for a cat from
the fissure at whose entrance Hernon lay to the plateau beyond. It was a
distance of twenty yards, past a hump in the cliff. Hernon was trapped.

He was perspiring. He turned his head and looked behind. When he saw
the smooth face of the cliff, where a minute before there had been a pile of
loose rocks and a path, his mouth opened wide and his eyes became fixed.
'Jesus, Mary and Joseph,' he said. Then he remained motionless for over a
minute staring at the smooth, dark-grey bulging face of the cliff that cut off
his return. He kept staring at it stupidly, as if expecting that the pile of rock
would rise again and cover it. But the only thing that happened was that tiny
rivulets of water oozed from it and began to descend slowly, dropping down
to the sea, just like the rest of the cliff. It almost immediately looked old like
the remainder of the cliff, as if it had been shaped that way for centuries.

'You horned devil,' muttered Hernon, suddenly becoming terrified of it
and crawling away up the fissure on his hands and knees. The fissure was
very low at its entrance. But it rapidly widened so that after ten yards or so,
a man could walk in it, stooping slightly to avoid an occasional boss of stone
that jutted down from the roof. Hernon, however, was so stupefied that he
kept crawling, long after he had passed the narrow strip, until he bumped his
head against a boulder that propped up the roof. Then he jumped up and
looked around him wildly.

Night had completely fallen within the caverns. It was pitch-black. But
looking out to sea over the edge of the cliff, he could still see the water and
the sky lit up by the twilight. He sat down on the rock to recover from his
shock and plan some means of escape. But instead of concentrating on how
he was to escape he kept remembering all the men in the district who had
been killed in the cliffs: Brian Derrane, who fell from the top of a cliff while
hunting a rabbit; John Halloran, who got entangled in a fishing-line he was
swinging out and got carried out with it; and several others. Gradually he felt a
curious longing to look out over the edge of the cliff and throw himself down.

He was not aware of the desire to throw himself down until he bent forward and looked down. It was about one hundred feet to the sea. He could
distinguish the forms of large boulders in the tide and flat rocks with seaweed growing on them. And as he looked at them he felt a sudden desire to
hurl himself down. That terrified him. He jumped up and crawled back, until he
pressed his body against the back of the cavern. He was quite helpless with
fear now.

He lay there for a long time quite motionless. It was pitch-dark now. All sorts of sea-birds were flying in and out. The whirring of their wings in the darkness was a terrifying sound, because they were invisible and they did not scream. They were all returning to their nesting-places for the night, in the interminable holes in the fissure. Hernon took no notice of this sound because he was used to it. Afterwards, when the moon rose and the place was lit up with a yellow light, he had intended to prowl among the caverns and club the sleeping birds. But now he was not thinking of the birds but of death.

It is extraordinary that physically fearless men like Hernon are always thrown into a panic like this when confronted by something they cannot understand. They are always eager to face danger when they can see it and understand its nature and touch it physically. But I have always noticed among our peasants that these rough, strong, unthinking men like Hernon are quite hopeless in a situation that demands thought if they have no one to guide them. Whereas the small, weak, cunning types of peasant, who invariably avoid danger, are always subtle and resourceful when placed in a dangerous position.

But very probably the danger of his position had been discussed beforehand around the village firesides, as is the custom on winter evenings, and he understood the hopelessness of it. It was absolutely impossible to reach the summit of the cliff. It was two hundred feet away and it bellied out, so that even if people came with a rope, the rope would dangle twenty feet away from him, absolutely out of reach. And it was equally impossible to throw a rope from the sea, up a distance of one hundred feet.

At last the moon rose. Gradually the yellow light lit up the sea, the cliffs and the caverns. It was very weird but it revived Hernon. He was quite used to the moonlight in the cliffs. It was something physical that he could understand. The birds were now asleep and there was perfect silence.

He got up and began to walk along the edge of the precipice, looking down and examining its face, seeking a path to descend. Even if he could get down to the sea he would have to swim over a mile in the night before he could get a landing-place, and there were sharks in the water. But he could not wait till morning, until perhaps a boat might come looking for him. He was too panic-stricken to wait.

The fissure, in which he was, wound irregularly through the face of the cliff for a distance of almost half a mile. But here and there it was so narrow that there was only a tiny ledge, a few inches wide, leading from one deep cavern to another. These passes were very dangerous even in broad daylight. But Hernon thought nothing of them. He had stopped crawling now. He dashed along, taking great bounds over pools, gripping the face of the cliff and swinging himself out over the edge of the cliff to reach another ledge. His figure, bending and bounding, looked wonderfully agile and beautiful in the half-darkness of the pale yellow moonlight; the mysterious bounding figure of a cliff-man. He had dropped his basket, his club and his sack. He had lost his cap. His fair hair shimmered in the mysterious moonlight.

Although he had been panic-stricken when he was crouching under the cliff, he was now perfectly composed physically. His limbs moved instinctively although somewhere in the back of his mind there was the picture of a skeleton that had once been found in these caverns. Some man, ages ago, had been wedged in among boulders at the back of a cavern and had died there, unable to extricate himself. That was a legend. It drove him on. But his body was cool and his limbs acted methodically, moving with supple ease, performing amazing feats of agility.

However, he went along several hundred yards without seeing the least sign of a path down to the sea. Then at last he turned a corner and came to a place called the Cormorants' Bed. Here there was an enormous cavern. Down from it to the sea there was a big black crack in the cliff. The cliff face was as smooth as elsewhere, but there was a long, straight stone, pointed like a wedge, running straight down. Hernon looked at it and wondered could he grip it with his knees and slide down slowly. His forehead wrinkled and he shuddered thinking of it. He looked down. There were rocks at the bottom. He would be smashed to pieces if he lost his hold. Yet without pausing he moved towards the cavern. He rounded a very narrow ledge and stumbled into a pool at the entrance to the cavern. Immediately there was a wild screech and hundreds of great black figures whirred past his head, flapping their wings. He stooped to avoid them, because these birds, going past on the wings, could knock him over the edge of precipice. Then when they has passed he groped his way to the wedge-shaped rock that ran down. He made the sign of the cross on his forehead, rubbed his palms together, grunted and stiffened himself. Then he gripped the rock savagely, swung his body around it and gripped with his knees. He hung on to it for a moment, like an animal crouched on its prey. Then he began to descend.

As soon as he moved downwards, he was seized with dizziness. His limbs shivered and he almost lost his hold. A prickly sensation went through his body to his heart, like a prod from a needle. But in an instant he stiffened himself and held his breath. The fit passed and he ceased to be conscious. His limbs moved mechanically and his eyes stared unseeingly at the wedge-shaped rock that he held. He went down and down inch by inch, each muscle rigid, moving with the slow, awkward movements of a bear, his broad back bent, his neck muscles cracking with the strain on his spine. His skin was perfectly dry, as if all the perspiration had been drained from the pores.

Then at last he found himself sitting on a rock at the bottom of the cliff. He still clung to the cliff, pawing at it, for several moments before he became aware that he reached the bottom. When he did become aware of it he uttered a loud oath, 'You horned devil,' and then perspiration stood out on his forehead once more.

But curiously enough, it was not through fear he was perspiring, but through pride. He had done a mighty thing. He had descended where no man ever had descended. Exalted with joy and pride, he waved his hand over his head and uttered a wild yell. The sound re-echoed again and again among the caverns of the cliffs, and before it had died, thousands of seabirds rushed from their ledges screaming. The air was full of terrifying sound. Hernon jumped from the rock where he still sat and, without pausing, plunged into the sea, terrified once more by the errie sounds in the devilish caverns from which he had escaped.

The sea was dead calm, shimmering under the moonlight that fell in it, making a broad silver path with golden rims, while afar it faded into blackness under a starlit pale sky. On a level with the sea, the cliffs seemed to reach the sky. The sea appeared to be walled in by them, like water in a deep basin. Afar off on the left there was a sharp promontory where the cliffs ended. Beyond that there was a rocky beach below the village. That was where Hernon could land. It was over a mile.

He began to swim with all his strength, swimming on his side, heaving through the water with a rushing sound like a swan. He was a great swimmer. His beautiful muscular shoulders rose out of the water, his long arm shot out circularly, he thrust forward his other arm like a sword-thrust and then he heaved forward, churning with his feet, while he shook his head and spat the brine from his panting mouth. In the water he was conscious of no danger. All his muscles were in action and he saw the open sea before him to traverse. In spite of his terrific exertion in the cliff and descending, he was quite fresh and he never slackened speed until he passed the promontory. Then he turned over on his back and let himself be carried in by the great rolling waves that drive to the rocky beach. Then he turned once more on his chest and swam to the low weed-covered rock on which row-boats landed. He mounted the rock and waded on to dry land. He was safe. He rushed up the shore and knelt on the pebbles. Crossing himself, he began to pray aloud, thanking God. But while he prayed he kept thinking of what the village people would say of his heroic feat.

MOTHER AND SON

Although it was only five o'clock, the sun had already set and the evening was very still, as all spring evenings are, just before the birds begin to sing themselves to sleep; or maybe tell one another bedside stories. The village was quiet. The men had gone away to fish for the night after working all the morning with the sowing. Women were away milking the cows in the little fields among the crags.

Brigid Gill was alone in her cottage waiting for her little son to come home from school. He was now an hour late, and as he was only nine years she was very nervous about him, especially as he was her only child and he was a wild boy, always getting into mischief, mitching from school, fishing minnows on Sunday and building stone 'castles' in the great crag above the village. She kept telling herself that she would give him a good scolding and beating when he came in, but at the same time her heart was thumping with anxiety and she started at every sound, rushing out to the door and looking down the winding road, that was now dim with the shadows of evening. So many things could happen to a little boy.

His dinner of dried fish and roast potatoes were being kept warm in the oven among the peat ashes beside the fire on the hearth, and on the table there was a plate, a knife and a little mug full of buttermilk.

At last she heard the glad cried of the schoolboys afar off, and rushing out she saw their tiny forms scampering, not up the road, but across the crags to the left, their caps in their hands.

'Thank God,' she said, and then she persuaded herself that she was very angry. Hurriedly she got a small dried willow rod, sat down on a chair within the door and waited for her little Stephen.

He advanced up the yard very slowly, walking near the stone fence that bounded the vegetable garden, holding his satchel in his left hand by his side, with his cap in his right hand, a red-cheeked slim boy, dressed in a close-fitting grey frieze trousers that reached a little below his knees and a blue sweater. His feet were bare and covered with all sorts of mud. His face perspired and his great soft blue eyes were popping out of his head with fright. He knew his mother would be angry.

At last he reached the door and, holding down his head, he entered the kitchen. The mother immediately jumped up and seized him by the shoulder. The boy screamed, dropped his satchel and his cap and clung to her apron. The mother raised the rod to strike, but when she looked down at the little trembling body, she began to tremble herself and she dropped the stick. Stooping down, she raised him up and began kissing him, crying at the same time with tears in her eyes.

'What's going to become of you atall, atall? God save us, I haven't the courage to beat you and you're breaking my heart with your wickedness.'

The boy sobbed, hiding his head in his mother's bosom.

'Go away,' she said, thrusting him away from her, 'and eat your dinner. Your father will give you a good thrashing in the morning. I've spared you often and begged him not to beat you, but this time I'm not going to say a word for you. You've my heart broken, so you have. Come here and eat your dinner.'

She put the dinner on the plate and pushed the boy into the chair. He sat down sobbing, but presently he wiped his eyes with his sleeve and began to eat ravenously. Gradually his face brightened and he moved about on the chair, settling himself more comfortable and forgetting all his fears of his mother and the thrashing he was going to get next morning in the joy of satisfying his hunger. The mother sat on the doorstep, knitting in silence and watching him lovingly from under her long black eyelashes.

All her anger had vanished by now and she felt glad that she had thrust all the responsibility for punishment on to her husband. Still, she wanted to be severe, and although she wanted to ask Stephen what he had been doing, she tried to hold her tongue. At last, however, she had to talk.

'What kept you, Stephen?' she said softly.

Stephen swallowed the last mouthful and turned around with his mug in his hand.

'We were only playing ball,' he said excitedly, 'and then Red Michael ran after us and chased us out of his field where we were playing. And we had to run an awful way; oh, a long, long way we had to run, over crags where I never was before.'

'But didn't I often tell you not to go into people's fields to play ball?'

'Oh, mother, sure it wasn't me but the other boys that wanted to go, and if I didn't go with them they'd say I was afraid, and father says I mustn't be afraid.'

'Yes, you pay heed to your father but you pay no heed to your mother that has all the trouble with you. Now and what would I do if you fell running over the crags and sprained your ankle?'

And she put her apron to her eyes to wipe away a tear.

Stephen left his chair, came over to her and put his arms around her neck.

'Mother,' he said, 'I'll tell you what I saw on the crags if you promise not to tell father about me being late and playing ball in Red Michael's field.'

'I'll do no such thing,' she said.

'Oh, do, mother,' he said, 'and I'll never be late again, never, never, never.'

'All right, Stephen; what did you see, my little treasure?'

He sat down beside her on the threshold and, looking wistfully out into the sky, his eyes became big and dreamy and his face assumed an expression of mystery and wonder.

'I saw a great big black horse,' he said, 'running in the sky over our heads, but none of the other boys saw it but me, and I didn't tell them about it. The horse had seven tails and three heads and its belly was so big that you could put our house into it. I saw it with my two eyes. I did, mother. And then it soared and galloped away, away, ever so far. Isn't that a great thing I saw, mother?'

'It is, darling,' she said dreamily, looking out into the sky, thinking of something with soft eyes. There was silence. Then Stephen spoke again without looking at her.

'Sure you won't tell on me, mother?'

'No, treasure, I won't.'

'On your soul you won't?'

'Hush! Little one. Listen to the birds. They are beginning to sing. I won't tell at all. Listen to the beautiful ones.'

The both sat in silence, listening and dreaming, both of them.

THE STOLEN ASS

The accused, Patrick Haughy, went into the witness-box and was duly sworn. Just as he was about to begin his statement, District Justice Murnihan interrupted him:

'What did you say your name was?' said the Justice.

The accused was a very disreputable young tinker with red hair and a pointed chin.

'Patrick Haughy, yer honour,' he said.

'Oh!' said the Justice. 'What I mean is, how do you spell it?'

'Begob,' said the tinker, shrugging his shoulders, 'I never spelt it in me life.'

There was laughter in court.

District Superintendent Clarke informed the Justice that the name was spelt H-A-U-G-H-Y.

'Oh!' said the Justice. 'In that case I should think the correct pronunciation is Aw-Hee.'

'It's usually pronounced HAW-Hee,' said Clarke.

'Or would it be Och-ee?' said the Justice. 'There were Irish kings of that name.'

'Yer honour,' said the accused, 'I was arrested by the pronunciation HAW-Hee.'

There was further laughter in court. The accused then began his statement.

'It was this way, yer honour,' he said. 'I started from Kilmacshanahan to go to Kilnamaramaragull with a black she-ass. The ass had cast one of her hind shoes, so she got lame in the way, an' begob I was afraid that I'd get taken for her if I carried her any farther, with the laws there be now about cruelty to animals. So I met another ass, he was a jackass with a great welt across his hind quarters, same as somebody struck him with a hot iron, maybe a blacksmith or some divil of a woman that found him atin' her cabbages; well, anyway, I said to mesel': 'I'll borrow this fellah an' lave me own ass in his place.'

Ye see, yer honour, my ass was a lot better of an ass, an' I only left her there so as I'd get her comin' back.'

'Where was this?' said the Justice.

'At Ballyfarnagaoran, yer honour.'

'I see,' said the Justice. 'So you stole a jackass at Bally-er-so-and-so?'

'No, yer honour,' said the accused. 'I didn't steal him. I just borrowed him.'

There was loud laughter in court. The accused continued:

'Well, I wasn't far on the road when I met a man comin' along an' he with another ass, a mangy-lookin' animal, that was knockin' his hind legs together and his nose to the ground blowin' up the dust with every step he took and coughin' his insides out, savin' yer honour's presence. Me an' this man started talkin', an' after a while he offers to swap asses with me an' five shillins into the bargain. Well, I thought to mesel' that I had left a better ass in the place o' the jackass I borrowed, an' so I'd be the loser anyway in givin' the other fellah's ass to this fellah —'

'What other fellow?' said the Justice.

'The fellah I took the jackass from,' said the accused.

'But you said you found him on the road.'

'Well, ye know, he must have belonged to somebody, so supposin' he did . . .'

Here the tinker scratched his head, wrinkled up his face and looked worried.

'What's the matter now?' said the Justice.

'Aw begob,' said the accused, 'ye got me all mixed up, yer honour, what with this fellah an' the other fellah that weren't in the story atall, only be way of comparison.

'What nonsense are you talking about?' said the Justice angrily. 'Now where are we?'

At this moment there was loud laughter in court. The Justice completely lost his temper and threatened to clear the court.

'Where were we, I say?' he repeated to the accused. 'I want no further nonsense.'

'It was at Ballymorguttery I met him, yer honour,' said the accused calmly.

'Whom did you meet at this village?' snorted the Justice.

'It wasn't exactly in the village but near it,' said the accused. 'The fellah that had the old crock of an ass, I mean.'

'Goodness gracious!' said the Justice. 'What an extraordinary story! Continue.'

'Well,' said the accused, wiping his mouth on his sleeve, 'after I left that fellah I set off with the old ass I bought from him, or it would be more like it with the ass he bought from me. No, but after lavin' him my jackass that I borrowed instead of my own ass. Ye see he gave me five bob, and anyway, I thought to mesel', five bob is five bob, an' if the ass didn't die on the way I could always get my own ass back on the return journey at Ballyfarnagaoran. But sure I might as well be lashin' a tin-can as that old ass for all the walkin' I could get out of him, an' after a couple o' miles he lay down in the road altogether. I got him up be pullin' at his tail and then I got him on another mile until we came to Kilnamaramaragull. An' there I saw an ass in a field an' I says to mesel': 'I'll take that ass an' lave this fellah in his place.' Ye see, be that means everybody 'd have an ass, because I'd lave the old fellah in the field instead of the one I'd take, and then I'd bring back the one I'd take to Ballyfarnagaoran, where I'd find my own black she-ass, and then I'd leave the ass I took out of the field instead of her and go home to Kilmacshanahan with my own ass.'

'Just a moment,' said the Justice, 'which ass do you mean?'

There was a titter in the court, but the Justice looked very stern. The tinker completely lost control of his memory. He just dropped his lower jaw and stared at the Justice.

'Now, better be clear about it,' said the Justice. 'Which ass did you . . . er . . . I mean what ass did you . . . er . . . look here, my man, what ass are you talking about?'

'There were several asses,' said the tinker, waving his arms in despair, 'but now I've no ass atall, an' is that fair, I ask ye honour? Mr Clarke arrested me an' I takin' the ass out o' the field an' he put the old ass in the pound an' he died there the following day so I got no ass to put instead of my own ass at Ballyfarnagaoran.'

'But how do we know it was your own ass?' said the Justice, leaning back and looking very cunning at the accused.

'The ass I bought is it, ye honour?' said the accused.

'Look here,' said the Justice furiously, again losing his temper and turning to the District Superintendent of Police, 'what do you make of this fellow?'

'I don't believe he had any ass in the first instance, sir,' said Mr Clarke.

'Ha!' said the Justice. 'Is that true, Haughy?'

'Yer honour,' said the accused, 'if ye give me time to go to Ballyfarnagaoran an' look around for her, I'd bring her to yer house tomorrow mornin'.'

There was loud laughter once more in court and this time the Justice was unable to stop it.

'Look here, my man,' he said to the accused, 'it's quite obvious you never had an ass and all these stories about asses are deliberately concocted to misdirect the court. I sentence you to fourteen days' hard labour without the option of a fine.'

'Many thanks, yer honour,' said the accused; 'but about me own ass . . .'

CHARITY

The parish priest was in his library, lolling in a chair by the window with his coat off. It was a dreadfully hot day and he had had a tough morning, visiting sick in an outlaying part of his parish. He was counting on half an hour's rest before dinner when suddenly a timid and prolonged knock came to the door.

'Come in,' said the parish priest wearily, sitting up and reaching for his coat.

Nicholas Reddon, an ex-schoolmaster and a notorious drunkard, slouched into the room. He had an extraordinary appearance, pathetic, yet contemptible and repulsive. His once handsome, slim figure was clothed in an assortment of shabby garments that looked still more shabby because they tried to be genteel. His long, thin, intelligent face was mournful, blotched and hardened by a fixed expression of defiant arrogance. His eyes were bloodshot and blinked continually.

He peered around the room suspiciously. Then he entered, closed the door quietly and made a slight bow, scraping his right foot. He stood facing the priest, twirling his cap on his right forefinger.

'Father Waters,' he said, 'I came to see you on a small matter. You will pardon the interruption when I —'

'Sit down,' said the parish priest, wrinkling his forehead and buttoning his coat.

The ex-schoolmaster sat down on the edge of a chair and placed his cap and his two hands between his knees.

'You've been drinking,' said the priest sharply.

'Father Waters —'

'You needn't deny it, Mr Reddon,' continued the priest, 'and I know what the small matter is.'

The priest stood up abruptly and waved his arms. He was a short, stout man, with a round face. His underlip stuck out aggressively.

'It's awful,' he said. 'Are you never going to pull yourself together? I suppose it's money you want.'

'That's not a charitable way of putting it, father. For a man in my condition who has been the unfortunate victim of . . . of cruel circumstances, I take it as an insult to be . . .'

He straightened himself and began to splutter.

'That's all rot,' said the priest. 'Listen. It's only last night I was talking to Mr Higgins and he told me about your disgraceful and thankless conduct. What did you do with the parcel of groceries he sent to your lodgings?'

'I dropped the contents at his hall door in his presence,' said Reddon, looking at the floor and sitting very motionless.

'Why, may I ask?'

'Because I am a gentleman and I refuse to accept charity from a shop-keeper whom I don't consider my social equal, an outsider, a mere nobody.'

The priest crossed his arms and stared at Reddon angrily.

'I've a good mind to kick you out the door and set my dogs after you,' he said bitterly.

Reddon suddenly burst into tears. He pulled out a handkerchief and pressed it to his eyes with both hands. His cap fell to the floor. He shook with emotion. The priest glared at him.

'Yes. I've a good mind to do it,' he continued. 'You're an unmitigated scoundrel and I know your kind. You feel insulted at this good man's charity, and now I'm going to tell you why he sent you that grocery. He sent it because he saw you stealing a rasher of bacon out of his shop that morning and he took pity on you. You are not too proud to steal from a man but you won't take charity from him. You won't take charity from Mr Higgins, but you'll come to me for money, and God knows I've little enough to spare for myself, not to mention any odd coppers I've got for the deserving poor that are starving all round me. Oh! You low, heartless wretch. I . . . I . . . I don't even pity you. You are beyond pity.'

The priest stopped breathlessly. He went over to the window and looked out, clutching his hands nervously behind his back. Reddon raised his head and his mournful, bloodshot eyes stared at the priest's back. His lips trembled for some moments and then he spoke.

'Father Waters,' he said pompously, with hanging lower lip, 'would you kindly allow me to defend myself?'

The priest did not reply or move. The ex-schoolmaster drew himself up, straightened his shoulders and put one hand on his knee.

'You deal with facts, Father Waters, but I deal with something that is more powerful than facts and that is the curse that is upon me.'

'Rot,' said the priest, without moving.

'So be it,' said the schoolmaster. 'Amen I say to that. It's all rot. I'm all rot and everything is all rot. If I held my position and if the inspector had not sent a report of drunkenness to headquarters, I'd be still a schoolmaster,

but what would that amount to? Nothing but rot. There would be still
drunkards and unfortunate wretches and liars and scoundrels. If it's not me
it's some one else. I'm not responsible. I may be a liar and a thief and an
ungrateful scoundrel, but I'm still a gentleman, and a gentleman never accepts
charity. I came to you because I considered that you are something beyond
me, something apart from the rest of the people, not a man but something,'
he waved his hand and glanced around wildly, 'something apart. I may be
wrong, but what are you for if not to stand between me and myself? Your
business is to deal with drunkards and scoundrels and thieves. Yes. If there
are no drunkards and scoundrels and thieves, then what is your business? If
there are no poor and no sick, what use are you? You belong to me because I
am a drunkard. That's my way of looking at it. That's why I come to you
for money and kick Higgins' groceries in through his hall door.'

He stood up arrogantly, swaying slightly, drunk through the efforts of his
outburst. He pulled himself up very fiercely and stood waiting for the priest
to turn round. But the priest did not move. His hands were still clutching.
His short, broad back was trembling slightly.

'I have the honour to bid you good day, Father Waters,' said Reddon.

He stepped back and made a pompous bow, which almost brought him to
his knees. Then he walked stiffly towards the door.

'Come here,' said the priest gruffly. He put his hand in his pocket and
held out two half-crown pieces. As soon as Reddon saw the money his eyes
glittered. He shuffled over, trembling and licking his lips, his quivering right
hand held out for the money. He grabbed it and put the coins to his lips.
Then he backed to the door quickly, bowing and simpering, his face in a
paroxysm of delight. His whole being had changed and he was now a cunning,
fawning drunkard, sneaking away with the price of another debauch. He
passed out of the door noiselessly, without uttering a word of thanks, but his
lips kept moving, forming some inarticulate words.

The priest never turned his face from the window. He stood still, clutching
his hands behind his back. But tears were rolling down his cheeks and he
was thinking: 'What am I to do? He'll come again in a few days and the
same thing will happen.'

THE SENSUALIST

It was nine o'clock. Night had fallen. There were stray lights in the village square. A few cabs still remained there. Their drivers sat huddled in their overcoats on the driving seats, waiting for stray passengers on their way to the hills. The motor-bus setting out on its last journey to Dublin was hooting around the corner making a great noise with its cumbersome engine. A herd of cows passed, lowing and shuffling and scraping the ground with their lazy hoofs. Around the village, the thronging tree covered hills were shrouded in a white mist. They seemed to have crept closer with the fall of night, cutting off the village from the rest of the world. There was a mysterious silence in the air, a country silence following the fall of night. 'Sleep, sleep,' it seemed to say.

A lawyer named Corcoran had finished his dinner in a little room over-looking the square at the Glenlee Hotel. Mrs Mallon, the proprietress of the hotel, was sitting at table with him. It had been a great feast. Corcoran had brought most of the provisions with him from Dublin that morning. On his way to the hills farther up the glen to attend the inquest on a murdered man, he had left provisions at the hotel, with orders to reserve the private room for him that evening and to pay special attention to the cooking. He had brought his own wine, fruit, fish and cigars. He had invited Mrs Mallon to partake of the feast.

During the meal they had drunk a small bottle of sherry only, but they were already slightly intoxicated with food. Mrs Mallon had only drunk one glass, but she seemed to be more intoxicated than Corcoran. She was sitting back in her chair with her two long plump arms stretched out over the white tablecloth, the fingers tapping the cloth dreamily, while she looked at Corcoran sleepily, her large blue eyes almost closed, her voluptuous mouth open. Her bust and shoulders, full and round and smooth, were covered with a close-fitting silk blouse of an orange colour. Her arms were bare almost to the shoulders, and even in the outline of the plump arms there seemed to be some vital attraction that caused them, as it were, to stretch some invisible tentacles, calling, calling for admiration and suggesting that in a mere touch of them there was a delirious pleasure. Except for her eyes, which had some mystery in their glossy blue surface and in their depth, none of her features had any particular beauty in them, no fine moulding inherited from beautiful ancestors, no suggestion of strength or subtlety or refinement of character. But her personality, her plumpness, her presence had that weird and mysterious animal magnetism that draws sensuous men towards it irresistibly and arouses intense dislike in women.

Corcoran was sitting opposite her, smiling broadly with the effect of his feast and abandoning himself completely to this devilish attraction. In all his life, he thought, he had discovered nothing like her. He was forty. He had lived freely, imposing only those restraints on his conduct, which educated men who make a cult of pleasure impose on themselves, in order that the palate may not become prematurely soured by promiscuous indulgence. But lately he had found it difficult to arouse any interest in himself for women, until he had met Mrs Mallon two months before. At the first meeting he had become enamoured of her. Since then he had deliberately set out to capture her. She had been to Dublin with him three times. He had given her expensive presents. He had made slight advances which she accepted with seeming alacrity, but silently and sleepily, without any of the giggling timorousness of other women, as if she were used to arousing desire in men and took these manifestations of her powerful attraction composedly. She had given no definite indication of . . . That's what excited Corcoran. That's what made this feast so piquantly exciting, because this night, now, he was definitely going to try a conquest. The mystery of the woman intoxicated him, her silence, her half-enticing, half-bored attitude.

The waitress cleared the table on an enormous tray and closed the door.

'Now,' said Corcoran, rising from the table, 'we are all to ourselves. Eh?'

'So it seems,' said Mrs Mallon, stretching backwards idly and showing her white teeth in a slight laugh.

Corcoran seized a large bottle, uncorked it, wiped the neck with his napkin and then stood laughing and thrusting out his chest. His face was fat and brick-red. His eyes were small and cunning as the eyes of lawyers always are, even when off duty. His body was short and plump, so plump that it was difficult to imagine how he had managed to get within his trousers. His arms were too short for his body and his body was too long for his legs. Altogether he was an unseemly man for a love affair. But his conceit overmastered his physical drawbacks.

He walked around the table breathing heavily, drew a chair very close to Mrs Mallon's chair and sat down abruptly. Without speaking he filled her glass and his own to the brim. Then he offered her a cigarette from a gold case. He put a cigar between his lips, struck a match, lit her cigarette and his cigar and puffed. Then he drew a long breath and leaned back, looking at her amorously.

'This is always the most pleasant part of a dinner he said, 'the aftermath. Eh?'

She just smiled, made a slight gesture with her shoulder nearest to him and puffed at her cigarette. Corcoran felt a thrill passing through his body. The shrug of her shoulder had caused it. That shrug, coming as it were from her body and not from her consciousness, seemed to say: 'Come. I am waiting.' He put his elbow on the table and turned his face close to hers. There was a silence of several moments. Then he raised his glass and invited her with a nod to drink. They clinked glasses, laughed and drank deeply, both of them. He seized her hand and pressed it. Her hand lay limply in his without answering the pressure. It was difficult to know what to make of it. Corcoran became more excited.

'Don't you find it lonely here,' he murmured, 'since your husband died?'

'No,' she said. 'Not very. It's near Dublin, and there are always plenty of people about.'

'Yes,' he said, 'of course. But you are a young and beautiful woman —'

'Thanks.'

'Don't mention it, my dear. And young and beautiful women should have a companion, I think.'

'I don't understand,' she said softly.

'Tosh!' he said. 'You know very well what I mean.'

'I hope you're not proposing marriage,' she whispered cunningly. 'That would be awful for a married man.'

'No need to remind me of my married state,' said Corcoran, with a pretence of irritation. 'If it were otherwise perhaps . . . But damn it, marriage. . . . Ever hear what the German philosopher called marriage?'

'Something nice, I'm sure.'

'Yes. He said: 'Even concubinage has been defiled by marriage!'

'Very good.'

'Yes,' chuckled Corcoran. 'Damn good. Eh? Come. Drink. Your health, madam.'

They both finished their glasses. Immediately Corcoran filled them again to the brim. Mrs Mallon tried to stop him filling hers, but he held her hand and filled it so fully that it overflowed on to the tablecloth, staining the white cloth rapidly. Both looked at the stain dully but neither spoke. Corcoran put down the bottle slowly and leaning over he put his arm around Mrs Mallon's waist. He pressed her towards him. She leaned her head away sleepily and he kissed her on the neck several times. Then he arose and was on the point of taking her altogether in his arms when a knock came to the door. Corcoran jumped back to his chair and Mrs Mallon rose to her feet, as rapidly as she could. But she was slightly fuddled with drink and excitement and the disturbance did not seem to make much impression on her. She went to the door and opened it.

The manager of the hotel was there, a young man with a plump pale face and a distant, sleepy look in his little eyes, a look that reminded one curiously of the expression of Mrs Mallon's eyes. His lips were opened in a curious, intimate smile as he looked at his employer, as if to say: 'We two understand one another, don't we?' He spoke in a sort of whistling, soft tone, as if his voice came from roof of his mouth and not from his throat.

'I've locked up the bar,' he said. 'These are the keys.'

He handed her the keys. She dangled them for a moment in silence and then looked at him intensely. He answered her look in the same curious manner. They looked at one another for several moments that way in silence.

Then she said: 'Everything's all right, I suppose?'

'Yes,' he said.

Suddenly Mrs Mallon broke into a silent laugh and bit her lower lip with her teeth. She bent forward and whispered something into the manager's ear. He nodded his head and then smiled. Then he nodded his head several times again and went off rubbing his lips one against the other. Mrs Mallon looked after him until he disappeared around the corner of the corridor. Then she smiled again and bit her lip as she smiled. She returned to the room and closed the door.

Corcoran was standing by his chair with his glass in his hand waiting for her anxiously. She smiled at him and nodded.

'It's all right,' she said. 'Sit down. It's only my manger, Mr Tobin. You look afraid. What of? Think it was your wife looking for you?'

She laughed and sat down looking at him and laughing. Corcoran sat down again beside her, very close. He was trembling slightly and looked agitated and worried.

'Hm. I see,' he said. 'Who is your manager? I mean what sort is he. Does he live here?'

'Oh, yes, Why?'

'Oh, nothing at all. Your health. Good Stuff, isn't it?'

'Yes. Tastes well.'

They both emptied their glasses. Mrs Mallon emptied hers eagerly and her attitude was now altogether more free, since she had been to the door to see her manager. She was continually smiling and breathing deeply, raising her shoulders up and down and fiddling with her feet under the table, shifting them about restlessly. Corcoran watched every movement she made and he kept thinking: 'The wine is going to her head. She's really a passionate woman.'

They both drank freely and smoked, talking in snatches all the time. Their conversation became more disconnected and ridiculous. They talked in riddles and Corcoran told extraordinary stories about love affairs and lovers, to all of which Mrs Mallon listened rapturously with her eyes almost closed, continually biting her underlip with her teeth. But Corcoran had not made any further attempts to embrace her, and sitting close beside her, his body seemed to be lax and overwhelmed by her presence and the passion she aroused within him.

At last Mrs Mallon looked at the watch on her wrist and said:

'It's eleven o'clock. It's time to retire.'

'Yes,' said Corcoran. 'I feel like it too.'

He seized her two hands and drew her to him. She did not resist. He leaned forward and whispered something into her ear. She drew away her head and burst out into a laugh.

'Naughty, naughty,' she cried. 'What a man! Oh, dear!'

'But —'

'Do let me get up. What would your wife say if she heard you?'

'Look here —'

'Please let me up. You know your room. Don't make a noise now. Please.'

'When may I —'

'Hush! Later. I'll come.'

'When? When?'

'In half an hour.'

'Hadn't I better come —'

'No, no. You mustn't. Not on any account. Wait. I have to do a few things first. Come on.'

She took his hand and led him out of the room. He picked up an unopened bottle as he left the table. Outside there was a long, narrow corridor. His room was the third on the left. She opened the door and thrust him in gently, smiling.

'Which is yours?' he said.

She did not reply but walked across the corridor and opened a door. Entering it she smiled at him again. Corcoran blew her a kiss excitedly and closed his door.

He undressed rapidly, got into his pyjamas and his dressing-gown, took his towels and soap and went off to the bathroom. The bathroom was at the far end of the corridor, facing the corridor. He entered and turned on the water. He was so excited that he didn't know which tap he had turned, the hot or cold. He stood for fully five minutes staring stupidly at the water trickling from the tap into the white tub, listening all the time to sounds in the corridor. He heard a door creak as it opened. He put his eye to the key-hole and looked. Mrs Mallon had come out of her room. She looked around slowly and then walked away. She was swaying slightly.

'Something to do,' thought Corcoran. 'I better hurry.'

He stripped hurriedly and plunged into the bath.

'Damnation!' he cried.

The water was ice-cold. He jumped out again, shivering and splashing. He wiped himself fiercely and dressed. Seizing his towels he rushed out of the bathroom and along the corridor into his room. There he sat on his bed, opened his brandy flask and took a deep swig. That revived him and again pleasant thoughts filled his head. He looked at his watch. He had still ten minutes to wait, but . . . hush!

The sounds of footsteps came creaking along the corridor. Was there one or two persons? It was hard to say. The sounds were very subdued and in-distinct, just slight creaks on the carpet. Corcoran jumped off his bed and was rushing to the door, when he stopped suddenly and thought: 'Suppose it's some other visitor. Seeing me come out like this. . . . Eh? Better wait.'

As he sat down on his bed, he heard a door creak, closing. Mrs Mallon's door, without a doubt. Would he go now? No. Better wait until she . . . Women hate to be . . . Five minutes more. He waited.

Then he arose, shivering with eagerness, opened his door, passed into the corridor, closed his door and tiptoed across to the other door. He made no sound in his stockinged feet. He was going to knock gently when he heard a sound that made him start. It was a man's voice, a soft whistling voice that seemed to come from the roof of the mouth instead of from the throat. Corcoran couldn't catch what the voice said, but his legs began to tremble with rage and his heart came thumping up into his mouth. Then there was another voice and Corcoran listened again. Mrs Mallon was speaking, dreamily, half asleep.

'Sure you turned the key?'

'Certain,' the other voice said softy.

'No danger then,' she said. 'The old codger can't come in.'

Soft, almost inaudible laughter followed, from two voices.

Corcoran drew back from the door, doubled up his fists and was about to hurl himself at the door, when another sound reached his ears and the sound seemed to knock all his senses out of him. . . .

Creak, creak, creak. . . .

Corcoran suddenly felt a sensation of intense cold permeating his whole body, as if he were sinking rapidly into an ice-cold pool. He shrivelled up. He went lax and his teeth chattered. A red blur came before his eyes and they filled with tears. Shame, shame, a terrible shame, such as he had never known in his life, such as he had not thought existed in his consciousness, overpowered him, struck him in every limb, in his brain, in his bowels, in the soles of his feet, as if his whole being were peopled with shrieking spirits that cried out: 'Shame, shame, shame.' As suddenly the whole world, a vast expanse of existence, immeasurable, immense, terrifying, thrust itself in upon him, all watching him and all crying out insanely: 'Shame, shame, shame.'

Drunk, terrified, humiliated, he did not understand this monstrous sensation of guilt, of ugliness, of things shrieking within him and about him: 'Shame, shame, shame.' He staggered across the corridor to his room, his eyes red and staring, his trembling hands crossed before his face. He opened his door and closed it softly behind him, lest he might make a noise to disclose his movements to these shrieking things. Then he dashed to the mirror and looked at himself, shaking like a palsied fellow.

When he saw his paunch and his bloated face and his stubby limbs and the bestial expression in his little eyes, fear and evil and lust, he grew calm. For a moment a soft, tender longing crept through his mind. He lowered his eyes and his lips moved, trying to murmur something.

But suddenly he burst into a peal of low, thick, senseless laughter. Fiercely laughing he seized his brandy flash and drained it. Then he threw himself on his bed.

YOUR HONOUR

Mr Patrick Gilhooley came out of Sinnot's riding-school in Park Gate Street at four o'clock in the afternoon. He had just taken his first lesson in horsemanship. He felt numb all over the body. Although he walked as usual, by pitching his flat feet out sideways like a motherly old cow, he felt sure that he walked like a cavalry officer. Therefore, in spite of his soreness and the memory of the smile he had seen on an impudent stable-boy's face during the lesson, he felt very proud of himself. His yellow top-boots had creases above the ankles. His brown riding breeches were made of the most expensive cord. His jazz pull-over was in the latest fashion. His smart bowler hat was perched at a daring angle. Phew! He felt a very fine and dashing fellow.

To the onlooker, of course, he looked perfectly ridiculous, with his flat feet and his undulating paunch, coming along like an advertisement for a cinema theatre.

Formerly he had been a small shopkeeper in a country village. His shop was a failure commercially because he spent all his time in political agitation. He was chairman of the local Rural District Council, and secretary to three different political organisations. At last, however, his hour struck. His second cousin, Mr Christopher Mulligan, the solicitor, was appointed by the government as Commissioner to administrate the affairs of a public body, suppressed for corruption. Immediately Mr Mulligan appointed all his cousins to fill subsidiary posts under the new, incorruptible administration. Mr Gilhooley became Assistant Deputy Commissioner.

Before Mr Gilhooley had walked fifty yards from the riding-school gate, he was accosted by a ruffian called the Cadger Byrne. Byrne was a very tiny man. He had a round, sallow face. His eyes were small, sharp and grey. His ears were diminutive and they protruded from the sides of his head instead of sloping in the usual manner. He was dressed in riding-breeches and gaiters. He had the manner and appearance of a disreputable racecourse tout. Exactly what he was.

'Pardon me, yer honour,' said Byrne, standing in front of Mr Gilhooley, and touching his cap.

'Eh?' said Mr Gilhooley, starting and halting abruptly.

Here is must be stated that the title 'your honour' is the property of a certain class of persons, now becoming defunct, i.e. Irish country gentlemen. In his youth Mr Gilhooley had been in the habit of touching his cap and saying 'Good morning, yer honour,' when the local landowner rode into the village mounted on an enormous hunter stallion. The landowner was in the habit of reining in his stallion, calling to Mr Gilhooley's father, then proprietor of the village shop, and without taking the trouble to dismount or to look at Mr Gilhooley's father, he ordered perhaps a box of matches to be sent at once to Ballyhooley Manor. Recently Mr Gilhooley loathed the title 'Your honour.' All his political agitation had been directed against the class of persons who held that title. But now when he heard himself addressed by that title for the first time in his life, an extraordinary thrill of pleasure permeated his whole fat body.

The thrill of pleasure passed in a moment, giving way to a suspicion that he was being insulted. A sense of inferiority passed over him, causing a little shiver down his spine and a lump in this throat, just as when he committed some *faux pas* in the drawing-rooms to which he had recently been invited on account of his new position. He looked at Byrne shrewdly.

But Byrne's upraised and expectant face was perfectly respectful. It bore that subservient smile which Mr Gilhooley recognised and understood very well, formerly of course. Mr Gilhooley became reassured. Undoubtedly the fellow mistook him, Mr Gilhooley, for one of the old caste.

'What do you want?' said Mr Gilhooley, stretching out his right boot with the toe upraised and staring at the toe, with a serious expression on his face.

He spoke sourly and rather arrogantly, but he was really very pleased.

'Would yer honour put in a good word for me?' said Byrne in a very fawning voice.

'How do you mean?' said Mr Gilhooley, staring again. Since the man wanted something he had ceased to be pleased. 'Where could I put in a good word for you?'

'In the stables, o' course, yer honour,' said Byrne, edging closer and looking at Mr Gilhooley with an almost impertinent smile of intimacy on his face.

'What have I got to do with stables?' cried Mr Gilhooley indignantly. He nodded his head backwards towards the riding-school and added ferociously: 'D'ye think I'm employed in there?'

Byrne waggled his head from side to side knowingly and the smile on his face broadened.

'Now, yer honour,' he said, 'sure ye know very well I didn't mane that? Don't I know a gentleman when I see wan? But, yer honour, what I'd be grateful to ye for is if ye'd put in a good word for me in yer own stables, yer honour.'

'Huh!' said Mr Gilhooley, now smiling broadly and swelling with a consciousness of a new dignity. 'I've got no stables.'

'Ah! That's all right, yer honour,' said Byrne in a tone that clearly indicated he didn't believe a word of it.

'Ho!' said Mr Gilhooley again. 'Did ye ever hear the like of it!'

He now looked at Byrne in a cheerful, friendly, patronising manner, and he really felt that he had been a landowner and a horse-owner all his life. Not only that, but he suddenly developed a suspicion, a momentary one, of course, that his ancestors had really been noble and that he was only coming into his own again. Ha! An aristocrat, by Jove! As good as the best of them and better.

'Now, yer, honour,' continued Byrne, 'I hope ye don't take it bad of me accostin' ye this way, but I been out of work for six months through victimisation. An' if his honour Sir John Corcoran was alive today 'tisn't here I'd be.'

'Oh! Ho!' said Mr Gilhooley.

He felt as if he had been a landlord and horse-owner all his life. Very pleasant sensation this; being solicited by a deserving poor fellow down on his luck. He mentally decided that Sir John Corcoran was the best of fellows, although he had never heard the name before. All this happened within Mr Gilhooley's mind during one second while Byrne prepared to continue his story.

The story was a long one, but Byrne told it rapidly, hinting at things and giving names of horses and calling public men by their nicknames. Mr Gilhooley kept nodding his head until Byrne had finished.

'I'm very sorry,' he said, 'but I'm afraid I can do nothing for you at the moment. Very sorry.'

'Thanks, yer honour,' said Byrne. 'I know yer honour would if he could. But if he have any loose change to help a poor fellow along I wouldn't mind mesel' but the children. An' indeed, yer honour, if Sir Joseph Corcoran was alive . . . thanks, yer honour, thanks. . . .'

Byrne uttered these thanks in anticipation, for he had seen Mr Gilhooley's hand moving slowly towards his right trousers pocket. The word of thanks hastened the movement of the hand. The hand entered the pocket and emerged with half a crown, which it dropped into Byrne's outstretched hand.

'Another one to make a pair, yer honour,' cried Byrne. 'Yer honour'll never miss it, and a fine gentleman like yer honour needs only to be asked, I know. Sir John Corcoran, God rest his sowl, never drew less than half a golden sovereign out of his pocket to tip a man. He was the elegant gentleman, yer honour. Thanks, yer honour, thanks.'

Again Mr Gilhooley's hand entered his pocket. This time Mr Gilhooley's mind had again begun to grow suspicious, and he experienced the sensation of slowly recovering from a fit of drunkenness during which he had imagined himself a millionaire and had been flinging his money about. He dropped the second coin — it was a florin — into Byrne's hand. Then he shrugged himself as if he had caught a chill, and set off at a smart pace. As he walked away he felt a shiver down his spine and he knew that he had made a fool of himself.

Byrne did not look after him. He just spat on both coins, hitched up his clothes, winked one eye and said in a curious, melancholy voice:

'Jay, that fellah was an easy mark.'

AT THE FORGE

An old farmer called Sutton was the first to arrive at the forge. He was a big man, with a black bead shaped like the head of a shovel. He was dragging a limping plough-horse by the halter. He brought the horse into the little yard off the road, and saw that the door of the forge was still locked and barred.

'Well, be the . . .' cried Sutton, uttering a long string of oaths, 'nine o'clock in the morning' an' still no sign of him. Holy Moses!'

Although the door of the forge was locked and barred with a heavy iron crowbar, it was quite easy to enter it through an enormous hole in the wall to the right of the door. Through this hole, three men could enter abreast. Tinkers and tramps passed in and out there regularly at night. Still the smith locked and barred the door scrupulously every evening.

Sutton tied his horse to the stone fence, looked in through the hole and saw nothing. He growled again, sat down and waited patiently for half an hour until Joe Tierney, who kept the 'Mountain Tavern,' five miles away the other side of the bog, arrived with his pony and trap.

'Morra, Joe,' said Sutton.

'Morra,' said Tierney. 'Where's Keegan?'

'The divil a bit o' me knows,' said Sutton. 'He's not here, anyway, where he should be at this hour o' the mornin'.'

'God! Isn't he an awful man,' said Tierney, getting out of his trap and going towards the hole in the wall. 'Look at that, will ye? The door is locked an' God Almighty could walk in an' out through this hole. Wha'?'

Sutton said nothing, thinking angrily of his ploughing and of the rating his wife would give him for not being back in time. Tierney stuck his lean, wrinkled face in through the hole and peered about the dark forge, smelling the rank odour of charcoal and twitching his nose. Then he came over to Sutton and sat down.

'Why doesn't he get a cottage near here?' said Tierney, 'and then he'd be in time every mornin'.'

'Huh!' said Sutton. 'That wouldn't suit him at all. The nearest public-house is in the village below in the glen, so he'd rather live there and walk the three miles back and forth every mornin' so as to be near his pint.'

'Me curse on him, anyway,' said Tierney. 'I have to be in the town at eleven o'clock an' it's six miles hard goin'. She'd never be able to do it with her two hind shoes off, not to mind that ould woman that's always on the road, watchin' for cruelty to animals. It's ten to one that I'd be had up for the Court unless I get shoes on her first. Where's this Keegan from, anyway? He's not a local man.'

'No. He's a Co. Carlow man,' said Sutton. Livin' in sin this twenty years with Mary Karney, ould Ned Karney's widow.'

'Lord! Oh, Lord!' said Tierney. 'It should be put a stop to, so it should. I wouldn't mind if he did his work, but when a man is livin' in sin, ye might say, though Ned is dead this twenty years, livin' in sin with another man's wife, it's the least he might do is to mind his work. Wha'? They should be made get married. Wha'!'

'So they should,' said Sutton, 'but . . . hech, hech . . . don't ye see the joke? If she marries him she loses her lodge that she had for nothin' from old Lord Marley on account of old Ned bein' his honour's coachman. Hech, hech, hech.'

'Aw! Be the hokey!' said Tierney. 'Did ye ever hear the likes o' that maneness?'

'Hech, hech, hech,' laughed Sutton in his enormous beard.

'An' he a strappin' young fellah, too,' said Tierney.

'Hech, hech, hech,' gurgled Sutton.

Laughing, the two old men forgot their irritation and their hurry. They launched forth into one of those interminable and senseless conversations in which mountaineers love to indulge on the most pressing occasions to the detriment of their work, and of everything else, about everything under the sun except the business in hand. Happily, with the eagerness of old woman discussing a scandal, they discussed the drought, the change of government, the decline of Lord Marley's fortunes, the fact that he had now only one riding horse, and only paid his coachman thirty shillings a week, although his wife paid two pound ten a week to the man that looked after her poodles (shockin', shockin'). Their faces beamed and they were very happy.

Then suddenly they were brought back to the realisation of the smith's continued absence by the arrival of Bridget Timmins with her donkey at a quarter-past ten o'clock. The donkey also had his two hind shoes off.

'Murdher! Murdher!' said Bridget Timmins. 'Isn't he here yet?'

'No, then, he isn't,' said Tierney. 'Are you too afther his blood?'

'I am, in troth,' said she. 'Two hind shoes off an' his poor old hoofs are as thin as a sheet o' paper, trampin' the roads for a month without 'em. But sure it's like this every Monday mornin'. I bet it's lying in bed he is yet; an' sure it's no wonder after last night.'

'How's that?' said Sutton excitedly.

'I wasn't there,' said Bridget, in a low, confiding tone, 'but I heard Joe Gleeson, the carpenter, tell Mrs Roddy that ye never saw such skin an' hair flyin' in all yer born life.'

Bridget Timmins stopped for breath and the old men gathered themselves together to listen, with their mouths open.

'It was how a charrybank full o' navvies and their girls came on an excursion from Dublin an' they all got drunk in Mahon's an' started to fight. Then Mahon called the Civic Guards, but sure ye might as well have brought five lame hens as them five policemen for a mob like that. It was nothin' but screamin' an' bottles flyin' an' people fallin' in all directions. Then out comes Keegan in his shirt an' trousers.'

'Aw! Lord! Oh, Lord!' said Tierney.

'Boys! Oh, boys!' said Sutton, licking his lips.

Mrs Timmins bent down and, raising her two hands, palms outwards, to her face, she flung them out with a dramatic gesture, as she said with great violence:

'He cleared the street in ten minutes with the handle of a spade.'

'Bravo!' cried Tierney, slapping his thighs.

'God be with him,' yelled Sutton.

At that moment a young farmer's son named Crow arrived with a broken plough on a cart. He had more definite news of the fight. Standing on his cart, with a hand on his hip, he began immediately to describe it with great vehemence. Another man came on a bicycle with a hoe that needed mending. A young woman stopped on her way to the village for groceries. The postman passed with the letters. He halted to listen. At eleven o'clock there was a crowd in front of the forge, all talking excitedly, boasting, swearing, laughing and cheering for Keegan.

And then somebody shouted: 'Here he comes. Here's himself.'

Everybody looked. He came around the corner, dressed in a blue sweater, with his coat thrown over his shoulder, his cap perched at the back of his curly, black head, swinging his arms, with his enormous chest expanded, his red face grinning humorously.

'Hurrah!' they cried. 'Hurrah for Keegan!'

THE WING THREE-QUARTER

There was a white frost on the ground. The whole field was covered with it. Here and there the turf had been cut and bruised by the tramping of feet during the practice matches of the past fortnight. And the frost had formed these patches of muddy, torn earth into hard cakes, pointed and sharp. The earth resounded under the feet of the fellows as they rushed out from the pavilion. You could see the fellows' breath, rushing from their mouths through the thin, freezing air in shooting columns, like puffs of stream from an engine.

A great cry arose from the crowd on the touchlines as the school team dashed out. All the boys waved their caps in the air and yelled out the school war-cry. It was the final of the schools' cup. 'Hurrah! Hurrah! Go on, Blackburn! Good old Fitz! Don't funk it, Regan!'

Regan rushing out with long strides heard this warning and shuddered. He ground his teeth and paced out at his full speed, dashing across the field like lightning to the far goal-post. When they saw him run the whole crowd burst into a wild cheer. God! He was as fast as a hare. If he weren't such a funk . . .

Regan stood by the goal-post stamping his feet and slapping his hands under his armpits waiting for the line-up. He was afraid to look at the crowd or at the white frost on the field. But he was acutely conscious of the crowd and of the frost. He didn't know which he feared most, the frost or the crowd. That dreadful sensation of being hurled down violently on to the ice-hard ground by a huge forward, the dreadful tackle about the knees, the sudden thump of hands clasping him about the knees and hurling his body into the air, the grunt and hot outrush of breath as the fellow clasped him and rolled with him to the earth, and then the louder thud as his own body hit the earth and all his members shook with the savage concussion. The frost and the tackle! Tackled in that frost. It was terrible. But he mustn't funk. If he did all that horrid crowd of boys would yell and boo . . . not only now but afterwards, during the whole term . . . That rotten funk Regan.

He looked splendid in his football outfit. A slim, tall fellow with long, sleek, fair hair combed back on his poll and a long, thin nose. But he was too neat and there were thick tape bandages on his knees, which none of the other fellows were wearing. They sort of sneered at him in the pavilion when he was putting them on.

The whistle blew. The captain waved his arm and cried out. Everybody rushed into line. A low murmur passed over the touchlines. Everybody waited. The other side looked very strong. Their forwards looked massive, lurched forward in a line behind their captain who was kicking off. Then there was a dull thud as the ball bounded off, then a roar and the whole field was in motion, rushing, panting and shouting, while on the touchlines the fellows shook rattlers and cheered.

The ball stayed in mid-field and Regan was left out on the right wing without anything to do. He kept running backwards and forwards as the ball advanced into the enemy's territory or switched back again towards his own line. He had positively no interest in the progress of the game and he kept praying all the time that it would not come near him. He was almost stupefied with terror and was only half aware of his surroundings, of the roaring and the rushing of feet. Then suddenly, after ten minutes' play, the enemy's backs got the ball from the scrum.

Regan's heart stopped beating, but he rushed forward to mark his man, a short, thick-set fellow, with a curly, dark head and square jaws. He saw the ball pass out rapidly to this man, as the out half and then the centre were tackled and felled. His man got the ball from a long pass, slipped it under his arm, lowered his head and dashed forward. A great cry went up. 'Take him, Regan. By the knees. By the knees. Down on him. Down on him.'

Thud, thud, thud-thud . . . The other fellow made for the touchline, running at a tremendous pace to get past Regan's flank. Regan flew up to him like lightning and then when he was within tackling distance he gritted his teeth and prepared to stoop for the fellow's knees. But just at that moment his heart failed. Instead of plunging in, he let himself fall limply and his hands just grazed the fellow's back. Regan stumbled forward and fell on his knees and as he arose he could hear a savage yell from the touchline and the cry: 'Funk! Ye funked it. After him. Funk!' He jumped to his feet again and sped after his man. The fellow was sprinting straight for the line but the full-back was waiting for him. Regan dashed on and reached his man once more, just as the full-back stooped to tackle him. They both got him and the three of them rolled over and over on the ground. Saved.

But the other fellows looked at him with angry faces and the captain rushed past him muttering something. Regan stood behind the scrum trembling.

The contact with the frost-covered fields had shaken him and he felt a terrific desire to rush off somewhere and hide. His teeth were chattering. But again he got a respite. The forwards took the ball on their toes and made a tremendous rush with it half-way up the field. For the next quarter of an hour it was again a forward game and Regan was left in peace.

Then a little before half time Regan got the ball from a scrum. He received the ball at mid-field from a line-up at touch and he had almost the whole width of the field to double past his opponent. The whole crowd raised a tremendous shout and several boys threw their caps in the air, because this was the very opportunity that always enabled Regan to score. His miraculous speed was his only asset, and here was an open field before him. In fact, a crowd broke from the railings on either side and dashed down to the enemy line to see the touch-down.

But Regan could not control his nerves. He dashed off well enough, and doubling in a wide arc, he passed the two centres three-quarters and came face to face with his own man on the wing. Then instead of spurting at his limit and going straight ahead, he ran in a still wider arc, going backwards instead of going forwards. Everybody shouted: 'Run straight. Run straight.' But Regan could not nerve himself to face his man. He kept doubling out until at last he ran into touch. There was dead silence. The fellows were too broken-hearted even to jeer at him.

Then, a few minutes later, after desultory play among the forwards, the half-time whistle blew. A servant ran on to the field with the lemons. The two teams gathered about their captains and trainers, and putting their heads together discussed plans. Regan threw himself on the ground and drooped his head. He could hear the babel of voices around him, but he didn't understand what was being said. He felt terribly ashamed and there was a red blur before his eyes. Somebody chucked a lemon towards him, shouting: 'Catch.' He didn't move to take it. It lay on the ground beside him. It was a very disagreeable situation. Then suddenly he heard his name called by the captain. He got to his feet and strolled over to the group. Everybody became silent. Then Regan heard the captain say: 'Take off that tape and go for your man or . . .'

He knelt down and unwound the tape. There were yards of it. He could hear somebody snigger viciously on the touchline: 'Oh, Lord! The baby is wearing bandages.' Then the whistle blew again. A cry arose: 'Come on, Blackburn. Give it to them, Bill. On the toes, forwards.'

The match became desperate now. Big Blackburn, the captain and the leading forward, with his skull-cap strapped around his skull and his huge arms swinging, broke away with the ball on his toes, down the centre of the field to the enemy's twenty-five. But the enemy full-back went down to the ball and then a mass of men all tumbled in a heap, struggling, until at last Blackburn's huge form arose in the centre, pushing men off him and struggling to break loose again. But they held on to his legs and back and he went down again, while the crowd cheered wildly. It was a great scene, and even Regan, shivering out on the wing, began to feel a thrill.

Away went the ball again. This time the enemy had it. They pressed up the field, passing and repassing cunningly, until they reached the home twenty-five. There was another scrum and then suddenly the ball was shot out, passed, once, twice rapidly. The right centre three-quarters got it, stood still, took deliberate aim and dropped a beautiful goal. This time the enemy team yelled and rushed around shaking one another by the hand. The home crowd on the touchlines were silent.

Again the ball was kicked off. There was only twenty minutes to go. The forwards were becoming exhausted and vicious. Several times in the next few minutes the referee had to warn men of both sides and there were five free kicks. The struggle became fearfully intense, and no sooner did a man get the ball than there were two or three pouncing on him and dragging him to the ground. The ball was kept all the time among the forwards and centres.

Then Regan got another chance to retrieve his honour. A terrific forward rush came down the touchline towards him. He heard the cry: 'Get down to it. Get down to it.' He stood trembling for a moment, and then, closing his eyes, he dashed straight forward and hurled himself on the ball, gripping it savagely in his arms. He rolled over and over on the ground and then a mass of men fell on him, grunting and panting, pulling at him and pushing. He almost lost consciousness, but he lay very still and clung to the ball. They formed over him and he was carried along the ground almost suffocated, until at last the referee blew his whistle and the press broke to form scrum. Then he struggled to his feet. As he arose he could hear a great cheer and a cry: 'Bravo, Regan.' Somebody clapped him on the back as he sprang backwards to his position.

But he took no notice of the cheer or of the clap on the back. He was in a fighting frenzy. This was the first time in his life he had gone down to a forward rush. It was his first good bruising on a hard field, and it awoke some element in him that nobody thought he possessed, of which he himself was unaware. Standing now, leaning forward, waiting for the ball, he felt that he wanted to fall upon the whole enemy team and lay them low. His face was covered with earth. His right knee was skinned. There was a big bruise on his left hip and his whole body tingled with pain after the mauling he had received. But his heart thumped with excitement and he felt fierce instead of feeling afraid. Afraid! He knew he would never be afraid again.

The ball was thrown into the scrum. There was a fierce push. The enemy go it. In a flash it was passed out to the centre, but almost before he had time to move off with it Regan had jumped clean on to his shoulders and brought him down. Another cry went up, and this time there was more wonder in the cry than joy. The ball dribbled away down the field, carried off by the home backs until play stopped again in a scrum on the home side of mid-field. Ten minutes to go.

'Let it out, forwards,' yelled the crowd. 'Give it to Regan. Regan. Go on, Regan.'

A wave of enthusiasm swept over the field and at last Regan was completely carried away by it. He felt himself a hero. And on such occasions it seems that chance also favours a man, for almost immediately Regan found himself running along, with the ball in the possession of his centre, who was running cleverly forward trying to make an opening. 'Pass, pass,' they cried. But he held on to it too long and he was tackled before he passed. The ball dribbled along the field and Regan had to turn back and pick it up. It seemed impossible for him to do anything with it but kick, as the whole field was now in front of him. 'Find touch,' somebody shouted. Regan hesitated for a moment and then decided to kick, but just as he was on the point of kicking, a forward rushed on him and again he felt a little thrill of fear at the possibility of contact with the burly figure and another fall to the ground. Suddenly, thrusting the ball under his arm, he dashed off.

The thing was so unexpected and impossible that he got ten yards ahead before there was any move made to stop him. Even his own men were amazed, because, instead of adopting his usual tactic of doubling out to the wing, he had plunged straight into the crowd, jumping like a deer and punching with his outstretched right hand. With this rush he broke through the enemy forwards and headed across the field towards the corner of the enemy goal-line. But he had still half the field to travel and the whole enemy back line doubled around to stop him. It was so unexpected that even on the touchline the fellows were silent, expecting him to be tackled every moment.

But he still went on. The scrum-half threw himself at his legs, but Regan vaulted right over the scrum-half's head and, suddenly swerving from the right centre three-quarters who was waiting for him, headed off the other way. Then the cheering began. He had still three men to pass, but he was going like a hare, swerving from right to left, jumping and punching. He reached the enemy twenty-five and then his own man came up on him from one side while the full-back approached from the other. There was a tense moment, and although the suspense lasted for only three seconds or so, it seemed a year to the fellows on the touchline who stood with their mouths open, stooping, with their caps in their hands. Then the clash came. The three men met at the same time. They all went down. But . . . Good Lord! Regan was up again and off like a shot straight for the goal-posts. He ran in at full speed, touched down without slackening speed and then raced back again, as if he had gone mad and wanted to score again at the other posts. But as soon as he reached his own men, they stopped him and slung him on to their shoulders.

But there was only a faint cheer from the touchline. Would the try be converted? The enemy was still leading. Not a sound was heard while the ball was placed. One, two, three moments. Then the ball sailed away. What? Straight through the posts. The flag went up. A wild cheer arose and then the referee blew his whistle.

Immediately the boys poured into the field over the ropes. Regan was hoisted on to Big Blackburn's shoulders and the whole school followed him to the pavilion shouting: 'Re-e-e-gan! Re-e-e-gan!'

THE REAPING RACE

At dawn the reapers were already in the rye field. It was the big rectangular field owned by James McDara, the retired engineer. The field started on the slope of a hill and ran down gently to the sea-road that was covered with sand. It was bound by a low stone fence and the yellow heads of the rye-stalks leaned out over the fence all round in a thick mass, jostling and crushing one another as the morning breeze swept over them with a swishing sound.

McDara himself, a white-haired old man in grey tweeds, was standing outside the fence on the searoad, waving his stick and talking to a few people who had gathered even at that early hour. His brick-red face was all excitement, and he waved his blackthorn stick as he talked in a loud voice to the men about him.

'I measured it out yesterday,' he was saying, 'as even as it could be done. Upon my honour there isn't an inch in the difference between one strip and another of the three strips. D'ye see? I have laid lines along the length of the field so they can't go wrong. Come here and I'll show ye.'

He led the men along from end to end of the field and showed how he had measured it off into three even parts and marked the strips with lines laid along the ground.

'Now it couldn't be fairer,' cried the old man, as excited as a schoolboy. 'When I fire my revolver, they'll all start together and the first couple to finish their strip gets a five-pound note.'

The peasants nodded their heads and looked at old McDara seriously, although each one of them thought he was crazy to spend five pounds on the cutting of a field that could be cut for two pounds. They were, however, almost as excited as McDara himself, for the three best reapers in the whole island of Inverara had entered for the competition. They were now at the top of the field on the slope of the hill ready to commence. Each had his wife with him to tie the sheaves as they were cut and bring food and drink.

They had cast lots for the strips by drawing three pieces of seaweed from McDara's hat. Now they had taken up position on their strips awaiting the signal. Although the sun had not yet warmed the earth and the sea-breeze was cold, each man had stripped to his shirt. The shirts were open at the chest and the sleeves were rolled above the elbow. They wore grey woollen shirts. Around his waist each had a multi-coloured 'crios,' a long knitted belt made of pure wool. Below that they wore a white frieze drawers with the ends tucked into woollen stockings that were embroidered at the tops. Their feet were protected by rawhide shoes. None of them wore a cap. The women all wore red petticoats, with a little shawl tied around their heads.

On the left were Michael Gill and his wife Susan. Michael was a long wiry man with fair hair that came down over his forehead and was cropped to the bone all around the skull. He had a hook nose and his lean jaws were continually moving backwards and forwards. His little blue eyes were fixed on the ground and his long white eyelashes almost touched his cheek-bones as if he slept. He stood motionless, with his reaping-hook in his right hand and his left hand in his belt. Now and again he raised his eyelashes, listening for the signal to commence. His wife was almost as tall as himself, but she was plump and rosy-cheeked. A silent woman, she stood there thinking of her eight-month-old son whom she had left at home in the charge of her mother.

In the middle Johnny Bodkin stood with his arms folded and his legs spread wide apart talking to his wife in a low serious voice. He was a huge man, with fleshy limbs and neck and black hair that had gone bald over his forehead. His forehead was very white and his cheeks were very red. He always frowned, twitching his black eyebrows. His wife Mary was short, thin, sallow-faced, and her upper teeth protruded slightly over her lower lips.

On the right was Pat Considine and his wife Kate. Kate was very big and brawny, with a freckled face and a very marked moustache on her upper lip. She had a great mop of sandy-coloured curly hair that kept coming undone. She talked to her husband in a loud, gruff masculine voice, full of good humour. Her husband, on the other hand, was a small man, small and slim and beginning to get wrinkles in his face although he was not yet forty. His face had once been a brick-red colour, but now it was becoming sallow. He had lost most of his front teeth. He stood loosely, grinning towards McDara, his little, loose, slim body hiding its strength.

Then McDara waved his stick. He lifted his arm. A shot rang out. The reaping race began. In one movement the three men sank to their right knees like soldiers on parade at musketry practice. Their left hands in the same movement closed about a bunch of rye-stalks. The curved reaping-hooks whirled in the air and then there was a crunching sound, the sound that hungry cows make eating long fresh grass in spring. Then three little slender bunches of rye-stalks lay flat on the dewy grass beneath the fence, one bunch behind each reaper's bent left leg. The three woman waited in nervous silence for the first sheaf. It would be an omen of victory or defeat. One, two, three, four bunches . . . Johnny Bodkin, snorting like a furious horse, was dropping his bunches almost without stopping. With a loud cheer he raised his reaping-hook in the air and spat on it, crying, 'First sheaf!' His wife dived at it with both hands. Separating a little bunch of stalks, she encircled the head of the sheaf and then bound it with amazing rapidity, her long, thin fingers moving like knitting needles. The other reapers and their wives had not paused to look. All three reapers had cut their first sheaves and their wives were on their knees tying.

Working in the same furious manner in which he had begun, Bodkin was soon far ahead of his competitors. He was cutting his sheaves in an untidy manner and he was leaving hummocks behind him on the ground owing to the irregularities of his strokes, but his speed and strength were amazing. His great hands whirled the hook and closed on the stalks in a ponderous manner, and his body hurtled along like the carcass of an elephant trotting through a forest, but there was a rhythm in the never-ending movement of his limbs that was not without beauty. And behind came his wife, tying, tying speedily, with her hard face gathered together in a serious frown like a person meditating on a grave decision.

Considine and his wife were second. Considine, now that he was in action, showed surprising strength and an agility that was goat-like. When his lean, long, bony arms moved to slash the rye, muscles sprang up all over his bent back like an intricate series of springs being pressed. Every time he hopped on his right knee to move along his line of reaping he emitted a sound like a groan cut short. His wife, already perspiring heavily, worked almost on his heels, continually urging him on, laughing and joking in her habitual loud, hearty voice.

Michael Gill and his wife came last. Gill had begun to reap with the slow methodic movements of a machine driven at low pressure. He continued at exactly the same pace, never changing, never looking up to see where his opponents were. His long, lean hands moved noiselessly and only the sharp crunching rush of the teeth of his reaping-hook through the yellow stalks of the rye could be heard. His long drooping eyelashes were always directed towards the point where his hook was cutting. He never looked behind to see had he enough for a sheaf before beginning another. All his movements were calculated beforehand, calm, monotonous, deadly accurate. Even his breathing was light and came through his nose like one who sleeps healthily. His wife moved behind him in the same manner, trying each sheaf daintily, without exertion.

As the day advanced people gathered from all quarters watching the reapers. The sun rose into the heaven. There was a fierce heat. Not a breath of wind. The rye-stalks no longer moved. They stood in perfect silence, their heads a whitish colour, their stalks golden. Already there was a large irregular gash in the rye, ever increasing. The bare patch, green with little clover plants that had been sown with the rye, was dotted with sheaves, already whitening in the hot sun. Through the hum of conversation the regular crunching of the reaping-hooks could be heard.

A little before noon Bodkin had cut half his strip. A stone had been placed on the marking line at halfway, and when Bodkin reach that stone, he stood up with the stone in his hand and yelled. 'This is a proof,' he cried, 'that there was never a man born in the island of Inverara as good as Johnny Bodkin.' There was an answering cheer from the crowd on the fence, but big Kate Considine humorously waved a sheaf above her head and yelled in her rough man's voice, 'The day is young yet, Bodkin of the soft flesh!' The crowd roared with laughter and Bodkin fumed but he did not reply. His wits were not very sharp. Gill and his wife took no notice. They did not raise their eyes from the reaping.

Bodkin's wife was the first to go for the midday meal. She brought a can full of cold tea and a whole oven cake of white flour, cut in large pieces, each piece coated heavily with butter. She had four eggs, too, boiled hard. The Bodkin couple had no children, and on that account they could afford to live well, at least far better than the other peasants. Bodkin just dropped his reaping-hook and ravenously devoured three of the eggs, while his wife, no less hungry, ate the fourth. Then Bodkin began to eat the bread-and-butter and drink the cold tea, with as much speed as he had reaped the rye. It took him and his wife exactly two minutes and three-quarters to finish that great quantity of food and drink. Out of curiosity, Gallagher, the doctor, counted the time down on the shore road. As soon as they had finished eating they set to work again as fiercely as ever.

Considine had come level with Bodkin, just as Bodkin resumed work, and instead of taking a rest for his meal, Considine and his wife ate in the ancient fashion, current among Inverara peasants during contests of the kind. Kate fed her husband as he worked with buttered oaten cake. Now and again she handed him the tea-can and he paused to take a drink. In that way he was still almost level with Bodkin when he had finished eating. The spectators were greatly excited at this eagerness on the part of Considine, and some began to say that he would win the race.

Nobody took any notice of Gill and his wife, but they had never stopped to eat and they had steadily drawn nearer to their opponents. They were still some distance in the rear, but they seemed quite fresh, whereas Bodkin appeared to be getting exhausted, handicapped by his heavy meal, and Considine was obviously using up the reserves of his strength. Then, when they reached the stone at half-way, Gill quietly laid down his hook and told his wife to bring the meal. She brought it from the fence, buttered oaten bread and a bottle of new milk with oatmeal in the bottom of the bottle. They ate slowly and then rested for a while. People began to jeer at them when they saw them resting, but they took no notice. After about twenty minutes they got up to go to work again. A derisive cheer arose and an old man cried out: 'Yer a disgrace to me name, Michael.' 'Never mind, father,' called Michael, 'the race isn't finished yet.' Then he spat on his hands and seized his hook once more.

Then indeed excitement rose to a high pitch because the Gill couple resumed work at a great speed. Their movements were as mechanical and regular as before, but they worked at almost twice the speed. People began to shout at them. Then betting began among the gentry. Until now the excitement had not been intense because it seemed a foregone conclusion that Bodkin would win since he was so far ahead. Now, however, Bodkin's supremacy was challenged. He still was a long way ahead of Gill, but he was visibly tired and his hook made mistakes now and again, gripping the earth with its point. Bodkin was lathered with sweat. He now began to look behind him at Gill, irritated by the shouts of the people.

Just before four o'clock Considine suddenly collapsed, utterly exhausted. He had to be carried over to the fence. A crowd gathered around and the rector, Mr Robertson, gave him a swig from his brandy-flask that revived him. He made an effort to go back to work, but he was unable to rise. 'Stay there,' said his wife angrily, 'you're finished. I'll carry on myself.' Rolling up her sleeves farther on her fat arms, she went back to the reaping-hook and with a loud yell began to reap furiously. 'Bravo,' cried McDara, 'I'll give the woman a special prize. Gallagher,' he cried, hitting the doctor on the shoulder, 'after all . . . the Irish race . . . ye know what I mean . . . man alive.'

But all centred their attention on the struggle between Bodkin and Gill. Spurred by rage, Bodkin had made a supreme effort and he began to gain ground once more. His immense body moving from left to right and back again across his line of reaping seemed to swallow the long yellow rye-stalks, so quickly did they fall before it. And as the sheaf was completed his lean wife grabbed it up and tied it. But still, when Bodkin paused at five o'clock to cast a look behind him there was Gill coming with terrible regularity. Bodkin suddenly felt all the weariness of the day overcome him.

It struck him first in the shape of an intense thirst. He sent his wife up to the fence for their extra can of tea. When she came back with it, he began to drink. But the more he drank the thirstier he became. His friends in the crowd of spectators shouted at him in warning, but his thirst maddened him. He kept drinking. The shore wall and victory was very near now. He kept looking towards it in a dazed way as he whirled his hook. And he kept drinking. Then his senses began to dull. He became sleepy. His movements became almost unconscious. He only saw the wall and he fought on. He began to talk to himself. He reached the wall at one end of his strip. He had only to cut down to the other end and finish. Three sheaves more and then. . . .

Best man in Inverara. . . . Five-pound note. . . .

But just then a ringing cheer came to his ears and the cry rose on the air: 'Gill has won.' Bodkin collapsed with a groan.

THE MOUNTAIN TAVERN

Snow was falling. The bare, flat, fenceless road had long since disappeared. Now the white snow fell continuously on virgin land, all level, all white, all silent, between the surrounding dim peaks of the mountains. Through the falling snow, on every side, squat humps were visible. They were the mountain peaks. And between them, the moorland was as smooth as a ploughed field. And as silent, oh, as silent as an empty church. Here, the very particles of the air entered the lungs seemingly as big as pebbles and with the sweetness of ripe fruit. An outstretched hand could almost feel the air and the silence. There was absolutely nothing, nothing at all, but falling flakes of white snow, undeflected, falling silently on fallen snow.

Up above was the sky and God perhaps, though it was hard to believe it; hard to believe that there was anything in the whole universe but a flat white stretch of virgin land between squat mountain peaks and a ceaseless shower of falling snow-flakes.

There came the smell of human breathing from the east. Then three figures appeared suddenly, dark, although they were covered with snow. They appeared silently, one by one, stooping forward. The leading man carried his overcoat like a shawl about his head, with a rifle, butt upwards, slung on his right shoulder and two cloth ammunition belts slung across his body. He wore black top boots. His grim young eyes gazed wearily into the falling snow and his boots, scarcely lifted, raked the smooth earth, scattering the fallen snow-flakes.

The second man wore a belted leather coat, of which one arm hung loose. With the other hand he gripped his chest and staggered forward, with sagging, doddering head. A pistol, pouched in a loose belt, swung back and forth with his gait. There was blood on his coat, on his hand and congealed on his black leggings, along which the melting snow ran in a muddy stream. There was a forlorn look in his eyes, but his teeth were set. Sometimes he bared them and drew in a deep breath with a hissing sound.

The third man walked erect. He wore no overcoat and his head was bare. His hair curled and among the curls the snow lay in little rows like some statue in winter. He had a proud, fearless face, bronzed, showing no emotion nor weariness. Now and again, he shook his great body and the snow fell with a rustling sound of his clothes and off the heavy pack he carried. He also had two rifles wrapped in a cape under his arm; and in his right hand he carried a small wooden box that hung from a leather strap.

They walked in each other's tracks slowly. Rapidly the falling snow filled up the imprints of their feet. And when they passed there was silence again.

The man in front halted and raised his eyes to look ahead. The second man staggered against him, groaned with pain and gripped the other about the body with his loose hand to steady himself. The third man put the wooden box on the ground and shifted his pack.

'Where are we now?' he said.

His voice rang out, hollow, in the stillness and several puffs of hot air, the words, jerked out, like steam from a starting engine.

'Can't say,' muttered the man in front. 'Steady, Commandant. We can't be far now. We're on the road anyway. It should be there in front. Can't see, though. It's in a hollow. That's why.'

'What's in a hollow, Jack?' muttered the wounded man. 'Let me lie down here. It's bleeding again.'

'Hold on, Commandant,' said the man in front. 'We'll be at the Mountain Tavern in half a minute. Christ!'

'Put him on my back,' said the big man. 'You carry the stuff.'

'Never mind, I'll walk,' said the wounded man. 'I'll get there all right. Any sign of them?'

They peered into the falling snow behind them. There was utter silence. The ghostly white shower made no sound. A falling curtain.

'Lead on them,' said the big man. 'Lean on me, Commandant.'

They moved on. The wounded man was groaning now and his feet began to drag. Shortly he began to rave in a low voice. Then they halted again. Without speaking, the big man hoisted his comrade, crosswise, on his shoulders. The other man carried the kit. They moved on again.

The peak in front became larger. It was no longer a formless mass. Gradually, through the curtain of snow, it seemed to move towards them and upwards. The air became still more thin. As from the summit of a towering cliff, the atmosphere in front became hollow; and soon, through the haze of snow, they caught a glimpse of the distant plains, between two mountain peaks. There below it lay, like the bottom of a sea, in silence. The mountain sides sank down into it, becoming darker; for it did not snow down there. There was something, after all, other than the snow. But the snowless, downland earth looked dour and unapproachable.

'It must be here,' the leading man said again. 'Why can't we see it? It's just under the shelter of that mountain. There is a little clump of pine trees and a barn with a red roof. Sure I often had a drink in it. Where the name of God is it, anyway?'

'Go on. Stop talking,' said the curly-headed man.

'Can't you be easy?' muttered the leading man, moving ahead and peering into the snow that made his eyelids blink and blink. 'Supposing this is the wrong road, after all. They say people go round and round in the snow. Sure ye could see it from the other end, four miles away in clear weather, two storey high and a slate roof with the sun shining on it. It's facing this way too, right on the top of the hill, with a black board, 'Licensed to Sell.' Man called Galligan owns it. I'd swear by the Cross of Christ we must be up on it.'

'Hurry on,' snapped the curly man. 'There's a gurgle in his throat. Jesus! His blood is going down my neck. Why can't you hurry on, blast it?'

'Hey, what place is that?' cried the leading man, in a frightened voice. 'D'ye see a ruin?'

They halted. A moment ago there had been nothing in front but a curtain of falling snow, beyond which, as in a child's sick dream, the darkening emptiness of the snowless lowland approached, tumbling like a scudding black cloud. Now a crazy blue heap appeared quite close. Suddenly it heaved up out of the snow. It was a ruined house. There was a smell from it too. From its base irregular tufts of smoke curled up spasmodically; dying almost as soon as they appeared and then appearing again.

The two men watched it. There was no emotion in their faces. They just looked, as if without interest. It was too strange. The *Mountain Tavern* was a smoking ruin.

'It's gone west,' murmured the leading man.

'Eh?' shouted the curly man. 'Gone did ye say?'

'Aye. Burned to the ground. See?'

'Well?'

'God knows. We're up the pole.'

Suddenly the curly man uttered a cry of rage and staggered forward under his load. The other man opened his mouth wide, drew in an enormous breath and dropped his head wearily on his chest. Trailing his rifle in the snow behind him, he reeled forward, shaking his head from side to side, with his under lip trembling. Then he began to sing foolishly under his breath. There were people around the ruined house. And as the two men, with their dying comrade, came into view, quite close, these people stopped and gaped at them. There was a woman in front of the house, on the road, sitting on an upturned barrel. She was a thin woman with a long pointed nose and thin black hair that hung in disorder on her thin neck, with hairpins sticking in it. She had a long overcoat buttoned over her dress and a man's overcoat about her shoulders. She held a hat with red feathers on it in her right hand, by the rim. Two children, wrapped in queer clothes, stood beside her, clinging to her, a boy and a girl. They also were thin and they had pointed noses like their mother. One man was pulling something out of a window of the ruined house. Another man, within the window, had his head stuck out. He had been handing out something. Another man was in the act of putting a tin trunk on a cart, to which a horse was harnessed, to the right of the house. All looked gaping, at the newcomers.

'God save all here,' said the curly man, halting near the woman.

Nobody replied. The other man came up and staggered towards the woman, who was sitting on the upturned barrel. The two children, silent with fear, darted around their mother, away from the man. They clutched at her, muttering something inaudibly.

'Is that you, Mrs Galligan?'

'Is it then,' said the woman in a stupid, cold voice. 'And who might you be?'

'We're Republican soldiers,' said the curly man. 'I have a dying man here.'

He lowered the wounded man gently to the ground. Nobody spoke or moved. The snow fell steadily.

'Mummy, mummy,' cried one of the children, there's blood on him. Oh! Mummy.'

The two children began to howl. The dying man began to throw his hands about and mutter something. A great rush of blood flowed from him.

'In the name of the Lord God of Heaven,' yelled the curly man, 'are ye savages not to move a foot? Eh? Can't ye go for a doctor? Is there nothing in the house?'

He stooped over the dying man and clutching him in his arms, he cried hoarsely:

'Easy now, Commandant. I'm beside ye. Give us a hand with him, Jack. We'll fix the bandage.'

The two of them, almost in a state of delirium, began to fumble with the dying man. The children wept. The dying man suddenly cried out:

'Stand fast. Stand fast boys. Stand . . .'

Then he made a violent effort to sit up. He opened his mouth and did not close it again.

The woman looked on dazed, with her forehead wrinkled and her lips set tight. The three men who had been doing something among the ruin began to come up slowly. They also appeared dazed, terrified.

'He's gone,' murmured the curly man, sitting erect on his knees. 'God have mercy on him.'

He laid the corpse flat on the ground. The blood still flowed out. The other soldier took off his hat and then, just as he was going to cross himself, he burst into tears. The three men came close and looked on. Then they sheepishly took off their hats.

'Is he dead?' said one of them.

The curly man sat back on his heels.

'He's dead,' he said. 'The curse o' God on this country.'

'And what did ye say happened?'

'Ambush back there. Our column got wiped out. Haven't ye got anything in the house?'

The woman laughed shrilly. The children stopped crying.

'Is there nothing in the house, ye daylight robber?' she cried. 'Look at it, curse ye. It's a black ruin. Go in. Take what ye can find, ye robber.'

'Robbers!' cried the soldier who had been weeping. 'Come on, Curly. Stand by me. I'm no robber. God! Give me a drink. Something to eat. Christ! I'm dyin'.'

He got to his feet and took a pace forward like a drunken man. The curly-headed soldier caught him.

'Keep yer hair on, Jack,' he said.

'Look at what ye've done,' cried the woman. 'Ye've blown up the house over me head. Ye've left me homeless and penniless with yer war. Oh! God, why don't ye drop down the dome of Heaven on me?'

'Sure we didn't blow up yer house,' cried the curly soldier. 'An' we lookin' for shelter after trampin' the mountains since morning. Woman, ye might respect the dead that died for ye.'

The woman spat and hissed at him.

'Let them die. They didn't die for me,' she said. 'Amn't I ruined and wrecked for three long years with yer fightin', goin' back and forth, lootin' and turnin' the honest traveller from my door? For three long years have I kept open house for all of ye and now yer turnin' on one another like dogs after a bitch.'

'None o' that now,' cried the hysterical soldier, trying to raise his rifle.

'Hold on, man,' cried one of the other men. 'She has cause. She has cause.'

He grew excited and waved his hands and addressed his own comrades instead of addressing the soldiers.

'The Republicans came to the house this morning,' he cried. 'So Mr Galligan told me an' he goin' down the road for McGilligan's motor. The Republicans came, he said. And then . . . then the Free Staters came on top of them and the firing began. Women and children out, they said, under a white flag. So Galligan told me. 'They damn near shot me,' says he to me, 'harbourin' Irregulars under the new act.' Shot at sight, or what's worse, they take ye away on the cars, God knows where. Found in a ditch. None of us, God blast my soul if there is a word of a lie in what I am sayin', none of us here have a hand or part in anything. Three miles I came up in the snow when Mr Galligan told me. Says he to me, 'I'll take herself and the kids to aunt Julia's in McGilligan's motor.'

'Where did they go?' said the curly soldier.

'I was comin' to that,' said the man, spitting in the snow and turning towards the woman. 'It's with a bomb they did it, Galligan said to me. Something must have fallen in the fire. They stuck it out, he said. There were six men inside. Not a man came out without a wound. So he said. There were two dead. On a door they took 'em away. They took 'em all off in the cars. And they were goin' to take Mr Galligan too. There you are now. May the Blessed Virgin look down on here. An' many's a man 'll go thirsty from this day over the mountain road.'

'Aye,' said the woman. 'For twenty years in that house, since my father moved from the village, after buyin' it from Johnny Reilly.'

'Twenty years,' she said again.

'Can't ye give us something to eat?' cried the hysterical man, trying to break loose from the curly soldier, who still held him.

'There's nothing here,' muttered a man, 'until Mr Galligan comes in the motor. He should be well on the way now.'

'They were all taken,' said the curly soldier.

'All taken,' said the three men, all together.

'Sit down, Jack,' said the curly soldier.

He pulled his comrade down with him on to the snow. He dropped his head on his chest. The others looked at the soldiers sitting in the snow. The others had a curious, malign look in their eyes. They looked at the dazed, exhausted soldiers and at the corpse with a curious apathy. They looked with hatred. There was no pity in their eyes. They looked steadily without speech or movement, with the serene cruelty of children watching an insect being tortured. They looked patiently, as if calmly watching a monster in its death agony.

The curly-headed soldier suddenly seemed to realise that they were watching him. For he raised his head and peered at them shrewdly through the falling snow. There was utter silence everywhere, except the munching sound made by the horse's jaws as he chewed hay. The snow fell, fell now, in the fading light, mournfully, blotting out the sins of the world.

The soldier's face, that had until then shown neither fear now weariness, suddenly filled with despair. His lips bulged out. His eyes almost closed. His forehead gathered together and he opened his nostrils wide.

'I'm done,' he said. 'It's no use. Say, men. Send word that we're here. Let them take us. I'm tired fightin'. It's no use.'

No one spoke or stirred. A sound approached. Strange to say, no one paid attention to the sound. And even when a military motor lorry appeared at the brow of the road, nobody moved or spoke. There were Free State soldiers on the lorry. They had their rifles pointed. They drew near slowly. Then, with a rush, they dismounted and came running up.

The two Republican soldiers put up their hands, but they did not rise to their feet.

'Robbers,' screamed the woman. 'I hate ye all. Robbers.'

Her husband was there with them.

'Mary, we're to go in the lorry,' he said to her. 'They're goin' to look after us they said. Fr Considine went to the barracks.'

'The bloody robbers,' she muttered, getting off the barrel.

'Who's this?' the officer said, roughly handling the corpse.

He raised the head of the corpse.

'Ha!' he said. 'So we got him at last. Eh! Heave him into the lorry, boys. Hurry up. Chuck 'em all in.'

They took away the corpse and the prisoners. There was a big dark spot where the corpse had lain. Snow began to fall on the dark spot.

They took away everybody, including the horse and cart. Everybody went away, down the steep mountain road, into the dark lowland country, where no snow was falling. All was silent again on the flat top of the mountain.

There was nothing in the whole universe again but the black ruin and the black spot where the corpse had lain. Night fell and snow fell, fell like soft soothing white flower petals on the black ruin and on the black spot where the corpse had lain.

THE BLACKBIRD'S MATE

A Blackbird was singing on a bough one morning early in the Spring. From his black voluptuous throat he sent aloft fair music in adoration of the rising sun.

The shining star was pouring down upon the dewy earth myriads of beams that rippled like the laughter of a happy God. Its rays danced on the glossy bellies of the naked trees. They warmed the wet buds that were already bursting on the topmost branches. From the earth sweet vapours rose, the smells of countless plants and herbs that were breathing their first breath. And loud like the clamour of wild torrents flowing over polished stones in mountain glens, a great chorus of birds made the very air drunk with joy.

Although the blackbird sang in ecstasy there was a strange pathetic cry in every note. His body, trembling on the bough, was calling for a mate.

And then, like a gift from the sun to which he sang, a hen bird dropped gently near him on the bough. She was less dark than he and her plumage did not shine in the sunlight. Her beak was not golden. But she had a beautiful, slender body. When he saw her, she looked good to him and her comeliness aroused a desire in him to spread his wings over her and caress her with all his force. So he sang his wildest and sweetest notes to charm her and make her come nearer.

She stretched out her neck and hopped towards him a little way. Then she became motionless, with outstretched neck, blinking her little eyes, as if dazzled by the beauty of his golden beak, his shining feathers and his voluptuous throat.

Then an overflowing passion made him hoarse and he ceased to sing. He too stretched out his neck and blinked his eyes. He spread out his wings and ruffled the feathers on his rotund breast. Uttering passionate cries, he trotted towards her. But instead of receiving him she fluttered upwards to another bough and then looked down with her head to one side, as if indignant.

He looked at her stupidly for a little while. Then his sudden burst of passion left him. He became subtle like the hen. He chirped and shook himself. He hopped away, raised his beak and sang a few notes very arrogantly, as if sending out an invitation for another hen.

That fetched her. She in turn grew excited and approached him once more with outstretched neck. Now he pretended not to notice her. But when she came quite near and made a little chirping sound, he again spread his wings and offered himself. Immediately she flew away from him, downwards, and then turning suddenly, she wound like a swallow through the trees. He became furious. Uttering a wild cry that re-echoed through the wood, he set off in pursuit.

They left the wood and followed the course of a stream that was lined with willow trees, until at last she hid in the bank among the wet roots of an overhanging bush. He found her there. She offered no resistance. Beak to beak, chirping, fluttering their trailing-wings, they united by the silent stream. Then they returned to the wood.

Now she followed him like a captive and when he hopped along the ground searching for food, she waited behind until he offered her a morsel, or shook a wriggling worm proudly before her eyes. Later she stood near him on a bough while he sang for her, and when night came she slept beside him in the ivy that grew around an old oak tree.

For many days they wandered through the wood, enjoying their young love without labour or anxiety. For food was plentiful. The hospitable earth opened her pores and offered to their prodding beaks a choice store of worms and insects and young sprouts. Except when he was feeding, the cock spent all day singing and playing with his mate. At dawn he sang when the sunrays were chasing the silent ghoulish shadows of the night. And again at noon he warbled when the sun was high. But his wildest song came with the fall of night, as if he called the departing sun, in fear that it would never shine again.

Then one day the hen bird began to search with great care among the branches of a hawthorn bush. At first the cock bird did not seem to understand her purpose, for he began to chirp and flutter about her as if in play. But she was very serious and not inclined for frolic, so she pecked at him angrily when he brushed against her. Then he stood on a twig and watched her with interest. At last she sat in a little hollow where three branches grew from a single stem, making a cosy nook. She turned around several times in this nook and pressed against the branches with her breast. Then, having finished her examination, she hopped upwards a little way and looked down, cocking her head from side to side very wisely. Then she flew around the bush and entered it very hurriedly from various angles. Then she went to neighbouring trees and bushes and looked about her, taking note of the surroundings. Finally she flew to the ground and hopped about. The cock followed her, uttering little cries, questioning her. She paid no heed to him. Now it appeared that he was the captive, following submissively in her tracks.

When she picked up in her beak a little cake of moist earth and grass and flew with it to the hawthorn bush he knew what she was about. He also made a little ball and followed her with it. They had begun to built a nest.

The making of the nest took a very long time because the hen bird insisted on doing all the designing. Whenever the cock added a piece of moss or a little chip of a twig, she caught it up and put it somewhere else. The business was carried on very secretly and both birds made wide circuits with material in their beaks in order to avoid being seen. Sometimes their work was interrupted by the necessity for driving away from their bush other birds. The smaller birds went quickly, but a pair of thrushes, that were also seeking a home, gave great trouble and were routed only by constant nagging that lasted a whole afternoon. Then at last the framework of the nest was finished. Then the hen sat in it and began to line it with feathers, until it looked very beautiful and it was hard to believe that it had not always been there, or that it had not grown like a flower, fashioned by some genius of the invisible world. Indeed, so beautiful was it that it was almost impossible to believe that two little birds could have made it with their beaks, using their breasts to plane it and compass its roundness.

Now the hen was very proud indeed. On a tree, within sight of the bush, she sat beside the cock, while he sang for an hour or more, rejoicing in the nest they had built.

They finished their work just in time, because next morning the hen laid an egg in the nest. She laid three more eggs and then she sat on the nest in a queer posture, as if she were in a swoon, or stricken with some sickness. The cock became still more tender. He fetched her food and roamed about the bush, protecting it from enemies.

For eight days after the hen began to sit on her eggs the sun continued to shine all day. The wood was merry with brilliant light and with the joyous smells of growth. Then the sun disappeared. The sky grew dark. The wind rose. Black clouds passed over the wood, dropping slow tendrils of grey mist from their sagging bellies. The air grew icy cold. At dawn the gloomy earth was covered with frost that closed its pores and drove the insects and worms deep into the soil. There was no food for the birds. Growth ceased and many buds that had been tempted forth by the sun withered on the branches. The blackbird began to sing less gaily. But the hen bird on the eggs still sat with the same look of drowsy happiness in her half-closed eyes.

It grew still more cold. A terrible silence spread through the wood, until the creaking of a branch or the passage of a thrush's wings became a sound of loud degree. The sky was shut out by a mist that had no colour. Then snow began to fall.

A little before dawn the first flakes began to drop in silence from the sky. But they fell so quickly that when daylight spread the earth was covered with an immaculate white coat. The trees assumed strange shapes. On the branches little mounds of snow gathered and then fell with soft thuds to the ground. Their falling was the only sound, for the birds were silent, shuddering in their hiding-places, terrified by the strange white flakes down from the dark sky.

The blackbird sat in the hawthorn bush above the nest on which his mate was sitting. He was terrified, for there was no more food and the wet snow came thudding through the bush on to his mate's back from the topmost branches. And the cold was intense. When day advanced and the snow still kept falling, he left the bush and flew away from the woods, across the fields, until he came to a house. There were many birds there, looking for food that might be cast out on rubbish heaps. But although he flew about for many hours he found nothing. Instead he was almost captured by a cat that lay in ambush behind the door of a shed. So he flew back to the nest. His mate was still there lying on the eggs. Night came. He stayed with her on the bush. She never moved or looked at him, but seemed to be still in a swoon of love.

Next morning the snow still fell. Again no bird sang. The wood was like a desert, with the great white hulks of the trees standing around like mummied ghosts. The blackbird was seized with panic and he tried to induce his mate to desert the next and fly away with him to the warmth of some shed in the plain. But she refused to move. The little creature was growing stiff with cold and hunger, but she could not leave the eggs that she felt warm against her breast.

The cock flew away again looking for food. He got nothing. He returned to the bush, cold and feeble with hunger. He perched above the nest, uttered a plaintive cry, closed his eyes and fell into a swoon.

He was awakened by a joyous cry that came from a thrush perched on a tree near by. He opened his eyes. Lo! It was morning and the sun was blazing in the sky. The white earth glittered. The melting snow was falling from the trees. Birds began to sing. He himself opened his beak and warbled. Then he looked at the nest. His mate still sat there motionless. He flew out from the bush, fierce with hunger. He left the wood and wandered down among the willows that lined the stream. There, sticking from the bank of the stream, he saw the head of a great worm. He pounced on it and pulled forth a large piece. He placed it on a stone and chopped it in two with his beak. He swallowed a piece and flew back with the remainder wild with joy.

When he reached the nest, he began to chirp and to bob his head, to draw his mate's attention. She did not move. He came nearer and bending down, he dangled the worm before her beak. She did not move. He dropped the worm by her beak on the edge on the nest. She did not move. He stood erect and uttered a queer cry. He bent over her, paused and pecked at her gently. She did not move. Then he hopped back in terror.

Then he rushed at her furiously and prodded her comb. He clawed at her and pushed against her with his breast, until he forced himself down into the nest and pushed her over the brink.

Her stiff body fell like a stone from twig to twig until it struck the earth.

For a few moments the cock sat still on the eggs. Then he felt them icy cold against his breast.

Uttering a piteous shriek he flew headlong from the wood.

THE OAR

Beneath tall cliffs, two anchored curraghs swung, their light prows bobbing on the gentle waves. Their tarred sides shone in the moonlight. In each, three stooping figures sat on narrow seats, their arms resting on the frail sides, their red-backed hands fingering long lines, that swam, white, through the deep, dark water.

There was a heavy silence there. There were strange shadows on the gently rolling bosom of the sea. The shadows came from the cliffs. Beyond, the Black Reef looked like a fallen spear, a clear black line with a pointed head. Above, the Drowned Man's Leap stood; a proud cruel cliff with a jutting beak, from which water dripped down its bulging, mossy belly. And round the frail, swaying boats, other shadows crept up from the deep, shapes of sunken rocks, where fishes roamed in lairs and beds of clustering yellow weeds.

There were no fish. The lines, baited with heated limpets, wandered idly through the languid sea. Strange too, although the moon shone fitfully, she wandered alone through the sky. Not a star was seen. The sky had no colour. There was no end to the languid sea, no horizon to its endless rows of slowly rolling waves.

The men sat on their narrow seats in silence, fingering their lines. A little while ago, just before nightfall, an enormous school of bream had come about the boats. They rose like mackerel, even to the water's edge and nosed the air, opening their gauzy red lips, like cormorants flying high in a breeze. As if terrified, they darted round the floating baits and nibbled at the lines. Each boat caught a couple and then they disappeared again. Dogfish came. The men were busy swiping the heads off the brutes with their knives and then throwing their carcasses over into the sea. Then the dogfish went away.

Excited by the enormous school of fish, the men waited now, although they did not get a bite. When the tide was full, they thought, the fish would come again.

Their greed made them pay no heed to the ominous silence and to the starless sky that had no colour. If those fish came again, they would fill their boats with them.

Now the tide was full. It became very hot. A man with a short red beard growing on his neck stood up in the prow of the boat farthest to the east. He tightened his belt round his waist. He coughed and shouted to the other boat:

'Are ye getting any bite, Little Martin?'

A voice coughed and answered:

'I think, Red Bartly . . . heh, I think now, that there is something to come out of that sky that has no colour in it, like a mist on a mountain.'

'Aye,' said Red Bartly. 'Maybe. That black reef over there, look at it. Ye'd think it was a long fishing-rod held out that way. And yet, my soul from the devil, by day, it's as broad as a boat is long.'

'Yes, yes,' the men murmured. 'Maybe we'd better pull up.'

But nobody moved, for their greedy imaginations filled their boats again and again from the enormous school of red-lipped fish that had risen like a miracle about them.

Suddenly it became still more silent. As when lead melts and flows in a silver stream, all smooth, so the wavelets melted into the sea's bosom. Now a motionless black floor supported the motionless coracles. Now there was no moon. Now a black mass filled the sky. From afar a bellowing noise came and then a wave simmered over a smooth rock quiet near. 'Tchee . . . ee . . . ee,' it said.

From each boat a wild cry re-echoed through the caverns of the mighty cliffs:

'In the name of God, cut. Cut. Oars out. Cut.'

With teeth bared, Red Bartly bounded into the prow of the curragh. He gripped his open knife, blade downwards. With one fierce stroke he cut the hairy yellow anchor rope. The fragile coracle shivered like an eased horse eager for the road. With a gay twirl of her high prow, she swung about to the east. Already an oar was out astern.

'Haul in the lines,' Red Bartly said.

'Damn the lines,' the others growled. 'Ha! What's that? Oh, Christ.'

Lightning flashed across the bellying sky, lightening the air with crooked knives of flame. Across its path, wild thunder crashed, reverberating. The leaden sea convulsed, swayed up the cliffs and moaned receding.

With loud cries, the two crews hammered their tholepins with sea-smoothed stones. Then they rowed, having knived their lines and their anchor ropes.

The oars cut the still-flat sea with a screeching sound. Red Bartly's curragh was in front. As they lay back, each crew hissed in unison. The whole strength of their wild hearts was in each stroke. And the light black boats, arching their gay prows, bounded like leaping salmon over the sea.

They rowed eastwards beneath the towering cliffs. To east and west, within them, long reefs and bastions of jutting rock stood out, chiselled like housewalls by the might of ancient storms. Southwards the ocean stretched; now a sloping mountain that had no summit.

Now the silent lightning flashed regularly and thunder followed its shooting rays. The boats lit up, stood out, white and small and then they passed with a rumbling swishing sound of moving oars again into the pitch-dark night.

When the lightning flashed on them the faces of the rowing men were white. But they no longer feared. They were fighting now and they murmured calmly as they rowed, wondering would they reach the rock-bound shore below their village before the sea rose in its fullness. The two boats rowed in a line, a few fathoms apart. And although it was pitch-dark, with ancient skill, they kept them, as straight as a rock-bird's flight, on the ancient course, along which their countless ancestors had rowed. They did not think. Every muscle of their bodies was taut with fierce courage.

Moving at great speed, the two boats reached the promontory of the fort. They passed it. Now they were coming abreast of the ancient fort of Aengus, perched on the cliff-top. Then the sea began to break. The wind came sweeping from the ocean, driving the sea before it. Then a loud cry came from the men.

'She's after us,' they said.

They crossed themselves hurriedly. Then they became silent. The long rolling waves broke into fragments. They became alive. Froth overspread them. They hissed as they clashed and cast their spume into the air. Some swayed and wallowed, towering high. Others raced along, with curved summits, as if consciously fleeing before the wind.

The boats no longer bounded forward. They rocked now, swinging their sterns across each following wave. Now the men did not pull fiercely but cautiously. They measured out half and quarter strokes, saving their boats from the foam-capped, monstrous waves that jumped at them from out the lightning flashes.

Still they passed on, tumbling black specks, past the Swan's Cliffs until they were abreast of the great reef that runs west of the Serpent's Hole. There were breakers there; for though it was full tide, the power of the sea swept its waters back afar, exposing even the black weeds that grow in deep caverns. And over the low-tide rocks, giant and beautiful waves came rolling under a shower of fluttering foam.

Then indeed the men trembled in their boats. Red Bartly shouted out with all his might:

'Strengthen your right hands and keep your faces to the sea. Lay her out.'

Now there was a sea in which heavy rocks could float.

They had to tack out into the wind. Blood burst from beneath their finger-nails and from their nostrils. The two curraghs, now quite close together, faced the sea with almost perpendicular prows. Their pointed beaks and rounded shoulders made them look like big black fish hauled quickly, resisting, over the surface of resisting water, from a distant high bank.

Then with a loud cry they turned again eastwards. Now the boats raced eastwards before the flying wind. They had gone a hundred fathoms when, lo! a mighty wave arose. Lightning flashed on it and on the boats. It arose close behind Little Martin's. As the lightning flashed Red Bartly and his crew saw it standing like a falling cliff over Little Martin's boat. Then the lightning passed. Red Bartly turned to receive the wave. In a moment it was upon them. Its spume filled their boat to the transom. As it passed and their boat fell away in its wake, lightning flashed again in three successive flashes.

Then indeed they saw a terrifying thing in the wild, enchanted light that spread red over the black sea.

First they saw an upraised oar, raised straight on high, its handle grasped by an upraised hand. Beneath it, they saw an upraised face in agony. The face looked up, with staring eyes, as if saluting Heaven with his upraised oar.

Then darkness came.

Again the lightning flashed. Again they saw the oar, now hurled aloft sideways. There was no hand grasping its handle.

Again darkness came.

The third time the lightning flashed, they looked and saw nothing but a wall of sea approaching them.

'Turn and save them,' cried one of Red Bartly's crew.

Red Bartly roared:

'Sense comes before courage. Three windows are enough. Row, you devils. Row.'

They passed the jutting reef. They reached the harbour's mouth. Now they rowed steadily making great way, through the rolling seas. Their eyes, against their cunning, life-loving wills, still pierced the darkness behind them.

They saw it once again, when lightning flashed, following them. The waves were tossing it. It stood like a mast and then fell, turning round and round into the darkness.

Then they heard shouting on the shore.

Up among the wailing women they were dragged. Hands were about their necks and prayers of thanksgiving whispered on their kissed cheeks.

But other voices shrieked in despair.

Red Bartly kept repeating in a crazed voice:

'We saw an oar by the Serpent's Reef. Raised up to Heaven with a hand grasping it. It followed us and no hand was grasping it.'

THE DITCH

He had a face like an ape. His forehead was wrinkled like that of an ape. His eyes were big and grey, with dead, white rims, utterly without expression. His ears were enormous and outstanding. His nose was short. Its point stuck upwards. His nostrils were like the mouths of little bells. He had flabby lips and a sunken chin. The colour of his cheeks was dark brown, like that of the uprooted earth when it is parched by the sun. His cheeks were dented with innumerable little lines, each line a mark of toil, furrows of pain. His rags were tied about him with cords. His boots were caked with dried earth. On his right shoulder he carried his coat, held limply by a great red hand. His left hand gripped the hanging mane of a horse that trudged beside him. He leaned against the horse's shoulder, his head near the horse's head.

His name was Michael Cassidy. He was thirty years old. He was a farm labourer.

It was after sunset. All day the hot summer sun scorched the earth. Both horse and man were exhausted with work. From dawn that day they had plodded back and forth through a field, stopping only to eat and drink.

They walked through a narrow lane that led to their master's farm-house. They made a soft, dull sound as their feet splashed heavily through the dry, loose earth. Sometimes the horse's harness jingled on his shoulder. Sometimes the horse snorted. Sometimes Cassidy cleared his throat and looked about him slowly, with upraised eyebrows and with an expression of pain on his face, disturbed by a wandering vague thought.

On either side of the lane, tall, flowering hedges hemmed them in. The branches brushed against their bodies and their nostrils were filled with the rich smell of exuberant growth. The brown of the dried, uprooted earth and the dark green of the hedges mingled in a grinning, sinister colour before their half-closed, weary eyes. Birds were singing. Beyond the walls of green hedges there were many other sounds of joy. Carts rumbled. Dogs barked. Cows lowed. People cried out. These sounds, in the calm of evening, heralded the fall of night and they were sweet and soothing and passionate. But they were remote from and alien to these two tired beings, trudging homewards, stupefied with work.

These two could not look above the tops of the hedges at the red blaze in the sky where the sun had set.

They came to a place where another lane cut across the one in which they were walking. There was a woman sitting on the grass, under the hedge, at the corner of the other lane, on the left. Neither Cassidy nor the horse saw her until they were within a few feet of her. Then she spoke.

'Is that you, Mick?' she said.

Cassidy started as violently as if he had been struck. Then he stood still. The horse stumbled against Cassidy, shook his head and then halted, drawing in a deep breath through his nostrils with a hoarse sound. Then both Cassidy and the horse looked at the woman.

She also was very ugly. She had a blotched, heavy, pale face, with a thick nose and big, black, stupid eyes. She wore no hat. Her black hair had been plaited and wound about her poll, but the plait had come loose and it hung across her shoulder, with a hairpin sticking from it. She wore an old grey overcoat that was fastened with safety-pins. There was a little white bundle on the grass beside her. She sat on the grass with her legs folded under her like a Turk. Her hands were crossed limply on her stomach. She looked with a strange, unhealthy fixedness at Cassidy. There was terror in her eyes. Her nostrils twitched. There were deep, vertical lines running from between her eyes to the centre of her forehead.

They stared at one another in silence for nearly a minute. The horse raised his head, stretched out his neck and smelt the woman. Then Cassidy spoke.

'Maggie!' he said in a hoarse whisper. 'Is that you?'

When he spoke, his knees began to tremble. Deep lines came in his forehead. A little light appeared in the iris of each of his eyes. The woman did not reply. She went on staring. Her hands moved on her stomach. The fingers interlaced. Then her hands strained, gripping one another closely.

Then Cassidy frowned. He stiffened himself.

'What the hell are ye doin' here?' he said in a fierce whisper. 'What brought ye? What are ye sittin' there for?'

The woman leaned her head forward, opened her mouth to speak and then remained silent. She shook her head, looked to one side and bit her lip. Then she looked at him. Now there was a terribly malign look in her eyes, a look of morose satisfaction and of hatred. Then she rose slowly to her feet, staggering heavily.

He opened his eyes wide when she reached her full height. His lower lip dropped. She slowly opened her shabby overcoat and exposed a black dress,

which was so threadbare that a white garment was visible beneath it. The
dress was loose above her stomach. On her stomach it swelled out in a balloonish
curve, very taut and unseemly.

'Jesus!' he said with great force.

Then he spat, looked about him and wiped his mouth on his sleeve.

She sank to the ground almost falling. She lay, half on her side with one
leg stretched out, staring at him. Her chin was sunk into her fat, loose-
skinned neck. Then she groaned and gritted her teeth, struck by a sudden
pain. She grasped her swollen breasts and looked about her wildly. Her
stomach moved. Something had jumped within it.

He looked away and then raised his face to the sky. His face writhed with
pain. He looked even more pitiful than the unseemly woman who lay groaning
on the grass. He was so ugly.

The sudden pain left the woman. She turned on him again and said savagely:

'What are ye goin' to do about it?'

He looked at her with equal savagery:

'How do I know?'

'What?' she said. 'What are ye drivin' at?'

'Why do ye come to me? That's what I'm drivin' at. How do you know?
There's more men than me in the country.'

She uttered an oath and said:

'Ye know well who did it. What are ye goin' to do about it?'

His eyes fell before her. His thighs were lax. He struck the horse a blow
on the chest with his elbow and muttered:

'Lift, damn you.'

The horse moved his left fore-hoof a little farther away. Suddenly the
woman began to speak at a great speed.

'You'll have to do something for me,' she said. 'By God! You will. It was
your doing, Mick Cassidy, and I swear by the mother of God that no man
touched me but you. For the love of God, Mick, have a heart in ye. I
dragged myself twenty miles since dawn. Christ! I'm sick. I've been with this
coming on me for the past three weeks. Me time is up 'now. I daren't go to
the doctor or say a word to the missus. She spotted me, I know, for I could
see her looking at me. So I told her I was sick and that I had to go home.
But where can I go? I can't go home. My brother is married in the house
and he gives my mother a dog's life as it is. Only for her old age pension
he'd send her to the workhouse. It's the door I'd get from him and his rat of
a wife. So I came here to you. God knows I wouldn't if I weren't put to it.
Ye told me ye'd stand by me and that I'd come to no harm. Ye'll have to do

something for me. What are ye goin' to do about it? Christ! Sure ye wouldn't let a sheep lie in a ditch, sick an' dyin', not to mind a human being. Anyway . . . By God! I'm desperate, Mick. Ye'll have to do something. There's a law in the land. Ye can't bloody well ruin a girl and then go by, so ye can't. Mother of God! What am I saying? Give us a drink. God! I have an awful pain. Can ye do nothin' for me? For God's sake, Mick, have a heart in ye. Ye won't? Eh? By Christ! I'll swing for ye. I'm desperate.'

She began to rise again, distraught. Then she fell prone, unable to rise. He became terrified.

'Hold on, Maggie,' he said.

He bent down towards her and then stood erect again. He rubbed his hands together slowly. The impulse to murder darkened his face; the brute instinct which urges all animals to slay the useless and sick of their kind. It passed rapidly, in a moment. It was followed by another impulse. He thought of the law and he grew afraid. With his lip quivering, he said to her:

'I can't take ye to the loft. They'd see ye comin' in and anyway . . . Can't ye go into the workhouse?'

She sat up and said wildly:

'The workhouse! God I'd rather drown myself. What would I do with this when I came out? Ye must do something for me, Mick?'

She uttered the last sentence in a peculiar manner that made him start and look into the distance. He looked back at her suddenly and started again.

'What?' he said. 'What d'ye mean?'

Her eyes were almost closed, but she looked at him cunningly.

'What?' he said again.

She did not reply. She just looked at him cunningly.

'All right,' he said softly. 'The tinkers that were here are gone since yesterday. We'll go up there.'

'Where?'

'The tinkers' ditch.'

'Isn't that dangerous?'

'What for?'

'Wouldn't I be seen there?'

'An' who's to know yer not a tinker? Sure nobody is goin' to prowl into a ditch after a tinker woman.'

'But wouldn't they hear it?'

'What?'

She pointed towards her body.

'What are ye after?' he said fiercely.

'By Christ!' she said in a fury. 'Ye must do something for me, Mick. Else I'll swing for ye.'

'Shut up or I'll choke ye,' he whispered.

She shrank back against the hedge. He turned away trembling. He leaned his head against the horse's neck and shuddered. Then he sighed.

'Come on,' he said. 'Can ye walk? Ye came this far, so ye can go a little farther, can't ye? We can't stay here. Somebody might come. It's only a couple o' hundred yards.'

She got up and followed him. The horse tried to turn up the lane towards home, but Cassidy lashed the brute and hauled him along to the right.

They went three hundred yards up a steep slope. They reached a copse of fir trees. There was an opening into it from the lane. A moor stretched beyond the copse to the left. Within the opening there was a patch of bare ground, stamped flat. On the close-cropped, stamped, withered grass, there were circular brown and black patches, burnt out; the marks left by fires. On the old patches, young blades of grass were sprouting. Beneath the hedge there was a wide, dry ditch, half full of leaves. Grey sacks, empty tins, rags and pieces of wood, that were once portions of carts and barrels, were strewn about there. In front of the ditch, there was a thick tree stump, with a few of the lower branches, chopped and naked of bark, sticking from it. Names had been carved on the stump. There was a big iron spike stuck in it. The tinkers used it for tethering their animals.

The place was a good shelter. The trees, in leaf, made a thick roof over it. It was dusky there, silent and sinister.

Cassidy pointed to the ditch and said:

'There you are.'

She looked at him and then she looked at the ditch. She went towards the ditch muttering. She kicked at the dead leaves, smelt them and then threw down her bundle. Then she turned to him and said:

'By God! You'll have to stand by me now. You'll have to do something for me. My time is up.'

'Shut yer gob,' he said. 'Don't make a row. Ye don't want to call in the whole village, do ye? Sit down there and be quiet. I'll leave the horse home and come back. I'll bring ye grub.'

She lowered herself heavily to the bed of leaves, sinking into them. She leaned her head against her right hand and closed her eyes.

'Is there anything ye want?' he said.

She opened her eyes, dropped her lower lip and said sombrely:

'I'll want nothing. It's up to you. It's you got me this way. Ye'll have to do something.'

'Well! Amn't I asking ye?' he said. 'Is there anything ye want?'

'Ach!' she said, dropping her head and closing her eyes.

'Ha!' he said.

When he was moving away with the horse, she raised her head and said in a startled voice:

'You had better be sure and come back. Else I'll . . .'

He made no reply, but he struck the horse on the side with his fist. She lay down, closed her eyes and began to sob hysterically.

'It's she all right,' he muttered to himself going away. 'Maggie Conroy. By the Holy, it is.'

He remembered how it had happened towards the end of September of the previous year. He had met her in a field as he was coming home from work. She was sitting under a hedge doing something. He just came towards her, looking at her. Neither of them spoke. He threw her down. She gasped and fainted. He got up afterwards and hurried away terribly frightened. He had looked back and had seen her, turned over on her face, with her hands stretched out. Next day the same thing happened. She went away to a farmer in the middle of October. Now she was here.

He reached the farmhouse, stabled and fed the horse and then went into the farmyard. He talked a while to his master about the day's work, while he washed his hands at the trough in the yard. He received his food from the woman in the kitchen. When he had eaten, he asked for some milk in a can and a piece of bread, saying he was going out that night with a dog. He went over to his loft over the stable and sat on his trestle bed until it was dark . . . trying to think.

After dark he left the loft bringing the food with him. He went by a path across fields to the ditch. He found the woman asleep.

It was now very dark in the ditch. He sat down near her. He could barely see the outline of her body. He heard her snore and the light rustling of the dead leaves as she moved restlessly in her sleep. There were bats roaming through the trees making a buzzing sound. It was very still and hot. Now and again, branches that had become entwined in their growth broke loose, making a queer, snapping sound. Little animals, scurrying through the trees, dislodged dead pieces of stick. All these sounds terrified him. He touched her and then drew away his hand. Then he looked around him, he became still more terrified of the wood. He shook her.

'Are ye hungry, Maggie?'

She awoke with a start and raised her head.

'What?' she said.

Suddenly he felt pity for her. He wanted to caress her and to say kind things to her. But his face remained brutal and he said nothing. Neither did he caress her.

'You're back,' she said. 'God! I'll die. Jesus, Mary and Joseph!'

Another pain struck her. She groaned and clutched her body.

'I brought ye some grub,' he said.

The feeling of tenderness left him when she groaned. He remembered the cause of these groans and that he must do something for her.

She sat up and bent forward and began to utter weird words, the strange mutterings of a woman in travail.

He became terrified again by these words.

'Hadn't ye better eat something?' he whispered.

'Who asked you?' she said fiercely. 'I didn't ask you. You must do something for me though.'

'For God's sake, Maggie,' he said, going on his knees, 'will ye be easy? Ye put the heart crosswise in me. What's the use o' going on like that? Sure ye can't change what's done. Can't ye be quiet now?'

'You must do something for me,' she repeated stupidly.

Then she reached out her hand towards the can.

'Give me that,' she said. 'Give me a drink.'

He handed her the can of milk and the piece of bread. She became possessed by a panic of hunger when she saw the food. She devoured it all, glaring about her and making queer sounds. She lay back when she had finished. Then she sat up and looked into the distance and said in a petulant tone:

'I'd love a bar of chocolate, so I would.'

She lay back again.

Suddenly it occurred to him that if she died here, he would get into serious trouble.

'Maggie,' he said. 'Will I go for a doctor . . . or a . . . or a priest?'

'Leave me alone,' she muttered. 'I hate the sight of you. Go away.'

'All right,' he said. 'I will.'

'Don't go,' she cried, sitting up. 'Stay here, Mick. Stay with me. Don't leave me. I'm terrified. The pain I have. God! You'll have to do something for me, though. Don't forget that. Otherwise I'll swing for you.'

She became very excited. She clawed the ground with her hands and began to toss about. He began to cry. Again he felt pity for her. He took her in his arms and whispered to her. But she struck her head against his mouth and bit his shoulder.

'Kill me,' she cried. 'Why don't ye put an end to me life? Gimme poison. God! I want to die. Curse the night I was born.'

Hush, hush,' he whispered. 'Don't shout. You'll be heard.'

'I don't care,' she screamed.

Then she blasphemed against the mother of God in a shrill voice.

He crossed himself and begged God's mother to forgive him and her.

Then she was quiet. It became very silent in ditch. Nothing moved. The moon appeared above the wood. Its yellow light crept down through the tangled branches. She began to rave in a low voice. She writhed with pain. She laughed. Her laughter terrified him. He gripped her tight within his arms, whispered to her, kissed her clothes and pressed his cheek against her stomach.

'Let me go,' she growled.

Making a great effort, she seized him by the throat and threw him from her with violence. He fell against the side of the ditch, stupefied. He shut his eyes and covered his ears with his hands, to shut out the sound of the cries she was now uttering.

Then, after a while, he became aware that something strange had happened. She was perfectly still. She was breathing heavily. He opened his eyes and looked at her. Now she was visible, in the yellow moonlight. Her face was towards him. It looked yellow, wan, tired, sinister. She did not speak and yet her eyes spoke to him, saying terrible things. Then he heard a cry. He started. Something had moaned beside her in the ditch. He looked at it. Staring at it, he struggled to his feet. She reached out her hand as if to prevent him from rising.

'Eh?' he grasped.

'Where are ye going?' she gasped. 'What did I tell ye?'

'Eh?'

'See?'

'What?'

'What are ye going to do?'

'Let me alone, damn ye.'

Her eyes held him. They terrified him. Again he looked at the thing that lay beside her in the ditch. For one moment he was possessed of a wild feeling of tenderness and pity for it; but at the next moment, he mumbled a cry of horror and covered his cheeks with his hands. Then he took away his hands, looked at her and hated the thing beside her. Raising his right hand above his head and swinging it as if to ward off a blow he muttered:

'Yes. I know. Let me alone. God strike me dead. I'll do it.'

His own words terrified him and he remained still. He again became aware of her sinister, mad eyes.

'Leave me alone,' he said angrily, but without any force.

He stooped and wiped his hands among the dead leaves. Then he groped about and found a sack. He stopped again.

'What are you doing?' she whispered in a dry voice.

'Have ye got a piece of string?' he said.

She did not reply. Again he heard a moan. He cursed and stepped across her body. He covered the thing with the sack and clutched the bundle fiercely against his chest. Then he strode away hurriedly through the wood.

She closed her eyes and clutched her throat and gasped as he went away. She listened eagerly to the sound of his departing steps. When the sound of his steps died away, she began to tremble. Then she burst into tears.

'God have mercy on me,' she muttered. 'Holy Mother of God, have mercy on me. Oh! Jesus, save me, save me.'

She heard a low cough. She became still. She listened. He was coming back. She sat up hurriedly and peered towards him through the trees. He came crouching towards her. She said nothing, but stared at him with hatred. Her eyes were fixed. There was a deep vertical line between them, reaching half-way up her forehead. He sat down on the edge of the ditch, with his head hanging.

'Where have you been?' she whispered.

He began to wipe his hands on the side of the ditch and remained silent.

'Where have you been?'

'Eh?' he said hoarsely. 'It's in the sack. I stuck it in under the root of a tree in a pool of water.'

There was silence for nearly a minute. Then she whispered in a dry voice: 'You killed my child. You murdered my child.'

He raised his head and gaped at her in amazement, still rubbing his hands against the side of the ditch. She became hysterical.

'Where's my baby?' she cried. 'What did you do with it?'

'Eh? What the . . . didn't you . . . Eh?'

'Curse you. May God . . . Give it to me. Give it to me. Where is it?'

'What? What are you saying? Didn't you . . .'

She staggered to her feet.

'Maggie, Maggie,' he whispered, clutching at her knees. She uttered a savage cry and struck at her rapidly with her palms. He began to blubber, dropped his hold and fell to the ground.

Screaming, she ran out of the ditch, into the lane. He raised his head, stretching out his hands and trying to utter her name, but his tongue clove to his palate. Trying to get out of the ditch, he stumbled and struck his head against the tree slump. That steadied him. He ran away through the wood towards his master's house, crying at intervals:

'Ha! Ha!'

A little after dawn police came to his loft and brought him to the barracks. Maggie Conroy was there with them.

'That's him,' she said coldly, pointing to him. 'Ask him what he done with it.'

'I put it in a sack,' he said to them,' under the root of a tree in a pool of water. She told me to do something for her.'

They gave him three years' penal servitude.

IT WAS THE DEVIL'S WORK

A ll the Peasants uttered a cry of horror. They uncovered their heads, crossed themselves and gaped at the two-headed monstrosity that lay dead on the grass. Even the cow gaped in wonder, as if offended by the trick nature had played on her; for she had laboured two days.

Tony Beag, a wise old man who acted as veterinary surgeon for the village, was the first to speak.

'By the hammers of Hell,' he said. 'It's the first freak I've seen. D'ye see? It's two calves and yet there's only one calf with two heads, on account of the way the two o' them are joined together. What's the cause of it? A blow on the side or a fall or something? Or maybe there's a growth on her insides, some sort of hidden disease that played Hell with her stomack.'

Red Bartly, the owner of the cow, began to wave his arms. He was almost in tears, but the light of rebellion shone in his eyes, keeping back the tears. A queer fellow, about forty years of age, life had gradually played the same trick on him that it had played on the twin calves before their birth. His body had withered and become twisted prematurely, as if leeches had drunk his substance.

'It's the devil's work surely,' he said. 'Two calves instead of one I've lost. It's not the loss of the calves entirely that's worrying me, but the shame and disgrace of it. To think that God should curse me and my house and make me look evil among the people. There's no justice in the world.'

'Faith! It's true for you,' said Michael Feeney, a melancholy old man who rejoiced in calamity. 'This is poor compensation for you and you after giving the priest double his dues last Easter. He read you out from the altar as an example to the whole parish. Now this has come to you. You are without calf and so you'll be without a yearling for next year's fair. It's very likely your cow's womb is torn so badly she'll remain a stripper for the rest of her life. By the Book! A man might as well pay his money to the village sorceress as to the priest, for all the protection he gets against misfortune.'

Red Bartly shouted at Feeney:

'Am I not bad enough without you reminding me of worse things to come? Some people take pleasure out of the misfortunes of their neighbours.'

'No offence,' said Feeney. 'I'm only saying what was in my mind. Sure I pity you. And maybe this is the best thing that could happen to you. It will prove to you that man is doomed to misfortune. I, too, was greedy and foolish and I believed in the goodness of this world, until the roof flew off my house in the great storm we had ten years ago in February. My horse died in the following month. The blight came on my potatoes and my wife had twins, all in the same year. That proved to me that I had nothing to hope for only misery and that the devil rules the world. I'm happy since then.'

'Come,' said Tony Beag. 'Let's bury this thing and then we'll take home the cow after she clears. We might have to strap her up, Red Bartly, for very likely she'll be sick to death.'

They buried the monstrosity and sat down on the grass watching the cow.

'By my soul,' said Strong Michael, the oldest man among them. 'It's queer. The cow is nearly as holy an animal as the sheep and yet strange things never come from a sheep. That's because she hid our Lord Jesus Christ under her wool when the Jews were after him.'

'Hell to that for a story,' said Feeney. 'If the sheep was blessed by God, why is she always suffering from disease? She's always sad, moaning in the night and in the day, in rain and in sunshine. She's a miserable and a cowardly and a trembling sort of an animal. Any mangy dog can tear her to pieces. Look now at the goat and you will see the world is ruled by the devil and that the wicked are rewarded. There is an animal for you. She betrayed the hiding place of our Lord to the Jews and God condemned her to have no wool because of that crime. But the devil came to her help and made her so hardy she doesn't need wool. She can stand the cold better than the Northern Dane. She has the nine lives of the cat. She is a thief and a destroyer, with no love for man. Yet she prospers. She is always gay, scampering and gaming from the day she is born till she dies. Her kids are a joy to behold, as merry and beautiful as the sunbeams on the ocean. They are always born without blemish. And that proves, as clear as the light of day, that the evil are rewarded and the good are punished.'

'Yes, yes,' said Strong Michael. 'But in the next world she'll be punished. In the next world, she'll be milked in Hell by Lucifer and all his devils, while the sheep will graze in the rich clover fields of Paradise.'

'Ha!' said Feeney. 'Little she cares where she's put. If she's put in Hell, she'll climb out of it and trespass in God's fields of clover. Aye! She'll eat the ivy and the briars off the walls of Heaven. It's only by robbery and breaking of the laws that all things prosper.'

'Begob,' said Red Bartly. 'I think it's true for you, Feeney. All the money

I've given to the priest is gone for nothing. I might as well have poured it down my throat in drink for all the protection God has given me against misfortune.'

'Say not so,' said Strong Michael. 'Can't you see, man alive, that this queer thing was sent to us all as a warning that the devil still lives, trying to make mischief? Unless we pray and fast and pay our dues to the clergy, wickedness will spread and destroy us. These things are sent to us in warning, same as the great flood and the potato blight and the cholera. That's the way God works, knowing man is sinful and that he doesn't respect the good until he feels the power of evil. But it's not often that he sends these misfortunes.'

'But why should he send them to me?' muttered Red Bartly. 'What harm have I done? Can any man here accuse me of sin? Haven't I lived like the virgin priest without lust and as busy as the running bee? Didn't I deny myself in every way since I was a child, so that I could count on my fingers all the times I've eaten meat, outside of Christmas and Easter and the feast of Saint Martin in autumn, when it's so ordered that every man kills a sheep or goat out of his share. But now, by the blistering fires of the arch devil, maybe it's otherwise I'll act. I've been put to shame and held up as a showboard before the eyes of the people.'

'No, don't talk nonsense,' said Tony Beag, 'and don't be led astray by anger and foolishness into a war with the priest, for you'll only get the worst of it, together with losing your immortal soul if you're obstinate. I've been tending cattle all my life and this is the first freak I've seen; but such things happened before and I believe they happened in the ordinary and that there's nothing against nature in them. It's all superstition, all this talk of sheep and goats being blessed or cursed. Men of travel and doctors say everything is according to the queer laws of nature.'

'Don't blaspheme,' said Strong Michael. 'I saw no freak either, but my father saw one in the village of Clash. A cow was sick with the disease of the eyes and when they cut away the corruption she fell down and twisted on the ground like a man with the colic. They got frightened and sent for the sorceress. She came and put the spell of the snakes on the cow. The cow got better but she had a calf with a fish's tail a little while later. Then typhus came to the village and destroyed nearly all the people. They say the sorceress was the cause of it for bringing in the devil. She was struck by lightning, they say, before she died.'

'I don't believe a word of it,' said Tony Beag.

'And what had I to do with the sorceress?' said Red Bartly. 'All I know is that I'm finished giving money to the priest. Along with paying my dues last year, I gave five pounds to the collection for putting a new roof on the church. Then I gave a pound to a strange priest that came making a collection for the conversion of the Chinese. Then I've been giving money these twenty years for Masses for my father that was drowned at sea. Now this has come to me. I've been robbed. That's how it is. 'Faith I'll eat bacon with the priest's money from now on and I'll fish on Sundays instead of going to Mass and if I roast when I die, I'll be in Hell with fine company, along with all the rich pagans of England and America.'

Later, they drove home the cow, remonstrating with Red Bartly and trying to persuade him that it was foolish and unprofitable to make war on the priest. But the obstinate fellow remained convinced that religion did not pay.

'Not a penny,' he kept repeating. 'I'd rather roast in Hell.'

So it happened that he ceased going to church. The villagers were amazed and shocked when they saw him going forth to fish on the following Sunday, while they themselves were going to Mass. Indeed he became brazen and waved his hand at them, saying:

'Hey! What a lot of fools you are, wasting a good day and the sea full of fish, so that they are climbing bone-dry on the rocks.'

The people were terrified at such profanity. Strong Michael shook his head and said:

'You'll bring a curse on the village.'

At Mass they discussed the affair with people from the other villages in the parish and it was the general belief that the two-headed monstrosity had been sent by the devil and that Red Bartly was now possessed by the Evil One. After Mass several strangers came into the village to look at Red Bartly, as at a public curiosity, such as a madman or being struck by an uncommon leprosy. But they found him in his yard helping his aged mother clean the fish he had caught. There was a great heap of fish. He was very gay and he sang, contrary to his wont.

'Hey!' he cried to them. 'Look at these fish. Never in the history of the village have such rock-fish been seen and the pollock are just as good. Upon my soul, there are twenty different kinds of fish. The sea was full of them, same as I told you. Now what do you say?'

The people marvelled, but Strong Michael said after some thought:

'My good man, bless yourself with Holy Water and throw this fish into the sea, for there's a curse on it.'

'Devil roast you for a fool,' said Red Bartly. 'I'll not throw it into the sea or give it to the pigs either, but I'll be fat all winter eating it.'

'You may be fat all winter,' said Strong Michael, 'but the time will come when you'll pay for this fish, roasting in the fires of Hell, with the red-hot marrow trickling from your bones.'

Red Bartly laughed and the people went away. The story spread over the whole parish and it became the general belief that Red Bartly had sold himself to the Evil One. The belief was encouraged by the parish priest, a wise old man who knew the peculiar character of his people. He took no actual measures against Red Bartly, knowing that time was on his side and that heresies are only given life by persecution.

Thus Red Bartly was left unmolested in the practice of paganism for a whole year. Nature, or the ancient gods of the country, came to his assistance in an extraordinary manner. Or it may have been just common chance; in any case he prospered exceedingly. His cow suffered no ill effects from her mishap. She conceived once more and gave birth to a healthy calf. His mare had a beautiful she-foal. Each of his eight sheep had two lambs. His goats had kids and they gave milk abundantly. During the year he reared three sets of pigs and sold them all at the highest price. His crops were excellent. When he fished he always returned with a full basket. During summer, when there was a little work to do on the land, he spent his time digging up the rocks in a barren field. He brought earth on his back from other fields which had a surplus of soil. Thus he made the rocky place fertile. And next spring the people were amazed when they saw the barren field in flower and preparing to bear fruit out of its new substance. Envy grew in them. There were some who wished to do as Red Bartly was doing. Paganism was about to get a grip on the peasants.

Then suddenly, that autumn, Red Bartly's old mother died. She died in the ordinary way, having caught pneumonia from walking around barefoot on the wet flags of the yard. But now Red Bartly was left alone in the house. He had nobody to care for him. It became necessary for him to take a wife. Then, indeed, it became apparent to him that, in spite of his prosperity, he was still in the power of the priest; for no woman would marry a man who was a pagan, sold to the Evil One. He approached several men who had daughters ready to get married. They all raised their hands in horror. So he had to spend the whole winter fending for himself, in a house that was rapidly growing like a wild beast's lair. Then, one Sunday in spring, he came to the people when they were squatting on the rocks in front of the village after Mass.

'Honest people,' he said, 'this is a bad way I am in now. For the devil a wife I can get, on account of the way the powers of this world are in the hands of the priest. It's clear to everyone, by the way all has gone well with me, that no man gains anything, either with his crops or with the living things that grow on his share, by giving money to the priest. But so the devil has arranged the government of this land, that the poor must let themselves be robbed or remain without a wife. I can hold out no longer. Still, let no man say when I went to the priest, that I changed my mind about what is right and what is wrong. It isn't fear that makes me go, but I want to get married.'

'Ah! Sure I told you,' said Feeney the cynic, 'that it's useless for any mortal being to try and get the better of the wickedness that rules this world Bow your head, my good man, and raise your hands above your head and let them take what you have and them go your road, glad they didn't take your life too. That's the best way for the poor to act.'

'That's nonsense,' said Tony Beag. 'God's mills grind slow but they grind sure. There's white bread in Heaven for the poor to eat, so let them not grumble here on earth.'

'Aye,' said Strong Michael. 'There are seven serpents tempting man to his destruction and religion is given to us, so that we may keep their tails in their mouths and prevent them from poisoning us with their bites. They lie that way, all coiled up and harmless, inside the saints that commit no sin. But in the wicked man they are twisting about in a horrid way, spitting and biting and they have constantly to be fed with sin. So that the wicked are always unhappy and nearly out of their minds, like the rich men in America that can't eat their food. Now here you are, Red Bartly, with one of these serpents let loose in you by greed. And now another one is let loose in you by the lust of the flesh. And before long the whole seven of them'll be tearing around inside you and your life'll be a horror, in a way your countenance'll look black and fearful to those that see you going the road. But go to the priest, brother, and bare your knees on the flagstones of the chapel. Then maybe you'll get peace from the wicked worms that are biting you. You'll get a wife too.'

They spoke to him at length, but the obstinate fellow shook his head and maintained that his paganism was justified.

'I'll go to the priest,' he said, 'because I have to get a wife. But it's robbery, I'm thinking. Now I have to put up with it. They catch a man no matter how he turns.'

He went to the priest on the following day, prepared for a dire sermon, threats and abuse. But the priest was a wise man and he received Red Bartly calmly, treating the affair as if it were an ordinary thing for a man to turn pagan. They discussed for an hour the amount of money that Red Bartly was to pay because of the insult he had offered to Divine Providence. Finally it was agreed amicably between them that, in recompense for the insult to God, Red Bartly was to walk barefoot around the parish chapel seventy-seven times, in the presence of the people, leaving a pebble in front of the door each time he passed. In recompense for his insult to God's representative on earth, he was to pay to the priest one tenth of what he had earned during his year of paganism. In addition, he was to pay treble the dues he had omitted paying during the aforesaid year. In addition, he was to pay for building a grotto at the holy well of Saint Brigid, which grotto was to be used by the faithful for making novenas, asking for the conversion of all pagans. Finally, he was in future to recognise and to state in public on all occasions, that the monstrous calf had been the devil's work, sent expressly to tempt him.

Red Bartly faithfully obeyed all these injunctions and the affair ended creditably for the priest. All thought of paganism vanished. And nobody doubted that it was the devil who had sent the monstrous calf, in order to tempt the people to their destruction. Even Red Bartly himself became extremely religious afterwards. He married and had children and finally became almost an object of ridicule by the excessive lengths to which he carried his religious devotion.

AN SEABHAC

Chroch sé suas é féin os cionn bruaich na haille faoi dhianruathar eitill agus rinne sé ar mhór-airde na spéire, ag cur timpeall agus timpeall ar bhord fada, nó gur mhothaigh sé íochtair sreamacha na néall ag gabháil go fuar fliuch thar dhroim. Isteach leis ansin caol díreach tríd an tír.

Cé nár thug sé anois ach corrbhuille fánach lena sciatháin agus é á scaoileadh féin go leisciúil le sruth an aeir, buailte suas le díon an domhain, bhí díocas agus saint mharfa an tseabhaic ina shúile buí; iad seo ag dearcadh síos go grinn ar urlár lonrach na talún a bhí sínte amach faoi bholg folamh na spéire; gan oiread na fríde i ndon é féin a cheilt ar a radharc damanta.

Scairt an ghrian aon uair amháin ar a dhroim agus é ag gabháil trasna idir dhá néall, trí ghlaineacht aeir. Ansin arís, ní raibh ann ach taise dofheisce ag gluaiseacht gan torann tríd an gceo; éan álainn an bháis, gan trócaire ná faitíos ina chroí, ag soláthar creiche in aoibhneas an mhaidneachain.

Gheit sé go tobann agus d'éirigh a chlog nuair a chonaic sé fuiseog ag teacht chuige aníos as móinéar glas agus an drúcht ag lonradh ar dhroim an éin chanta faoin solas glégeal. Scaoil sé chun siúil é féin ar an bpointe a leag sé súil ar an gcreach. Choinnigh sé air chomh tréan agus ab fhéidir leis, nó go raibh sé díreach os cionn na fuiseoige. Ansin do thosnaigh sé ag cur timpeall go mall, gan cor as a sciatháin sínte agus a shúile ataithe le dúil. Bhí a chraiceann ag creathnú faoina chlúmhach tiubh; ar nós gadhair atá ag faire ar leaba dhearg.

D'ardaigh an fhuiseog go místuama ar dtús agus gan le cloisint uaithi ach corrghíog gan rithim idir léimeanna. Ansin do thosnaigh sí ag canadh go hálainn le lán a scornaigh agus d'ardaigh sí caol díreach gan stró, mar bheadh bua a glóir á tarraingt suas ar neamh. Anois bhí sí ag eiteall ar nós an fhéileacáin, le mionchraitheadh sciathán. Bhí an spéir lán lena ceol.

D'fhan an seabhac nó go raibh an fhuiseog chomh fada suas agus ab fhéidir léi gabháil. Thog sé marc uirthi ansin agus scaoil sé a neart. Tháinig sé anuas ina mullach ó na néallta mar bheadh lasair tintrí. Bhris an ceol ina scornach nuair a chonaic sí an seabhac ag déanamh uirthi. Lig sí scread agus léim sí i leataobh. Ní baileach go raibh sí sách sciobtha le iomlán an ruathair mharfa a sheachaint. Is beag nár baineadh an t-anam aisti le gach ar theangaigh léi den bhuille. Chrap sí a sciatháin agus scaoil sí síos í féin i ndiaidh a cinn, ag iarraidh talamh a bhaint amach sula mbuailfeadh a namhaid an dara buille. D'fhág sí slám clúmhaigh a stróiceadh as a heireaball ag snámhán ar an aer ina diaidh.

Nuair a chonaic an seabhac gur chinn air an marú a dhéanamh den chéad iarriadh sin, d'oscail sé a sciatháin agus leag sé iad in aghaidh na gaoithe lena ruathar a chosc. Ansin do chuir sé timpeall arís os cionn na creiche, thóg sé marc go deifreach agus scaoil sé a neart. An babhta seo ní raibh an fhuiseog i ndon aon cheo a dhéanamh leis an mbuille a sheachaint. Criogadh í, ar nóiméad díreach a buailte. Síos léi bun os cionn, a cuid sciathán ag seachrán agus a ceann casta timpeall ar a scornach fhada, as ar tháinig ceol álainn tamaillín beag roimhe sin.

Lean an seabhac titim na fuiseoige, ag gabháil timpeall agus timpeall ar bhord gearr, luite isteach go dlúth leis an gcreach; nó gur bhuail siad talamh araon ar thrá bheag ghainimheach le taobh abhann. Ansin do chuir an t-éan troda cos go gaisciúil ar bhrollach na fuiseoige mairbhe. D'fhan sé seasta mar sin ar feadh tamaill, a shúile beagnach dúnta, a theanga gháirsiúil ag sliobarnaigh lena ghob agus a chroí ag bualadh go tréan faoi na barraí dubha ar a chliabh. Nuair a bhí a scíth ligthe aige, rug sé greim crúibe ar an gcorp agus chroch sé leis é suas san aer. As go brách leis ansin go dtí a nead, ina raibh a chéile suite ar gor.

Bhí an nead déanta in áit fhíor-ríoga, istigh ar thulán buí faoi bhruach bolgach aille móire, ag an bpointe ab airde de chuan fada cúng. Bhí sé chomh fada suas sin os cionn na farraige nach raibh i mórthorann feargach na dtonn ach sioscadh ciúin nuair a shroich sé an tulán. Ní raibh torann ar bith eile le cloisint sa gcró ard siúd a d'éirigh suas caol díreach ón uisce; leac aoil leagtha os cionn leice dá samhail ar feadh cheithre chéad troigh. Dhá mhí roimhe sin bhí plod mór éan ag maireachtain sa gcuan; éanacha de gach saghas dá bhfeictear ag neadú i bhfarragáin aille. Ansin do tháinig an dá sheabhac óg as an aer thoir agus iad ag gabháil lena chéile faoi chuthach macnais.

Lán le scanradh, sheas na héin aille ó mhaidneachan go dtí ard na gréine agus iad ag faire ar choimhlint cholla na seabhac; iad seo ag déanamh ruathair i ndiaidh ruathair ghrá tríd an aer os cionn an chuain; ag scaoileadh a nirt ar a chéile anuas ó na néallta go dtí bruach uisce agus ag cur timpeall in éineacht arís suas; iad ag casadh agus ag iompó ar a chéile; brollach le brollach agus sciathán le sciathán; mar bheidís á gceangal féin le cion. Ar uair an mheán lae, chonaic lucht na faire an bhaineannach ag tabhairt an fhireannaigh isteach i bprochlais agus chualadar a scréach nuair a chuaigh an bodach ina teannta. Bhí fios acu ansin go raibh an dá éan troda go braith air nead a dhéanamh sa gcuan agus nach raibh aon rogha, dá bharr sin, ach teitheadh; rud a rinne an slua ar fad gan mhoill. Faoi ard an tráthnóna agus an dá sheabhac ag siamsa go fánach agus ag déanamh aeir ar fuaid an chuain, ní raibh aon chréatúr eile fágtha ina ngaobhar. Bhí an áit álainn sin ar fad mar ríocht ag an gcúpla barbartha. Ag gabháil faoi don ghrian, thug an t-éan fireann leis a chéile suas go dtí an tulán buí; áit a raibh dhá fhiach ina gcónaí sular imíodar ar a dteitheadh uaidh an anachain.

Anois, nuair a chaith an fireannach bródúil corp na fuiseoige síos ar an tulán le taobh na nide, níor tugadh aird dá laghad air. Bhí a chéile chomh suantrach sin le gor go raibh mothú thar a cumas. Is beag nach raibh sí ina codladh ar an nead mídhéanta; a gob leagtha ar chipín agus í ag breathnú síos ar an bhfarraige trína súile leathdhúnta. Thosnaigh seisean á dúiseacht. Scaoil sé a sciatháin síos le cois agus chuaigh sé timpeall ar an nead go basach, ag glaoch uirthi go ceanúil, á maoidheamh agus ag brú in aghaidh a taoibh lena ghuaille. Thus sé corrphrioc lena ghob dá cír agus chimil sé a droim le clúmhach síodúil a scornaí. Chuaigh sé thart timpeall uirthi ceithre bhabhta sular dhúisigh sí i gceart. Ansin d'ardaigh sí a ceann go tobann, d'oscail sí a béal agus lig sí scread. Chuir seisean scread uaidh freisin agus chuaigh sé de léim i mullach na fuiseoige. Scuab sé an ceann di go tapaidh, tharraing sé an clúmhach lena chrúba agus thairg sé an fheoil úr fhuilteach dá chéile. D'oscail sí amach a béal agus shloig sí an phlaic d'aon iarraidh amháin. Nuair bhí sin déanta aici, leag sí a ceann arís ar an gcipín, scar sí amach a corp os cionn na n-ubh agus thug sí don ghor iomlán a coinsias.

Sin é an uair a thosnaigh an seabhac fireann ag déanamh gaisce go rícheart; an bodach leitheadach ag siúl go basach anonn agus anall ar an gcarraig fhuilteach; cnámha nochtaithe faoi chois agus screamhóga de chraiceann tirim greamaithe den chloch agus mealltracha beaga aisig curtha i dtaisce ar storráin le n-ithe arís; bréanbholadh uafásach ag líonadh an aeir thart timpeall ar uachais an mharfóra. Níor léir dó siúd ach áilleacht san áit damanta. Bhí a anam barbartha lán le áthas agus ríméad, faoi bheith ag comhlíonadh iomláin an daulgais ceaptha amach dhó ag a nádúir.

Ar nós gadhair atá sínte amach ina chodladh os comhair tine mhór agus é ag brionglóidigh ar fhiach an lae, chuaigh an t-éan troda trí lúcháir agus macnas a chéilíochta; ag cuimhniú ina shiúl ar a scaití cola agus ar na huibhe a bhí á mbeochan sa nead. Anois agus arís sheas sé ar bhruach an tuláin, bhuail sé a sciatháin in aghaidh a bhrollaigh agus lig sé gáir ghaisce; ag breathnú síos amach uaidh ar an ríocht a bhain sé amach dhó féin agus dá chéile.

Briseadh a ríméad go tobann, nuair a chuala sé gleo beag thuas ar bharr aille, scathamh soir ón tulán. Sheas sé ar an bpointe a chuala sé an torann agus d'éist sé go grinn. Is gearr arís gur chuala sé an gleo beag céanna. Chreathnaigh sé taobh istigh dá chlúmhach, suas agus anuas le barr a chraicinn; go díreach mar chreathnaigh sé nuair bhí sé seasta os cionn na fuiseoige lena neart a scaoileadh faoi ruathar an mharfa. Bhí a chroí ag bualadh chomh tapaidh anois leis an am eile sin, ach ní dúil sa marú a bhí á shaighdeadh. Bhí fios aige gur ghleo cainte daonna a bhí ansin thuas agus bhí sé lán le faitíos.

Scaoil sé síos é féin go mear ón tulán agus rinne sé mioneiteall cúramach siar go dlúth le héadan íochtarach na haille. Chuaigh sé achar mór siar sular chas sé amach os cionn na farraige. Ansin do thosnaigh sé ag cur timpeall agus ag ardú ar bhord fada, nó go raibh sé as amharc thuas imeasc na néall. Soir leis arís agus é i bhfolach, thuas faoi dhíon na spéire, nó go raibh sé díreach os cionn na háite ina raibh an gleo. Sheas sé ansin agus bhreathnaigh sé síos go faiteach ar thriúr fear, a bhí ag obair go deifreach ar bhruach na haille. Bhí bun téada ceangailte acu de mhodhlaer mór cloiche eibhir agus eiris déanta den cheann faoi ascaill an fhir ba hairde. Bhí mála beag donn ceangailte dá chrios ag an bhfear céanna.

Nuair a chonaic an seabhac go raibh an fear ard á ligean síos le taobh na haille ag an mbeirt eile, go dtí tulán beag caol a bhí cothrom le tulán na nide agus scathamh fánach soir uaidh, bhí sé cinnte go raibh lucht na téada ag iarraidh é a scrios. Bhí drogall air, ina dhiaidh sin, a neart a scaoileadh in aghaidh an t-aon namhad amháin a bhí i ndon faitíos a chur air. Sé an chaoi d'ardaigh sé scathamh beag eile suas agus é ag craitheadh. Thosnaigh sé ag gabháil timpeall ansin agus ag breathnú síos go cráite ar na daoine, gan fonn dá laghad ar a intinn a neart a scaoileadh fúthu.

Tar éis an tulán thoir a shroichint do shiúil an fear ard go dtí an gob ba faide siar agus rinne sé comhartha lena chairde. Tharraing siadsan an fuílleach téada. Shocraigh sé é féin ansin go cúramach, bhuail sé cos ar bhruach an tuláin agus siar leis; uachtar a choirp ligthe amach in aghaidh na téada agus é ag cosaireacht le héadan maol na haille. Shroich sé cor thoir de thulán na nide; áit ina raibh an chráin seabhaic agus an nead ceilte ar a radharc ag bolgán cloiche. Bhagair sé arís ar a chairde agus scaoileadar chuige fuílleach téada. Siar leis ansin, ag cur orlaigh bealaigh i ndiaidh orlaigh agus é buailte isteach le éadan cloiche mar bheadh bairneach.

D'imigh an faitíos den seabhac nuair a chonaic sé an fear i ngar don nead. Síos leis ar nós an philéir lena chéile a sheachaint ar a contúirt. D'oscail sé a sciatháin nuair a bhí sé ag bruachaireacht leis an tulán agus leag sé trasna é féin, i bhfoisceacht dhá throigh don chráin ghoir. Bhéic sé uirthi, chomh ard agus bhí ina cheann, ach níor thug sí aird dá laghad air. Chuaigh sé soir agus siar thairsti, arís agus arís eile, ag glaoch agus ag screadaíl go cráite, sular chuala sí a ghlór. D'ardaigh sí a ceann agus lig sí scread. Thug sin misneach damanta don éan troda. Amach leis chun na farraige agus thosnaigh sé ag ardú.

Suas leis arís, nó gur mhothaigh sé íochtair sreamacha na néall ag gabháil go fuar fliuch thar a dhroim, i dtost na firmiminte. Ansin do leag sé a shúile buí ar a namhaid agus iad ag fiuchadh le gráin síoraí. Thóg sé marc go haireach agus líon sé amach a chorp le haghaidh an ruathair. Ar an nóiméad sin na fírinne agus é seasta i gcóir chatha, ní uaibhreas nirt ná col an mharfa a bhí á shaighdeadh chun na troda. Níor mhothaigh sé á mhaíomh ach an gean cráite a bhuail a chroí nuair a chuala sé scread a chéile.

Dhún sé a sciatháin go dlúth agus scaoil sé a neart. Síos leis, síos amach, in aghaidh an fhir aird, gan faitíos ná trócaire; éan álainn ag soláthar báis ar mheán lae. D'fhógair an bheirt charad ar an bhfear nuair a chonaic siad ruathar an éin. Bhreathnaigh fear an téada suas agus shocraigh sé é féin in aghaidh na haille. Ar an bpointe sin b'iad súile an fhir a bhí faiteach. Ansin do chaith sé suas uille os comhair a éadain agus an seabhac ag bualadh. Briseadh ruathar an éin ar an éadach. Caitheadh thairis an corp agus buaileadh é go trom in aghaidh na haille. Síos leis ansin, bun os cionn, gan treo gan deifir; éan álainn an bháis gan luaithneas ná neart.

Nuair a shroich an fear áit na nide, d'éirigh an chráin suas agus í ag screadaíl. D'ionsaigh sí é go cróga. Rug sé uirthi, chuir sé snaidhm ar a cuid sciathán agus chaith sé isteach í sa mhála a bhí lena chrios. Ansin do thug sé leis na huibheacha.

Thíos amuigh, bhí corp an tseabhaic ag imeacht ar bharr uisce; a sciatháin briste agus a cheann ag seachrán lena scornach casta. Bhí sé á chrochadh amach chun farraige leis an scruth.

THE HAWK

He breasted the summit of the cliff and then rose in wide circles to the clouds. When their under-tendrils passed about his outstretched wings, he surged straight inland. Gliding and dipping his wings at intervals, he roamed across the roof of the firmament, with his golden hawk's eyes turned down, in search of prey, toward the bright earth that lay far away below, beyond the shimmering emptiness of the vast blue sky.

Once the sunlight flashed on his grey back, as he crossed an open space between two clouds. Then again he became a vague, swift shadow, rushing through the formless vapour. Suddenly his fierce heart throbbed, as he saw a lark, whose dewy back was jewelled by the radiance of the morning light, come rising toward him from a green meadow. He shot forward at full speed, until he was directly over his mounting prey. Then he began to circle slowly, with his wings stiff and his round eyes dilated, as if in fright. Slight tremors passed along his skin, beneath the compact armour of his plumage — like a hunting dog that stands poised and quivering before this game.

The lark rose awkwardly at first, uttering disjointed notes as he leaped and circled to gain height. Then he broke into full-throated song and soared straight upward, drawn to heaven by the power of his glorious voice, and fluttering his wings like a butterfly.

The hawk waited until the songbird had almost reached the limit of his climb. The he took aim and stooped. With his wings half-closed, he raked like a meteor from the clouds. The lark's warbling changed to a shriek of terror as he heard the fierce rush of the charging hawk. Then he swerved aside, just in time to avoid the full force of the blow. Half-stunned, he folded his wings and plunged headlong towards the earth, leaving behind a flutter of feathers that had been torn from his tail by the claws of his enemy.

When he missed his mark, the hawk at once opened wide his wings and canted them to stay his rush. He circled once more above his falling prey, took aim, and stooped again. This time the lark did nothing to avoid the kill. He died the instant he was struck; his inert wings unfolded. With his head dangling from his limp throat, through which his lovely song had just been pouring, he came tumbling down, convoyed by the closely circling hawk. He struck earth on a patch of soft brown sand, beside a shining stream.

The hawk stood for a few moments over his kill, with his lewd purple tongue lolling from his open beak and his black-barred breast heaving from the effort of pursuit. Then he secured the carcass in his claws, took wing, and flew off to the cliff where his mate was hatching on a broad ledge, beneath a massive tawny-gold rock that rose, overarching, to the summit.

It was a lordly place, at the apex of a narrow cove, and so high above the sea that the roar of the breaking waves reached there only as a gentle murmur. There was no other sound within the semicircle of towering limestone walls that rose sheer from the dark water. Two months before, a vast crowd of other birds had lived on the lower edges of the cliffs, making the cove merry with their cries as they flew out to sea and back again with fish. Then one morning the two young hawks came there from the east to mate.

For hours the rockbirds watched them in terror, as the interlopers courted in the air above the cove, stooping past each other from the clouds down to the sea's edge, and then circling up again, wing to wing, winding their garland of love. At noon they saw the female draw the male into a cave, and heard his mating screech as he treaded her. Then they knew the birds of death had come to nest in their cove. So they took flight. That afternoon the mated hawks gambolled in the solitude that was now their domain, and at sundown the triumphant male brought his mate to nest on this lofty ledge, from which a pair of ravens had fled.

Now, as he dropped the dead lark beside her on the ledge, she lay there in a swoon of motherhood. Her beak rested on one of the sticks that formed her rude bed, and she looked down at the distant sea through half-closed eyes. Uttering cries of tenderness, he trailed his wings and marched around the nest on his bandy legs, pushing against her sides, caressing her back with his throat, and gently pecking at her crest. He had circled her four times, before she awoke from her stupor. Then she raised her head suddenly, opened her beak, and screamed. He screamed in answer and leaped upon the carcass of the lark. Quickly he severed its head, plucked its feathers, and offered her the naked, warm meat. She opened her mouth wide, swallowed the huge morsel in one movement, and again rested her beak on the stick. Her limp body spread out once more around the pregnant eggs, as she relapsed into her swoon.

His brute soul was exalted by the consciousness that he had achieved the fullness of the purpose for which nature had endowed him. Like a hound stretched out in sleep before a blazing fire, dreaming of the day's long chase, he relived the epic of his mating passion, while he strutted back and forth among the disgorged pellets and the bloody remains of eaten prey with which the rock was strewn.

Once he went to the brink of the ledge, flapped his wings against his breast, and screamed in triumph, as he looked out over the majestic domain that he had conquered with his mate. Then again he continued to march, rolling from side to side in ecstasy, as he recalled his moments of tender possession and the beautiful eggs that were warm among the sticks.

His exaltation was suddenly broken by a sound that reached him from the summit of the cliff. He stood motionless, close to the brink, and listened with his head turned to one side. Hearing the sound again from the summit, the same tremor passed through the skin within his plumage, as when he had soared, poised, above the mounting lark. His heart also throbbed as it had done then, but not with the fierce desire to exercise his power. He knew that he had heard the sound of human voices, and he felt afraid.

He dropped from the ledge and flew, close to the face of the cliff, for a long distance towards the west. Then he circled outwards, swiftly, and rose to survey the intruders. He saw them from on high. There were three humans near the brink of the cliff, a short way east of the nest. They had secured the end of a stout rope to a block of limestone. The tallest of them had tied the other end to his body, and then attached a small brown sack to his waist belt.

When the hawk saw the tall man being lowered down along the face of the cliff to a protruding ledge that was on a level with the nest, his fear increased. He knew that the men had come to steal his mate's eggs; yet he felt helpless in the presence of the one enemy that he feared by instinct. He spiralled still higher and continued to watch in agony.

The tall man reached the ledge and walked carefully to its western limit. There he signalled to his comrades, who hauled up the slack of his rope. Then he braced himself, kicked the brink of the ledge, and swung out towards the west, along the blunt face of the cliff, using the taut rope as a lever. He landed on the eastern end of the ledge where the hawk's mate was sitting on her nest, on the far side of a bluff. His comrades again slackened the rope, in answer to his signal, and he began to move westwards, inch by inch, crouched against the rock.

The hawk's fear vanished as he saw his enemy relentlessly move closer to the bluff. He folded his wings and dove headlong down to warn his mate. He flattened out when he came level with the ledge and screamed as he flew past her. She took no notice of the warning. He flew back and forth several times, screaming in agony, before she raised her head and answered him. Exalted by her voice, he circled far out to sea and began to climb.

Once more he rose until the under-tendrils of the clouds passed about his outstretched wings and the fierce cold of the upper firmament touched his heart. Then he fixed his golden eyes on his enemy and hovered to take aim. At this moment of supreme truth, as he stood poised, it was neither pride in his power nor the intoxication of the lust to kill that stiffened his wings and the muscles of his breast. He was drawn to battle by the wild, sad tenderness aroused in him by his mate's screech.

He folded his wings and stooped. Down he came, relentlessly, straight at the awe-inspiring man that he no longer feared. The two men on the cliff top shouted a warning when they saw him come. The tall man on the ledge raised his eyes. Then he braced himself against the cliff to receive the charge. For a moment, it was the eyes of the man that showed fear, as they looked into the golden eyes of the descending hawk. Then he threw up his arms, to protect his face, just as the hawk struck. The body of the doomed bird glanced off the thick cloth that covered the man's right arm and struck the cliff with a dull thud. It rebounded and went tumbling down.

When the man came creeping round the bluff, the mother hawk stood up in the nest and began to scream. She leaped at him and tried to claw his face. He quickly caught her, pinioned her wings, and put her in his little sack. Then he took the eggs.

Far away below the body of the dead hawk floated, its broken wings outstretched on the foam-embroidered surface of the dark water, and drifted seawards with the ebbing tide.

THE PAINTED WOMAN

One lone star was following a little half-grown moon across an open space in the dark sky. All around, the firmament was full of sagging clouds. Some were black with hanging tails of rain that fell in far-off lands. Others were pale with the light of waning day. The stark earth was swept by a bitter wind. The dying light of the hidden sun lay brown upon its back, like the shroud upon a corpse.

Yet birds were singing in the wintry dusk. They smelt some tender current in the bitter air, telling them that spring was coming with sunlight and with flowers; as if a strange spirit passed upon the wind over the bleak rocks and the naked fields, whispering:

'Soon. Soon now. Lambs are kicking in the womb.'

Already people were preparing the ground for the sowing of their crops. Since an hour before dawn, Martin Bruty and his brother Patrick had been carrying seaweed on their mare to a field where they were going to plant potatoes. Now they were coming home, exhausted and drenched to the skin by the showers of hail that had fallen. Their hands were numb. Their sodden clothes were stained with the congealed slime of the weeds.

The mare walked quickly, with her neck stretched forward, shivering. Her hair was as smooth as a seal's fur. She was straddled. A long piece of canvas stuffed with straw lay on her back from tail to mane, with a basket hung on either side from two pegs in a wooden yoke. Wisps of straw from the straddle's packing trailed under her belly.

Martin Bruty sat sideways on her haunches, reclining on the canvas as on a couch, his left forearm encircling the wooden yoke. He was forty years old, tall, lean, ungainly, with big muscular limbs and a beautiful face. His eyes were soft and wistful like those of a child. His countenance was pure, like that of a young virgin. His hair was grey at the temples. He looked at the sky, at the dim, stark land, at the horse and at passing birds with wonder and awe. Whenever a bird sang, he looked towards the spot whence the sweet sound came and his lips parted. He looked simple, kind, gentle, without care.

Patrick walked behind the mare, stepping very quickly in order to keep pace with her. He was five years older than his brother, yet he looked much younger. He was small and stout, with very short legs. He walked nervously, taking tiny steps and looking in all directions without noticing anything. He frowned and sniffed. There was a greedy look in his little blue eyes. His large white eyebrows moved up and down and he twitched his forehead with he sniffed. His cheeks were as red as beetroots. His cap was stuck at the back of his round skull, showing a bald patch over his forehead. He looked restless, unhappy, unpleasant, completely out of harmony with nature that was whispering of spring, young buds, sunshine and happiness.

He carried two pitchforks on his left shoulder. In his right hand he had a can of milk. They walked in silence. The canvas of the straddle creaked against its wooden yoke. The horse's hoofs rang against the loose stones of the road. The wind whistled. The sea moaned in the distance. There were sounds of other horses, afar off, coming home and of people calling, in the village, at the top of the winding road that was bound by grey stone fences, ascending. The village was dimly visible at the summit of the hill, on the border of a wide barren crag. People were lighting their lamps and fowls were cackling as they waddled home from the pond.

Near the village, they overtook a woman who was walking with a little boy. She answered their salutation in a gay voice. They passed on. When they had rounded a corner, Patrick leaned against the fence and said to his brother:

'I'll be up after you. Bring the horse to the field. I'll light the fire and have tea ready when you come back.'

'All right,' said Martin, without looking at his brother.

He rode on. After a few yards, he suddenly sat erect, struck the horse in the flank with his foot and urged her on with an oath. She broke into a quick trot. His face darkened. He rode into the village at a gallop.

Huddled together, surrounded by stone fences, the houses were coloured like the savage wilderness about them, grey and bleak. In the dusk, their thatch and their whitewashed walls, drenched with rain that dripped from their eaves, looked as grey and desolate as the stones. The wind howled among them, sweeping across the naked crags from the cliffs beyond. To left and right, the rocky land rose in terraces to the black horizons. There was a smell of peat on the wind, acrid, making the scene still more melancholy.

Yet there was peace there and birds sang upon the gables of the houses, singing of golden, mellow summer dusks.

He rode the mare, through a gap in the fence, into the yard of a house in the centre of the village. The mare halted at the closed door of a barn on the left side of the yard. She shuddered and began to munch at wisps of straw that lay on the ground. Martin dismounted, opened the barn door, brought out a dish of raw potatoes and gave them to her. She whinnied and began to gobble them up, gripping them with difficulty between her soft, thick lips. He uncovered her. She spread out her four legs, shook herself and cleaned her nostrils with a loud noise. Then he rubbed her from head to foot with a bunch of straw. Where the straddle had lain, her hide was hot and moist with perspiration. There was a big bay patch there. The rest of her hide was dark with rain. Everywhere he touched her hide, rubbing her, the hide trembled violently.

Now and again, while he worked, he glanced over his shoulder down the road. Each time his face darkened and he muttered an oath. Then again, as he turned to the mare, his face grew tender and he spoke to her as he rubbed her.

He bound up the straddle with a rope, hung the baskets on pegs in the barn wall, put the straddle into the barn, closed the door, mounted the mare and rode away. Now the mare snorted, straining at the halter, trying to break into a gallop. He brought her to a field among the hills, a mile from the house. It was pitch-dark when he returned.

There was a light in the house. Smoke rose from the chimney. Smoke also issued in gusts through the door, buffeted by a contrary wind. The house looked dreary. There were no curtains on the windows. The yard was wild, muddy, overgrown with weeds. The walls were almost black for want of whitewash.

When Martin entered, Patrick was on his knees on the hearth, blowing at a newly-made peat fire, over which a kettle was hanging from an iron hook. Little red flames ran to and fro among the sods of peat when he blew. When his breath died away, the flames vanished and a cloud of smoke arose from the fire. He did not look up when Martin entered.

'This fire is enough to break the heart in a stone,' he said. 'The rain must have come in on it in the barn. Strain the milk.'

'Isn't the kettle boiled yet, then?' said Martin. 'Is it only now you're lighting the fire?'

'How could I have it lit?' said Patrick angrily, without looking up. 'I'm only just coming in.'

'What kept you then?'

'I had business.'

'Blood an' ouns.'

Martin strode to the dresser and seized the can of milk violently. His eyes were flashing.

'You had business,' he muttered. 'A fine business you had. The parish is talking about you.'

Patrick went on blowing the fire.

'Throw a little paraffin on that,' said Martin, as he poured the milk through a cloth into another can.

'No,' said Patrick, jumping to his feet. 'I'll go out to the barn and chip a few slices of that plank we got from the wreck last year. It's no use wasting paraffin.'

Martin looked after him angrily as he went out. He muttered to himself:

'We could buy a lot of paraffin with all money he spends on drink and chasing after every strip of a woman in the parish.'

When Patrick returned with the chips, he said: 'This is no life, returning hungry to an empty house.'

'I've heard you say that often enough,' said Martin. 'We weren't put on this earth to enjoy ourselves, but to save our souls.'

'Ach!' said Patrick sourly, as he stooped over the fire with the chips. 'A man would be better dead than listening to your grumbling.'

'Who is doing the grumbling?' said Martin.

'That's enough of it,' said Patrick. 'That's enough now. Be putting the things on the table.'

'I'll take off my wet things first,' said Martin.

''Twill be years before that kettle boils.'

He began to strip off his clothes.

The fire blazed up, making a brighter light than the tin paraffin lamp that hung on a nail in the wall. The delft on the dresser shone. Now there was no smoke. Patrick shut the door. Then he too began to strip.

'These three years since mother died,' he said, 'are worse than all the hardship I ever had in my life. A house without a woman is worse than hell.'

'Say Lord have mercy on her, when you speak of her,' said Martin.

'Every damn thing I say, you pick me up,' shouted Patrick. 'What have you against me? Eh?'

Naked, Martin walked to the hearth and took dry clothes from a line that stretched across the chimney.

'Mind the kettle,' he said. 'It's going to boil.'

They dressed in dry clothes and hung their wet ones on the line. They laid the table for a meal of tea and bread and butter. Patrick made tea. They sat down to eat. The table was without a cloth. The cups had no saucers. The loaf lay on the naked board. The butter was also lying on the board, with a bedraggled thin paper about it. The milk lay in the three-quart can into which it had been strained.

They ate hurriedly, in silence. Then Patrick went to the hearth to refill his cup from the teapot. At the fire he said:

'I'm not going to stick this any longer. One of us has to stir.'

'Pour some into this,' said Martin, reaching over his cup.

Patrick returned to the table and continued to eat. He kept glancing at his brother furtively, his white eyebrows moving up and down.

'What did you say?' he muttered after some time.

'Me?' said Martin. 'I said nothing.'

'Didn't you hear what I said?'

'What did you say?'

'I said it was time for one of us to get married.'

Martin pushed away his empty cup, put the can of milk to his head and drank a large quantity of the milk. He wiped his mouth, crossed himself and went to the fire.

'You have something on your mind,' he said. 'Out with it.'

He took a piece of tobacco from his waistcoat pocket and bit it. Patrick also drank some of the milk, crossed himself, put on his cap and came to the fire. He lit his pipe with a coal. They both sat in silence, on stools, one smoking his pipe, the other chewing.

'Well!' said Martin at length, spitting into the fire. 'Out with it.'

'Well!' said Patrick. 'I have this on my mind. It's time for one of us to bring in a woman here. A man would be better dead than living this way. There's nobody to clean or wash or get a meal ready for us after the day's work. We haven't had a pig this last year. There's money lost. Potatoes are going to rot in the barn. I'd rather let them rot than sell them for the few shillings they give for them in the shops. We could feed ten pigs in the year. Sheep too. We can't keep a sheep because we have no time to run after them over the rocks. We're losing money, along with the loneliness and misery of an empty house.'

'Money!' said Martin. 'You can't bring it to the grave with you. Haven't we enough to eat? But you may do as you please. You've been driving at this a long time and I'd rather have anything than hearing all the tongues in the parish jeering at our name on account of your blackguarding.'

'What blackguarding?' said Patrick angrily.

'You and Kate Tully,' said Martin in a loud voice. 'You follow her whenever she goes.'

'Well!' said Patrick. 'I'll follow her no longer. And less of your tongue, I'm telling you. You don't know what you're saying.'

'How?'

'How? This is how. I asked her coming up the road and she agreed.'

Martin spat his chew into the fire, looked at his brother with open mouth and then said:

'Tare an' ouns! You asked Kate Tully to marry you?'

'I did. What about it?'

Martin's face suddenly lost its angry look. His eyes became sad and weary. His jaw dropped.

'Eh?' said Patrick. 'What's the matter? Were ye . . . were ye thinking of asking her yerself?'

'Me?' said Martin, flushing and raising his head. 'I'd rather lie with a dog than with the woman,' he added fiercely.

'Be careful of what you are saying,' said Patrick in a low voice.

'I'll say what's in my mind,' said Martin. 'Now is the time to say it, isn't it? She's been fifteen years in America without tale or tidings of her. Then she returned last year with a boy and no husband.'

'Her husband is dead,' said Patrick angrily. 'What are you driving at?'

'Maybe he is,' said Martin. 'A woman doesn't go about here with a painted face, though, if she is right. What for does she paint her face and lips and terrify every decent man with her language and her free ways, unless . . .'

'Unless what?'

Martin shuddered and became silent. Patrick was watching him with glittering eyes.

'God knows,' said Martin sadly, 'it's hard to think badly of her, after what she was before she went away. Ye'd stand in the snow looking at her lovely face and she was so shy and modest that she blushed when a man bid her the time of day. Now she is . . . Ach!'

'Now, listen to me here,' said Patrick. 'I've had enough of this. Remember what I'm saying. I'm going to marry Kate Tully. If you don't like it, there's the door. You can take your share of the land and money and get a wife for yourself.'

'You're not marrying her,' said Martin. 'You're marrying her fortune of three hundred pounds.'

'Well, there you are now,' said Patrick. 'Think over it. I'll have no argument. I've wasted the best of my life, each of us watching the other. You always had a sour mouth whenever I thought of a woman. But I'll wait no longer.'

'Marry her then,' said Martin, jumping to his feet. 'Marry her. But I'll stay here. This is my father's house. You can't put me out of it. Marry her and the devil take you and her.'

He strode to the door. Patrick jumped up and shouted:

'Where are you going? Take back what you said.'

Martin turned back and looked at his brother gloomily. Then he shuddered, bent his head and murmured sadly:

'I'm sorry, Paddy. I . . . I . . . Tomorrow we can . . . I'll go out for a bit.'

He went out. Patrick sat down again by the fire and smoked. His face twitched. Then he also jumped to his feet and left the house. He visited his uncle. He returned at midnight and went to bed. Martin had not yet returned. At two o'clock in the morning he was awakened by hearing Martin come into the room.

'Where were you till this hour?' he said.

'I was over to the cliffs to see was there any wreckage,' said Martin.

'How could you see in the dark, man alive?'

'Never mind,' said Martin. 'I was listening to the sound of the sea.'

'Ugh!' said Patrick, turning towards the wall. 'You're out of your head.'

Maybe I am,' said Martin.

He got into bed beside his brother, but he lay awake all night, thinking.

Next day, while they were at the seashore loading seaweed on the mare, Martin said to his brother:

'Have you still got a mind to do what you were talking of last night?'

'I have,' said Patrick.

Martin brought the loaded mare to the field, dropped the load and returned. Then he said:

'Very well. We better go home at noon and dress ourselves. A settlement has to be made.'

'We'll do that,' said Patrick, 'in the name of God.'

'I hope God will bless it,' said Martin gloomily.

In the afternoon, Patrick went on the mare to the town and returned with a bottle of whiskey. After dark, they went with their uncle and another man to the house where Kate Tully lived with her married brother. They made the match. Martin agreed to everything they said. He appeared to be quite satisfied. It was decided to have the marriage in a week's time. Next day they went to the parish priest to sign the agreement.

There were thirty acres of land, a horse, a cow, a bullock, a yearling calf, the house and furniture and a boat. Martin gave his share of all this property to his brother, excepting his share of the boat. The boat was to be owned in common by the two of them. In return, Patrick gave Martin his share of their common savings, which amounted to four hundred pounds. It was arranged that Martin should go on living in the house until he married. He was to receive one-fifth of the house's earnings, in return for his work.

The priest tried to point out to them that this arrangement might cause some difficulty later on and that it was better that Martin should at once set about making a home of his own, but Martin refused to hear it. He said he was now too old to marry.

Kate Tully also had a clause inserted in the agreement to the effect that, in case of her death, her son Charles should inherit the property equally with any children she might have by Patrick. Patrick agreed to this after some argument.

After they had signed the agreement, they went to celebrate in the town, but Martin refused to accompany them. Neither did he give any assistance in the preparation for the wedding. He went about his ordinary work.

Patrick, on the other hand, went about in his best clothes, talking loudly, drinking, superintending the preparations, treating all his friends with the extravagance of a mean man carried away by a sudden passion. He hardly slept at all.

'Why don't you drink with me?' he said to Martin. 'Why are you gloomy? Have you anything against me?'

'This is not a time for drinking and merrymaking,' said Martin. 'It's your prayers you should be saying approaching a sacrament, instead of leering at the thought of your marriage bed.'

'Pruth!' said Patrick. 'Bloody woes! What a monk you are!'

Martin heard the people whispering and mocking at his brother, because he was going to marry a withered woman, who already had a child. Children, as is the custom when there is marriage in a house, used to call after him, shouting: after him, shouting: 'Kate Tully.' Instead of paying no attention to this harmless teasing, he was deeply mortified.

Patrick spent money freely on the preparations. His uncle's wife and two other women were brought in. They scoured out the house, whitewashed it, put curtains on the windows, delft on the dresser, new sheets on the beds. Whiskey, porter, wine and a large quantity of food was purchased. A sack of flour was baked into bread.

The whole countryside came to the wedding. The kitchen and the two bedrooms were packed with people. Only a few had room to sit in the kitchen. The rest stood, row behind row, around the little space in the centre where couples were dancing. A man sat on a chair near the fire playing an accordion. Three men went round serving whiskey and porter. Out in the yard there was a group of young men, drinking heavily, boasting and discussing feats of strength. In the bigger bedroom, where the marriage bed was prepared, people were eating in relays. Women passed back and forth, carrying teapots from the kitchen fire. Other women hustled guests to the table. Patrick went around shouting, already quite drunk, urging everybody to be merry. There was an air of reckless savagery and haste about the whole thing, and the older people noticed a lack of decency and of respect. They were whispering to one another.

Martin, sitting gloomily in a corner of the hearth, noticed that people had no respect for the house or for the marriage. He heard the whispering. He felt terribly ashamed and angry. He thought it was about him they were whispering, that they were jeering at him. So he refused to eat or drink. He sat without movement, with his eyes on the fire. He wanted to get up, leave the house and stand on the cliffs, looking out at the sea; but he would not move, lest they might jeer still more at him for running away. And yet it was a torture to stay. He was aware of the little boy, Kate's son, who was sitting in the opposite corner of the hearth. He was aware of Kate herself, who sat in triumph near the musician. He hated them all. Henceforth they would all be in the house with him. He would stand naked before the people, a butt for people's scorn. So he thought.

Every time Kate spoke in her loud, gay, rasping voice, he shuddered. And yet he could hardly restrain himself from looking at her.

Everybody was watching her and she seemed partly to enjoy the attention she attracted and partly to resent it. She sat with her legs crossed. Her dress was so short that a red garter showed on her thigh above the knee. She kept tapping her foot on the floor and pulling down her skirt that refused to go any farther than the brink of her knee. Her legs were beautiful. She wore silk stockings. Her dress was gaudy. It was red. Her cheeks and lips were painted. She was very slim and she had an exquisite figure. But her broad shoulders were bony. Her chest was flat. Her hair was dyed a yellowish colour. Her face bore the remains of great beauty. But her eyes were hard and her mouth was coarse. Although she was only thirty-five years of age she looked old. All that was left of her youthful beauty was a skeleton. She had, however, that power of attraction which comes of knowledge. The coolness of her manner, the cynical, brusque way in which she spoke, the glitter in her strange eyes were more exciting than the freshness of young beauty. She kept smiling. Her smile was contemptuous. With her mouth she enjoyed her triumph. But her eyes sometimes had a look of fear in them.

Her son was even more strange than she. He was six years old, pale, deli- cate and shy. He looked alien. His skin was yellow. His ears were large and strangely fashioned. His neck was long and thin. He had hardly any chin. His wrists were like spindles. His thin legs bent inwards at the knees. His upper teeth protruded. He kept eating sweets from a paper bag and looking casually at the dancers, without any excitement.

Patrick kept going up to his wife and putting his arm around her and saying:

'I have you now.'

Then he got so drunk that they put him lying on the marriage bed in the big bedroom. Then Kate danced with the young men and drank punch in the little bedroom with the women.

When it was nearly dawn, Patrick awoke from his drunken sleep, drank some whiskey and came into the kitchen. He went up to his wife and began to caress her passionately in front of the people, mumbling:

'I have you now.'

The guests began to leave. Martin heard them laugh as they went away, shouting: 'I have you now.'

Before they had all left the house, Patrick dragged his wife into the bedroom and locked the door. The little boy lay asleep in the corner of the hearth, forgotten. The uncle was the last to leave. He said to Martin:

'Where is little Charley going to sleep?'

'His bed is in his mother's room,' said Martin.

The uncle tittered drunkenly and said:

'You had better take him into your bed tonight, Martin, in the little room. It's not right to disturb a couple on their marriage night.'

Then the uncle went away. It was daylight. Martin took the little fellow in his arms and carried him into the little bedroom. The boy woke up and started on finding himself in a stranger's arms. He began to call for his mother. He struck at Martin's chest with his little fists. Martin put him into his own bed without undressing him. Then he lay on the bed, soothing the child. The child fell asleep.

Then Martin went into the kitchen and sat by the fire. He heard Patrick snoring. He jumped to his feet and dashed out of the house, leaving the door open. He went up to the cliffs and wandered around there. He came back to the house, took the can and milked the cow. When he returned with the milk, Kate had arisen. She was busy tidying the house and getting breakfast ready.

'Hello!' she said gaily. 'You didn't go to bed?'

She was full of energy and yet she looked horrible, like an old woman. There was no paint on her face. Her cheeks were hollow. Her lips were cracked and yellow like those of a corpse. She was wearing a loose wrap, belted at the waist. She wore slippers without heels on her bare feet. Her hair was bedraggled, streaming around her neck. He looked at her in amazement and said nothing. Then he sat in the corner of the hearth, waiting for his breakfast.

She took no notice of him. She hummed a tune as she worked and she worked at great speed, deftly. She gave him his breakfast and brought tea into bed to her husband. Martin heard his brother growl when she wakened him. Then his brother called out:

'Martin.'

'What?'

'Start cutting potato seeds. We'll begin sowing tomorrow.'

Martin said nothing. But he thought:

'He orders me like a servant before her.'

He became inflamed with anger. He left his breakfast and went out. He stood outside the door, trying to rebel against his brother, but it was alien to his nature. He could not do so. The child awoke and began to cry.

'What the devil is the matter with that child?' grumbled Patrick.

'I'll run in and see,' said Kate. 'He probably finds himself strange.'

Martin walked away. He entered the barn and began to cut potato seeds. Later, Patrick joined him. They worked together in silence. Neither referred to the wedding. Patrick looked cross and discontented. The child came out of the house and began to play in the yard, uttering loud cries and calling his mother to look at things which he found strange.

'He won't live,' said Patrick. 'What do you think?'

Martin said nothing.

'No. He won't live,' said Patrick. 'His father was a foreigner. They have bad blood in them.'

At dinner the child was cranky and refused the food that was given him. His mother suddenly lost her temper and beat the boy. The boy went into hysterics. Patrick jumped up, cursed and left the house.

'Tare an' ouns,' Martin called after him. 'Have ye no more nature in you that to curse at a child?

'Mind your own business,' shouted Patrick from the yard.

Martin took the boy in his arms and began to soothe him.

'Don't spoil him,' said Kate. 'It's just temper.'

Martin looked at her angrily. She dropped her eyes, caught the child from his arms and began to kiss it. Then she sat down and burst into tears, rocking the child and murmuring:

'You poor little orphan. I don't know what to do with you.'

Martin went out. That evening, when the child was being put to bed, Patrick said:

'Hadn't you better put his little bed into Martin's room?'

'Why so?' said Martin.

'Nothing,' said Patrick. 'Only . . . only I thought he might keep you company. You never liked being alone at night.'

Martin looked at his brother savagely.

'Do what you like,' he said. 'You're master here.'

They put the child into Martin's room. That night, when he came in after visiting in a neighbour's house, he stood for a long time over the little bed, in the dark, listening to the child's breathing. He pitied the child and at the same time hated his brother. He realised that his brother was jealous of the child.

A few days later, while they were working in the field sowing potatoes, Patrick said:

'You're spoiling that child. You had better not be coddling him. He's nothing to us anyway. His father was a foreigner.'

'Every child was made by God,' said Martin. 'Kindness won't spoil anything.'

'It's time you were thinking of getting a wife for yourself, then,' said Patrick, 'as you're so fond of children.'

The Spring came. The dark earth became a paradise. It was good to smell the wind that was scented with the perfume of growth. Bird music was triumphant. The cold sunlight glittered on the black earth uprooted by the sowers. Each dawn was wild with the cries of living things going forth to labour. Each dusk was full of tender murmurs, as tired men happily sought their beds and cows lowed for their milkers and sheep bleated over their new-born lambs. All evil passions were silenced by man's frenzied efforts to satisfy the energy born of the earth's awakening.

Yet it was a false peace that fell upon the house. The silence grew as menacing as a dark cloud that hangs in the sky on a sultry day, foretelling thunder.

A great change came over Kate. She no longer put paint upon her cheeks and lips. She cast aside her foreign clothes and dressed in the manner of a peasant. She did the housework with enthusiasm and skill. She left nothing undone. She dropped her brusque, gay manner. She became serious. She no longer talked of anything but of the house, the crops, the cattle. She no longer looked alien. She became a peasant woman again. She grew bold in the house and spoke curtly to her husband. She put on flesh. Her eyes lost their strange, lascivious look. Instead, they became avaricious. Her cheeks, that had been hollow and yellow like the cheeks of a corpse beneath the paint, now filled out and became tanned brown by the healthy air and wind. Her lips and fingers no longer twitched nervously. She was no longer taken by hysterical bursts of passion. She became like a rock in which there is neither softness nor passion. Now she did not inspire desire. Although her attraction still remained great, she reacted differently on men. Women of the village began to speak well of her.

She treated both men with equal coldness, as if neither were her husband. And in the evening, when they had returned from work and were sitting by the fire before going to bed, she talked to her child instead of talking to them.

Neither did the child become friendly with either of them. He still remained an alien. He improved in health and became bold, playing about the house as if he had been born there; but whenever he looked at the brothers there was a vacant stare in his eyes, as if they were strangers to him. When Patrick scowled at him, he sighed and went to his mother. When Martin tried to play with him or gave him toys which he had whittled with a knife, he remained silent and as lifeless as a girl with a man whom she does not love.

Yet Martin was not offended by the boy's manner. His kindness to the boy pleased him because it irritated his brother. He was pleased also with the change that had taken place in Kate. He was pleased with her coldness towards her husband. He was pleased with the gloomy, discontented look that had settled on his brother's countenance. He had become bitter. He no longer found pleasure in the sea, nor in the singing of birds, nor in watching the starry sky at night. A mocking, malicious spirit had taken possession of his mind, driving out all other pleasures but that of making his brother unhappy.

Spring passed. Now warm breezes sang among the swaying fields of corn. People became idle watching the growth of their crops. It was good to lie in a glen in the sunlight among the wild, sweet flowers.

The brothers stayed about the house, drawn irresistibly towards the cause of the bitter enmity that was growing in their minds.

One morning, Martin was making a top for the little boy by the fire. The boy stood near, watching. Patrick sat in the corner of the hearth, smoking. Kate was out in the yard, attending to young pigs they had just bought.

Suddenly Patrick said to the child:

'Hey, Charley, did you have a top in America?'

'Yes, I had,' said the child. 'I had three.'

'Who made them for you?' said Patrick. 'Your father?'

'No. Mammy bought them in a shop.'

'Didn't your daddy make any toys for you?'

'No,' said the child. 'I don't remember my daddy.'

'Leave the child alone,' said Martin angrily.

Patrick's little eyes gleamed. He sniffed and moved his white eyebrows up and down.

'What was you daddy's name?' he continued.

'My daddy's name was John.'

'John what? What was his other name?'

'John Smith,' said the boy.

'Bloody woes,' said Patrick. 'That's handy name to have. Where was he from?'

'Leave the child alone,' shouted Martin.

'What's up now?' cried Kate from the yard.

'Wasn't your daddy called Martin?' continued Patrick.

The child began to cry. He ran out into the yard to his mother. Martin jumped to his feet and cried:

'You leave that child alone. Do you hear?'

Patrick jumped up and shouted:

'Whose house is this? Clear out if you don't like it. I'll have none of your impudence.'

Kate came in, holding the boy by the hand.

'What's this?' she cried. 'What were you doing to the child?'

'I asked him a civil question about his father,' shouted Patrick. 'Haven't I a right to know who the brat's father was, seeing I'm keeping him?'

Kate ran to the hearth and picked up the tongs.

'I'll brain you with this,' she hissed, 'if you say another word.'

Martin caught her.

'Don't you hit him, ' he cried. 'Let me deal with him.'

'So that's it, is it?' cried Patrick. 'You've changed your mind about her since the night you said you'd rather lie with a dog than with her.'

'Liar,' shouted Martin, turning pale.

'You can have her now, then,' said Patrick. 'She's a dry bag. I've been sold a blind pup. There was nothing in her womb but that sick vermin that doesn't know his own father. My curse on the house.'

He rushed out. As he passed the child he made a kick at it. The child screamed. Kate dropped on to a chair, put her fingers between her teeth and bit them. Martin stood before the hearth, trembling. Then he cursed, took his tobacco from his pocket and bit at it. He began to chew. Kate began to tremble. Then she began to sob hysterically.

'Look here,' said Martin to her angrily. 'I did you wrong. He said the truth. I said what you heard just now. But don't you be afraid. I'll do right by you now. That savage won't raise a hand to your child while I'm here.'

He left the house.

All that day, Patrick went among the neighbours, complaining that his wife treated him with cruelty, that she was barren, that there was a scar on her stomach, that her womb had been extracted in an hospital, that she favoured his brother, that she was robbing him in the interests of her child. He returned late at night. His wife was waiting for him. She received him as if nothing had happened and gave him his supper.

Martin returned from a visit while Patrick was having his supper. He glanced with hatred at his brother and immediately went into his room.

Patrick called after him:

'We'll begin tomorrow making a field of that crag beyond the Red Meadow. There is going to be no one eating the bread of idleness in this house.'

'All right,' said Martin calmly from his room.

Then he stood near the bed of the sleeping child, listening to the child's breath, in the darkness. His face broke into a smile and his eyes glittered. When he got into bed he kept laughing to himself. He kept waking through the night and listening to the child's breathing and laughing to himself.

Next day they brought crowbars and a sledge and they went to the crag beyond the Red Meadow. They began to quarry the rocks. They worked savagely, excited by their hatred of one another. Patrick ordered his brother about, treating him like a servant. Martin obeyed meekly and smiled in a strange manner at his brother's oaths

That evening, while they were having supper, he said suddenly to Kate:

'I've been thinking, this while back, that I should make a will. No man knows when his hour is going to come and it's best to put things in a way that there'll be no quarrel over my few pounds after I'm gone.'

Patrick looked up suspiciously. His little eyes flashed. His neck became florid. His white eyebrows moved up and down. Then he said:

'It's not of your death you should be thinking, but of getting a wife. If you had the guts of a man you'd look for a wife.'

Martin smiled faintly and went on talking to Kate. Kate's eyes became small. She watched Martin like a bird.

'I've been thinking,' he said, 'this while back, that little Charley has been a great comfort to me since he came into the house. I'd like to think that maybe when he grew up and I'm gone he'd have something to think well of me for. So, I'm thinking of making a will.'

Then he arose from the table and went out. Kate put her apron to her eye, as if to wipe away a tear. But her eyes were dry and her face was flushed.

Patrick looked at the table with his mouth open. Then he caught up a piece of the bread that Kate had baked, crushed it between his fingers and growled:

'Do you call that bread? It's like putty. I wouldn't give it to a dog.'

He threw the bread at the child and said:

'Here. Catch that.'

Then he cursed and went out of the house. Kate showed no sign of resentment in her cold, hawk-like countenance.

Next day, while they were digging out the stones from the crag, Patrick said to his brother:

'Wake up, you fool. Don't loaf around. Is it thinking of your will you are? Did you make that will yet?'

'I'm thinking about it,' said Martin calmly. 'I want to put it in a way that nobody can touch my money but the child. I have to think about it.'

'The curse of God on you,' said Patrick with great violence.

He dropped his crowbar and left the crag. He came home and shouted at his wife:

'Give me some money.'

She gave him a pound note.

'I want more,' he said.

'That's all there is in the house,' she said quietly.

'I'll have a look then,' he said.

He rushed into the bedroom and tried to open her trunk. She ran in after him and said:

'Leave that alone.'

'What have you in it?' he cried. 'Why do you keep it locked?'

'It's none of your business,' she said. 'I gave you three hundred pounds when I came into the house. That's all you bargained for.'

'Ha!' he cried. 'You have money in it. You kept money from me. You are stealing the money of the house for your bastard child. You have taken my land. You got around my fool of a brother to leave you his money and now you —'

'Shut up,' she hissed at him, 'or I'll brain you.'

He rushed at her and felled her with a blow of his fist. Then he became terrified and fled from the house. When Martin returned from the crag, Kate was going about her work calmly. He noticed that she had a black bruise on her cheek. He asked her what had happened. She told him.

He smiled strangely and said:

'I'm going into the town.'

When he returned in the evening, he handed her a document.

'That's the will,' he said. 'In case God sends for me, Charley will have every penny I own. Look after that.'

She kissed his hand and brought the will to her trunk. Putting it in, her eyes glittered and she sat for a long time before the open trunk, sucking her lips and smiling.

Patrick returned drunk that night, but he went to bed quietly. Next day, when they were working on the crag, Martin said to him:

'I didn't see you in the town yesterday.'

Patrick looked at him and said nothing.

'I went in to make that will I was talking about,' said Martin calmly.

Patrick remained silent.

'It's all settled now,' continued Martin quietly, 'so my mind is at peace.'

'Listen,' whispered Patrick savagely.

Martin looked at him.

'Watch yourself,' whispered Patrick.

They glared at one another. Their faces were white with hatred.

'I'm satisfied,' whispered Martin through his teeth.

After that they became silent and avoided each other. Kate assumed complete charge of the house. She ordered them about.

'The horse need water,' she would say. 'One of you go and bring her to the well.'

Again she would say:

'The cow is starving in that field. Change her, one of you, to the Red Meadow.'

She never called either of them by name, but spoke to them in common, as if they were strangers. It was she who treated with neighbours about cases of trespass and she paid the rates and the rent that came due in summer.

Neither of the brothers paid any attention to her. They watched one another ceaselessly. Their eyes became fixed.

Suddenly a wild hurricane came raging over the ocean. The sun, moon and stars were hidden day and night behind a wall of black clouds that belched rain upon the earth and clashing in their flight from the shrieking gale, set the firmament on fire and shook the cliffs with the thunderous echoes of their bursting. The sea rose to the summits of the cliffs and its foam was carried to the wind far into the land. Even the wild seagulls fled into the village and stood upon the gables of the houses and screamed in horror.

For three days the storm lasted. Then the wind died. The sun appeared. The sky grew clear. The waves began to fall, heaving like wounded animals, into the sea's back. Rafts of curdled foam and torn weeds, speckled with jetsam, floundered to the shore. People came to look for wreckage.

In the evening Patrick said to his brother:

'Be ready at dawn. We are going in the boat to look for wreckage.'

Martin answered him:

'I'm satisfied.'

They both went to bed. Neither slept. Each kept rising in the night and going to the window to see if dawn had yet broken. Kate also lay awake. A cock crew an hour before dawn. At once both brothers began to put on their clothes hurriedly. Kate also arose and threw a coat over her night-dress:

Martin was the first to get to the kitchen. He cried in a loud voice.

'Are you ready now?'

Patrick came into the kitchen, followed by Kate.

'You had better take some bread, one of you,' she said. 'You'll be hungry before you get back.'

'We don't need bread,' said Patrick. 'Get the rope, you. Where is the rope?'

'I'll get it,' said Martin, going out to the barn.

Patrick began to fumble in the pockets of his waistcoat.

'Why have you on your new waistcoat?' she said. 'You have your new cap on too.'

'Mind your business,' he said. 'Give me my old waistcoat.'

She brought it to him. He took it aside and took a knife from its pocket. He put it furtively into the pocket of the waistcoat he was wearing. She saw him, but said nothing. Her eyes became fixed.

Martin came in, carrying a coil of rope on his arm.

'Are you ready now?' he said.

Without speaking Patrick moved to the door.

'Wait,' said Kate, 'till I sprinkle the Holy Water on you.'

They both went out without answering her. She picked up a little cruet of Holy Water that hung on a nail in the wall by the window. She ran out into the yard after them and shook Holy water on each of them with her forefinger. Neither of them blessed themselves.

Then she returned to the house, went into the child's room and stood by his little bed, watching him and listening to his breathing.

The brothers walked in silence through the village and along the rocky road over the crags to the shore. Their boat lay bottom upwards within a fence of stones above the mound of boulders that lined the shore. They knocked down the fence at the prow and at the stern. Then they raised the prow. Martin crawled under the boat, raised it higher and rested his shoulders against the front seat. Patrick crawled in astern, put his shoulders against the third seat and straightened himself.

'Go ahead,' he said.

They moved off, carrying the boat on their shoulders. Its black, canvas-covered hulk, with their legs sticking from beneath, moving slowly over the rocks, made it look like a beetle. They brought it to the brink of the tide and stepping into the water, they laid it, mouth upwards, with a splashing sound, upon the waves. Patrick held it to the shore while Martin brought the oars and the rope. They put the oars on the thole-pins and threw the rope into the stern.

'Keep your hand on her,' said Patrick, about to step aboard.

'You hold her,' said Martin. 'I'm going in the prow same as I always do.'

'No,' said Patrick in a whisper. 'I'm going in the prow today.'

They looked at one another coldly. Their eyes were fixed.

'Go ahead,' said Martin. 'It's all the same to me.'

'Why so?' said Patrick through his teeth.

'Go ahead,' said Martin, 'seeing you want to go in the prow.'

'It's all the same to me too,' said Patrick softly. 'I'll go in the stern, same as I always do.'

'You'll go where you said you'd go, said Martin, 'or I'll stay on the rock.'

They glared at one another again. Then Patrick stepped into the boat, sat on the front seat and seized the oars. Martin pushed off the boat and jumped aboard. They began to row eastwards towards the cliffs.

The sea was still disturbed. Although its dark surface was unbroken, there were deep hollows between the waves that came rolling quickly to the shore. The light coracle bounded from wave to wave, bobbing like a little bird in flight against the wind.

The sun began to rise as they turned a promontory. The sea glittered. They rowed close to the cliffs that rose above them precipitously. There was a loud sound of birds coming forth to fish from their caverns. Seagulls soared about them. The sea was littered with refuse. Now and again, the fin of a shark cut the surface. Gannets swooped from on high and fell like bullets, with a thud, into the floating rafts of weeds.

Masses of weeds, shining in the sunlight lay among the broken rocks at the base of the cliffs.

They rowed quickly, searching the sea and the shore for wreckage. They had rowed three miles when at last they saw a great beam floating near the shore in a raft of weeds.

'There's a beam,' said Patrick. 'Put a noose on the rope.'

Martin shipped his oars and made a noose with the end of the rope. He tied the other end to the central seat. They rowed towards the beam. The beam rushed back and forth, on the ebbing tide. There was a heavy swell. The great piece of timber sometimes raised its head aloft from the mass of floating weeds, like a great sea monster nosing at the air. They rowed around it, seeking a chance to encircle its snout with the noose as it rose upon a wave.

Martin hurled the noose three times without success. Then at last the beam came rushing at them, carried on a great receding wave and as Patrick wheeled the boat to avoid its crashing into them, it passed close to their quarter, with its barnacle snout raised up. Martin threw the noose. It caught. Patrick groaned and lay on his oars. The rope went taut. The boat shivered. The beam swung round, held by the taught noose and turned its snout to the boat's stern. Martin caught his oars and began to row. They turned towards home, followed by the wallowing beam.

Its great weight swung the boat from side to side when the heavy swell came against it. Again it came rushing with upraised snout at the boat when the swell came with it. Rowing with all their force, they had to tack to and fro to avoid its crashing into them. The rope, tied to the vacant seat amidships, passed under Martin's seat, and ran through a notch in the stern to the log, rasping against the wood. Now it lay buried in the water, slack, as the log was hurtled towards them by the sea. Now it hung taut above the waves, dripping with brine.

Now there were many fins of sharks following the boat, keeping pace. Overhead, seagulls soared on still wings, looking down, cackling.

Patrick watched the fins of the sharks with fixed eyes. His lips were drawn back from his clenched teeth. His white eyebrows were raised up on his wrinkled forehead. Suddenly he dropped his oars, took his knife from his pocket and opened it.

Martin's back quivered. He dropped his oars and stood up, uttering a strange, wild shriek. He turned on his brother. Patrick was crouching in the prow, gripping the open knife. They rushed at one another. The boat swung round. The beam, carried on a tall wave, came crashing into it.

The brothers, just as they were about to grapple with one another, saw the beam, with upraised snout, looming over them. They raised their hands and uttered a cry of horror. The knife dropped from Patrick's hands into the sea. They threw their arms around one another in an embrace, as the log fell, smashing them and the boat beneath its weight.

Clasped in one another's arms, they began to sink.

The sharks' fins came rushing through the water towards the wreck. Then they dived.

The brothers rose once, still clasping one another in a tight embrace. Then they were tugged sharply downwards and they rose no more.

A mass of weeds gathered around the wrecked boat, with the log, snout upwards, astride it, while seagulls soared all round, screaming.

Sources of Stories in Volume 1

The following were first collected in *Spring Sowing* (1924), London: Jonathan Cape.

A Pig in a Bedroom	His First Flight	The Bladder	The Struggle
A Pot of Gold	Josephine	The Cow's Death	The Tramp
A Shilling	Selling Pigs	The Doctor's Visit	The Wave
Beauty	Sport: The Kill	The Fight	The Wild Sow
Benedicamus Domino	Spring Sowing	The Hook	The Wren's Nest
Blood Lust	The Black Bullock	The Landing	Three Lambs
Colic	The Black Mare	The Rockfish	Two Dogs
Going into Exile	The Blackbird	The Sniper	Wolf Lanigan's Death

The following were first collected in *The Tent* (1926), London: Jonathan Cape.

A Red Petticoat	Poor People	The Old Hunter	The Wild Goat's Kid
At the Forge	Stoney Batter	The Outcast	The Wing Three-
Blackmail	The Conger Eel	The Reaping Race	Quarter
Charity	The Fireman's Death	The Sensualist	The Wounded
Civil War	The Foolish Butterfly	The Stolen Ass	Cormorant
Milking Time	The Inquisition	The Tent	Trapped
Mother and Son	The Jealous Hens	The Terrorist	Your Honour
Offerings	The Lost Thrush	The Tyrant	

The following were first collected in *The Mountain Tavern and Other Stories* (1929), London: Jonathan Cape.

The Blackbird's Mate	The Ditch	The Mountain Tavern	The Oar

The following were first published in *Dúil* (1953), Baile Átha Cliath: Sáirséal agus Dill.

An Charraig Dhubh	An Fiach	Bás na Bó	Daoine Bochta

Fód — Uncollected

Sources of Stories in Volume 2

A Dublin Eviction — *The Weekly Westminster*, 13 December 1924, p. 216.
A Public Scandal — *The Manchester Guardian*, 9 September 1925, p. 16.
An Extraordinary Case — Unpublished.
Making a Home — *Home Topics*, 23 January 1926, pp. 7-8.
Non-Stop — *The Manchester Guardian*, 21 May 1928, p. 20.
One Hundred Pounds — Unpublished.
Pay on Cruiser — *The Tatler*, 30 October 1929, p. 246.
The Last Horse — *The Manchester Guardian*, 25 January 1926, p. 16.
The Library — *The Manchester Guardian*, 9 July 1925, p. 18.
The Lost Child — *The Manchester Guardian*, 11 February 1924, p. 12.
The Night Porter — Story 30, January/February, 1947, pp. 23-32, (adapted from Chapter 3 of Liam O'Flaherty's autobiographical *Two Years* (1930)).
The Renegade — *The Irish People*, Vol. 1, No. 6, November 1923, p. 5, Boston.

The following were first collected in *The Mountain Tavern and Other Stories* (1929), London: Jonathan Cape.

Birth	The Black Rabbit	The Letter	The Strange Disease
Mackerel for Sale	The Child of God	The Little White Dog	The Stream
Prey	The Fairy Goose	The Painted Woman	
Red Barbara	The Fall of Joseph	The Sinner	
The Alien Skull	Timmins	The Stone	

The following were first collected in *Two Lovely Beasts and Other Stories* (1948), London: Victor Gollancz.

Galway Bay	The Beggars	The Mouse	The Tide
Grey Seagull	The Challenge	The New Suit	The Touch
Life	The Eviction	The Old Woman	The Water Hen
Light	The Flute-Player	The Parting	The Wedding
The Bath	The Lament	The Seal	Two Lovely Beasts

The following were first collected in *The Wild Swan and Other Stories* (1932), London: Furnival Books.

It Was the Devil's Work   The Wild Swan   Unclean

The following were first published in *Dúil* (1953), Baile Átha Cliath: Sáirséal agus Dill.

An Beo   An Chulaith Nua   Teangabháil
An Chearc Uisce   An Luchóg

Sources of Stories in Volume 3

A Grave Reason — *The New Leader*, 16 October 1925, p. 12.
A Public-House at Night — *T.P.'s & Cassell's Weekly*, 15 November 1924, p. 151.
An Ounce of Tobacco — *T.P.'s Weekly*, 8 October 1927, p. 739.
Brosnan — *Harper's Bazaar* (US), 1 September 1938, p. 74.
Field of Young Corn — *John O'London*, 9 September 1933, p. 793.
For Love or Money — Unpublished.
Idle Gossip — *The New Leader*, 19 February 1926, p. 11.
In Each Beginning Is An End — *Fascination*, Vol. 1, July 1946, p. 32, (adapted from Chapter 23 of Liam O'Flaherty's autobiographical *Two Years* (1930)).
Indian Summer — *Good Housekeeping*, Springfield, Mass., Vol. CXX, May 1945, p. 34.
Limpets — *The Weekly Westminster*, 30 January 1926, p. 312.
Match-Making — *Cassells Weekly*, 20 June 1923, p. 443.
Moving — *The Manchester Guardian*, 16 November 1925, p. 16.
The Accident — *Fortnightly Review*, Vol. CXLIII, February 1935, p. 155.
The Backwoodman's Daughter — *Mademoiselle*, Vol. 22, April 1946, p. 150, (adapted from Chapter 19 of Liam O'Flaherty's autobiographical *Two Years* (1930)).
The Black Cat — *The Humanist*, July, 1926, pp. 237.
The Black Sheep's Daughter — *Housewife*, Vol. 15, April 1953, p. 38.
The Cake — *The Irish Statesman*, 19 December 1925, p. 455.
The Cutting of Tom Bottle — *Charles' Wain: A Miscellany of Short Stories* (1933), London: Mallinson, pp. 139-160.
The Good Samaritan — *The New Leader*, 27 August 1926, p. 8.
The Intellectual — *The Weekly Westminster*, 22 August 1925, p. 428.
The Tinker-Woman's Child, *T.P.'s & Cassell's Weekly*, 3 October 1925, p. 759.
Tidy Tim's Donkey — *The Weekly Westminster*, 5 January 1924, p. 316.

The following were first collected in *Short Stories: The Pedlar's Revenge* (1976) Dublin: Wolfhound Press.

A Crow Fight	Fishing	The Arrest	The Salted Goat
A Tin Can	King of Inishcam	The Caress	The Test of Courage
All Things Come of	Lovers	The Fanatic	The White Bitch
Age	Patsa, or the Belly of	The Flood	Timoney's Ass
Bohunk	Gold	The Mermaid	Wild Stallions
Enchanted Water	Proclamation	The Pedlar's Revenge	

The following were first collected in *The Stories of Liam O'Flaherty* (1956), New York: The Devin-Adair Company.

Desire	The Hawk	The Post Office
The Blow	The Mirror	

The following were first collected in *Dúil* (1953), Baile Átha Cliath: Sáirséal agus Dill.

An Buille	An tAonach	Mearbhall
An Scáthán	Díoltas	Oifig an Phoist
An Seabhac	Dúil	Uisce Faoi Dhraíocht